The Blood of Father Time, Book 2

THE BLOOD OF FATHER TIME DUOLOGY #2

The Blood of Father Time, Book 2

THE MYSTIC CLAN'S GRAND PLOT

Alan M. Clark, Stephen C. Merritt, & Lorelei Shannon

FIVE STAR

An imprint of Thomson Gale, a part of The Thomson Corporation

Detroit • New York • San Francisco • New Haven, Conn. • Waterville, Maine • London

Set in 11 pt. Plantin.

LIBRARY OF CONGRESS CATALOGING-IN-PUBLICATION DATA

Clark, Alan (Alan M.)
The blood of Father Time. Book 2, The mystic clan's grand plot / Alan M. Clark, Stephen C. Merritt & Lorelei Shannon. — 1st ed.
p. cm.
ISBN-13: 978-1-59414-604-6 (alk. paper)
ISBN-10: 1-59414-604-7 (alk. paper)
1. Time travel—Fiction. 2. Tennessee—Fiction. I. Merritt, Stephen C. II. Shannon, Lorelei. III. Title. IV. Title: Mystic clan's grand plot.
PS3603.L3554N493 2007
813'.54—dc22 2007005379

First Edition. First Printing: July 2007.

Published in 2007 in conjunction with Tekno Books and Ed Gorman.

Printed in the United States of America on permanent paper
10 9 8 7 6 5 4 3 2 1

Inspired by the dastardly deeds of Big and Little Harpe, the true-life adventures of our great American hero, Virgil A. Stewart, and the notorious land pirate, John A. Murrell.

ACKNOWLEDGMENTS

Many thanks to Beth Massie, Susan Stockell, Jack Daves, Diana Rodgers, Dan Carver, Jeff Oliver, Ken Bryant, and Bovine Smoke Society.

1

The more Joel Biggs thought about it, the dumber he felt about telling his cousin Moss that he had traveled back in time when he was a boy.

Joel leaned back on the lumpy couch and rubbed his forehead. *Moss let me come here, under his roof with his family, to dry out. Now he must think he's harboring a lunatic as well as a drunk.*

Joel opened his eyes a slit, and saw that Rachel, Moss's seventeen-year-old daughter, was staring at him. Again. Joel gave her a weak smile, but her expression didn't change. *Why does she think I'm so goddam interesting, anyway?* She wasn't giving him the usual "what a freakshow" look he got from the kids back home. It was almost like she was studying him with those intense eyes.

Whatever Rachel's motivation, her stare spooked him a little. He was glad when she silently left the room.

Joel sighed, feeling stupid all over again. He knew he couldn't afford to worry about what his hosts thought of him. Moss had given him a great opportunity to get his shit together. *And it's not like Moss didn't know I had problems when he invited me to stay.* But Joel did care what Moss thought of him. Not a real cousin, but a close friend of the family, Moss had been like a big brother when Joel was little. He'd showed almost endless patience, letting the younger boy follow him around like a puppy, even patching him up sometimes after Joel's dad had used him as a punching bag.

Joel closed his eyes and saw a little boy, dorky shorts and scabby knees, running to catch up. But it wasn't Joel at all, it was Billy.

Billy. Pain skewered Joel's heart, sharp and immediate.

Joel looked down at the book in his lap, *The History of Matthew Crenshaw and His Adventure Exposing the Great Land Pirate, Jarrett Cotten and the Mystic Clan,* the book Billy had sent him just before he died. When he was a kid, Joel had been obsessed with this historical account of the local Tennessee hero, Matthew Crenshaw, written in the early eighteen-hundreds. As an adult and a history professor, he found the Crenshaw story fascinating, and the book itself was a hot topic of controversy with the literary set because of its unusual, almost modern narrative writing style. Joel hadn't seen another actual copy of the book since he was a boy. But his thoughts were too far away to concentrate on it, and he found himself looking out the window at the fall color in the hills of twenty-first-century Tennessee. He thought about the day he and Billy had come home from the eighteen-hundreds, how terribly happy and sad that day had been.

After they returned, Billy had become Joel's best friend. They had stood together against all the questions from Mark's parents and the police, as well as from their own parents and friends: What happened? Where had they been? Where was Mark? Where had they gotten the strange clothing?

Joel and Billy agreed that no one would believe the truth, so they came up with an alternative. Their story was simple: They had all three become lost while exploring the woods near the Maxwell farm. Their clothing had become ruined when they struggled through a thorny bramble and they'd found the clothes they were wearing in an old, abandoned farm house. At one point, needing a rest, Joel and Billy stopped and sat on a log, but Mark continued the search for a way out of the woods. Joel and Billy got tired of waiting for Mark to return and went in search of him, eventually finding their way home, but never seeing Mark again. As far as they were concerned, this had all taken place in an afternoon.

Since they had been gone for a month and a half, no one was prepared to believed them. A psychologist was in attendance when the police questioned Joel and Billy. She said the boys were obviously traumatized and that that could account for their lapse in memory. The questioning continued, hour after hour. Finally Billy broke down in tears and began to tell the truth. He started with the Indians and pirates, then began to tell about the cave, the battle and the earthquake. The psychologist gently interrupted him and asked to speak with the police in private. After that the boys were released to their parents. A few more questions were directed to Joel, but only by the psychologist, and she was so friendly and sweet that it creeped Joel out. He stuck to his original story.

The frantic search for Mark went on for at least a month. Then over time, with no results, no leads, it evaporated. To this day, Joel knew, teenagers told wildly varying stories of Mark's disappearance and the strange loss of time Joel and Billy had experienced. Some kids said the boys had been abducted by aliens. Others said they had been enslaved by traveling hippies, or survivalist weirdos. Still others blamed it on possession by the Bell Spirit. (That particular creepy bit of Tennessee folklore still cropped up all the time, and people only half-jokingly blamed it for everything from failed crops to unexplained car failure.) Strangely, even the truth was told—that the boys had wandered into some sort of time portal—though none of the folks who passed on that particular version of the tale knew they were actually telling the truth.

It was all so unbelievable. To this day, Joel had trouble believing it himself. When his drinking was at its worst, he had been certain it was an alcoholic delusion. How could he expect Moss to believe otherwise, the way he'd dropped the story on him so casually?

Joel decided he'd better tell Moss he was kidding, or find a way to convince him. He turned the book over in his hands. Earlier that morning, he'd damn near had a heart attack (and given Lynn one in the process) when he'd found the names "M. Ryder" and "J. Biggs" in its pages. *I could just show that to Moss. It's black-and-white proof that Mark and I were known to someone back then.*

Or proof that I'm not just delusional, I may be psychotic.

Shit.

Was he trying to convince Moss, or himself?

The sound of an engine came through the open window and Joel got up from the sofa to take a look. Moss had said he was going into town to pick up a sports car he'd ordered. As frugally as the Phelpses lived, that seemed a bit odd, but Joel hadn't thought much about it at the time. *Too damn self-absorbed, as usual.*

Joel caught sight of the "sports car" and burst out laughing. The laugh felt good, but weird. Joel couldn't remember the last time he'd *really* laughed.

The two Phelps boys, Brian and Caleb, stopped playing on the rope swing and raced along beside their father. Joel stepped outside to join them as Moss pulled up next to the house.

Moss turned off the engine and stepped down. "How do you like my new sports car?"

"It's a tractor, fer chrissakes," Joel said, chuckling. "What are you doing with that?"

"What are you talking about?" Moss said, his expression deadpan. "Hell, this was the hottest thing they had down at the John Deere dealership. Hop on, I'll take you for a ride!"

"I'm not gettin' up on that thing!"

"Aw c'mon, Joel. She's my little Italian baby, you'll hurt her feelings!"

"You're an idiot!" Joel said, laughing in spite of himself.

"Take *us,* Daddy," Caleb and Brian squealed, "take us for a ride."

"Okay, boys, hop on! You don't know what you're missin', Joel. This baby can really fly through the turns!"

Moss climbed up on the tractor and turned it on, gunning the engine several times and beaming at Joel. The boys climbed up on either side of him and the three rode off across the yard. Joel watched the bright green vehicle bouncing absurdly across the lumpy ground, hauling the laughing trio, a proud father and his sons. They made several laps around the yard and Joel was still laughing when Moss brought the tractor back and turned it off. He climbed down and smiled at Joel.

"Here ya go, buddy," he said, holding out the keys, "take 'er for a spin. Ya can drive 'er into town an' see if ya can pick up some chicks—ya know how the ladies like a fast piece of machinery."

"It's got a torque converter on the rear end, you dumbass!"

Moss burst out laughing. "It sure does. Ain't many sports cars can claim that, an' if you're clever enough, you an' a lady friend might figure out somethin' fun to do with it."

"That's not funny," Joel said, laughing. But as he looked at his "cousin," he felt the years vanish—eye to eye, he could once again feel the connection they'd shared in childhood. Until that moment, he hadn't realized just how isolated he'd become, or what he'd been missing.

2

After a dinner of roasted chicken, corn on the cob, fried okra, and black-eyed peas, Joel and the Phelpses went outside and built a fire. They sat on logs arranged in a circle around a fire pit and roasted marshmallows (except for Rachel, who plucked blades of grass and stared off into space). Caleb and Brian chattered endlessly about the tractor as they immolated one marshmallow after another. Soon the boys were such a sticky mess that Lynn took them inside to clean them up.

Moss fed another log to the fire. When it settled, a shower of sparks leapt up into the darkening blue dusk.

"What a life," Joel said, half-aloud, "you've really got it nice out here, Moss."

His "cousin" smiled, nodding his head as he took his seat again.

"I mean—having a fire, a campfire, right outside your front door—how many of us get to do that?"

The weather had cooled a bit, and Joel was hit with a sudden wave of nostalgia for childhood, Halloween, camping out, and the smell of burning leaves. Fall was finally here. While growing up, he'd felt this same wonderful and indefinable *something* at the same time each year. It had been a decade since he last felt it, but with the smell of woodsmoke the feeling returned, and Joel shivered with anticipation as waves of pleasant memory passed through him. He smiled, feeling no desire to drink, feeling very nearly normal.

Been doing a lot of smiling today, he told himself. *It's a hell of an improvement.* There was a sharp snap, and Joel looked up. Rachel had stopped plucking grass and was now breaking small twigs. She looked oddly out of place, sitting on a log in her dark, goth-punk clothing. Loneliness seemed to come off of her in waves. Joel felt suddenly, deeply sad for her.

Presently, Lynn came back outside without the boys. "Can you imagine it?" she said, sitting beside Moss. "The boys would rather play a game of monopoly in their room than sit around the campfire with us."

Nobody responded. Joel tried to think of something to fill the lengthening silence, but couldn't. All he could think about was how to convince Moss that the story he'd told him about his childhood time travel was real. And suddenly he couldn't stand it any longer—he knew he had to let it all out. He'd told Moss the short form. Here was his opportunity to give it life. If Moss believed him, fine. If not, well. . . .

"Now that we're sitting around the fire, I thought I'd tell a story," Joel said. He had once felt comfortable telling stories. Hell, the history classes he taught were nothing but storytelling, but that seemed like a lifetime ago and he found himself a little nervous.

"Hey, that's just the thing," said Moss. "Isn't it a law somewhere that if you have a campfire, you gotta tell stories?"

"If there ain't," Lynn said, "there oughta be."

"This is a story about three boys from my neighborhood in Dexter. Their names were Joe, Mark and Billy, and they traveled back in time to eighteen-eleven. . . ."

Joel looked at Moss, who returned his gaze, nodding his head as if to show he understood. He saw Rachel roll her eyes, but noticed she was in no hurry to get up. Joel cleared his throat. *Here we go. . . .*

"The creek they played in had recently been rerouted to follow a deep, straight cut through Billy's yard and into the woods beyond. It had been dug out with a backhoe, and it was so deep that when they were in the bottom of it, all they could see over the banks were the treetops and the sky. They called it 'The New Cut,' and, on that first day of summer, the three boys set out to explore it.

"In the late afternoon, the boys were tired and hungry and wanted to go home. They crawled out of the creek, and found they had somehow gotten themselves lost. They tried to backtrack, but it was no good—nothing looked familiar. Without knowing any better, they headed off into the virgin wilderness, desperately seeking someone to help them.

"Billy got separated from Joe and Mark. The little boy was alone and terrified, until he was found by a couple of Indians who were hunting in the area. He hung out with them for the next few days, until they were attacked. One of the Indians was killed, and the one called Willawic was gravely wounded. Billy ran off looking for help for his Indian friend.

"The same night Billy got lost, Joe and Mark found the cabin of a frontier family and were taken in. The father was a cruel man who intended to force the boys to work his land, so in the middle of the night, Joe and Mark ran away. The next day, the two boys were captured by the river pirates that plagued these parts back then—you know, the criminal gang at the Outlaw Cave over on the Mississippi. These pirates preyed on the river traffic, the flatboats and such carrying goods down to New Orleans. They would attack the boats, kill everyone aboard, and steal their goods."

Joel heard the softest "cool" come from Rachel, but couldn't see her face in the shadows. He smiled to himself, knowing he had her hooked.

"When the outlaws caught the boys, they were gonna tie 'em to some trees and leave 'em to die in the wilderness. But Joe was a resourceful kid and got away and almost freed his friend. The head outlaw, a big fella named Wesley Pike, was impressed with Joe's gumption. He thought the boy was a lot like himself and felt fatherly toward him, in his own harsh way. He decided the boys should live.

"You see, Joe was something of a bully. When he finally had it figured out that they'd traveled back in time, he was pretty excited about the prospect of living out some of the things he'd only read about. He saw the pirates as a bunch of fun-loving, if violent, swashbucklers and envied their way of life. And, although he was frightened of them, he thought they were pretty cool.

"Mark was so disturbed by the pirates' violence, he withdrew into himself and talked all kinds of gibberish for a long time. Because he was so weird, the pirates wanted to do away with him, but Wesley decided Mark was funny and adopted the boy as his dog. 'An' nobody hurts my dawg,' the outlaw would say.

"In a short while, though, Mark came out of his funk and was his old self again."

Rachel leaned forward, poking a stick into the fire. Joel could see her face, but couldn't make out her expression. He liked to think she was hanging on his every word. (Why he liked the idea, he wasn't entirely sure.)

"During the time they lived with the outlaws, Mark and Joe learned all kinds of things—useful back then, but not so useful now—like how to load and shoot a flintlock rifle, how to hunt, ride a horse, and all that kind of frontier stuff. But they also saw things that no kid should ever have to see.

"Like what?" Rachel asked. Joel heard the challenge in her voice.

You don't want to know, little girl, Joel thought. A thousand images flickered through his mind, red-drenched and unspeakable. "Death by murder," he said flatly. "Some brutally impersonal. Some viciously intimate. The boys saw a lot of both and couldn't decide which was worse."

Rachel nodded, shrugged nervously, looked away.

"About this time," Joel continued, trying to smile, "Billy caught up with Joe and Mark and got them to help him with Willawic. When they got to the spot where Billy had left Willawic in the forest, Joe saw that the Indian was wearing Nike brand athletic shoes."

Joel heard Rachel snort a laugh in the darkness. He smiled. It did sound pretty nutsy. But he was on a roll.

"Joe knew that, somehow, Willawic had a connection with their own time. Perhaps the Indian could help them find their way home, if only they could learn to speak a common language.

"The three hauled the wounded Indian down to the Pirate Cave. They carried him in a back entrance and hid him and Billy in a forgotten side chamber.

"Now Wesley had a brother named Virgil Pike, who was as mean a man as you'd ever care to meet. Virgil, although a full-grown man, came to hate Joe for taking his role as Wesley's little brother and vowed secretly to kill him.

"Wesley decided it was time to take Joe on an adventure and make a man of him. There was a Tennessee militia that had been stepping on the outlaws' toes and generally givin' 'em hell. Now, Wesley wanted to run 'em to ground and do 'em in. So one bright morning, Joe set out with Wesley, Virgil and fifty of their cutthroats. They traveled for a couple of days to a spot where they could ambush the militia. Wesley gave Joe a gun and expected him to get right in there with the fighting and do his part. Hell, Joe expected the same thing, but when the killing began, he froze up.

"This wasn't at all what he'd thought it'd be like. People

were really dying in front of him, people with families and lives and personalities, right before his eyes. The screams, the blood, the viciousness—it was horrible. Joe found he couldn't bring himself to fire his pistol. But Virgil was the only one who saw this.

"Joe suddenly realized he wasn't at all what he thought he was, and this was the start of a big change in him."

"He was growing up," Moss said, "isn't that right, Joel?"

"That's right, Moss—could be the only growing up he ever did."

Joel paused to catch his breath and kicked at a log in the fire, sending a shower of sparks skyward.

"The pirates slaughtered most of them, at least forty men. Joe never forgot what he saw that day—it was burned into his brain."

Joel swallowed hard, trying to shove the grisly images out of his mind.

"When they got back to the cave, Joe was too busy keeping an eye on his friends, who weren't near as savvy as he was in the outlaws' ways, and maintaining his relationship with Wesley to see how bad Virgil hated him. That is, 'til one day, when Wesley left the cave on some business and Joe was left alone with Virgil. The outlaw attacked the boy and he barely got away with his life. Joe took off into the forest, Virgil hot on his tail.

"Let me tell you a little bit about Virgil. He was small, not much bigger than Joe himself. But he was vicious to the bone and crazy as a rabid dog. Some even said he was a cannibal. And it was Joe's blood he wanted."

Joel paused and looked his audience over.

"Well?" Moss said.

"Yeah, Joel," Lynn said, "what happened?"

He chuckled, pleased with himself and the success of his tale.

"He managed to elude the outlaw for a day, and then laid a

clever trap for 'im deep in the bottom of a deadfall. He sharpened a stout branch, and lay in wait. Pretending he was hurt, and stuck under all the fallen wood, Joe lured Virgil out on top of the pile of rotten branches. Just as he'd hoped, the branches snapped under the weight of the man and he fell, impaling himself on Joe's spike. The boy crawled out, leaving Virgil for dead, and made his way back to the cave."

"Yea!" Lynn said, clapping.

Rachel was looking him in the face, obviously intent on the tale. Firelight reflected in her eyes.

"Joe was happy all the long way back to the Outlaw Cave, for he'd done away with his tormentor. In fact, he was pretty darn full of himself. But his happiness was short lived. When he got back, there was Virgil, wounded, but alive! He had somehow gotten to the cave before Joe."

"Oh my!" Lynn blurted. "How awful."

"Yes, it was. But Joe thought he was safe for a while, at least 'til Virgil healed up. Virgil's pride had prevented him from telling anyone what Joe had done to him. The evil little man was hurt badly, or else Joe knew he'd be dead already.

"Mark and Billy had been trying to figure out how to speak to Willawic, but weren't having much luck. The Indian spoke French, and, of the three boys, only Mark had ever studied the language. However, Mark's French left much to be desired, and Joe worried that the language barrier would not be crossed before Willawic healed up and left them.

"By now, Billy was thoroughly sick of being cooped up in the little side chamber. He had taken to roaming around the cave by himself. Joe knew it was only a matter of time before he was caught. So, he introduced Billy to the outlaws as *his* dog. Wesley was flattered that Joe was trying to be like him, and the big man silenced all naysayers.

"At any rate, the pirates were too busy to deal with Joe and his friends. They had bigger things to deal with. The surviving Tennessee militia was now under the leadership of a man named Thomas Fellowes. Fellowes was a hard man, but honest. He had been scalped by Indians and survived it, though he bore a horrendous scar—"

"Thomas Fellowes?" Lynn said. "That name sounds familiar—"

"Lynn," Moss said, gently, "let him tell his story."

"Sorry," Lynn said sheepishly. Joel tipped her a wink.

"Now, as I was saying, the Tennessee militia had a new leader, and they had gotten a whole bunch more volunteers together to rout the pirates from their cave and make 'em pay for all that they had done.

"The night the militia surrounded the cave, Willawic took off, and the three boys had no idea what had become of him. He wasn't there to help Joe when Virgil finally came for him."

Lynn gasped. Her hands flew to her mouth.

"Virgil wanted Joe dead like he wanted his next breath. He almost beat the boy to death. But Wesley stopped it. Wesley killed his own brother to save Joe."

"Wicked," Rachel whispered.

"The militia fought the outlaws for three days. Joe and his friends thought that as soon as the militia killed off all the pirates, they would be rescued and maybe even find help getting home. But no."

"Whaddaya mean, no?" Lynn asked.

"Yeah," Rachel said, "c'mon, what happened?"

"It was a horrible, bloody battle. The militia suffered great losses and were pissed, and the men began to question Thomas Fellowes' leadership. Most of the pirates escaped, and when the militia captured the cave and all those who'd stayed behind, they turned out to be just as bad as the outlaws. You see, the militia had mutinied against Thomas Fellowes. They picked a new leader, one that would let 'em do what they wanted, which was to plunder the cave and rape and kill the survivors. The boys were imprisoned along with the surviving outlaw women and children."

"Oh no!" Lynn said, leaning her head on her husband's shoulder and gripping his arm tightly.

"Now calm down, Lynn," said Joel, "it's gonna get better."

"Yeah, Mom, chill out."

"The boys knew they didn't have long to live if they couldn't figure out some way to escape. Well, Thomas Fellowes had been watching and listening. He snuck in to see the boys, and revealed that he was from the twentieth century as well. In their conversation, it came out that he was a neighbor of theirs who had mysteriously disappeared some years back—his house was situated along that creek where the boys got lost. The boys decided that he did look familiar, except for the big scalping scar.

"Fellowes told them that Willawic was in the woods nearby, looking for them. With Fellowes' help, the Indian freed the boys and led them into the forest. Fellowes joined them not long after, and together they struck out into the wilderness, hoping to find the way home.

"That night, Mark finally managed to, more or less successfully, communicate with Willawic. Mark told the Indian that he and his friends had come from the place where Willawic's Nikes had come from. Willawic agreed to take them to that place.

"As they followed the Indian through the forest, Wesley Pike popped up, pretty pissed off 'cause Fellowes and the militia trashed his setup at the cave. He and Fellowes went at it, the ugliest fight you've ever seen. Each man was trying his damndest to kill the other.

"Right about this time, a massive earthquake hit. Joe remembered his Tennessee history, and realized it was the quake that formed Reelfoot Lake.

It seemed like the world would end. There was a great flood. The Mississippi ran backwards. Forests were flattened, hills sheared off while great waves washed away everything in their path. Wesley Pike and Thomas Fellowes tumbled into the water as they fought and were lost. Trying to save Fellowes, Mark fell into the deluge and was carried away as well. The others tried to rescue him, but Mark was gone and they never saw him or the two men ever again."

As the last sentence left his mouth, Joel grew suddenly embarrassed. *Well that sounded like a big, steaming pile of horse shit.*

"Oh, how sad," Lynn said, sniffling, "I thought it was gonna have a happy ending."

"Geez, Mom!"

"Now, Lynn," Moss said, "hesh up an' let Joel finish his story."

"Joe was devastated by the loss of his friend, but he decided he had to keep going. If nothing else, he had to help Billy get home.

"They found the creek and followed it until they began to recognize things again. Suddenly, they were back home. Willawic waved good-bye to the boys as they passed back into the present."

"Were they home, really?"

"Shut *up*, Mom!"

"Don't talk to your mother like that, Rachel. Lynn, hesh your mouth an' let him finish the damn story."

"Yes, Joe and Billy *did* make it home and they grew up, never telling anyone but me about their adventure. And from then on, for the rest of his life, Joe went down to that creek *every day*, hoping that eventually, Mark would return. But Joe never saw his friend again."

"Ooh, what a spooky story," Lynn said, hugging herself.

"I thought it was *cool*," said Rachel.

"And it's all true," Joel said, and everyone laughed. When they realized he wasn't joining in, a sudden silence descended. Joel saw a troubled expression on Moss's face, and forced himself to laugh. The others let go, laughing with him.

Rachel got up and walked over to where Joel sat. "Hey, that was *really* a great story," she said, putting a hand on Joel's shoulder.

Her eyes then flashed with something that, as a teacher, he'd seen many times before. The girl had a crush on him! *Oh, Christ, just what I need.*

"Thanks a lot," she said.

"You're welcome, Rachel."

She smiled—the first he'd seen from her—and it transformed her face from sullenly pretty to beautiful. She turned and headed for the house, looking over her shoulder just once. Joel watched her go and then turned back to the fire.

"I think you scored some points there, Joel," Moss said. "Wish *I* knew how to do that."

"Aw, she's tired," Joel said. "She'll forget all about it in the morning."

"I'm afraid you may be right. Well, I'm off to bed." Lynn abruptly stood, and waddled toward the cabin. "You comin', Moss?"

"Yeah, be right there. How 'bout you, Joel. You comin' in yet?"

"No, thought I'll stay out here with the night a bit."

"Okay then, see you in the morning. Don't get y'self et by a bear or nothin'."

Moss started for the cabin, then paused and turned back. "So that's the story, is it, Joel? That's what happened?"

"Yeah, that's about it."

"You know, you scared Lynn this morning, screaming and yelling and waving that book around. What was all that about?"

Joel grimaced, then grinned weakly at Moss. "I, uh, I found the names Thomas Fellowes, Mark Ryder, and Joel Biggs in the book. I can show you. I've been looking for evidence that we'd been back there in eighteen-eleven for so long. I just couldn't believe my own eyes when I found it. I needed Lynn to read it aloud to me, to make sure I wasn't crazy. I'll have to apologize to her in the morning."

"I'd like to see that book." Moss nodded his head and shuffled off. "G'night."

After Moss had gone, Joel pulled out the Crenshaw book. As much as he'd wanted to show it to Moss tonight, Joel wanted his "cousin" to sleep on the story first. To think about it. Moss knew that Joel had vanished along with Mark and Billy that summer. Everyone knew. Moss had even come out with his parents for a while, and joined the search party looking for Mark. Joel had only seen Moss a couple of times during that stressful period, and the older boy had been kind but awkward, almost embarrassed around him. Joel had always figured it was either because Moss thought Joel had been in the clutches of a pervert for a month and a half, or that Joel was crazy, or both. Now that he'd finally told Moss the truth, would he be able to accept it?

Of course he won't. Would you believe something like that, if it hadn't happened to you?

Joel sighed. He knew it was ridiculous, but he hoped that somehow, his story would seep into Moss's brain as he slept, and convince him of its truth.

Joel opened the book. By the light of the fire, he reread the testimonial letter by Thomas Fellowes. He had to see those names again.

State of Tennessee, Shelby County, 1833

The man going by the name of Matthew Crenshaw

requested that I, Thomas Fellowes, make this statement attesting to an incident which occurred in the township of Wallace in the state of Tennessee on the twenty-seventh of November, 1833. The gentleman in question, while passing through the town in the company of Jarrett Cotten, came to see me on a matter of great urgency.

Before I continue, I must state and attest that I have known the man going by the name Matthew Crenshaw (hereafter referred to as Crenshaw) since he was a youngster. I do know his true name, and that he is now well beyond his thirtieth year. Furthermore, I should say here that prior to the date aforementioned, I knew the name Jarrett Cotten as belonging to one who was an infamous outlaw.

My friend sought me out in my general store to speak privately, saying that he was passing himself off to Jarrett Cotten as Matthew Crenshaw, a man of desperate temperament; and through this deception, hoped to put himself in good stead with Cotten. Crenshaw said he told the man he was a complete stranger to the territory and told me that if I were seen with him, to feign unfamiliarity.

He was pursuing Cotten after the man had stolen two negroes from the farm of Crenshaw's good friend, Hume Stogdon, in Madison County, Tennessee. Being under the guise of an outlaw, Crenshaw hoped that Cotten would lead him to the stolen negroes.

Crenshaw wanted to be seen by me on this day to leave some record of his passing, being afraid Cotten had seen through his disception and was soon to do him in. I agreed to prepare this letter and gave him a loaded pistol so that he could defend himself if Cotten turned on him. We were together but a very brief time before he rejoined Cotten.

This is the extent of my knowledge on the subject, but it

has been suggested to me that Mr. M. Ryder and Mr. J. Biggs were witness to a good deal more and if found, would be of great assistance in this matter.

If it serves the cause of justice, then I freely give this account of the events thus known to me. Penned by my hand and entered into record at Alexandria, Tennessee on the tenth day of May, 1833.

THOMAS Q. FELLOWES
(SEALED)

Joel had always dreamed that Mark had gone on to have a life in the eighteen-hundreds. He'd tried to imagine it was a good one, but in the back of his mind he knew that Mark had probably drowned in the flood following the New Madrid earthquake.

But there it was, written on the page in front of him. Possible evidence that Mark *had* survived. Fellowes had written his testimonial twenty years after Mark was lost. Thomas Fellowes had obviously survived the flood. Why couldn't Mark?

But he didn't just mention Mark, he wrote my name too. What the hell does that mean? And why don't I remember it from reading this when we were kids? I'd remember that, wouldn't I?

Joel couldn't get the sentence out of his head: "*. . . it has been suggested to me that Mr. M. Ryder and Mr. J. Biggs were witness to a good deal more and if found, would be of great assistance in this matter.*"

Joel's head was starting to hurt. *Why should I think M. Ryder is really Mark? J. Biggs obviously isn't me. I left Fellowes behind in 1811. We never saw each other again. Maybe he's just using our names as code. Or maybe it's another Biggs. Biggs's have been in this area forever. But M. Ryder . . . could it be Mark? Really?*

Joel tried picturing Mark as an adult, but all he could manage was his friend's dimpled chin and that dumb-assed smile of his. Joel shook his head, and tried to return his attention to the book.

> The day had grown warmer as Crenshaw and Cotten worked their way south. At dusk, Cotten shared out more provisions, indicating that they would eat in the saddle once again. The outlaw's long silence and unresponsiveness through the afternoon had made it clear to Crenshaw that he was expected to follow Cotten unflinchingly.

Joel's eyes wandered from the page, and into the dark woods at the edge of the Phelpses' yard. He imagined Mark bursting from the trees, waving, smiling. *"I'm back, Joel! I'm back!"* He could almost see the figure of a man, tall and slim, in his mind's eye. But for some reason, Joel couldn't imagine Mark's face at thirty-two. *I can't think of him as anything but a child, and that child couldn't have survived to adulthood in the eighteen-hundreds.* The thought pressed down on him heavily. With a sigh, Joel looked back down at the book.

> As the last of the sun's brilliant colors faded from the sky beyond the distant hills, Cotten came to rest where the road climbed gently toward a heavily forested hill. He dismounted and scanned the underbrush without offering an explanation. Crenshaw waited uncomfortably, fearful that Cotten had somehow discovered his efforts to keep a secret journal and was planning to lead him off into the wilds to do him in.
>
> When the outlaw returned and sat astride his horse once again, there was a self-satisfied expression on his face, and Crenshaw felt his worst fears were about to be realized. He almost spurred his mount to bolt away, but managed to calm himself. The pistol in his coat gave him some small

measure of comfort, but Crenshaw knew that he had little chance of prevailing in a direct conflict with the notorious criminal. Cotten was known for his speed and skill with weapons of all sorts.

Cotten led him along a rough trail through heavy undergrowth. The low-lying boughs of bordering trees attempted to wrest them from their mounts. When at length the outlaw did nothing to threaten him, Crenshaw realized that Cotten had merely been looking for this secret trail, not plotting his demise.

Crenshaw thanked providence that, as yet, he had not been revealed.

"The Mississippi state line," Cotten announced, as they crested a steep hill and turned onto another thin trail.

A benighted valley lay before them, and they descended into it. The air grew more chill and Crenshaw gathered his greatcoat more tightly about him. Since leaving the road, they were no longer slogging through a quagmire. With fatigue and the rocking of his horse, Crenshaw found himself beginning to doze. He was uncertain how much time had passed when Cotten startled him to wakefulness.

"Come along, young Crenshaw," the outlaw said. "The mysteries of the night hold us within their ephemeral grasp."

Joel smiled faintly. He remembered reading this passage from the Crenshaw book to Mark, up in the tree house. When he had glanced at his friend, he saw that Mark was asleep. With a tinge of shame, Joel remembered how angry he had become.

I was such a miserable bully.

But it wasn't all my fault. Mark could be such a baby. He couldn't think on his own, had no spine, couldn't stand up for himself, and never had an original thought in his head.

Trying to throw off his sleepiness, Crenshaw shook himself, and nearly fell from the saddle.

"You promised that we would pass the time in conversation," Cotten said, amiably. "Yet tonight, you have offered nothing to our intercourse but your abominable snoring."

"I was more fatigued than I had thought. Please forgive me."

Cotten's fearsome white teeth shone as he smiled in the moonlight. "I trust you are now well rested?"

Crenshaw nodded his head, forcing himself to smile.

"Well then, good sir, fill your pipe and we will talk."

Soon the fragrant smell of tobacco wafted on the cool night breeze. Crenshaw held his pipe tightly in his gloved hands, the warmth helping to thaw them out.

"I first visited New Orleans as a young man," Cotten said. "I had a great desire to become involved in speculation, but had no experience."

Speculation, Joel thought. *Such a genteel word for robbery, murder, and deceit.*

"I thought I might find easy prey in New Orleans because I'd heard many rich and foolish people lived there, as well as many who preyed upon them. I was also impatient to meet others of my kind. I had little success, until late one night, while returning to my inn, three men brandishing pistols approached and politely asked for my money. I handed them my pocketbook, and I explained how glad I was to meet them.

"The first one said, 'We've been watching you for many

nights. You seem to be a student of speculation, but one who is at a loss as to how it is done.'

" 'That is true,' I said, then introduced myself and pleaded with them to educate me. They agreed and returned my pocketbook to me. Thus began my initiation into a career of brilliant wickedness.

"At that young age, I was quite taken with them. We fell in together very naturally, and they showed me the town. We spent a month in an extravagant frolic through countless taverns and many a comely wench.

"I was made known to all the speculators in New Orleans and was given the name of every fellow engaged in speculation on the Mississippi.

"I was taught many a criminal art. But the most valuable lesson I learned was the art of killing.

"The only victim I ever allowed to keep his life was my first. He boarded at the tavern where I stayed. He was a Louisville dandy, all flash and glitter. I was determined to rob him and devised a plan with my new friends. I would take him on a bender. My friends were to fall upon us both as we were returning to our lodgings. The event unfolded just as planned. My friends beat the fellow within an inch of his life. How the sight of his blood thrilled me! I longed to join in, but to maintain our ruse, I had to play the victim as well. I would never be put in such a position again. The robbery so disgusted the Kentuckian that he left New Orleans that very night, vowing never to return. He had no idea just how lucky a man he was."

Cotten chuckled in such a fashion that it made Crenshaw's blood run cold. "The booty was substantial. We split four ways. It allowed me to live comfortably for a year. During that time, I prowled the great cities of the South, from New Orleans to Cincinnati, from Memphis to Charleston, making acquaintances of all the speculators I could find. These numbered some four hundred.

"It was with these clever souls in mind that I first conceived of the Mystic Clan.

"Then one day I was in a small town in Alabama when rumors of a slave uprising began to circulate. The townsfolk were well acquainted with news of the recent revolts in the West Indies and the horrors suffered by the planters there. They were prostrate with fear.

"The idea occurred to me that this was a powerful weapon. I thought back to my first time in New Orleans when, having seen the grand houses of the very rich, I had told myself, 'This could all be mine, if only I had the right weapon.' Watching that Alabama town become a slave to its own fear, I knew that I had found it. Cause a slave revolt throughout the South and in the confusion that would follow, my Mystic Clan could go to work, robbing the wealthy of everything they had."

Joel's headache had grown worse. He rubbed his forehead hard. Unwanted, twelve-year-old Mark Ryder's face appeared behind his eyes once again. Joel shoved it away with a hot rush of anger. *If I hadn't been there, Mark never would have survived. Fuck the goddam sonofabitch! He's not worth it.*

The outlaw had at last fallen silent, and Crenshaw did his best to commit everything Cotten had said to memory so he could set it down in writing on the morrow when there would be light enough to do so.

Light enough. . . . The fire had died down, and the pages had grown hard to see. Joel felt suddenly very tired. Mark still haunted his thoughts, hovering at the edge of his consciousness, as he almost always did. The anger Joel had felt for his friend drained away. *What the hell am I getting mad for? Mark was just a kid, a simple, trusting kid. And he needed me. Why did I let him get away? Why couldn't I save him?*

Because I was just a kid too—that's why. I swear, Mark, I swear to you that I did my best. . . .

Joel closed the book and slipped it back into his jacket pocket. He leaned back into a pile of leaves, memories of Mark swirling through his mind. He was sleepy and knew he should get up and go inside to bed, but even so he allowed his eyes to close.

3

The red clay of the trail was imprinted with hundreds of hoofprints, but it was hard and dry now. It looked to Joel like no one had traveled this way in twenty years. He was glad to see Willawic, Mark and Billy just ahead. It felt good to be back with them.

Then the voice of a dead man filled his head. "Yer yella, boy, a coward."

It was the voice of Virgil Pike and now everything was wrong, a dreadful déjà vu. The forest towered dark and menacing on either side, the horseshoe-imprinted, cracked clay of the winding trail the skin of a venomous snake. He froze in his tracks and turned to go back.

"C'mon, Joel, whadya stop for?" his three friends voiced in unison.

He turned back to find them staring intently at him.

"Nothin', I jus' figured I don't belong here."

"Why would you think that? What's wrong with this?"

"I don't know. It's just too hard, too dangerous."

"Jeez, Joel," Mark said, "you can really be a goober sometimes."

They turned and walked on. Joel's sense of dread intensified as he watched them pass beyond the curve in the trail. Something told him that around that curve the ground was roughed up and bloody.

"There was an old lady who followed a fly," Mark, Billy and

Willawic sang together, "I don't know why she followed a fly. Perhaps she'll die."

"Aw, hell," Joel told himself, "what's a little bloody ground?"

"There was an old cat who swallowed a horse. I don't know why, it's stupid of course. Perhaps a divorce."

The trail climbed a slight rise as it curved and what lay beyond was obscured by a row of maples.

"There was an old house who swallowed its dick. I don't know why but that's real, real sick. Perhaps a lick."

Mark was laughing as Joel caught up with him. He was holding a copy of *Big Hooters* magazine and he thrust it in Joel's face. Joel eagerly took the magazine, glad for the distraction—he knew he didn't want to see what was in the field just ahead.

"Hey, Joel," Mark said, "when we get back let's get some action figures and play war just like this!" Mark tore the magazine out of his grip, and Joel looked where his friend was pointing, at the stinking, mutilated corpses.

Like black ash falling from the sky, buzzards dropped upon the corpses and tore at them. A storm of flies swarmed about the clearing, blurring the view.

Crying, Joel stumbled forward into the midst of the dead. His shame was tangled with the torn-out throats, the tattered clothing, the rent flesh. Mark caught up with him and swung him around.

"What's going on?" he asked. "Did you do this?"

Joel shoved him away and Mark fell to the ground. Joel walked to the middle of the battlefield, turned around in a tight little circle as he looked at the cadavers surrounding him. A tight knot of pain lodged in his throat. He tried not to collapse, tried not to give in, but the wormy mass of shame came apart in his head. The explosion forced a single agonized howl from his throat and hurled him to the ground. And then he was crying in great uncontrollable sobs.

Mark approached, knelt down beside him, and put a hand on his shoulder. “I know what you did,” he said, “but it’s not your fault.”

“Yes it is,” Joel said, “I made this happen.”

“What are you talking about?”

“This is what happened on that *great* adventure Wesley Pike took me on.” Joel’s sarcasm scalded his throat. “This is where we ambushed the Tennessee militia!”

“It’s not your fault, Joel—we’re just little boys.”

“You are, Mark,” Joel said, “but I’m all grown up now and this is just a dream.”

4

Joel woke at dawn with leaves clinging to his clothing. His shirt and pants were soaked through with early morning dew. Yawning, the sharp tang of the sodden campfire caught in his nose and, for a moment, he saw the others, the Pikes and a few of their cutthroats asleep in their bedrolls around him. He looked off into the mist-shrouded trees and saw a boy standing on the edge of the woods.

No, this is the Phelpses' property, he thought, sitting up and brushing the leaves away. Then reality shifted behind his eyes, and he was alone by the firepit again. The woods thinned out—the trees losing their Herculean dimensions—and the sounds of the virgin forest faded from his mind.

He rubbed his eyes to clear out the sleep and the vision, but the boy remained. At first he thought it must be Brian or Caleb.

Then he got a better look.

"Mark?" he heard himself whisper.

The boy turned, walked into the mist and was gone. Joel rose to his feet and took a couple of steps after him, but then sensed he would never reach him.

No goddammit, I'm through chasing that little boy. I need to find the man.

Stiff and sore, Joel walked back to the Phelpses' log cabin and entered. He was padding through the house, headed for the loft for a couple more hours of sleep, when something caught his eye. Dozens of tabloid magazines were scattered all over the kitchen table. One tabloid, the *World News Weekly,* famous for Bigfoot photos and Elvis sightings, was open, with a note from Lynn on top of it:

> Hey Joel,
>
> When you were telling about the Indian in Nikes, I thought I remembered this—just had to look it up. Some imagination you've got! You should go to work for the World News Weekly!
>
> Lynn

Joel moved the note. The headline glaring at him read "160-Year-Old Indian Skeleton Discovered—Wearing Nike Shoes!"

Joel stared. His heart started to pound. There was a grainy photograph of a skeleton, curled up on its side, with the remnants of what could be Nike athletic shoes on its feet. In contrast to most of the other photos in the tabloids, this one didn't look Photoshopped. The article was brief, stating that the man in the Nikes was believed to be between fifty and sixty years old, dead of natural causes. Several paragraphs were dedicated to "experts" declaring the authenticity and age of the impossible shoes. Silly. Ridiculous, even.

Joel's eyes suddenly stung with tears. "Willawic," he whispered. "Good to know you had a long life, buddy." His fingers grazed the cheap paper, remembering Willawic's rare smiles.

He made up his mind on the spot. He was going back.

5

The sun was still an orange ball on the horizon when Joel, without awakening Lynn or Moss, managed to slip up to the loft for his belongings. He was halfway down the ladder when he heard Rachel come out of the bathroom.

"Hey," she said sleepily, "y'okay?"

Joel froze, his mind a blank. "Be quiet, now," he whispered at last, "you'll wake your parents." He stepped off the ladder and reluctantly turned to face her. God, she was adorable. Her hair was tousled, and her long legs were bare under the well-worn Reverend Horton Heat T-shirt she slept in. Joel looked quickly away, and felt like a sleaze for having looked at all.

"But where y'goin' so early?"

"Don't worry 'bout me, I'm just goin' for a mornin' walk."

"But you have your suitcase."

Shit. Shit. Shit. Joel took in a deep breath. "Rachel—something's come up. There's something I have to do back home."

She scowled, some of the sleep clearing from her suspicious eyes. "You're leaving? Why? How come you said you were jus' goin' for a walk, then?"

He took her gently by the shoulders. The girl's eyes went wide. "Rachel . . . I said that because I'm a cowardly shit. I didn't know how to tell your dad that I was leaving after everything he's done for me. I didn't know how to tell you. I'm sorry."

Suddenly she pressed up against him. "Take me with you, Joel."

His eyes bugged. *Well. Didn't see that one comin' didja, smart guy.* He stepped back, away from her. "I can't do that. You're just a kid. And—and you're my cousin!"

"You know we're not really related." She was smiling, but there was desperation in her eyes. Joel wondered what was going on with her. He wished he could help her. *But I can't. I can't.*

"No." He said it quietly, but firmly. "I'll see you again, Rachel. I'll come back and visit when I've done what I've gotta do. Then we'll talk, okay?"

She didn't say anything. She just gave him an angry, betrayed look and walked away.

Joel walked out the door and closed it quietly behind him, feeling like hell. He'd send a thank-you note, or call later, he promised himself as he hiked into town.

He had his seat on the first bus back to Dexter within an hour. He settled in, opened the Crenshaw book and read as the miles passed beneath him.

State of Tennessee, Madison County, 1833

I, McHenry Lake, was entreated by a man going by the name Matthew Crenshaw to testify as to what happened on the day he and Jarrett Cotten called at my house on the bank of the Wolf River in the latter part of November, 1833.

When they arrived at my door, Jarrett Cotten introduced himself to me as Parson Jeremy Wode and Crenshaw as Jonathan Gurdy, and they shared a meal with me and spent the night. After they had left the next morning, Crenshaw briefly returned alone, having given Cotten the excuse that he'd left his pipe and tinderbox at my cabin.

Crenshaw explained that he needed to speak with me in order to gain verification of his visit. He asked me to prepare a letter so it could be used to gain an arrest warrant for Jarrett Cotten. He said the Crenshaw name was also false and that he must withhold his real name. He was masquerading as Matthew Crenshaw to gain Cotten's confidence, and through this, hoped to find evidence that would enable charges to be brought against him.

He also informed me that Cotten had stolen my red barb mare.

This document sworn out before Judge Thomas Erwin in the courthouse at Alexandria, Tennessee, on this, the second day of December, 1833.

McHenry Lake

State of Tennessee, Madison County, 1833

I, Thomas Erwin, Judge of the Supreme Court of Madison County aforesaid certify that the preceding testimonial of McHenry Lake is a true and perfect copy, in word and letter, of an instrument of writing filed in my office, to be read in evidence against Jarrett Cotten upon his trial for horse-stealing, at the July term of our said court, 1834.

In testimony whereof I have hereunto subscribed my name and affixed my private seal (there being no public seal of office) at office in Alexandria, this second day of December, A. D. 1833.

Thomas Erwin

Joel was home by ten-thirty that morning. He opened the front door, which he'd forgotten to lock—forgotten, hell, who'd want anything of his anyway—and peered into the half-light coming through the grimy curtains. He wrinkled his nose; the place stunk. It smelled like booze and rotten food, with an undertone of puke and despair. Joel held his breath as he walked through the door.

He was ashamed by what he saw. Bottles and cans littered the floor and coffee table. Food wrappers, bits of popcorn, stacks of paper from when he still had a job and a life. Joel closed his eyes for a moment, wishing he were anywhere else in the world.

Goddam. I need some coffee. He did need it. Joel thought, *If I drank enough hot, sweet java, the cesspit I live in won't drag me back down into a bottle.*

Joel loaded up his elderly Mr. Coffee machine with stale, cheap French Roast and fired it up. On impulse, he grabbed a green plastic garbage bag from under the sink and moved through the house, gathering his empties and trash. He cleared the debris of his recent drunks, gathering liquor bottles and beer cans, scraping a splash of dried vomit from the carpet, sweeping up the shards of a broken tumbler. He threw out dishes so dirty they'd never be clean again, a filthy undershirt, mountains of papers without even looking at them first. When he was done, the garbage bag was stuffed. He carried it out to the garbage, then dragged the vacuum cleaner out of the closet and cleaned the floors.

When he was finished, he remembered the coffee. Joel poured himself a mug, dumped in plenty of sugar. The milk in the fridge had gone sour before he'd even left for Moss's house. The relative cleanliness of his living room gave Joel a curious, cool wave of peace for a moment. Looking around the cluttered kitchen, he decided he would clean it up next, and then he would start on the bathroom.

What the hell's come over me?

I really feel good for a change.

At least physically.

Of course, it didn't matter if he scrubbed the whole damn

house with Pine-Sol and painted it puce. The truth was, there really wasn't anything here for him; no job, no friends, no family. Nothing had changed.

The thought of drinking turned his stomach and made his flesh crawl, but the thought was inescapable. He had come home to the same world he had left, and Joel knew it was only a matter of time before he drank again.

I'll always be wearing my father's dirty genes—just as shiftless as he ever was.

Goddam.

When he'd read his name and Mark's in the Crenshaw book, he'd found what he'd been looking for all his life. Proof that he really had gone back in time. Proof that Mark had survived childhood in the brutal eighteen-hundreds; that he might still be alive. All he had to do was walk down that creek.

Doing just that had made perfect sense when he left the Phelpses at the crack of dawn this morning. But it had been easy to feel confident and optimistic there, away from his shitty, drunken life. Now, faced with staring down the weird, time-ripping length of the creek, well . . . he was afraid. No, not afraid. He was scared shitless.

Joel opened the Crenshaw book at the flimsy square of toilet paper he'd used as a marker and read over the testimonial of Thomas Fellowes once again. He looked at the names, M. Ryder and J. Biggs, for the hundredth time.

What if I decide not to go? Will my name vanish from the book? He stared at the letters that formed "J. Biggs," stared at them until they didn't make sense anymore. They didn't move.

Of course they didn't. Because it's all a coincidence. A fuckin' weird one, for sure, but just a coincidence. He must have read the names in the book as a kid, and his booze-addled brain had lifted them and inserted them into his grandiose, alcoholic fantasy about his childhood. There probably never was a Mark

Ryder. He slammed the book and pushed it away.

He kicked the chair across the table from him and it fell over backwards with a jarring clatter.

But suppose it's real. Suppose it is. I'm too damn old and sick to survive in the eighteen-hundreds. I'd get killed in the first five minutes, probably.

And so what if I did? It'd be better than dying here, in this shit-pile.

He gulped the last of his coffee and got a mouthful of grounds. The more he thought about it, the more ridiculous the whole thing seemed.

If I did make all of this crap up, then everything I remember about my childhood is bullshit. That's hard enough. But if all of this is just a load of crap, then everything I believe about myself is wrong, and I can't take that.

Shit. If only Billy were alive . . . well, he could tell me if I were fuckin' nuts or not. The thought of his friend brought an unwanted, painful lump to his throat.

Joel rested his head in his hands, closing his eyes. The world seemed to be shifting under his feet. Reality was a treacherous, slippery thing, eluding his grasp like a watersnake, and just as likely to whip around and sink its fangs into him.

A cold panic gripped Joel's heart. Suddenly, desperately, he wanted a drink.

It had been one of those nights when he'd drunk so much and felt so bad that he was sick of the whole fucking thing. He'd promised himself, yet again, that he was going to give it up and had stashed what remained of the fifth in the back of a file cabinet. He knew full well that, although he would forget where he put it in the morning, he would remember it in a time of need.

Apparently, that time had come.

Joel went into the study and retrieved the whiskey, and

returned to the kitchen for a glass. It seemed stupid, pouring cheap, stinking booze into a glass just to pour it down his throat and get shitfaced, but some tiny, remaining shred of dignity wouldn't allow him to drink straight from the bottle. Though his hands had been steady for the last couple of days, when he tipped the bottle toward a tumbler, fear caused his hand to shake and half the whiskey missed its mark and drooled down the outside of the glass.

There was the softest plop as he lifted the glass from its amber puddle and brought it to his lips.

A knocking came from the front door. Joel jerked around and the tumbler slipped from his hand, falling to the floor with an explosion of glass. He froze, hoping it wasn't Moss. He kicked away the broken glass and went to peer through the living-room window. A police car sat in the driveway. His heart missed a beat.

"Who is it?" he asked. *As if I don't fuckin' know.*

"It's the *po*lice," said a voice, young and nasal. "We need ta have a word with ya."

"What about?" Joel's voice came out unsteadily and a fist gripped his stomach and yanked.

"Would you open up the door please, Mister Biggs?" came a second voice with the soft, local drawl.

"Uh . . . just a minute," Joel said, stalling while trying to remember what he'd done. He jumped when he heard the rude squawk of their radios. "I'm not dressed."

"Just open the door, please."

He saw his life sliding downhill into ruin: jail time, sanitariums, delirium tremens, and dying his father's long, slow death—a raving lunatic, his internal organs failing one at a time as he drowned himself in his own ninety-proof embalming fluid.

Quietly fitting the chain latch into position, Joel opened the door a crack and peered out at the two police officers. One was young, with dark, greasy hair and acne. The other was middle-aged, with the puffy, slitted eyes of an alcoholic. They were both overweight and tense.

"What do you want?"

"Yor neighbor, Missus Devereaux, said ya assaulted 'er. She swore out a warrant for yor arrest."

Joel slowly backed away. "Let me put on some pants."

"No, Mister Biggs, jus' open the door."

Joel made a dash for the back of the house. He heard from behind him, "He's makin' a run for it!"

With a burst of adrenaline, he flung the kitchen door open and sprinted across the side yard. Out of the corner of his eye he saw a dark-blue uniform starting after him.

"He's headed for Missus Devereaux's!"

If Joel hadn't been so intent on running he would have laughed—did they think he was on his way to finish off the old bitch? *That's me, Joel Biggs, ravening serial killer. . . .*

He leapt through the hedge, its sharp twigs tearing at him, and into Mrs. Devereaux's back yard. He was speeding across her patio, knocking lawn furniture out of his way, when she caught sight of him.

"He's over here!" she screamed, as he rounded the corner of her house and started for the road. "BOO!" Joel roared on his way past. She let out a satisfying shriek.

A glance to his right and he saw one of the pudgy officers cut across the yard toward him. Behind, he could hear the jingle of equipment on the other's belt as he chugged around Mrs. Devereaux's house from the other side.

Joel put on a burst of speed, crossing the road and running along the edge of the creek bank, the younger officer almost upon him. Something strange had happened inside him once he began to run. He was no longer afraid. He ran with a wild exhilaration, his heart pounding with savage freedom. He was going to get away. He was going to make it. And if he didn't, well . . . Joel would fight. He'd grab for the young officer's gun, and the older one, the one with the eyes of a drunk, would shoot him. Either way, he'd end up free.

Joel leapt off the eight-foot bank and landed in a crouch, water spraying in all directions. Pulling his feet free of the silty sand and gravel, Joel was amazed he hadn't hurt himself. His shoes were filled with stones which dug into his feet as he sped away.

There was no splash behind him, just curses. Joel grinned. *Knew you couldn't make it, didn't ya, you fat fuck.* He heard the older cop's raspy voice say, "Let him go, Hank—it's just a misdemeanor warrant." The other officer made a response, but Joel was too far away to hear what he said.

Suddenly, he was aware that he knew what he was doing and where he was going.

A tangle of barbed wire snagged his shirt and spun him sideways. He stopped to free himself.

The barbed wire led to a tangle of driftwood, exposed roots, and garbage that blocked the way. Joel only hesitated a moment before climbing the barricade. He slipped a few times and cut his shin on a soup can lid, but he made it over the top. Once again, he followed the water.

Stumbling on over the exposed bedrock, trudging through the shallows and deep water, he felt disconnected from the world around him, as if he were in one of the many dreams he had had over the years about The New Cut. As in the dreams, he felt he couldn't stop, but this time he didn't want to.

Joel wasn't twelve anymore and was now tall enough to see above the high creek bank. Would he be able to see the changes as they occurred? Perhaps nothing would happen as long as he could see above the line of the banks. He couldn't tell—were the trees becoming larger, more numerous? Where were the neighboring houses, and the cars for that matter? Everything was a blur as he stumbled on.

He turned for one last look behind him. He squinted at the endless green, at the strange, hot shimmer in the air. Or was that just his overheated imagination? The flesh on the back of his neck began to crawl. As Joel turned back around, his chest slammed into a heavy root protruding from the bank. The breath was knocked from him, and he fell and went under. He thrashed around for a panicky moment, unable to find the surface. Then his feet found purchase and he stood, face breaking the water, sucking in air with a spluttering gasp. *Since when is the creek so goddam deep?* he thought. Then Joel remembered that long ago this creek had been a river.

Pulling his feet from the sucking mud, he noticed that the banks were more shallow. A heavy mist crept off the surface of the water, swirling around his legs, caressing him with ghostly fingers. There was a chill in the air. The cold bit through Joel's soaked clothes to his clammy skin, and he shivered. He wished he'd brought a jacket. *Hell, I wish I'd brought a lot of things, like food, and water, and a big fucking gun.*

The birds and animals recovered from the rude surprise he'd given them and started chattering again. The heavy forest muted the sound, making it hard to tell where each cry and twitter came from. Joel remembered the deceptive nature of the deep woods, and he shuddered.

Although the trees had lost their leaves, the heavy tangle of branches and twigs filtered out much of the light. The wind whistled through the dead limbs and, in the distance, he heard the groaning and creaking of trees rubbing against each other.

Joel crawled up the bank and looked around at the drifts of brown leaves. Here and there, he saw burrows among them, some disturbingly large. Hugging himself against this bitter, gray world, Joel walked lightly, so as not to awaken the hibernating animals.

He shivered, stuffing his wet hands under his arms and realizing just how alone he was, just how stupid he'd been to come here utterly and completely unprepared. He felt he'd been eaten by the woods, a helpless, toothless, clawless morsel swallowed whole and soon to be digested. Joel slumped against a tree and closed his eyes.

Fuck, it could be worse. At least I don't have any booze here.

6

Joel was in no shape to travel. He was soaked to the skin, freezing, and although it had only been late morning when he fled from his home, he was suddenly exhausted. He found himself a hollow between the roots of a massive tree, and lined it with dried leaves. He curled up, pulling more leaves over himself until only his face showed through, and went to sleep.

He woke up disoriented, blinking in the filtered late-afternoon sunlight. He emerged from his bed of leaves like a zombie from the grave, yawning, stretching, shaking out his nearly dry clothes. Joel's stomach let out a tremendous rumble. He foraged around until he found some late-season huckleberries, overripe and mushy, but sweet. He ate all he could find, but was still hungry. Joel pulled the small pocket knife from his pants and stared at it, wondering how it could help him. At last he sharpened a long stick, and waded into the river to fish.

It took more than a few tries, but Joel finally managed to skewer a small fish. He held it over his head and whooped, sending birds flying from the trees. He had his Zippo in his pocket (thank God) and made himself a small fire. Although the fish was bony and bland, he found it delicious.

After a drink from the river and a piss in the woods, Joel was ready to go. He started walking down the riverbank, whistling softly. He could do this. He could survive. Joel smiled up at the sky, finally at peace with himself and his decision.

"Joel!"

He scowled. Had he heard someone call his name? No, of course not. He kept walking.

"Joel, wait! Goddam it, wait up!"

There was no mistaking it that time. The voice was young, female, and on the edge of panic. *Oh fuck. It's Rachel.* Joel turned around to see her far down the creek, stumbling along under the weight of a heavy backpack. With a sigh of resignation, he walked back down to meet her.

Joel watched Rachel silently as she threw her backpack into the weeds along the riverbank, then slogged out. He made no move to help her. She gave him sideways looks as she tried to scrape the mud from her Doc Martens onto a scrubby bush.

"What the hell do you think you're doing here?" It came out angrier than he meant it to. Joel realized that he deeply resented Rachel's intrusion on his personal quest. He crossed his arms and glared at her.

Rachel hung her head, looked at him through her dark hair. " 'M sorry," she muttered.

"Jesus, Rachel. You don't know what you've walked into. This place—"

"I don't care." Her voice was so soft he barely heard her. Joel scowled.

"What did you say?"

"I said I don't care! I just want to be with you!" Rachel looked at him, her face streaked with tears. Before he could answer, she ran to him and threw her arms around him. Joel hesitated, then wrapped his arms around her as she sobbed into his chest.

"It's okay, honey. We'll get you home."

"No! I want to stay with you!"

"Rachel—"

And then she was kissing him. Her little hands were on his face, on his back, around his waist. Her mouth was soft and warm, her tongue flicking his upper lip. Joel couldn't breathe.

He felt himself rising to the occasion, and he pushed Rachel roughly away.

"Nina—"

"It's Rachel." She looked at him curiously, then smiled up at him. "It's okay. I want to."

Somebody shoot me. Right now. "Rachel . . . your first time should be with somebody special. You don't even know me, not really."

She slumped against a tree and gave him an incredulous look. "Jesus Christ, Joel, I'm seventeen. You don't really think I'm still a virgin, do you?"

"That—that's not the point. I'm not gonna sleep with you, Rachel. You're just a kid, and you're my cousin—"

"No I'm not! Just 'cause I used to call you that doesn't make it so."

"Rachel—"

"Mama used to call her fat ol' hound dog her baby, but that sure as hell didn't make her my sister."

"Whatever! It's not going to happen! Ever!" Again the words came out more harshly than he'd intended. Rachel stared at him balefully for a moment. Then her face crumpled, and she started to sob. He took her gently into his arms. "C'mon, Rachel, what is it?" Joel asked, his voice softening. "Tell me about it. I-I'm sorry I yelled at you—it's just that I wasn't expecting you and . . . this isn't exactly the safest place."

"It's not that," Rachel whispered, pushing her hair out of her eyes. "It's, well, you got something I want and I don't know how to ask you for it."

"Aw, Rachel, I just can't—"

"Not sex, that's not what I mean."

He smiled at her. Her eyes were so wide and earnest. "Well whatever it is, I'm not going to think you're stupid, I'm not going to laugh, and I'm not going to be insulted by anything you ask me. I promise."

Rachel took a deep breath. "You're a . . . you're an alcoholic."

Joel swallowed hard, and tried to keep the shame off of his face. "Yep."

"But, like, you're staying sober. I-I gotta learn how to do that. See, uh . . . I been, like . . . getting into drugs—smoking some dope—you know—drinking sometimes, cocaine, crack, crystal meth. . . . And I was gonna go over to a friend's house this weekend—his mom's going away, and he's got some heroin."

Joel felt his insides turn to glass. Through his grip on the girl's shoulders, he could feel Rachel shaking. He wanted to say something to comfort her, but kept his mouth shut, knowing how important it was for her to get this out in the open.

"It started slow," Rachel said, her voice defeated, tears streaming down her cheeks, "then I was . . . like . . . doing something almost every night—whenever I got together with my friends. Now it's every day. Even if I have to do it alone. I gotta have something . . . every day. Doesn't matter what, long as it's something. And I'm scared, Joel—real scared."

Jesus Christ. She's just a fucking seventeen-year-old kid. Joel inhaled slowly and deeply before responding, then looked at the girl with as level an expression as he could manage. "If you're so scared, Rachel, then quit. Just quit. Do it now before it's too late."

"I-I can't. That's why I came looking for you. 'Cause I can't quit on my own."

What the hell am I supposed to do? I mean, I can't even quit. The only reason I didn't pour that booze down my throat was the cops came for me.

"Rachel, you've gotta go home. I can't help you. We gotta get you back down the creek."

"But you've gotta help me." Her voice was small and hopeless.

"I—I'll try. But we have to get you home first. You're not safe here."

She wiped her eyes, then looked at him with a mischievous little grin. "Not safe here? You mean the eighteen-hundreds?"

"Yes." Joel didn't smile back.

Her grin slipped a little. "You're shittin' me, right?"

"No. That story I told was true. Every bit of it."

"I knew it! I just knew it!" Her eyes sparkled. "Can't we stay a little while?"

"Not if you want to live to see eighteen. C'mon, let's start walking." He picked up her backpack, and grunted with the weight of it. "Holy shit. What do have in here, anyway?"

"Oh, I thought I might have to spend some time on the road, or in the woods, so I brought some stuff. Energy bars, matches, water, binoculars, a gun, stuff like that."

"A *gun?*"

"Yeah. I found it in the attic, and kinda borrowed it. It's older'n dirt, but I've got bullets for it, two full clips."

He stared at her. "You believed my story, didn't you?"

She blushed. "I guess I sorta did. I wanted to believe it, anyway."

"You're somethin', you know that, Rachel?"

She beamed. "So are you."

"Yeah, I sure am. Somethin' the cat dragged in." She laughed, loud and long, as they started walking along the creek.

Joel and Rachel hadn't gone far when he heard it. A rustle of leaves, far off. The sharp snap of a stick. He froze.

"What?" Rachel's voice sounded loud in his ears, and Joel shushed her as he took the pack from his back. He opened it and rummaged around until he found the binoculars.

"What is it?" she whispered excitedly. "Indians?"

"No. They were gone from this area by the eighteen-thirties.

That's now." He scanned the ocean of green with the binoculars, trying to keep his hands from shaking.

"Isn't it eighteen-eleven?"

"No, as far as I know, time passes here at the same pace as at home. When Billy and I got home twenty years ago, we'd been missing for over a month; just about the same amount of time we'd been here."

"You know a lot about this time, huh?"

"Shh. I see 'em." Four men—no, five. Joel's stomach went cold looking at them, at their tangled hair, their buckskins, their rifles and hunting knives. One of the men, a wiry, rat-faced little guy, let out a distant, shrill laugh, and Joel's heart lurched. *Virgil!*

Joel was immediately ashamed of the foolish thought and his own fear. Virgil was twenty years dead. But these men weren't trappers; they didn't run in packs. A hunting party? Not damn likely. They had the look, Joel thought, of outlaws. He lowered the binoculars.

"Let's get the hell out of here," he whispered.

"Who are they?" Rachel squinted at the distant figures, getting closer by the moment.

"I don't aim to find out. Let's go." He shoved the binoculars in the backpack and shouldered it.

"Uh, Joel?"

"What?"

"They're waving at us."

He whipped around to see. They weren't waving, exactly. They were pointing, talking to each other excitedly. Then they started trotting toward the river, toward Joel and Rachel.

"Run!" he shouted. Rachel froze, confusion on her face. Joel grabbed her wrist and took off.

They ran through the woods, away from the river, through vines and bushes and shrubs with tearing thorns. They ran until they were both panting and Joel doubled over, his side lanced with agonizing pain.

"Do—do you think we lost 'em?" Rachel looked around fearfully.

Joel took another moment to catch his breath. He rested his hands on his knees. "Prob'ly. They're not gonna waste too much time looking for us." *I hope.*

Joel remembered the gun Rachel had mentioned and he rummaged around in the backpack until he found it and one of the clips. It was Colt .45 semi-automatic. He knew this type of pistol had a long history. This one was pretty old too, probably military issue from World War II, but it looked to have been kept clean and in good working order. He slid the clip into the handgrip until it clicked home.

"Are you going to use that thing?"

Joel realized he didn't know how to use the pistol even if he wanted to. He remembered how to load and fire a musket, but a gun from his own time was something of a mystery to him.

"Who were they? Some famous outlaws?"

He was suddenly embarrassed. There was no sign they were being pursued at this point. Why had he run like a rabbit, anyway? *Because you can't be too careful, that's why.* "No. Just some rough-looking characters. But they were probably up to no good. And if they'd seen you were a girl. . . ."

Joel's throat tightened. The idea of something horrible, unspeakable happening to Rachel made him feel sick.

The color drained from the girl's face. "Omigod. I never thought of that." She looked down at her boots. "Let's get out of here, Joel. Let's go back where we belong."

He nodded slowly. He couldn't bring himself to tell her that he had no idea where the river was now.

7

They wandered for almost two days. Rachel's protein bars and overripe huckleberries they found got them through. But even with the little tin compass she'd packed, they didn't find the river.

Joel had expected Rachel to be angry with him, but she was surprisingly subdued. She'd been terrified during the dark night they'd spent in the woods. He had held her in his arms as she slept, her sweet breath on his neck. He'd stroked her hair, not wanting to make love to her, only wanting, with all his heart, to keep her safe. Now, as they trudged through dense woods that all looked the same but totally unfamiliar, he felt like he had failed her utterly.

"This sucks," she grumbled. "It's like the fuckin' *Blair Witch Project.*"

"The what?"

Rachel went around behind Joel and dug in the backpack. She came up with a plastic bottle half-filled with water, their last. She took a gulp. "The Blair Witch Project! The movie! Where you been, Joel, in a barn?"

"Nope. A bottle." He laughed darkly. She handed him the water, and he took a little sip, then put it away.

"Well, you're out now. No chance of falling off the wagon here, huh." She smiled.

"Ain't it the truth." Before he could stop himself, he brushed a strand of hair from her face. "How about you? How are you holding up, girl?"

She sighed. "Okay, I guess. It's not like I'm a tweeker or something. But there've been a few times . . . well, a few times I'd kill for a joint. Or anything else, you know." She looked away from him, face tight and a little embarrassed.

"Well hell, let's find you some jimson weed! You chew on that, you'll get a buzz. Of course, you'll froth at the mouth, bark at the moon, puke yourself inside out, and probably die. . . ." He shot her a sideways grin.

She tried to glare at him, then burst out laughing. "Fuck you!"

"What a mouth! Is that any way for a sweet young lady to behave?"

"Sweet? I haven't had a shower in three days." Still chuckling, she stomped off through the trees. Joel took a deep breath, hoping to God that he could get her out of here alive.

"Joel! Joel, c'mere!"

He rushed to catch up. Rachel was standing in the middle of a thin dirt road, grinning like a possum.

"Nicely done!" Joel smiled. "You found the local superhighway!"

"I rock," said Rachel. "Which way should we go?"

Joel looked right, then left. Nobody coming or going. "Let's figure that out in a minute. First, let's step off the road. There's something we need to do."

"Ow! Joel, that hurts!"

"Sorry, I'm trying to be gentle. I've never done this before."

"Don't quit your day job."

Joel used his knife to saw through the last long hank of Rachel's hair. Now it hung raggedly just below her ears. He stepped back and inspected her.

"Well, how do I look?" she demanded. "Do I look like a boy?"

"Not really. You're too pretty." Joel wanted the words back the second he said them, and he blushed deeply. Rachel grinned. He cleared his throat and continued, a little gruffly. "But if you keep that flannel buttoned over your tank top, you'll probably pass as one. Folks around here can't really imagine a young lady running around in trousers and boots."

Rachel looked down at herself. "Aren't they going to think our clothes are a little weird?"

"Well, sure, but they're not gonna think we're visitors from the future, now are they. They'll just think our mamas dress us funny."

"Our mamas?" She raised an eyebrow.

"Hmm. Maybe we'd better say I'm your dad."

Rachel made a face. "How about my uncle?"

"Okay, sure."

"How does my hair look, anyway?"

Joel winced. "When you see it, just don't beat the crap out of me, okay?"

"I make no promises!"

They started down the road. Rachel was in a good mood, joking and laughing. She was excited about seeing a real frontier town. Joel had his worries, but he kept them to himself. *No reason to borrow trouble.*

"So, Joel, how do you stay sober?"

Joel's mouth snapped shut. The question took him completely by surprise. "I—" Joel began, then stopped, deciding it was best not to say he had no idea. "I guess I take one day at a time. I was in A.A. for almost a year. That helped, but then something happened . . . and I had to get away to get sober again. Rachel, I was drinking every day, all day before I came to your house to visit."

"What happened?"

"Billy died and there was a charge against me at the university I didn't know how to handle."

"Billy was one of your friends from the story, right?"

"Yeah."

"What kind of charge?"

Joel realized he didn't want to tell her. Rachel was nearly the same age as Nina Bryant. He tried to turn away, but he couldn't seem to get away from the question in Rachel's eyes.

"I stuck my neck out to try and help some of my students. It was stupid. Billy said so. So did my A.A. sponsor. I told my students I was going to A.A., trying to straighten myself out, and that if any of them were troubled about the future and needed someone to talk to, I would make myself available. But the university let me know that an on-campus group was out of the question."

Rachel frowned. "Why?"

"It wasn't part of the image they wanted to present to the outside world."

Rachel shook her head. "Dumbasses."

"You said it. So I started a mixed Alcoholics Anonymous and Narcotics Anonymous meeting at my house. I knew it was inappropriate, but I was newly sober and not thinking clearly."

Joel smiled grimly. "There was a girl, Nina Bryant, showed up at a meeting one day. She was a student in my History of Native American Cultures class. She'd been flirting with me all semester."

"Mm." Rachel nodded. "Druggie?"

"I don't think she had a substance abuse problem at all. I think she was a troubled young woman who needed a lot of attention. And she was used to getting it."

"Attention whore," Rachel grumbled, almost making Joel smile.

"Over the course of the semester, Nina came on to me more

and more, and got madder and madder when I wouldn't take her up on it. Sometimes after class, I'd have to be rude to get rid of her."

Rachel eyes showed suspicion. And something flickered beneath it; jealousy? "Uh-huh," she said. "Except for that one time when you just couldn't help yourself."

"No! Never! Nina Bryant set me up," Joel said, too defensively. "She stayed after the meeting and asked to use the bathroom while everyone else was heading out the front door. I was cleaning up empty coffee cups and dumping ashtrays when she called to me from the bedroom. I shouldn't have gone in there."

"But you did."

"Yeah, I did. She was undressing and when I came in she jumped me."

"Jumped you?" There was that suspicious look again, this time with a sly smile.

"She was all over me, trying to kiss me. She grabbed my—" Joel closed his mouth, wishing he'd never opened it.

"That's why you called me Nina the other day." Rachel was grinning openly.

"Yeah, I guess." Joel muttered, wondering how the hell Rachel had gotten control of this conversation.

"I was trying to get her to put her clothes back on when another girl new to the meeting, Clara Dobbs, came back for a book she'd *accidentally* left behind. She came into the bedroom while Nina was half-naked. I found out later she was Nina's best friend."

Nodding, Rachel put away her smile.

"I got them out of my house, thinking I might have some explaining to do, but no more."

"Dumbass."

"Yeah, I know. Anyway, Nina lodged a sexual-harassment accusation against me with the university provost. Her story was that I lured her to my house and offered to improve her failing grade if she'd have sex with me. She said that when she refused, I ripped her blouse off and would have raped her if Clara Dobbs hadn't interrupted. Apparently Clara was her 'witness.' "

The smile was back. "Was Nina pretty?"

"Oh yes," he said a little too enthusiastically. "Lovely."

"And you wanted her?" Rachel was positively beaming as she bounced on her feet.

Joel looked away. "Sure. Yes. . . . Okay? I'd have enjoyed having sex with her, but I sure as hell wasn't going to. It would have been seriously wrong."

"But they fired you, even though you didn't boink the bitch?"

"No, but I was sure they were going to fire me. They'd been looking for an excuse for a long time. The Dean placed me on paid administrative leave while they investigated Nina's charge."

"But then you had that reputation. . . . All the girls thought you were a total horndog!" Her eyes were sparkling. "I'll bet half of them wanted you anyway."

Joel sighed and closed his eyes. "I talked to my A.A. sponsor about it, but his response just made me feel like an idiot. I put off phoning Billy for a week or two. I didn't want him to know what a stupid mess I'd gotten myself into. Finally I couldn't take it any longer and I called him."

"And he said you were an eedjit too."

"Billy's mom answered the phone. He'd been killed in a car wreck the day before."

The grin fell from Rachel's face. She looked a bit ashamed. There was an uncomfortable pause and then she spoke up. "So it wasn't the thing with the girl that got you drinking again. It was Billy's death, right?"

"Even Billy's death was an excuse. Truth is it was just *me*. Sure I was under a lot of stress with it, but if I hadn't taken that first drink, eventually things would have gotten better."

Rachel nodded her head solemnly.

Joel had the impression she was glad to hear that he hadn't gotten drunk just because a young woman wanted to have sex with him. Perhaps she felt she still had a chance with him. That made him deeply nervous.

"Once I have that first drink, there's no stopping me from having another," Joel said. "I try not to think about it. The longer I go without a drink, the easier it gets."

"Well, I guess it's good we're here, then. Nothing around here to get high on. Just so long as we don't think about it."

"I'm not thinking about it," Joel said. "Are you?"

"No. Are you?"

"No. You?"

"No. Yes! I'm ready to smoke one of those friggin' squirrels!"

Joel burst out laughing.

Late afternoon, and the sun streamed through the trees in spikes of pure gold. Joel was worried about what might happen when the sun went down. Rachel was inspecting a fungus growing out of a tree trunk.

"They call those fairy platforms," said Joel.

"I know. I've just never seen one quite that color before." She prodded it gently, then curled her fingers around a frond of an enormous fern. "All the plants here are amazing. They're so—so big and healthy. Like Jurassic plants or something!"

Joel had to smile. "Do you like plants?"

"Yeah," Rachel muttered, looking embarrassed. "I do. And I like to draw 'em."

"Really! I didn't know you were an artist."

"I'm not! I mean, I just draw plants, is all. I like the way they look up close. When you look really, really close at a flower, it's like something from another planet. Or a fern, the way the leaves curl." Her face turned red. "Shit, I sound like an idiot."

"No you don't! I think that's great, Rachel. I'd love to see your drawings sometime. Would that be okay?"

She grimaced. "No way!"

"I've been thinking about that pistol in the backpack," Joel said slowly.

"Yeah, some good protection I brought, huh?"

"Yeah, well that's just the thing—it's a little too good. I've been thinking maybe we should bury it somewhere."

"Bury it? That's my daddy's gun. It's also the only way we have to defend ourselves."

"That's true, but if it fell into the hands of someone from this time, it could change history. Then we might not have a home to go back to."

"Yeah—I saw something like that in an episode of the old *Twilight Zone*."

"Since I don't know where we are, I can't bury it and hope to recover it later, and, as you say, it's our only means of defense. So let's just make sure it stays in the backpack unless we need it to defend our lives."

They walked until dusk. Joel found a little clearing twenty or so feet from the road, and started a small fire. They ate the last of Rachel's protein bars, and some desiccated strawberries they'd picked along the way. Joel leaned against a tree, and Rachel leaned against him, her head on his shoulder. As he always did when she was close to him, Joel was overwhelmed with the need to keep her safe. And there was something else, too. A deep, tugging feeling that came from the very core of him, reaching out for Rachel and basking in her nearness, making him feel bare and exposed.

Jesus. Don't do it, you moron. Don't you dare fall in love with her.

But on some level, Joel knew it was already too late.

Joel was quiet on the road the next morning. He was unsettled and more than a little ashamed of what he was feeling for Rachel. He avoided looking at her. Rachel seemed to be in a fine mood, joking with Joel, asking questions, making comments about the plants and the animals and the weather. Joel answered her in short, abrupt sentences.

Finally, she trotted in front of him and stopped in the middle of the road, fists on her hips. "Joel Biggs, are you pissed at me or somethin'?"

"No." He tried to smile at her.

"Then what are you so damn grouchy for?"

Anger flashed over him, and he didn't have the strength to fight it. "What for? I'll tell you what for, goddammit. We're out here in the middle of dogass nowhere, we're out of food, we don't know where we're going, and somebody or something might pop out of the woods and kill us at any second. Is that a good enough reason to be grouchy, little girl?" He didn't realize he was yelling until it was too late for him to take it back.

He expected her to shrink from him, to start crying maybe. He felt a sick little rush of power at the thought, and hated himself for it.

But she didn't. Rachel took a step toward Joel and glared up at him, her face inches from his. "Now you listen here. I know we're in a world of shit, I'm not an eedjit. I realize I shouldn'ta followed you, an' now you think you're stuck with me. But guess what, Joel, I've been helpin' you. Whose food bars have we been eatin', anyway? Whose binoculars did we use? If I wasn't here, you'd be eatin' bugs and rotten berries. So you can talk to me with a little respect, Joel, or you can kiss my ass!" Her eyes blazed into his, challenging him to answer.

Joel couldn't help it. He started to smile. Then he started to laugh.

Rachel's face flushed crimson.

"If you're laughin' at me, you son of a bitch, I'm gonna pop you one!"

"I'm not!" he laughed. "I swear, Rachel, I'm not. You're just—you're just somethin' else. You're amazing, is what."

She blinked, then grinned. Rachel threw her arms around him and hugged tight. "Okay," she said. "I guess I don't have to kick your ass. You done bein' a sourpuss now?"

"Yup." He kissed the crown of her head.

They walked for two hours, Joel plodding along, Rachel zipping back and forth across the road, pointing out this plant or that animal. Joel again found himself astonished by her. He never would have guessed, by her sullen demeanor at home, that she had so much personality, or so much enjoyment for life. *It's this place,* Joel thought. It stripped off the layers of dead skin, the soundproof shell that twenty-first-century people built around themselves to slow down the constant assault on their senses. In some rough way, it let you start fresh, if you'd let it happen. He silently hoped Rachel would be able to do that, before it was too late for her.

She caught him staring at her. Her hands came up to her ragged hair and smoothed it down. "What?" she asked.

Joel smiled. "I was just wondering how the hell you found me. I didn't exactly leave you a map."

Rachel's eyes sparkled. "I followed you all the way to the bus station. I'm surprised you didn't turn around and see me, but you just kept ploddin' along like one of the zombies from *Night of the Living Dead.*"

Joel mock-scowled. "Thanks a lot."

She ignored him. "Then I hitched into Dexter, got your ad-

dress out of the phone book, and went to your house. When I saw the door standing open and you weren't there, I kinda figured something happened. And then I saw the creek."

He shot her a sideways look. "You really believed the story I told that night?"

"No, not exactly. Not consciously, anyway. But I wanted it to be true, Joel. I don't know why, but I did. And when I saw The New Cut, I knew that was where you'd gone. So I went after you."

Joel laughed. "Well, you clever little wench!"

Rachel's mouth quirked up. "Wench?"

Joel felt himself starting to flush. "I didn't—"

"Joel Biggs, you're the only person I've ever met who'd even think of using the word 'wench' in a normal conversation."

"We were talking about time travel. That's not normal."

"True."

"Rachel?"

"Yeah?"

"Never hitchhike again. It's really dangerous."

"Yes, mom." She kicked his shoe, and, for a fleeting moment, he was ridiculously happy.

8

Not ten minutes later, they saw a little wagon in the distance, coming toward them down the road.

"Should we hide?" asked Rachel, eyes wide.

Joel slowly shook his head. "No. We need to find out where we are, and where we can get some supplies. You just stay behind me, okay?"

She nodded, looking frightened and excited.

"Hallooo!" Joel called, waving. The man driving the wagon waved back. It was a small, shuttered contraption, pulled by a huge, rawboned gray nag. A tiny child sat atop its swayed back. A woman walked alongside the wagon, a small army of children trailing behind her.

"Tinkers," Joel said to Rachel.

"What?"

"They're probably tinkers. People who travel from place to place fixing things, trading small items, selling charms, things like that."

"Oh. Gotcha."

"Good day, friend," the man on the wagon said to Joel as they approached. He had light, thinning hair, a broad smile, and a thick Irish brogue.

"Good day," Joel said.

"Me name's Padraig Kilkenny, sor. This here's me good wife Brid, and all these young monkeys are mine as well."

"Pleased to meet you. I'm Joel Biggs, and this is Ruh—Reed.

My, um, nephew."

Rachel was making faces at the golden-haired toddler sitting on the horse, and the little girl was giggling wildly. Joel nudged her shoe with his, and she looked up and smiled. "Oh. Hi."

Kilkenny looked at her curiously, then beamed at Joel. "My good sor, can I interest ya in some fine flints? Or have ya any knives that need sharpenin'? A timepiece which needs repair, perhaps?"

"Thank you, Mister Kilkenny, but I'm afraid we're but two poor, lost travelers with no money to spare. Would you be good enough to direct us to the nearest town?"

"Oh, aye. We've just come from Alexandria. It's not but three miles down the road. Are ya truly lost, then?"

Joel was momentarily distracted by Rachel chuckling. Two small boys who looked like twins were inspecting her Doc Marten boots, poking and tugging. "Oh, um, yes, I'm afraid we are. We were set upon by robbers, and had to run for our lives. In our rush to escape, we lost our way."

Brid Kilkenny, a tall, angular woman with pale skin and startling blue eyes, pulled the little boys away from Rachel with an apologetic smile. A girl of about eight peeked around her skirts at Joel.

"In that case," said Kilkenny, "I suggest ya pay a visit to the Silver Horse Inn. The owner's a kind man, and he'll help ya to get back on your feet."

"Thank you, Mister Kilkenny."

Rachel was now surrounded by three boys, the oldest about fourteen, the youngest maybe ten. Joel realized they were staring at the silver eight-ball earring that hung from Rachel's left ear. Joel coughed, trying not to laugh.

"Reed was, ah, born in France. The young people dress differently there. . . ."

"Oui," Rachel said, nodding solemnly.

"I see. He's a handsome lad, Mister Biggs." Kilkenny winked at Rachel. "All the lasses must be mad for him."

They parted ways with the Kilkenny clan and started down the road toward Alexandria, Tennessee.

Alexandria, Joel thought, trying to place the town. Then it hit him. *Oh my God! Alexandria was an early name for Jackson.* He smiled, imagining what the newborn community must look like.

Rachel was full of nervous energy, eyes wide with excitement. She danced backwards down the road in front of Joel, grinning at him.

"Joel, you're really good at that! I mean, you really knew how to talk to those people. You sounded just like a guy from back then! Now, I mean."

"I probably sounded like a stiff. I'm out of practice."

"I can't believe you told them I was from France!"

"Well, I had to say something. Take out that earring, would you?"

"We're from France," said Rachel in a monotone, taking the earring out and sticking it into her pocket.

"Very funny, Miss Conehead."

"OmiGOD, Joel! You got a pop-culture reference! I think I'm gonna faint!"

Joel and Rachel walked into Alexandria as the last crimson rays of the sun lit up the western sky. Rachel was excited, her eyes sparkling in the dying light. Joel was less thrilled. With every step, the stench of his garments and his unwashed body puffed in and out of the neck of his shirt. This mingled unpleasantly with the smells of cooking food, the moldering vegetable scent of horse manure, and numerous wood fires rising from the town ahead.

Joel felt he should be thrilled to walk along the muddy street of a bump-in-the-road town that would one day be a bustling city, but instead he was on edge and nervous. He feared this era and the dangers it held. With every step he remembered another horror from his boyhood; another man he saw die.

As they drew closer, the road became a mire, and houses as well as places of business sprang up on either side. Rachel cursed under her breath as her boots sank ankle-deep into the stinking mud. The tinking sound of a blacksmith at work blended with the clatter of wagons, the whinnying of horses, and distant sawing. Cursing, a tow-headed young man in torn homespun breeches and shirt wrestled with his mule, trying to get it to pull his wagon from a ditch where it had fetched up.

Rachel grabbed his elbow. "This is so fucking cool!" she whispered. Joel nodded, hoping his face didn't betray his tension.

A middle-aged man passed him in a hurry. By the fellow's well-worn and dirty clothes Joel took him for a farmer, perhaps heading for the tavern to strike a deal or just to have a drink and shoot the breeze with his friends. When the man said, "Hello," Joel mumbled a reply and automatically looked down, avoiding the man's gaze. Rachel looked at him curiously, and shame burrowed into his gut.

Dammit, why do I have to be such a coward?

Because I'm a weak, soft, twenty-first-century man, that's why. It was a goddam miracle I survived this place as a kid. He knew his alcoholism had weakened him both physically and mentally, and he wasn't up to par with the men of this time.

But I have Rachel to protect. She's depending on me. I have to be up to the task. I just have to.

The road widened as they moved into town. Its mired surface had been churned up by the passage of countless horses, wagons, and men. Rachel moved to the center of the road where the mud was a little more packed down, and Joel followed. The glow of candle and lamplight drifted out of windows they passed, lending warmth to the chill.

"Joel," Rachel breathed. "It looks just like a movie."

"Yeah. A movie that can reach out and bite you."

"Don't worry, we'll play it cool. We'll just blend in."

He looked at her, with her innocent, clear face, her modern clothes and boots, her slender, almost fragile body. "You keep quiet, okay? I'll do the talking. Until you get used to how people around here speak."

"No problemo."

Joel winced.

"Look! Look!" Rachel was pointing at a sign hanging out over the street. It read "Silver Horse Inn," but the creature on the weathered board looked more like a pig with a mane than anything equine. "Can we get a room? I, uh, I mean, a place to stay? I've got almost two hundred dollars in my bag."

Joel had to laugh. "I don't think the proprietor will be impressed with your modern paper money," Joel said.

Rachel frowned.

"I'm afraid we'll have to rely on the kindness of strangers," he said.

"Ah always rely on the kindness of strangahs," Rachel purred, batting her eyes.

"Better deepen that voice, Reed." Joel winked at her. Rachel drew herself up tall, then began to walk with a pronounced swagger.

The Silver Horse Inn was a small, dimly lit place, rich with the smell of cooking meat and strong beer. The owner, a Mr. Charles Treemount, was indeed a kind man. A short, round fellow with bushy brown hair, he listened to Joel's story of highway robbery with a furrowed brow. Without hesitation, he offered Joel and Rachel—Reed, as he knew her—a room and board until they could get back on their feet. Joel was enormously grateful, and offered to work in any capacity he was needed. To his surprise, Rachel offered to care for Treemount's horses. Smiling, the stout man shook hands. After a dinner of thick, brown stew, Treemount's tiny wife Martha directed Joel and Rachel to their room.

There was only one bed. Joel offered to sleep on the floor.

"Don't be an idiot," said Rachel. "I won't molest you."

Reluctantly, Joel got into bed with her.

Rachel went on about the blanket for a while; a coarse, colorless thing which stunk of mildew and rodents. Then she pulled it up to her chin and went to sleep. Joel smoothed her ragged hair, and let himself rest.

9

Their time in Alexandria went surprisingly well. Joel helped Treemount around the inn, cleaning, serving food and drinks, and occasionally cooking. Rachel groomed and fed Treemount's horses and those of his guests, even cleaning stalls without complaint.

Rachel played the part of Reed well—cussing, spitting, and swaggering with the best of the local boys. Baths were a problem, of course. Rachel took them outdoors in a washtub, freezing while Joel kept watch for anyone who might see her and discover her secret. As the weather grew colder, she started washing indoors with a cloth and bowl. "I barely have tits," she informed Joel. "I don't really want to freeze them totally off."

A week went by, then two, then a month. Treemount noticed Joel's command of the language, and asked if he might tutor his children, and a few of his friends. Joel quickly agreed.

He knew they should leave. They should pack up as much food as they could carry, and head back down the road, looking for The New Cut. But Joel didn't want to. He was sober, for one thing. He was sober, and he was as happy as he could remember ever being, because he spent every day with Rachel. He spent every night lying next to her, hearing her soft breathing, feeling her warmth. He couldn't bear the thought of not having her next to him, so he said nothing about leaving. And surprisingly, neither did she.

Rachel was sober too. There were no drugs available, of

course, and, despite the constant presence of strong ale, wine and whiskey, she didn't drink. She'd made friends with several of the local boys, fishing in a nearby creek with them, and sometimes riding a borrowed horse through the woods with her buddies. Joel tried like hell not to be jealous. There was a rosiness in her cheeks that hadn't been there before, and an outgoing confidence that he would never have associated with the quiet, sullen teenager from Moss's house. She never mentioned home.

Joel had been astonished to discover that they'd arrived in the very year that Matthew Crenshaw set out on his historic journey with Jarret Cotten. He sometimes daydreamed about trying to find Crenshaw, maybe helping him bring down the infamous outlaw. But what would he do with Rachel?

He knew he should be looking for Mark at the very least. Joel asked around town about Mark, even though he knew it was tremendously unlikely that anyone in this sleepy burg would have met him. Of course, no one had. He told himself that once he'd safely returned Rachel to her own time, he'd set out in search of his old friend. Someday.

For now, Joel was content. He and Rachel settled into a comfortable routine. Until the day Joel got a letter from one Hume Stodgen:

Dear Mr. Biggs,

Mrs. Harriet Blakely, cousin to Mr. Charles Treemount, has recommended your services as an educator. If you are looking for a position within a household, I would be most pleased if you were to come to my home in Adairville for an interview. Mrs. Blakely offered that she had paid you a short bit per week. I can offer one bit per week, room and board.

My son Stephen and I eagerly await your response.

Sincerely,
Hume Stogdon

The address was written below.

Joel knew that Matthew Crenshaw worked for Hume Stogdon during the time he had met the outlaw Jarrett Cotton. He had been thinking of looking up Stogdon in the hopes of meeting up with Crenshaw, but that had been relegated to the realm of someday. Now that Stogdon had contacted him, the possibility of meeting Crenshaw became very real. Joel thought of Matthew Crenshaw as a true American hero and felt it was a damned shame that so few knew about him. Within the next year, Crenshaw would perform a great service for his fellow countrymen, be left penniless for his efforts, and hounded out of the country by the surviving members of Jarrett Cotten's Mystic Clan. But perhaps with Joel's help, the hero might fare better.

Wait a minute—tutoring the Stogdons is the job Crenshaw is supposed to be doing. Maybe history has the dates wrong, and Crenshaw hasn't been offered the job yet. Or perhaps he works for the Stogdons in some other capacity.

What if I take the job and it's never offered to Crenshaw? What would that do to history?

What if I'm *Crenshaw?* Thinking of all the man's brave deeds, the many dangers he faced and survived, Joel shook his head and quickly pushed the idea aside.

Now that he knew exactly where Stogdon lived, it seemed he must make a decision. Could it be that if Crenshaw shows up at the Stogdons, Joel might indeed be able to help him in some way? Now that he was sober and beginning to feel good about himself, shouldn't he do something with his life, something selfless and meaningful?

But what about Rachel?

With his heart a lead weight in his chest, Joel brought up the subject of returning home with her. He told her the weather would soon be turning bitter, and they'd better travel while they could. He reminded her of how much her family must miss her, how they must be frantic with worry over her. It was time to go back.

To his surprise, she flatly refused. There was something akin to panic in her eyes.

"I can't! I'm not ready, Joel. I have to be sure . . . I have to be sure I won't go back to doing what I had been. I feel like I'm worth something here. Do you get what I'm saying?"

He nodded. Of course he understood. How could he not? She grabbed his hands in her small, cold ones. "We'll go back, Joel. But not yet, okay?"

So, feeling like he should have argued harder, he brought up Hume Stogdon instead. Rachel was thrilled. As much as she liked the inn and the horses and her days with her friends, she was bored. "They're nice kids, Joel, but they don't know much of anything. And I'm sick to death of holding in my pee because I can't whiz like the boys. I think my bladder's stretched out to the size of a bowling ball by now." She was up for a change.

In September of 1833, Joel bought a nag with the money he'd saved up from tutoring, and he and Rachel headed for Hume Stogdon's place. It was a pleasant journey. Rachel sat on the horse in front of him, and they chatted and talked and pointed out birds and animals to each other. Rachel took excellent care of the rawboned, swaybacked horse, whom she had dubbed Warthog, brushing him down nightly and finding him sweet clover when she could. There was a kindness to Rachel, Joel realized, which was as much a part of her as her sudden smiles.

Adairville was much smaller than Alexandria. Joel could see the disappointment on Rachel's face. But Stogdon didn't live in town; he lived on a farm to the west of the settlement. Rachel seemed to like the idea of living on a farm for a while.

Turning onto the road that fringed Stogdon's land, Joel had a rush of anxiety. He patted his breast pocket to make sure he still had the letter from Stogdon. As he drew near the cabin, he began to wonder about the position. If he accepted and took the job, would he be treated like a servant? And what would Stodgen think of Joel bringing along his "nephew" unannounced?

He looked around the property as they rode up. Stogdon and his son, Stephen, had a modest log cabin and four rough outbuildings, three acres cleared for planting, two piglets, a handful of chickens, and a couple of elderly horses in a small paddock. Three black men were working in the field near a smoking tobacco barn.

"Holy shit," Rachel whispered over her shoulder. "Are those slaves, Joel?"

"Yeah," he said. "Those are slaves. You've seen slaves before, in Alexandria."

"Yeah, but that was in town. Here they're working in the fields, just like in the movies."

Joel would never get used to the slavery either. It went against everything he believed, but he felt powerless to do anything about it. He had seen few free blacks. Even the ones he knew to be free were subservient to whites in all situations. It made him profoundly uncomfortable.

Something in him, however, was relieved to see the Stogdons had slaves to perform the hardest manual labor. Perhaps he wouldn't be asked to contribute to the work in the fields. He immediately felt guilty for the thought. *Lazy sonofabitch. A little hard work would probably do you some good.*

Hume Stogdon, a tall, gray-haired man, rounded the corner of his cabin and waved. "That you, Mr. Biggs?" he called out in a deep baritone.

"Yessir," Joel answered, climbing from his mount and offering Stogdon his hand. He then helped Rachel down from Warthog.

"Ye found us—good!" Stogdon turned to look at Rachel. "And who might this be?"

"Oh, this is my—"

"Wife. I'm Joel's wife, Rachel. Please pardon my clothing, good sir. My only dress was eaten by goats." She beamed sweetly.

Joel's stomach froze. Why in the hell had she said that? *Too late to do anything about it now.*

Stogdon laughed. "Well, Missus Biggs, I'm sorry to hear about your dress. But I believe I've got half a bolt of calico stored away, if you'd like to make a new one."

"Thank you so much, sir!" Dear God, had she actually batted her eyes?

"That's a charming bride you have there, Mister Biggs."

"Please, call me Joel."

"Yes, Joel!"

The man's smile was infectious, his handshake firm, and Joel found his anxiety melting away.

"You have a nice home," Joel said, looking around. "I hope I can be of assistance to you, Mister Stogdon."

"Hume, please," the man said with a wide smile. "All my friends call me, Hume. An' don' worry, there's plenty o' work ta be done."

There was that anxiety again, and Joel laughed uncomfortably. "A bit of schooling. That shouldn't be too difficult."

Stogdon swallowed and reddened. "Not unless Stephen an' me prove to be slow learnin'. I gather I didn' tell ye neither one of us got our letters. Well, truth is I had schoolin' when I was a boy, but it didn't take. My neighbor, Lehman Cobb, wrote that letter ye received from me."

He smiled uneasily and Joel broke out laughing.

Stogdon looked as if he were becoming angry.

"I'm sorry, but I thought ye were gonna have me workin' in the fields!"

Stogdon relaxed. "Well, that too!" he said, smiling slyly and bursting out with his own rumbling laughter. He clapped Joel on the shoulder.

Joel liked Hume already.

"I kin tell right now we're gonna git 'long famously," Stogdon said. "I hope ye takin' on double duty like this—me and Stephen both—won't be askin' too much."

"I can handle it. I just hope you don't mind me bringing my, uh, wife along unannounced—"

"Tha's just fine," Stogdon said. "The place could use a purdy woman around. C'mon in an' let me introduce ye ta my son, Stephen."

Joel tethered Warthog to the rail out front, and he and Rachel walked with Stogdon toward the cabin.

"Do you have another boarder, a Matthew Crenshaw?" Joel asked, holding his breath.

"Crenshaw?" said Stogdon. "No Crenshaw staying here?"

"Ah, I must be mistaken," Joel said. Rachel was looking at him curiously. He glared at her, and she gave him a sweet smile and a wink.

Perhaps Crenshaw hasn't arrived yet. Maybe I misremembered the dates. . . . If he had not left the Crenshaw book on his kitchen table back in Dexter, he'd be able to check. Well, all he could do was get to know the folks in the area, ask after the man, and try to discover his whereabouts. Crenshaw would turn up sooner or later.

A tall, strapping teenager stepped out of the cabin, blinking in the late-afternoon light. He was a good-looking kid, with sandy hair and dark-blue eyes.

"Mister Biggs, Missus Biggs, this here's my son Stephen," Hume said.

"Pleased ta meet ya." Stephen held out his hand to Joel. The boy's hands were strong and callused. Joel realized that a boy of this era could probably kick the ass of a man from his. Then Stephen caught sight of Rachel. His face turned red. His mouth opened, then closed. He lowered his head. "Ma'am," he mumbled.

Stogdon laughed. "Stephen don't see too many women 'round here, much less ones as purdy as you, Missus Biggs." The boy's face turned redder. He muttered something and headed out for the fields.

Stogdon took them to one of the outbuildings, which had been outfitted with a rough table, two chairs, and a narrow rope bed.

"I hope ye'll be comfortable here," Stogdon said.

"I'm sure we will be," Rachel smiled. "It just needs a woman's touch."

As soon as the door shut behind Hume, Joel grabbed Rachel by the arm and led her over to the corner by the fireplace. "What the hell do you think you're doing?" he hissed.

Rachel glared at him and yanked her arm away. "In the first place, don't you manhandle me, Joel Biggs, or I'll kick your ass. And I'll tell you what I'm doing. I'm turning back into a god-dam girl."

"But Rachel—"

"But nothin'. I'm sick and tired of pretending to be a boy. I'm sick of never takin' a bath because somebody might see my tits. I'm sick of chewing tobacco so the boys don't think I'm a wuss. And I'm sick to death of pissing in huckleberry bushes so nobody figures out I don't have a dick. You know somethin',

Joel? I've learned to pee standing up. You wanna know how I do it?"

"NO!" Joel hollered, putting his hands over his ears.

She started laughing, then he did too.

"I'm sorry, Joel. I know I should have said something to you first. But I was afraid you'd say no."

"I probably would have."

"Nothing's changed. We just have to pretend we like each other around other people, that's all." She winked at him.

"Hmm, I don't know, Rachel. You're asking a lot of me. . . ."

She punched him in the shoulder so hard he yelped.

10

After a month's work, Hume and Stephen could read a primer and write their names as well as simple sentences. Hume proved to be the quicker of the two, though Stephen was dogged in his pursuit of the written word. Hume remarked on the "near-magical" way Joel had of teaching. With amusement, Joel realized he may have been the only phonics teacher in the nineteenth century.

Joel liked the Stogdons more each day. They were simple and straightforward, and soon came to treat him and Rachel as family.

Rachel liked them too. She spent her days caring for the horses and wandering the farm and the surrounding woods drawing, Joel guessed. In the evenings she'd sit in the main house with Joel and the Stogdons, sewing and chatting. She'd done a decent job with the cloth Hume had given her, managing to make two simple dresses and a skirt. Hume insisted he was capable of doing all the cooking himself; he'd done it for years since his wife had died. But sometimes Rachel cooked anyway, because, she said, she wanted to contribute something to the household too. She seemed to be developing a quiet maturity that astonished and delighted Joel.

Matthew Crenshaw never showed up, and Joel found no one who knew the man. Again he worried that his presence in this period of history had changed things, somehow altered the course of events.

One way or the other, Joel's situation was good, and he had no desire to leave the Stogdons. Hume never asked him to do anything but teach them to read and write, and life on the farm moved at an easy pace. However, that autumn, in spite of himself, Joel readily volunteered when the Stogdons needed help in the fields. He slowly regained his health and some vitality. Rachel teased him mercilessly about the new muscles in his arms and the broadening of his chest. He was secretly delighted.

Rachel wanted to work in the fields too, but Hume Stogdon wouldn't hear of it. "You're a lady, Missus Biggs. The fields ain't no place for you." Rachel was disappointed, and Stephen Stogdon seemed to be too. It had become painfully obvious over the past few months that the boy had a severe crush on Rachel. He was an honorable young man, and Joel didn't think he'd try to put the moves on her, but he often saw Stephen watching Rachel from a corner of the room, his eyes wide and moony.

So Rachel was on her own during the day, left completely to her own devices. That worried Joel a little; she seemed to be growing slightly bored and restless lately. But Joel was too busy during the day to think about it, and each night he collapsed, exhausted, into the narrow bed he shared with Rachel, often before she did. Most mornings, he was up and gone before she awoke.

On the twenty-third of November, Joel and Rachel awakened to a commotion. Two of the Stogdon's slaves, Macklin and Briley, were missing.

"Good for them," Rachel had whispered to Joel. "I hope they're halfway to Canada by now."

But Hume Stogdon insisted that the men wouldn't have run off. "They was loyal fellas," he said. "I treated 'em good, an' they was happy here." Joel thought the word "happy" might have been an exaggeration, but it was true that Stogdon was a kind, fair man. There were many worse masters. Much, much worse.

With Joel's and Rachel's help, they spent the next day and a half scouring the countryside for the missing slaves. They each went in a different direction—except for Joel and Rachel, who rode together—talking with all the neighbors and spreading the word. Late in the afternoon on the twenty-fourth, Joel came upon their neighbor, Lehman Cobb, on the road back to the farm. When asked about the slaves, Cobb said he'd seen Jarrett Cotten and a couple of his men around Stogdon's property near dawn.

"I know 'e looks the gentleman, but 'e's jus' as rough as the men as does 'is bidding, an' twice as shrewd. I'd steer clear o' Cotten an' 'is men. There don' seem ta be anythin' fer it. They steal from anyone they want, an' if'n ye gits on 'em 'bout it, they jump ye. Some say it's best ta make friends wit' 'em. But if ye 'ave ta do somethin' 'bout it, I hear Cotten's headin' out fer Memphis tomorrow an' if'n ye follow 'im, 'e might lead ye ta the negroes."

Until that moment, it hadn't occurred to Joel that the day's event was the very thing which was supposed to prompt Crenshaw to pursue Cotten. Where was he, dammit?

That evening at the dinner table, Stephen and Joel made their plans to pursue Cotten. They hoped to catch up with him at the Vess River ferry, or at least hear word of him along the way.

In any event, I'll have Stephen with me—I could never do this alone. And yet, I wonder if we're up to it even together.

Rachel, standing by the fireplace with her arms crossed, announced, "I'm coming with you, Joel."

"No!" Joel and Stephen cried at once.

Rachel opened her mouth to protest, when Hume Stogdon set his big hand on her shoulder. "Yer so much like my late wife, Rachel. She were a strong one, too. Stubborn as the day was long, an' jus' as lovely. I hear from Stephen that you kin ride like a man, an' I have little doubt of it. But Cotten an' his men . . . they got no respect fer ladies. If they was ta catch ye—well, it doesn't bear thinkin' on."

"Hume and Stephen need those men for their farm to survive," Joel said gently. "And not only that, Cotten might hurt Macklin and Briley. He's got no respect for human life."

"Or niggers either," said Stephen. Rachel and Joel winced.

"I'll take good care o' ye, Rachel," Hume said. "Ye kin even work the fields, if ye really have a mind to. Heaven knows I kin use all the help I kin get."

Rachel glared at Joel steadily and fiercely. "All right," she said. "Please excuse me." Before Joel could say a word, she was gone.

"Ah, she'll get over it," Hume said with a smile. "She jes' loves ye a lot, that's all."

Joel wished that were true. He wished it with all his heart.

The next morning when Joel awoke, he found Stephen in the depths of a fever. He remembered the same from the book. The young man tried to rise, but when it was evident he was too sick to travel, Joel told him to lie back down and rest. Rachel brought a cool, damp cloth and pressed it to Stephen's forehead.

It was strange, Joel thought, to see evidence of history playing out on such a seemingly insignificant level, when what he would have thought an important element—Matthew Crenshaw—was still missing.

"Don' fret about it, Stephen. I'll tend to it—I'll get the slaves back."

As Joel gathered up his traveling gear—heavy coat, hat, a portmanteau full of extra clothing—the wind rattled at the shutters and door.

"Cold out," said Hume, "freezin' rain all las' night. Ain't weather fit fer travelin'."

Rachel was bustling around the kitchen, silent anger coming off of her in waves as she made coffee and fried eggs.

"Well, it'll have to do," Joel said, smiling grimly, stuffing a loaded pistol Hume had given him into his belt. "If it's good enough for Cotten, it'll have to be good enough fer me. Only thing for it is to try and head him off."

"Least ways, wear this," Hume said, handing Joel his good hat. "It's got a quilted linin' to keep ye warm."

Joel took off his hat and replaced it with Hume's.

"And I want ye to take Gailey. She's what ye need out in this weather. That nag o' your'n ain't a-gonna make it a half mile."

Joel nodded his head. "She's a good horse."

"You be sure to brush her every night," Rachel snapped.

"I will."

Hume smiled a little. "You git as far as Wallace an' need help, you stop in at the general store and ask for my friend, Thomas Fellowes. You tell 'im I sent ye, and he'll do what he kin."

"Thomas Fellowes?"

"Tha's what I said."

Joel knew that Crenshaw was supposed to meet up with Fellowes, but had not been able to remember in what town this took place. He knew there was no time for further questions and he let it go. Knowing Fellowes was out there, though, gave him a small measure of comfort. Whether or not he found himself in Wallace, he would eventually look him up. *How old must he be now? At least sixty,* Joel guessed.

"Ye take care o' ye'self, now, Mister Biggs." Hume placed a hand on Joel's shoulder. "An' I thank ye fer this, I surely do."

"Now, Hume, don't go on about it. You'd do the same for me." He walked over to Rachel, tried to take her hand in his. She pulled away.

"Good-bye, Rachel," Joel said, and he suddenly felt a great, heavy sadness in his chest. She wouldn't look at him.

Joel opened the door and the wind howled into the cabin. He stepped outside, slipped on the icy step, and landed on his backside. Hume helped him to his feet, stifling a laugh.

"Ye sure ye don' wan' ta reconsider?"

"Just a minute!" Rachel pushed past Hume and grabbed Joel by the elbow. She held something wrapped in a scarf in her left hand. With a grin, Hume went back inside and closed the door behind him.

"I gotta do this, Rachel," Joel said, looking into her eyes.

"Take this," she said, handing Joel the bundle in the scarf.

"Please don't make me leave with you mad at me."

"You son of a bitch," she said, then threw her arms around his neck and kissed him full on the mouth. For a few moments, Joel Biggs was warm from his hair to his heels.

11

Inside the scarf, Joel found the .45 pistol and the two full clips of ammunition. He had doubts about taking it with him. If Cotten and the Mystic Clan got their hands on it and gave it to one of their gunsmiths. . . . Still, he knew he would need protection. He slid one of the clips into the handgrip of the pistol and put the gun and the other clip into one of the inner pockets of his great coat. This pocket connected with the outer pocket through a tear in the fabric. He would be able to get to the pistol fairly easily, but its outline would not be evident. Joel patted the gun, secured his supplies, mounted Gaily, and set out into the frigid half light.

The sun had never come up so slowly and never was there a day so cold and gray. Joel had been on the road for an hour and a half, and felt he'd never be warm again.

The road wound through bejeweled trees, each twig sparkling with a coating of ice. Gailey had little trouble with the ice on the road, the animal's weight being sufficient to break through the thin layer and into the mud beneath. Each breath of the cold air seared Joel's lungs. Each exhalation was a white cloud that tickled the frost on his nostril hairs.

Perhaps, Joel thought, *I'll meet up with Crenshaw along the road.* It could be that history had misplaced him, that instead of the Stogdon home, he was with some other family in the area and was keeping a low profile. *And maybe,* Joel told himself, *Cotten stole slaves from that family about the time he stole those from the Stogdons. Maybe Crenshaw is pursuing the outlaw along this very road, right now!*

So far, he had encountered no other travelers on the road. The world was silent, and he was alone until he heard the low roar of the Vess River. Slowly, as Joel and the river moved eastward, they came together. As he and the Vess converged, the road dropped into a gully until it met the level of the water. Just around the curve ahead, on a rock outcrop above the water's edge, stood the ferryman's cabin. Blue smoke curled from the end of a blackened pipe that pierced the shake roof of the tumbledown shack at an odd angle. Dim golden light shone in the single window, making Joel feel colder. The ferryman's barge was tied to a large steel eye that had been driven into the outcrop supporting the shack.

Joel dismounted, tethered his horse to the eye, and carefully climbed the icy steps cut into the rock. He pounded on the door of the shack, the impacts sending needles of pain along his frozen arm.

Someone stirred within while Joel shivered in the cold. The door was swung violently inward by a sour-faced old man. His clothes were mussed as if he'd been sleeping in them, and his greasy white hair stood out in all directions. He gave Joel an appraising look, yawned and ran a hand through his hair.

"There's nothin' that side o' the river this time o' the mornin'," the ferryman said, "nothin' there at all. Come back later. When it's warmer."

He started to close the door in Joel's face.

"Hold there, sir! My mission is an urgent one! I'm after the man who stole my slaves."

The ferryman held the door open a crack and eyed him hesitantly. "Stole yer niggers, eh?"

Joel frowned at the man's choice of words and nodded his head. He knew the term was standard in this time, but he'd never get used to it.

"Well, all right then," he said, shuffling into a threadbare coat, "ye'll have ta help me break 'er loose. Now let's git goin' afore we let all the warm out."

He took up a couple of axes, handed one to Joel, and they walked down to the barge. As they broke the craft free from the ice, Joel asked him if he'd seen anyone else on the road that day.

"Ain't seen nobody," the ferryman growled. "Been asleep. None but you's stupid enough ta be travelin' in this 'ere weather."

"You know a man name of Matthew Crenshaw?"

"Ne'er heard o' him."

"How 'bout a man name of Jarrett Cotten?"

"Sure I know 'im."

Joel looked him in the eye.

"Well, not very well," the man said, "and only from a distance. At least I reckon I'd recognize 'im."

Joel gave him a questioning look.

"Come ta think o' it, I guess I don' rightly know, when it comes right down to it."

"Chicken shit," Joel muttered under his breath.

The sound of a horse's hooves on the road caught Joel's attention and he turned to check on his mount. Beyond Gailey, he could see a well-appointed rider approaching, the man dressed for the weather in fine furs and a beaver hat, his horse—a shiny black stallion—one of the finest mounts Joel had ever seen.

He turned back to the ferryman and whispered, "That Cotten?"

The man winked knowingly and went on with his work.

Joel thought of the .45 automatic in his pocket and took some comfort from the knowledge that it was there. Their work on the ice almost done, he pitched his axe into a nearby stump and untethered his horse. Then he mounted up and waited next to the other rider.

The gentleman did not look much like the drawings he had seen of Jarret Cotten in history books, but Joel wasn't surprised by that. He'd often thought that nineteenth-century artists and woodcutters all suffered from severe astigmatism. Cotton was handsome in a thin-faced, ferrety way. His dark eyes were those of a predator. His mouth was wide, and seemed permanently set in a sardonic smirk. The dark hair curling beneath his hat was clean, though oily and untangled. The outlaw obviously thought a great deal of himself.

At first Joel found it difficult to speak to the man. Since he occupied such a lowly station in life—this being readily indicated by his belongings—Joel was unsure how his words might be received by a man of such an affluent and aristocratic bearing. However, he knew he had to somehow manage to fall in with Cotten, and there was no way, he told himself, that he would give up the chase so easily after coming this far.

"The weather is foul, sir," Joel said, trying to follow the script he had read not so long ago and feeling like an idiot. "Is it not?"

The gentleman looked him up and down and Joel shifted nervously in the saddle under the probing gaze.

"Yes it is," he said at length. "However, it does have its own mysterious beauty. The King and I have enjoyed seeing it."

The gentleman must be referring to his horse as *The King,* Joel decided. *Or maybe he has an imaginary friend.* Joel suppressed the suicidal urge to laugh.

Joel looked around at the miserable, frozen landscape. Already, he couldn't feel his toes, the cold knifing into his lungs was likely to give him pneumonia, and if his horse slipped on the ice and he fell from the saddle, Joel might break his neck.

What he wanted the most, he realized, was to crawl back into his warm bed with Rachel.

Pompous ass, he thought, and then, forcing a smile, said, "Indeed."

The ferryman was finally ready and beckoned them to board his barge. The gentleman went first, riding aboard and paying his fare, and Joel followed after him. As the ferryman began hauling away at the cable that spanned the river, the barge moved slowly toward the opposite bank.

"Shall we travel together, sir," Joel offered timidly, his stomach fluttering, "as long as we share the same road?"

The gentleman gave him another appraising stare, then nodded his head curtly. "A companion on the road is always preferable to traveling alone."

12

Joel and his companion left the ferry and rode in silence for several miles. Watching the rosy morning light dancing off the veil of ice, Joel was beginning to understand the gentleman's appreciation for this deadly landscape. Occasional crashes in the forest on either side punctuated their passage as limbs, overburdened with ice, gave way and fell with a sound of breaking glass.

As they proceeded, Joel struggled to find the words that might entice his reticent companion to speak and, perhaps, divulge some useful information. However, it was the gentleman who spoke first.

"If you don't mind my asking, sir, what business takes you abroad in such weather?"

"I am trying to find a horse that wandered away," Joel said, "—or was stolen from my property—not a week hence," he added, trying the gentleman's vernacular.

"If it wandered off in this bitter weather, it has surely perished."

The wind shifted, cutting through the gaps in Joel's clothing. He bundled the collar of his coat up around his ears and pulled his hat down over his brow.

"Yes," he said, then thought of how Crenshaw was supposed to draw the man out. "I would rather some resourceful fellow had taken the poor beast than that." He gave the man a conspiratorial glance.

The man nodded with a slight smile. "I am from Denmark, thirty miles west of here in Madison County. Do you live nearby? Are you acquainted with the country hereabouts, the people and goings on?"

Joel decided he should stick to the script. "No sir, not at all. I am from Adams."

The gentleman cocked an eyebrow. He shifted uncomfortably in his saddle, dropped the reins and rubbed his gloved hands together. "You must love this horse very much to so stubbornly pursue it."

"He's practically all I've got. The horse I ride now is *borrowed.*" He gave the gentleman a knowing wink as he patted the animal affectionately on the neck.

"You say you're from Adams," the man said with a troubled expression. "Then you must know something of the dreaded Bell Spirit there."

Yes, Joel was very well acquainted with the history of the haunting. "I've had an encounter or two," he said, noting the man's discomfort with the subject and storing it away. *Just like in the book.* "How far are you going on this road and what is your business?"

"I am engaged in several errands at once," the gentleman answered, "and depending upon my people, I will get more or less done. But tell me, sir, if you would, is there much speculation in your part of the country?"

"Speculation, sir? What do you mean?"

"Thievery and such. You know, those clever and resourceful fellows who live off of the fat of others."

"Ah," Joel said, trying to show interest, but concealing his excitement. This was so much like the Crenshaw story! Should he deliver the next line? Could he do it? Would Cotten respond the way he would to Crenshaw?

What if Crenshaw shows up later and asks the same thing? But if he doesn't turn up, the chance to get Cotten will be lost. Just how far am I willing to go? I can stand in for Crenshaw a little bit longer, but he'd better show.

Joel took a deep breath and opened his mouth. "It is a pleasure to meet a man whose mind is of a similar bent."

His heart leapt in his chest. He cleared his throat and said, "As to your question—not so much. There's not much to steal thereabouts, being but a frontier town. I had hoped for better, and may be moving on soon. The pickings are slim in Adams."

His companion's gaze sharpened, and Joel saw him make the slightest of nods, as if the man were pleased by what he heard. Joel relaxed a little.

"I am Jarrett Cotten, good sir, and, likewise, it is a pleasure," the outlaw said, riding closer and extending his hand. Joel clasped the proffered hand and Cotten bore down hard as he leaned toward him and spoke, gazing intently into his eyes. "There is a rogue band prepared to conquer this countryside."

Joel felt his resolve withering beneath the man's predatory gaze. He wanted to pull away, to grab the .45 in his pocket and blow Cotten away, but was trapped by both that intense stare and the hand painfully squeezing his own. He fought to keep his features composed.

"Their organization," Cotten said, "has so many members in high places that they are invincible. No one can do anything with them, as anyone who speaks out finds the world turned against him. A friendly young man, such as yourself, however, couldn't help but prosper in their midst."

Cotten gave him a slow, malevolent wink and released his hand.

Where the hell was Crenshaw? Things were moving too fast and Joel was suddenly having trouble keeping everything straight in his head. He felt like he was losing control of the situation—if he was to keep from being found out, he was going to have to think fast on his feet.

Joel discreetly shook out his hand to restore the circulation.

"Tell me, young man, what is your name?"

"Jo—" he started to say, then caught himself.

No, not my real name. Too many around here know me. He had to think fast!

"My name is Matthew Crenshaw," he said, and felt a sudden chill run through him—he *knew* it was the truth.

His stomach dropped and his mouth dried up. The Crenshaw story flashed through his mind all at once, the man's pain and suffering.

No, mine, he told himself, *my pain and suffering.*

Oh, holy shit. I'm Matthew Crenshaw. It was me all along. Sick unreality washed over Joel. Beads of sweat popped out on his forehead, and he quickly brushed them away.

"I noticed the hesitation," Cotten said. "Is Crenshaw one of many names, then?"

Does he see through me?

"An adventurous man cannot survive on one name alone," Joel said, surprising himself with the facility of his response.

"How true," said Cotten. "You please me, sir, as I've always placed much value on meeting men such as ourselves—those of the pure grit."

Oh God, I can't do this! What if it turns out wrong? There are countless ways for this adventure to kill me. And even if it turns out the way of history, I'll wind up penniless and exiled to Europe for my efforts.

The blood drained from his face and Joel began to shiver, quaking from fear, not from the cold.

After a time, Cotten slowed his horse. "Let us rest here a moment and have a draught to warm ourselves. You look frostbitten."

He led the way to a log beside an old firepit set some distance away and concealed from the road. They dismounted and Cotten pulled a brandy flask from his portmanteau and took a seat on the log, gesturing for Joel to join him. Joel had the distinct impression that Cotten had stopped here many times before.

"You seem to know the area quite well," Joel said.

"Yes," Cotten said, pulling the stopper on the flask and taking a sip. "I pass this way with regularity." He passed the brandy to Joel.

What was he going to do? Of all times to go off the wagon, this was not the one. He would need all his wits about him. And he knew that if he took that first drink, there would be no stopping him from having more and more until he was drunk. But in refusing the drink, he didn't want to seem weak. All *real* men drank. All real men were able to handle their liquor. What could he say that would garner respect rather than contempt?

"No thank you," Joel said. "I make it a practice to keep a clear head when entering into new situations. I am new to this part of the country and must appraise it. Also I sense that you have much wisdom to offer concerning speculation, as you referred to it. I do not wish, through lack of attention, to fall prey or lose any such opportunities."

Cotten slowly pulled the flask back.

Shit, Joel thought. *Now I'm finished.*

"You are perceptive, Crenshaw, for I am one to whom you might have fallen prey," Cotten said finally. "Perhaps overly cautious, but it is certainly better to err on the side of caution when dealing with rogues."

Joel let out the breath he'd been holding.

Cotten took another sip. "We'll rest here 'til you've warmed yourself."

The outlaw shifted to a more comfortable position. "Let me tell you something about that rogue band of which I spoke. They are the Mystic Clan and their leader—a noble bandit I have known all his life—is a bold Tennessean. Their main enterprise is slaves, but not in the way one ordinarily deals in that particular commodity. The Tennessean has his confederates positioned throughout the land, and they are constantly on the lookout for the most malcontent of negroes. These they approach with promises of freedom and even money to entice them to slip away in the night to a prearranged meeting place, where they are taken into the possession of the Mystic Clan.

"Now, let me explain to you the law of negro stealing, as I know something of it as well. If a negro has escaped and his master puts up a reward inviting any man to catch said negro, such an advertisement constitutes a power of attorney, empowering the captor to take the slave into possession and act for the master. Since such a commission entrusts the captor to take the negro as his own for a time, then if the captor puts the negro to his own use, instead of returning him, no theft has been committed and the only redress for the master is to be had in civil action. The bandit leader and his confederates hold nothing but contempt for such trifling suits."

Cotten took another drink.

"Tell me more of this fascinating fellow and his bold Clan," Joel said.

"The Mystic Clan makes a fortune by selling the slaves time and again. Before each sale, they arrange a meeting place so they can steal them back. Early on, the Tennessean found the promise of eventual freedom kept them loyal. The Mystic Clan never courts disaster—after four or five sales, when the risk becomes too great, they simply kill the slaves. The fish of the Mississippi have become fat on their corpses."

Though he knew the history, it was quite another thing to hear the outlaw speak so matter-of-factly about such butchery, and Joel had difficulty concealing his shock. He began to cough. "What a waste," he said finally.

Cotten gave him a cold stare. "I have oft heard the noble bandit say, 'If I can't afford to kill a negro, I won't steal him, and if I can't afford to kill a man, I won't rob him.' "

Joel took that in, forced himself to nod as if in agreement. *Does he really think I don't know he's talking about himself?*

"Shortly after setting his mind upon a career of speculation, this Tennessee bandit killed his first man. He was walking the Natchez Trace, for he had sold the nag he had been riding in order to purchase provisions for his journey. He had it in mind to steal a new horse if the chance arose. Having walked for several days, the Tennessean had become weary and desperate, yet no opportunity to steal a horse had presented itself. Finally, while he was stopped for a rest and a bite to eat beside a stream, there approached a horseman astride a magnificent steed. From the quality of the man's accoutrements the bandit took him to be a merchant traveling from New Orleans, and imagined that he was carrying more than could be seen on the surface. He made up his mind to take whatever the man had.

"Once the horseman had drawn near, our bandit hero brandished half of an exquisite dueling set he had pilfered and ordered the man to dismount and disrobe. When his apparel lay at the Tennessean's feet, the hapless man was instructed to turn around and march toward the creek, which he did. As the two proceeded, the man inquired of the bandit if he were planning to murder him.

"The bandit said, 'Stop here,' and the man fell to his knees at the edge of the stream. 'If I am to die at your hand, sir,' the fellow begged, tearfully, 'please give me time to pray and put my soul in order.'

"Before he could say another word, the Tennessean took his brains away, shooting him in the back of the head and watching the contents spout from the front of his face. The man collapsed by the stream and the bandit gutted him, reeling his entrails out into the water. He filled the cavity in his belly with stones and thus sank him in the stream—a trick he'd learned from the legendary Pikes."

Yes, Joel remembered this method of weighting a corpse to keep it underwater. It was, in fact, a favorite method of Wesley's. Joel's mouth went dry and he averted his gaze, trying to hide the horror that surely could be seen in his eyes. "What a brazen fellow! Surely there was never a man so bold! You must introduce me to him someday."

"This is not a man met lightly, Crenshaw. He surrounds himself with only the most adventurous knaves.

"In his younger days he haunted the Trace, filling his pockets with the gold of unwary travelers. But why was he never caught, you may ask yourself? Because he has the grit to kill."

Cotten fixed him with his flat, reptilian eyes, and Joel felt the hairs prickling on the back of his neck.

"I've known many a good thief who was caught and hanged because he showed mercy to those he robbed when he should've done 'em in, like crushing a beetle 'neath one's heel. Not our bold Tennessean, sir. I have never known him to leave behind any who could deliver evidence against him."

Although Joel felt his disguise was still in place, he couldn't help but think Cotten referred to him, and it was difficult to contain his fear. He would have thought he knew something about this man, but hearing the indifferent tone with which he discussed killing people, his casual depravity as he talked of using people until they were used up, was a singular and dreadful experience. He had serious doubts about going through with the ruse. *But how the hell can I get out of it now?*

And who would take Cotten on, if not me? I know Crenshaw's story and if things get too rough, I'll find a way to get out. I have to try. If I don't, God knows how many people are going to die.

"Oh, what a life he must lead," Joel gushed. "Would that

mine were half as thrilling!"

Cotten's appraising eyes showed a hint of a smile.

Why did I have to be Crenshaw? Shit!

After a meal of cold bacon and dried apples provided by Cotten, they mounted their horses and took to the road again. Having accepted his role—no, his *identity*—and his mission, Joel found it easier to relax with the outlaw. Though still wary and vigilant, he had lost some of his unease. His task was to don a persona so flattering to Cotten that the outlaw would take him into his confidence without hesitation. He would imitate Cotten's high-flown speech and exhibit a cruel, predatory streak that would be attractive to the criminal.

The day had grown slightly warmer, and Joel was relieved that the cold's bitter edge was gone. The sun never came out, but remained a yellow blemish in the even gray of the overcast sky.

"Have you had any thoughts concerning where you'll take shelter this evening?" Cotten asked him.

Let Cotten think that, but for his help, I would be left out in the cold.

"No," Joel said, "I trusted I would find something along the road."

"Sir, I am surprised at you," Cotten said, casting him a sly smile. "That is poor planning. In this country such an undertaking would prove most dangerous with all the rogues prowling about." Cotten gave him a wink.

"Truth be known," Joel said, "if I were not to find accommodations along the way, I would be one of those rogues."

The comment had the desired effect, and Cotten's face lit up in a wicked smile. "Truly you are of the pure grit, as I suspected, and since I am a goodly judge of character, and am sure my confidence in you will be vindicated, I will tell you that *I* am the

Tennessean of whom I spoke." Cotten beamed smugly.

"Could it be, sir, that I have the great fortune to make the acquaintance of so accomplished a fellow? My life until now has been merely a hapless one, and I had begun to despair of ever finding the good life. It is providential that I happened upon you when I did, that I might have the chance to study with a *master.*"

Boy, that one reeked, Joel thought, *but I bet Cotten swallows it whole.*

Smiling toothily, the outlaw turned to him with a condescending expression. "You'll find many privations in following through your wildest schemes, including those of which you haven't yet dreamt. With me, you'll learn to withstand these hardships and surmount the impossible. That is what this glorious old veteran and consummate artist may bestow upon you."

What a pompous ass, Joel thought. *If he weren't so deadly, I'd laugh in his face.*

No telling how many loaded pistols he's got under that coat of his, though. I should be laughing at myself—Cotten's eloquent speech is contagious and I sound the poodle as well. But it will impress him, unless he sees it as mockery.

No, not this man—he will take it as the sincerest form of flattery.

"I am speechless, sir," Joel said, "and humbled by your eloquence, and I know there is more than mere words behind you."

"Indeed, say the word and it is all yours."

Don't seem too eager, Joel reminded himself.

"I am honored, but I must pursue my horse."

"Your horse be damned, man!" Cotten turned on him viciously, his eyes flashing. "I offer you the world and you would trade it for a piece of mere horseflesh? Why, damn it to hell, man, I can teach you more than you could ever hope to learn in a lifetime. Follow me and you'll have your choice of the finest of horses. I will provide for us both and teach you the secrets of the good life."

"Sir, I am flattered that you, who are obviously such a great man, consider me worthy of your company."

"I am confident that I will find you an apt and able student, and that you will never let me down. I feel the truth of it! Sir, the Mystic Clan is a noble band of princely bandits. We may bedevil the world, but we are true to each other, with such fidelity as no fraternity has ever experienced. And that is how we get things done. I would consider it the singlest honor if you would join us, and, for now, accompany me on my errands."

"And where do your errands carry you?"

"South, near the Mississippi state line. I have many friends there. And do you recall what I told you of the Mystic Clan's slave trading?" Cotten punctuated this with a wink as Joel nodded his head. "Well, there is a bit of that business in which I am currently engaged. Recently the Mystic Clan struck in Madison County on the farm of an old man named Stogdon. My confederates and I carried away two of his negroes while all in the house slept."

When Joel heard the outlaw mention Hume, he was taken off guard, and had to struggle to suppress his surprise.

"I was planning to stay the night at a house belonging to some of my confederates, those who have taken charge of the negroes."

For a moment, Joel couldn't believe his good fortune. If he played his cards right, tonight, while all were sleeping, he could run off with the slaves and return to the Stogdon household a hero.

But then he remembered that in the Crenshaw story the slaves were not at the confederates' house when they arrived. And besides, that was no longer his only mission.

"My friends will put us up for the night and you can come

along as we dispose of the slaves. This will be your first lesson, and a valuable one, for I know of fewer methods of making money that require less effort or risk."

"Certainly," said Joel, with a slight nod of his head, "I am eager to learn the method, for it is most delightfully devious."

"You will like my fellows, Mister Crenshaw," Cotten said.

Distracted, Joel didn't respond to the name at first, but then realized he must never let this happen again.

"I promise to you, sir," said Cotten, "that I will introduce you to all of them. I will tell you of our plans. You will know our strengths and will become a part of my inner circle, my Grand Council. I will make a brilliant man of you and put you on your way to riches."

The day having warmed a bit made for more pleasant conditions for the men, but it was more taxing for the horses, as the road was a mire. The slow pace at which they moved proved to be a vexation to the outlaw, and he became sullen and withdrawn as the day wore on.

Toward noon, Cotten took another intersecting road. "I had hoped to make it to my confederates this evening," he said, suddenly turning to Joel, "but the road is so bad, I fear we will have to travel all night getting there."

Joel didn't understand what the hurry was all about, but with Cotten in such a dark mood, he thought it imprudent to question him.

Cotten was hunkered down in his saddle, his hat pulled down low over his brow. Joel wished he knew if the outlaw was just brooding over the weather. He feared that he had somehow tipped his hand, and even now his murderous traveling companion was leading him into the wilderness to do him in!

I should try to let someone know I have passed this way, to look out for my return, and notify the authorities if I don't come back.

Joel thought he knew where they were and he had an idea.

"Does this road take us through the town of Wallace?" he asked.

If I can find Thomas Fellowes, I could leave word with him.

"We will be passing through the very heart of it," said Cotten. "How do you know Wallace? I thought you were unfamiliar with this territory."

"I have but traveled through it, and no more," Joel replied smoothly, despite the tightness in his chest and throat. "I do remember the general store in Wallace. Would we have time to stop there?"

"Certainly, it would give me a chance to refill my brandy flask at the Walker Tavern. What purpose do you have there?"

Joel's mouth went dry and he groped. "Nothing pressing. I know you say he is just a horse and I should abandon my search, but I have raised him from a colt and am very fond of him. I thought to put a notice in the general store."

"For all the good it will do you. I suppose there was a time when I experienced kindred feelings, but if you expect to follow me, you will have to learn to abandon all such attachments. If need be I would abandon *The King*. . . ." Cotten patted the neck of his horse. ". . . without a moment's hesitation, or put a shot through his skull."

"It may well be that I am sentimental, but it would do my heart good to try."

"I have heard that a curse upon the sentimental is to haunt the dark and wretched places of the Earth after death."

Joel nodded his head as if considering this sage advice, but it also gave him an idea and an opening for something he wanted to explore. He wanted to find out just how uncomfortable Cotten might become with the subject of the Bell Spirit. It gave him a thrill to think that he had found a chink in the great outlaw's armor. "Several years ago," he said, "I was invited by friends to attend a picnic on the farm belonging to John Bell, in my hometown of Adams."

Cotten looked away.

"We were not invited by the Bells, but it was common knowledge that anyone who came to their farm would be welcomed and allowed to enter into discourse with the spirit who haunted that family."

Slowly shaking his head, Cotten took a deep breath, and let out a long sigh. Joel tried his best to ignore him.

"As I'd been told there might be, perhaps twenty persons were there, meandering about the Bells' property and in and out of their cabin, without a thought to the feelings of their poor hosts. There was even a Frenchman there who had traveled all the way from Paris to debunk the phenomenon. He was knocking on the solid logs of the cabin's walls looking for secret passages, and even asked for a pry bar so he could check under the floor. Can you believe the man's audacity?"

"A man after my own heart," Cotten said insouciantly.

"Be that as it may, Mister Bell retrieved the instrument for him and allowed him to pull up the floor. And that was just like Mister Bell—no matter how brazen his uninvited guests became, he treated them with respect and good humor. Being a puncheon floor, something this fop of a Frenchman was unused to, he didn't get very far before giving up.

"After the picnic, we were allowed to come into the cabin and speak with the spirit. I must tell you it was the most disturbing thing—the voice seems to emerge from a pinprick hole in the air. It is but a whisper, strangely shrill, and can converse on any subject, even events which have not yet taken place. I hear Andrew Jackson honored the Bells with a visit. He too was curious about the spirit and spoke to her for some time."

"I would think such a great man above common superstition," said Cotten.

Joel noticed tiny beads of sweat on the outlaw's face. "Oh, then you don't believe?" Joel asked. He knew Cotten was feigning disinterest to cover his fear. Part of the thrill for Joel was finding out just how far he could take it. "Let me assure you, I have spoken with the spirit, and she told me of the troubled souls who are the victims of murder and what they—"

Joel allowed his voice trail off.

"Well, come on," Cotten said, after a moment. "Finish your bit of unpleasantness and let's have done with it."

"No," Joel said, in a mysterious tone, " 'tis best not to."

"Dammit," Cotten said, "do you think that, with as many men as I have killed, I really want to hear about the dead?"

"I apologize," Joel said, pretending acquiescence, "I will never breathe another word of it."

Cotten nodded curtly.

Joel was satisfied with the effect of his words. They rode in silence for a while. Presently they came to Wallace, a small town bordered on the east by a broad stream. It was a sleepy little village of few buildings; the Walker Tavern, near the center of town, being one of the most prominent. The two men dismounted and tethered their horses to the rail out front of the tavern.

"If you don't object," Joel said, "I will stop at the general store across the street and leave my notice there—I am out of tobacco and now I have an excuse to stop for more."

Cotten, apparently having regained some of his humor, grinned and slapped him on the shoulder. "I will see you shortly, then."

He stepped inside the tavern and Joel hurried across the street to the general store where he hoped to find Thomas Fellowes.

It was warm and bright inside, neatly ordered and filled with foodstuffs, tools, farm implements, bolts of cloth and other sundries. A potbellied stove sat against one wall, a white-haired man rocking in a chair beside it. Sitting near the front window, a pair of heavily creased old fellows shared a game of checkers.

Behind the counter, wearing an apron, was a thin, balding man and there beside him was Thomas Fellowes. It gladdened Joel's heart to see the friend who had once saved his life. With his grotesque scalping and cheek scars, the apron seemed out of place on Fellowes. Joel was shocked at how much the man had aged. He was probably only in his early sixties, but he looked older, his skin deeply lined, dark shadows under his eyes. He was always slim, but now Fellowes was downright bony, arms roped with sinewy muscle.

Joel wanted to tell Fellowes who he was and all that had transpired since they had last met. He wanted to ask if he knew anything about Mark. Hell, he wanted to throw his arms around the man's neck. But he knew there was no time for that, and he didn't want to get Fellowes more involved in this mess than he had to. What name could he give that would be accurate yet not give away to Fellowes just who he was? He had doubts about what he came up with, but it was all he had. He just hoped Fellowes would not immediately recognize him.

Joel approached the counter and, speaking low, addressed Fellowes. "My name is J. Biggs. I am a friend of Hume Stogdon's. I urgently need your assistance. Hume said I could count on it."

Fellowes did not seem to recognize the name Biggs. Joel was both relieved and disappointed. "I will do everything I can to help," he said without hesitation.

Joel asked for paper, pen, ink, tobacco, a small journal, and a few pencils.

Fellowes asked the balding man—his employee, Joel decided—to gather these items. After they were presented to Joel, Fellowes asked the balding man to check on something in the back room. As Joel wrote out two notices for a lost horse, he spoke in hushed tones to Fellowes so they wouldn't be overheard. First he told of the theft of Hume's negroes, then about his pursuit.

"Do you know of Jarrett Cotten and his criminal activities?"

"I've heard tell."

"I am engaged in a deadly masquerade with him and have told him my name is Matthew Crenshaw. After I have recovered Hume's slaves, I aim to bring the law to Cotten and his criminal fraternity. The man thinks I am with him, that I am one of his breed, and I hope to carry the masquerade to his fraternity itself, learn their ways, and expose them all. If you see me with Cotten, do not acknowledge my presence. He does not know my real name. If I do not return this way, you must notify the proper authorities."

"I will! But why the hell are you talkin' that way?"

Joel gave a questioning look.

"Ye sound like ye got a corn cob stuck up yer arse."

"Oh, never mind—it's Cotten. His bullshit rubs off on you. Will you help?"

Fellowes hesitated, looking at Joel curiously. "I said I would," he said, finally, "I'll do anything for a friend of Hume's."

"Thank you. If you would, also prepare a letter attesting to my appearance here today and what we spoke about. It will be important evidence. Make two copies. Mail one to Hume and the other to Judge Thomas Erwin at the Supreme Court of Madison County with whatever explanation you can provide."

Fellowes agreed to do this. Joel paid for his supplies and stuffed them into the outer pockets of his coat except for the journal and one pencil which he sharpened and placed in an inner pocket.

"Oh, and post this if you will," Joel said, handing Fellowes one of the notices. "There is no such lost horse, but it bears the signature of J. Biggs and the date on the back. That will help establish that I was here."

Without another word, and before he lost the nerve to continue, Joel spun on his heels and left the store, hurrying across the street to the tavern.

He hoped he would live to return, and tell Fellowes everything.

The Walker Tavern was built of rough-hewn logs and had a puncheon floor covered with sawdust. Daylight knifed into the smoky room through thin cracks in the windows. A fire burned in the hearth and tallow candles glowed smokily atop puncheon tables scattered throughout the cramped space. The room was quite noisy, although only about half the tables were occupied. The bar was made of the only finished wood in the room, planks set atop logs standing on end. Cotten stood there, two glasses before him, and when he saw Joel, he motioned him over.

Joel stopped to speak to the barkeep, giving him the other notice before joining the outlaw.

"Would you care for a drink," Cotten asked, as Joel joined him, "before we continue our journey? It surprises me to find such a fine liquor in this place."

This bastard's going to ask me to drink with him several times every day.

"They wouldn't have enough for me here," Joel said, half joking, then immediately regretted saying it.

Cotten was silent a moment, looking at Joel. "Ah . . . I begin to understand," he said.

Joel's stomach knotted up. He tried to remain composed.

"Once you start, it is difficult to stop."

Joel nodded his head, wondering if this admission had blown his chances of continuing on with Cotten. A part of him hoped this was the case and he could return to Rachel and their quiet life with the Stogdons.

"I have seen the problem many times. It has been the downfall of many a great man."

Cotten had locked eyes with Joel again, and there was that intense appraisal. Joel struggled not to flinch.

"You are wise to consider your limitation and to take such action to avoid disaster. Would that some of my colleagues did the same. . . ." He sighed heavily, and dropped his gaze.

Joel immediately felt a weight lifting from him.

"Ah, well . . . you mustn't reveal this to anyone else—some foolish men consider it weakness. I will provide your excuse."

Joel nodded, dumbfounded by the depth of Cotten's understanding.

"I trust you have seen to your business?"

"Yes," Joel said, "and I thank you for indulging me."

"Certainly," Cotten said, draining his glass. "I do not wish to seem overeager. However, I am in a hurry."

With a growing sense of doom, Joel followed the outlaw outside to their horses.

13

The outlaw shared out some of his provisions, and they ate an afternoon meal while in the saddle, Cotten unwilling to lose any time by stopping.

"Crenshaw, you must be mystified as to how I knew to approach you concerning speculation. But a short time spent with a man and I know him as a brother. I knew within that same time that you and I are cut from the same bolt, and that I could trust you with my life."

Joel, struck by the irony, struggled to suppress a smile.

"You have but to practice—I will instruct you—and you will excel at penetrating the thoughts and souls of others. You start the exercise by watching the reaction of a fellow as you tell of villainous exploits such as one might read about. If he warms to the subject, you pursue him. Otherwise, you retreat and choose another subject."

As they continued on their way throughout the afternoon, Cotten boasted of the Mystic Clan's deeds, divulging names, dates, and the sites of their criminal exploits. And just as in the Crenshaw book, he began to tell of the Clan's "Grand Plot." Joel's excitement nearly overshadowed his fear and he had to counsel himself to take deep breaths and remain calm and vigilant. As the outlaw took the lead, it was an easy matter for Joel to use one of his pencils to record these particulars in the journal he had secreted in the inner pocket of his greatcoat.

The point of Joel's pencil broke for the third time and, stifling a curse, he once again fumbled his jackknife out of his pocket. Under his greatcoat, he furtively began to whittle a new point on the pencil. The effort was hampered by the movement of his horse as they proceeded along the muddy road. The blade slipped and thudded into his saddle horn.

Cotten turned his head at the sound. "Pardon me, sir?"

"No—nothing," Joel said, breathing deeply to steady his nerves. "What was it you were saying about the fraternity's 'Grand Plot?' "

Cotten turned to him as if suspicious, and Joel reminded himself not to seem overeager.

"Yes, the slave uprising. Well, as I've explained, our activities with the slaves have never been limited to financial gains alone. We are always on the lookout for just the right type. Those negroes vicious enough to commit murder, yet clever enough for us to train to excite other slaves to action. We recruit them as officers for our army. We win them over by explaining to them that all of Europe has abandoned slavery and that the slaves in the West Indies won their freedom through a similar revolt as the one we are proposing. We tell them that their masters and, indeed the entire country, have fattened themselves on the fruit of their labors, and that, should they win their freedom, they would be on an equal footing with the whites and could even marry their women.

" 'There are thousands of white men willing to die alongside you, fighting for your freedom,' we tell them. Then we swear them to secrecy with a long, drawn out ritual—full of fire, Latin words, and sleight-of-hand tricks to prove our connection with the magical world—in which we make use of a painting I had commissioned for this purpose. It depicts a terrible visage, the demonic being the negroes must face if they fail to keep our secret. I have found the negro to be much given to superstition, and have made good use of it."

Unlike you, who nearly pissed his pants over the Bell Spirit, Joel thought with a wry smile.

"Once we are sure of them, we sell them to planters with large holdings to act as our liaisons with other slaves, instructing them to incite their fellows to rebellion."

Cotten faced forward once more and continued, gesturing expansively now and then to illustrate one point or another.

"All up and down the Mississippi, these officers are busy fomenting discontent among their fellow slaves and offering them freedom for a price. Finally, on Christmas Eve of next year, we will give the officers enough money to purchase liquor so that all the slaves might have a dram—I know of no surer method to bring the negroes together. Once they are liquored up, our officers will promise their fellows that the day of vengeance and freedom is at hand. They will order their 'troops' to kill all the whites in the households the next day, but for a few who will join them in battle. Those negroes who refuse to fight will be killed.

"On December twenty-fifth, we will bring the rich to their knees and while the country fights to put down the slave revolt, we will loot the South."

To reduce the possibility that the outlaw might catch him taking notes, Joel had cut a slit in the lining of Hume's hat, and as each page of the small journal was filled, he discreetly tore it out and stuffed it behind the quilting. He had just slipped a page into it and was returning the hat to his head when he dropped it. His heart skipped a beat as he caught it. Cotten continued obliviously.

"You may ask why Christmas Day was chosen. Traditionally, the whites are less vigilant during the Yuletide celebrations. As you know, the slaves are often freed from their duties and allowed to celebrate their own festivities. That is when the slaves will strike!"

"How will the slaves be armed for this?" Joel asked. "How will you get the weapons to them?"

"The Mystic Clan has set aside twenty percent of our considerable income to purchase guns and ammunition. These are cached throughout the countryside in strategic locations. On Christmas Eve, they will be distributed amongst the slaves. The arms will of course be in limited supply and the negroes will be expected to use their farm implements as well—sickle, pitchfork, or adze. A family sleeping in the black hours of morning is easy prey. And, as they proceed, they will gather additional arms.

"New Orleans, Natchez, Atlanta, Nashville—all the great cities of the south will be destroyed. Pretty white women have been promised to the negroes as an incentive. All others—men of course, but children as well—will be put to the sword. In the midst of this revolt, in the confusion and rubble, my Mystic Clan will sack the burning cities. The plunder will be unimaginable.

"We will let the pitiful negroes fight for us, all the while thinking they are fighting for their freedom. This will be a glorious massacre, but for them, it will all be for nothing, as their cause is hopeless. The whites will destroy them utterly, once they recover from the Christmas attack.

"In the aftermath, I will revel in the knowledge that I have caused more destruction, shed more blood than any other conqueror history has known.

"And I *will* succeed."

Joel shuddered.

"I'm sure this seems the most outlandish of plots to you, Crenshaw, but I pride myself on its audacity. It is this very quality that has made my every effort successful. You see, I learned a valuable lesson as a young man—I was publicly flogged for an amateurish horse theft—and the experience awoke the animal within. I learned to strike with such viciousness and cunning that none could stand against me. I have not failed at any crime I have undertaken since."

Joel knew something about that horse theft from his reading, but he couldn't quite remember what it was. Something about gloves. He looked down at the pair he was wearing. Cotten was wearing a pair also, he knew. What was it?

He remembered that the outlaw was still a teenager when he was caught trying to sell a neighbor's horse. Because Cotten was nearly an adult and had been in trouble with the law several times already, he was treated like an adult. He was tried in Nashville and received a sentence of forty lashes and a stint in the pillory outside of the courthouse where the townsfolk were allowed to further humiliate him.

Oh yes, that was it—they had also branded his thumbs with the "HT" of horse thief, and after that, Cotten was never seen without his gloves.

"I count all Americans among my enemies," Cotten said, "and life for me is meaningless if not dedicated to their ruination."

Joel's pencil broke again and he was relieved—he had writer's cramp and would not have been able to go on much longer, anyway. Although he knew the story already, he wanted to make damn sure that he put down all the particulars.

He started whittling a new point on his ever-diminishing pencil and realized that he was no longer cold. The ice had all melted and the world was a slushy mire. Now he would have gladly traded the warm muck of the road for the clean ice of their earlier travels.

"The Mystic Clan is invincible," Cotten continued, "and I hazard to guess that we are already five thousand strong from New Orleans to as far north as New York. Some of my inner circle are men of influence, each in a position to contain a leak, should anything about us get out. With threats and ridicule, they can make small of such matters. One gentleman, Art Clayton, was once the Attorney General for the State of Georgia. He is my second in command."

Joel got a point on his pencil just in time to start a list of the "inner circle" and their positions within the community as they were enumerated by the outlaw.

In trying to keep up with Cotten's rapid-fire speech, Joel used a shorthand he had developed over the years while taking notes from historical texts. He discovered that since he hadn't used that skill for some time, he had forgotten much of it, and now had to improvise to fill in the gaps.

The problem is, he thought, *I'm not being very consistent.*

He hoped he had as much paper and pencils as Cotten had words, and when the time came to transcribe all this for publication, he hoped he could decipher his shorthand as well.

14

The day grew warmer still as Joel and Cotten worked their way south toward the Mississippi state line. At sundown, Cotten shared out more provisions, indicating that they would eat in the saddle once again.

As the last crimson rays of sunlight dwindled behind the distant hills, Cotten stopped at a point where the road climbed a gentle rise toward a heavily forested crest. The outlaw dismounted and carefully scanned the surrounding underbrush without offering a word of explanation. Joel waited apprehensively, fearing once again that Cotten had somehow discovered his furtive notations and was planning to lead him off the road into the wilds to murder him.

When Cotten leapt back into his saddle with a smirk on his face, it seemed Joel's worst fears were about to be realized. He almost set spurs to his mount and bolted away, but managed to restrain himself. Even so, his fingers nervously traced the contours of the .45 in his pocket.

Quietly, Cotten led them along a barely discernible trail through choking undergrowth. After a time, when the outlaw did nothing to threaten him, Joel began to relax, realizing that Cotten had merely been looking for one of his secret trails.

"The Mississippi state line," Cotten suddenly announced as they crested a steep hill and turned onto another thin trail.

A darkened valley lay before them, and, as they descended into it, the air grew more chill and Joel gathered his greatcoat tightly about him. He noted, with satisfaction, that since leaving the well-traveled road, they no longer slogged through a quagmire. With his fatigue and the steady rocking of his horse, he was presently lulled into a doze, and was uncertain how much time had passed before Cotten startled him to consciousness.

"Wake up there, Crenshaw," the outlaw said. "The mysteries of the night hold us within their ephemeral grasp."

Joel shook himself awake and nearly fell from the saddle.

"You suggested yesterday," Cotten said amiably, "that we might pass the time in pleasant conversation. Tonight, however, you have had nothing to contribute to our intercourse but your damnable snoring."

"I apologize. I was more fatigued than I had realized."

Cotten smiled, his fearsome white teeth flashing in the moonlight. "I trust you are well rested?"

Joel nodded his head, smiling ruefully.

"Why, sir, then fill your pipe and let us talk."

Their pipes filled and lit, the fragrant smell of tobacco soon wafted on the cool night breeze. Joel cupped the pipe in his gloved hands, the warmth thawing them out.

"When I was a young man visiting New Orleans," said Cotten, "I was much desirous to become involved in speculation, but had little practical knowledge. I thought to find prey in New Orleans because I'd heard many rich fools lived there—ready plunder for my willing hands—and I was anxious to meet others of my kind. At first I had little enough success, until late one night, while returning to the inn where I boarded, three men brandishing pistols approached and politely asked for my money. When I handed them my pocketbook, they could not help but notice how delighted I was to meet them.

"The first one said, 'We've been watching you for many nights, as you seem to be a student of speculation. We thought to teach you how it was done, since you seem to be in a quandary.'

" 'Thank you!' I said, then introduced myself and pleaded with them to teach me everything they knew. They returned my pocketbook to me, and so began my introduction, my initiation into a career of brilliant wickedness.

"At such a young age, I was quite taken with them. We fell in together quite naturally, and they showed me the town, an extravagant frolic through countless taverns and many a comely wench.

"I was indoctrinated into the art of pilfering by legerdemain, counterfeiting, audacious thievery, and cozening. My specialty was posing as an itinerant preacher and taking collection after delivering a fraudulent sermon. You have never heard a heartrending sermon such as I can give. But it was the art of killing that was their most valuable lesson.

"I was made known to all the important speculators in New Orleans and was given the name of every fellow with that career on the Mississippi, from New Orleans on up to all the western ports.

"The only victim I have ever allowed to keep his life was my first. One of my fellow boarders at the tavern where I stayed was from Louisville and he was quite the dandy, all flash and glitter. I determined to rob him and so devised a plan with three of my new friends. I would take him on a bender through all the local dives. My friends were to fall upon the both of us as we returned to our lodgings. The Kentuckian was so disgusted with the robbery that he left New Orleans that very night, vowing never to return to such a despicable hive of villainy.

"The take was sizable and, though split by four, allowed me to live comfortably for a year, during which time, I prowled the great cities of the South, from New Orleans to Cincinnati, from

Memphis to Charleston, making acquaintances of all the speculators I could find. These numbered some four hundred and it was with these clever souls in mind that I first conceived of the Mystic Clan.

"Shortly thereafter, I was in a small town in Alabama when rumors of a slave uprising began to circulate through that small community. The townsfolk had heard of the recent revolts in the West Indies and the dire consequences suffered by the planters, and so were prostrate with fear. The idea occurred to me that this could be a powerful weapon. My thoughts returned to New Orleans when, seeing the grand houses of the very rich, the posh elegance of their lives, I had told myself, 'I could have all this, if only I had the right weapon.'

"Watching that Alabama town enslaved by fear, I knew that I had found it. Turn all the slaves of the South to revolt and I could sweep the wealth of the whites right out from under them as they scurried about trying to put out the fire I had started."

Joel remembered reading about most of this in the Crenshaw book. He was witnessing history that he already knew and thought he would be more excited than he was. But then, he was very tired.

Cotten jabbered on about his early exploits, his philosophies, and his successes with women. Joel did his best to commit everything to memory so he could set it down in writing when there would be light enough to do so, but he couldn't keep his eyes open.

He dozed fitfully, awakening periodically to hear the outlaw still chattering away, oblivious to the fact that Joel wasn't paying any attention.

By sunrise, Joel was wide-awake again, thinking about meeting up with Hume's slaves and the danger of being recognized. The last thing he needed was for one of the slaves to pipe up, "Hello, Mister Biggs, sir."

He tried to think of a signal he could give them, but that was too risky—if they misunderstood, they could all end up dead. Then his thoughts turned to methods of disguising himself—he hadn't shaved for several days now, and perhaps the growth of beard. . . .

No, that's ridiculous! Those men are probably scared, but they're not stupid. I'll just have to hang back, hope they don't get a chance to see me.

I should trust the Crenshaw story I know, Joel told himself, *and try not to worry.* Even so, he was unable to put the thought out of his mind and questions tormented him as the morning wore on.

In his journal he entered what he could remember of Cotten's disclosures from the night before. Each time he discreetly slipped a page into his hat, he worried that his actions were obvious, that, although he performed the maneuver while Cotten wasn't looking, the outlaw might turn his head suddenly, or catch Joel's movements out of the corner of his eye and become curious.

He had just put a page into it and placed the hat back on his head when Cotten turned and looked at him. He opened his mouth as if to speak and then stopped. Joel felt his insides turn to ice while the outlaw's cold eyes seemed to pierce the felt of his hat.

"That's the most decrepit-looking hat I've seen in a long while," Cotten said. "Seems to me it gets lumpier by the hour."

Joel didn't know what to say—fear took control of his tongue. "It's the quilted lining," he nearly shouted, "uh—that's torn loose, uh, and all bunched up."

"I see," said Cotten, "hand it to me and I'll cut the lining from it for you."

"No! By Christ, it's *my* hat, and I'll not hand it over to any man!"

Cotten stared at him, speechless, his fragile expression that of a man who has just discovered his companion is a raving lunatic. The outlaw turned away and they rode on in silence as Joel gradually regained his composure.

"I apologize for taking that tone with you," Joel said. "My—my father gave me this hat, is all."

"You truly are sentimental about your belongings," Cotten said quietly. "We'll have to work on that."

Toward midday their road dropped through a river basin.

"We're coming up on the Hatchie River," said Cotten, "where we will meet our confederate."

"I was thinking I would wait for you on the bank of the river. I have some accouterments for fishing and thought to try my hand here."

"The fish are always available, the business we have with our confederate cannot wait."

As their destination came into view, Joel was shocked. He had been expecting the well-appointed home of a wealthy man—in the Crenshaw story he knew, it was—but instead, he found a run-down cabin; sagging shakes on the roof, chinking falling out from between the logs and smoke seeming to pour out of every hole but the chimney. The ground before it, where it was not rocky, was churned mud and appeared lifeless.

"My stomach is ailing me," Joel said. "Must be something I ate. Perhaps I could just lie down on that rock by the water and rest."

"It is nothing, I'm sure. Now stop your womanish whining and come along. There is our destination just ahead!"

The nearby trees looked as if they had retreated upslope to escape the filthy squalor of the place. Broken bones, shards of pottery, rotting garbage littered the ground around the cabin.

"The weather has warmed such that I could bathe in the river if we had the time. I'm rather unpresentable."

Cotten turned to him with an exasperated look. "Crenshaw, you will now follow me without another word and perform as I dictate."

Joel's mouth snapped shut. Now there was no way out. He could only hope for the best and be prepared to defend himself. He gripped the automatic through the tear in the fabric of his pocket.

Some distance from the cabin was a small outbuilding, its door bearing a stout lock, and Joel wondered if this was where the slaves were kept.

Three horses stood within a paddock. One of the animals nickered as they approached and dismounted.

The man who came outside to greet them was one of the filthiest Joel had ever seen. His britches were patched and threadbare, mud caked to his stockings and the flaps of leather tied to his feet. His shirt had almost ceased to exist, surviving only as strips of mismatched cloth hung over his shoulders and gathered with a frayed rope.

As Cotten introduced him, Joel scanned the property for any sign of the slaves. He pulled his hat down low and turned the collar up on his coat, desperately hoping to elude detection.

The man, introduced as Ned, removed a greasy, shapeless hat and bowed deeply to Cotten and Joel, muttering something that couldn't be understood.

This is the great man's empire? This is the type of man whom he chooses for his vaunted fraternity?

Of course, he picked me, a drunk who plans to betray him. . . .

Ned turned his doughy, sweating face upward. "We gots ever'thin' jes as ye ordered, Cap'n," he said in a cloud of sour whiskey vapors.

"And the negroes?" Cotten asked, dismounting.

"Aw, there's a bit o' a problem. McAllister says he's got ta lay low fer 'while. The slaves are still in the shed."

Cotten turned and punched the man in the face, knocking him off his feet. He swore at him while Ned cowered in the mud.

"McAllister!" Cotten shouted, "Where are my goddam niggers?"

Joel climbed down from Gailey.

I can't believe this guy! One minute he's acting the lord of his domain, the next he's having to beat the help like a common foreman.

Coughing, a small weasel of a man appeared from inside the cabin. His bearded face was angular, its seams well defined by dark stains. As he approached, there wafted from him a heady stench of body odor.

"M-mister Cotten!" he said, his face bobbing up and down obsequiously.

"McAllister," Cotten said in a flat voice, "I hear you haven't been moving the merchandise. Kindly explain to me why this is so. What about our agreement?"

"W-well sir, it's like this. My, uh, picture is on an ad-advertisement fer some o' our stolen negroes. I-I cain't go nowhere. I'm holed up here, a-afeared ta show m-my face."

The only evidence of Cotten's displeasure was his cheeks flushing . . . and then the pistol. It came swinging out from behind the outlaw's coat, rose level with McAllister's head, and fired.

The man's head seemed to blow inside out.

"Well, sir, then you're of no use to me," Cotten told McAllister as the lifeless body slumped. The man's head struck the dirt with the sound of a split melon.

Ned, still on the muddy ground, was dumbstruck. Cotten raised another pistol and blew his brains out as well.

Joel stared at the death around him, rigid with shock. This is what saved him, as Cotten seemed to take his emotionless stance as cold acceptance. Joel read this in the outlaw's eyes, and to further this deception, he forced himself to curtly nod his head.

"If an arm of my conspiracy has a canker, 'tis better to amputate the limb entirely than to risk exposure to the rest of the body," Cotten said.

He stooped and removed a key from a ring on McAllister's belt. Straightening, he put away the second pistol and drew yet another.

"Follow me," he ordered, turning and heading for the locked outbuilding. "Do you have a pistol, sir?"

"Yes," Joel replied automatically.

"Then draw it, cock it, and be prepared."

Joel almost pulled out the .45. Then he gathered his wits and pulled out the pistol Hume had given him. He cocked it and followed in silence, not trusting himself to speak, his legs moving mechanically, as if in a dream. He stopped several feet from the shed as the outlaw unlocked the door and went inside.

Cotten emerged with Hume Stogdon's slaves in tow. They were filthy and haggard, their eyes downcast. The one nearest Cotten—Joel recognized as Briley—lifted his eyes and focused on Joel, a spark of recognition lighting up his face. Joel's stomach clenched in apprehension, but Cotten raised his pistol and pulled the trigger before the slave could say a word. The other slave, named Macklin, was horrorstruck and looked at the outlaw, his body trembling.

"You must now kill the other, Crenshaw," Cotten said as he handed a surprised Macklin a bowie knife, then stepped quickly out of range.

But there aren't any advertisements about these slaves, Joel thought, and almost said as much, but bit his tongue. He stared at Macklin, not knowing what to do, the pistol dangling in his grasp.

Macklin looked blankly at the knife and then lifted his gaze to meet Joel's. There was recognition, and then there was anger.

Did Cotten see that?

The slave, shifting his grip on the blade, crouched to spring.

The loud report startled Joel back to himself.

There was a pistol at the end of his arm, held shaking in his white-knuckled grasp.

And it was smoking.

Macklin, who was no longer a slave, fell back against a woodpile, the scar of his death a splash of vivid crimson against the splintered, gray wood of the shed.

Cotten slowly nodded his head with evident approval. "A lesser man would not have reacted so swiftly."

Joel could only nod his head in agreement.

"It seemed to me he might have recognized you at the end," Cotten said.

"He did look a little familiar."

Joel felt like he'd been hit hard in the gut. Though he walked away from the scene, he couldn't shake the image of Briley lying dead, Macklin's ruined face retreating from the smoking barrel of his pistol. He took deep, slow breaths to try to keep from puking.

This wasn't supposed to happen. It's not in the story! If I hadn't been trying to control what was going on, this might not have happened.

But am I really changing history? Am I doing it right now? Should I try to impose my will, or should I just let go and trust that it'll come out all right? Is it my fault, what happened, or did it take place long before I was born?

Damn Cotten to hell! He knew the theft of Macklin and Briley was not widely known. But they were ultimately disposable to him, and he just wanted to test me.

The outlaw led the way into the cabin. The stink of the cramped single room took Joel's breath away. It took him a moment for his eyes to adjust to the dimly lit interior, longer still before the miasma of odors numbed his protesting nose. Vermin crawled freely over the walls and floor; insects, rodents and small, dark, scuttling things in the corners.

"We'll get some sleep and then move on," Cotten said.

Joel knew he wasn't going to be able to sleep, not after what he had just done. Though he told himself that Cotten had deftly orchestrated that murder, it was impossible to put out of his mind the fact that he had just killed an innocent man.

Cotten was quiet and seemed tired, and Joel was grateful for that. He didn't want to have to talk to the man. Cotten gave Joel a blanket and then retired to the room's only bed, a rope and wood frame affair with a mattress of straw-stuffed ticking thrown on.

This place is a goddam shithole. Why would Cotten choose a place like this when he could have anything he wanted?

Joel lay down by the drafty fireplace. The smoke burned his throat, but at least he was warm. The blanket stank and was stiff with filth. He tried to ignore the smoke and the noises—Cotten's snoring, the scuttling of insects and mice—and put his mind to rest. He would need his wits about him when it came time to continue their journey.

He craved sleep and release from his dark thoughts, but each time he felt himself drifting off, his imagination told him he might be killed while he slept, and he came instantly awake. Joel was still staring into the fire when he heard Cotten stir and rise from his sleep and prepare to depart.

"Up, young Crenshaw," he said. "We must be about our business."

15

Sleep-deprived and in shock, Joel moved mechanically, doing as the outlaw instructed. They loaded all the bodies into the cabin and set it on fire. They watched to make sure it would burn, then mounted their horses and moved on.

That was when it hit Joel that he had just helped Cotten destroy the evidence of the crime for which he hoped to have the man arrested. *Goddammit, this is all one great big mistake. How could I have believed I could pull this off? Now my evidence is gone. It's his word against mine. I just need to get the hell away from Cotten.*

He knew he couldn't just take off—Cotten would not tolerate that after taking him into his confidence—so Joel followed in troubled silence as the outlaw led them back along the road to Tennessee. They were headed for the Mystic Clan's hidden stronghold on an island in the Ghost River, hurrying to make it to a meeting of the Grand Council. This was all the more frightening to Joel now that he was looking for a way to get out of his present situation. Instead of getting away, he was moving toward the heart of Cotten's criminal enterprise. The closer he got, the more difficult it would be for him to escape.

The more Joel thought about Macklin and Briley, however, the angrier he became. He had spent time with these men, had grown to respect them. Despite the fact that the Stogdons kept them as slaves, these men had treated themselves with respect. While working together on the Stogdon farm, Joel had found

Briley and Macklin to be good companions. They were intelligent and compassionate, even to their masters, and each had a good sense of humor. The more he thought about the cruelty of their murder, the less afraid Joel became.

As he broke from his reverie, he became aware that Cotten was explaining something about their destination.

"The Ghost is merely a stretch of the Wolf River," the outlaw said, "that becomes several miles wide as it spreads through a swamp. The current seems to disappear as the river passes through, hence the name, Ghost."

Hence the name . . . hence the name! Listen to this smug bastard. He thinks he's above everything that holds humanity together. Joel's anger had turned to outrage, and he reminded himself that there was a reason he was headed into the snake pit. He would just have to find other evidence to use to put Cotten away. If he had to, he'd invent it!

Although the day remained warm, there was heavy rain and they traveled in miserable silence. At one point, the outlaw taught Joel the secret hand signal of the Mystic Clan, a subtle yet complicated gesture. Joel suppressed a smile, wondering what would happen if he showed the signal to a Crip or a Blood.

"Use the phrase, 'America's Powder Keg,' along with the hand signal to identify yourself to other members of the Mystic Clan," Cotten advised.

The phrases and hand signals of the Mystic Clan might have been cool when I was a kid, but now it all seems so lame. Cotten just loves the melodrama.

Near sundown, they arrived at the Wolf River.

"I fear that it is too dark now to chance this swollen river," Cotten said, "and, furthermore, I do not relish traversing the benighted swamp."

After dismounting, Joel and Cotten led their horses east along the muddy riverbank for an hour, until, long past sunset, they came to a cabin.

If this is the cabin along the Wolf River that's in the Crenshaw book, Joel thought, *it will be the home of McHenry Lake.*

The latch string had been withdrawn and the hole stoppered with a cork to keep out the cold. They knocked on the door and waited in the rain while a terrible racket emerged from within, followed by a gruff voice. "State yer name!"

"Parson Jeremy Wode," said Cotten, "and my protégé—."

"—Jonathan Gurdy," Joel said.

"What bus'ness 'ave ye?"

"We're caught in the weather and are cold and wet beyond endurance."

There was a grumbling from behind the door and then it opened to reveal a man, tall and gaunt—very severe in appearance, Joel thought. He held two pistols at the ready. On the floor beyond the man was an overturned washtub and broken dishes in a puddle of gray suds.

"Hope we didn't startle you," Joel said. *So this is McHenry Lake. He doesn't look anything like I imagined.*

"I ain't happy ta be puttin' ye up," the man said in a somber tone, lowering his weapons. "But as a Christian man, I reckon I oughter."

"We hate to take advantage of you like this," Cotten said, his voice swimming with forced regret, "but there doesn't seem to be anything for it."

"Ye kin put yer animals in the paddock out back. When yer done, leave yer greatcoats on them hooks under the eaves, there."

After the man had shut the door, Joel chuckled mirthlessly. "Friendly fellow."

Cotten's servile attitude vanished instantly and he became cold, obviously angry with the delay. "I've heard of this sonofabitch—he's given my men a hard time on occasion. This being close to one of our routes through the Ghost, he has plenty of opportunity. If he becomes more of a problem, I'll have him removed."

I've got to find a time when Cotten's not around so I can speak to Lake, Joel thought as they led their horses around to the back of the cabin. *Perhaps he hates these outlaws enough to help me.*

While putting their mounts inside the paddock, Joel noticed Cotten eyeing one of Lake's horses. "I've a mind to take that red barb. She's a beautiful high horse."

Now speaking to Lake had taken on life-and-death importance, as Joel knew that if Cotten decided to take the horse, he would most likely kill the man.

When they returned, the door's latch string was out, and they hung their coats on the hooks, opened the door, and stepped inside. The man greeted them with blankets and suggested they warm and dry themselves and their shoes by the fire.

"My name's McHenry Lake. Sorry I was so ornery before, but that's what happens to a man lives on 'is own. Also, there's dangerous men hereabouts." Lake leaned forward, eyeing them with an expression that indicated he thought his guests might be of that type. Cotten seemed to take no notice. "But the Christian thing is ta comfort those as needs it," Lake continued, "ain't that right? Had a wife as taught me that, but she died."

"She was a wise woman," Cotten said with a wisp of a smile. "Without Christian charity on the frontier, there is nothing but the evil of this savage wilderness."

Cotten oozed into his pious routine, and Joel, warming his butt by the fire, ignored him. The outlaw rambled on for a good hour and a half, Lake dutifully, if impatiently, listening. Finally their host found a way to stop Cotten's mouth—by giving the outlaw something to put in it. Lake prepared a meal of fried cornbread and catfish and, for an all too brief stretch of time, there was silence as they ate. Afterward, Cotten started in again.

After a time there was another pause and Joel leapt at the opportunity to find a way to speak to their host in private. "Mr. Lake," he fumbled, "could you show me to the outhouse. I fear that I might fall in the river looking for it in the darkness."

Lake looked impatient. "There's a lamp there," he said, pointing, "an' if ye go out the door an' go right, it's fifty feet up the hill."

Joel fidgeted impatiently.

If I could just get in close enough to whisper to him.

"Well, is there anything I can help you with? I-I mean it's only fair, us forcing ourselves on you, and all."

Cotten gave him a curious frown.

Lake stared at Joel a moment, then shrugged.

They spent the rest of the evening sitting across the cabin from one another while Cotten paced and ranted on and on about God, Jesus, the sins of man, and the devil.

Joel tried to think of ways to catch Lake's attention by using covert gestures, but the few he tried out received only looks of disgust, and, try as he might during the brief pauses in Cotten's tirade, Joel couldn't engage the man in conversation.

He thought of getting his writing materials from his greatcoat hung outside and writing a note and slipping it to the man, but discarded the idea when he realized that Lake might not be able to read.

Besides, if Cotten ever found that note, my fate would be sealed. No—all I can do is hope to get up early, before either Lake or Cotten has risen. I don't know how, but I'll just have to.

"Don't ye need ta go ta the outhouse?" their host asked at length.

"The need has passed," Joel said.

"Follow me," Cotten ordered Joel. "Do you have a pistol?"

"Yes," Joel replied automatically.

"Then draw it, cock it, and be prepared."

Joel did as he was told, and followed in silence, his legs moving mechanically. He stopped several feet from the shed as the outlaw unlocked the door of the structure and went inside.

Cotten emerged with Hume and Stephen Stogdon in tow. They were filthy and haggard, their eyes downcast. Stephen lifted his eyes and focused on Joel, a spark of recognition lighting up his face. Joel's stomach clenched in apprehension, but Cotten raised his pistol and pulled the trigger before his friend could say a word. Horrorstruck, Hume looked at the outlaw, his body shaking.

"You must now kill the other, Crenshaw," Cotten said as he handed Hume a bowie knife.

Joel stared at Hume, not knowing what to do, the pistol hanging all but forgotten in his grasp.

Hume looked blankly at the knife and then lifted his gaze to meet Joel's. There was recognition, and then there was anger.

Did Cotten see that?

The old man, shifting his grip on the blade, crouched to spring.

The loud report startled Joel back to himself.

There was a pistol at the end of his arm.

And it was smoking.

Hume fell back against a woodpile. The scar of his death was a splash of vivid crimson against the splintered, gray wood of the shed.

Cotten slowly nodded his head with evident approval. "A lesser man would not have reacted so swiftly."

Joel could only nod his head in agreement.

Sweating and shaken, Joel was roused from sleep just before dawn by Cotten.

"Up, Crenshaw," the outlaw whispered, then moved toward the ladder to the loft where Lake was sleeping.

Joel was certain Cotten would kill Lake so he could take his horse without leaving a witness behind. *But he might not be so quick to climb that ladder,* Joel thought, *if Lake is awake up there.* Joel stumbled off his pallet and proceeded to stomp his feet on the puncheon floor. "To get the circulation going," he stage-whispered as Cotten shot him a look that said, *Shut the hell up, you idiot!*

From the loft, Lake's snoring continued, and the outlaw turned back to the ladder.

Joel pretended to struggle with his boots and dropped them one after the other, glancing apologetically at a glowering Cotten.

The snoring continued.

Joel tried a coughing fit without results and then decided he would have to take a dive, tripping over a footstool and knocking over a chair.

There was a stutter in the snoring and then it stopped.

Cotten, his face flushed, turned away from the ladder and seized Joel by the collar. Hissing dreadful oaths under his breath, he shoved Joel toward the door, opened it and threw him out of the cabin. Joel tumbled outside onto the ground.

Cotten gathered up their possessions and exited the cabin. Joel accepted his portmanteau from the outlaw and remembered he had left his pipe and tinderbox on the table in the cabin and decided to leave them behind so he would have an excuse to return for them. They moved to the paddock. Joel set about preparing Gailey for travel. Cotten saddled and bridled The King, then pulled a hackamore with a short lead from one of his packs and slipped it over the head of Lake's red barb mare. They mounted their horses, and with Cotten leading the mare, left the paddock, riding south along the riverbank.

A quarter of an hour later, Joel reined in his horse and Cotten turned to him. "I forgot my pipe and tinderbox," he said, with what he hoped was appropriate exasperation. "I must return for them."

"Well, hurry on about it. You've caused no end of trouble this morning. If we'd been engaged in a bit of the 'What If,' we'd surely be jailed by now."

And what is horse theft, then? Joel wondered. "I'll be a more apt student once I've awakened."

"If Lake is awake and has noticed his horse is gone, you'll have to kill him. I would have taken care of that myself, but, with all the noise you made, I was unsure if he was lying in wait in his loft against that very possibility."

Joel turned his horse around and headed back to the cabin, sneaking glances to see if Cotten were following. But the outlaw was ranting silently and gesticulating to the air.

Upon reaching the cabin, Joel saw the door was still open and heard Lake snoring obliviously in the loft. He stepped inside and slammed the door shut. When this failed to rouse the man, he climbed the ladder and shook him. Lake came awake and immediately slugged him in the face, and Joel fell backward down the ladder. He landed on his tailbone.

Lake was down the ladder and hauling Joel to his feet in an instant. "What's the meaning o' this?"

"I-I-I-I n-need you to know I am a law-abiding man. But I'm mixed up in some dreadful business with the outlaw, Jarrett Cotten."

"That 'im wit' ye? I know all 'bout that man's bus'ness on the river."

"Yes sir. He's on down the road waiting for me." Joel rubbed his sore tailbone. "I told him I had to return for my pipe and tinderbox there on the table. I needed a chance to talk to you where he couldn't hear me. I'm not really Jonathan Gurdy. My name's Joel Biggs, but you must keep that as a closely guarded secret. Cotten knows me only as Matthew Crenshaw. I've adopted this disguise in an effort to bring Cotten down."

"Now I know why you was actin' so queer last night," Lake said, handing Joel his pipe and tobacco.

"You see," Joel said, nodding his head, "Cotten stole a couple of slaves from a good friend of mine, but he's also mixed up in a slave uprising, and I wanna help the law lock him up, so I'm pretending to be one of his men with the hope I can get something on him."

"So why ye tellin' *me* all this, son?"

That was a good question, Joel realized. Just what did he want from Lake? He couldn't remember the story well enough at this point to know what to do next. How could Lake help? All Joel could think to ask for was some sort of documentation of events.

" 'Cause I need more than just my say-so to convince the sheriff of Madison County that Jarrett Cotten should be arrested. Can you write a letter describing all of what happened last night and this morning, our talk and everything? Just don't use my real name in it. Refer to me as Matthew Crenshaw."

"Anythin' ta git that outlaw an' 'is filth offa this 'ere river!"

"Thank you sir," Joel said, scampering out the door. "I'll be back for that letter."

Then he stopped because he thought of something from the Crenshaw book. It wasn't a part of his recent reading—he hadn't gotten to that part yet—so he couldn't be sure of it. If he hadn't left the damned book on his kitchen table, then maybe he'd be able to check to make sure. He thought he remembered from reading it twenty years ago that Cotten's negro-stealing was never proven and that the outlaw had to be convicted of a lesser offense, that of horse theft.

"Cotten has stolen your red mare—"

Lake's eyes narrowed and his chest puffed up.

"—but if you'll trust me," Joel quickly added, "and let us

move on now, I guarantee she'll be returned to you, and we'll have Cotten imprisoned for the theft."

Lake let out his breath as if relieved. "She's blown, and no good to me anyway. I was going to sell her, but was feeling guilty about that. This way, at least she'll serve a good purpose."

"Yes sir."

"You come back for me and I'll go with you to the law and swear out a warrant."

"That I will."

Now Joel had more than just his word against Cotten's. He mounted his horse and rode back to rejoin the outlaw.

16

Cotten led them along the riverbank for about an hour until it seemed to broaden out into a morass. He then took a turn onto an almost non-existent trail that led into the trees. They came to a small, hidden paddock containing six horses, where Cotten insisted they leave their mounts before continuing into the wetlands of the Ghost River. Joel was uneasy about leaving Gailey behind, but there was a trough of water and a manger filled with feed for the animals. She would be all right there for several days if need be.

Joel and Cotten spent the next several hours slogging into the autumnal swamp carrying their portmanteaus. Though the day was chilly, Joel had to roll up his sleeves and loosen his blouse to stay cool.

Cotton stopped at a point that seemed arbitrary to Joel. He struck an elegant pose, cleared his throat, and gestured toward the swampy forest ahead of them.

"There it is," he exclaimed proudly. "America's Powder Keg. Just beyond those cypress trees lies the heart of the Mystic Clan."

Joel smiled broadly, but didn't much care, wanting only to be out of the ankle-deep muck. He could certainly see why the outlaw considered it an impregnable fortress, for the approach alone had exhausted him.

Peering through the orange and gold wooded swamp, trying to see the spot where Cotten was pointing, Joel saw only a green heron perched on a cypress knee before he was forced to return his eyes to his footing. His left boot was being sucked off his foot by the sopping tangle of dead mosses, lichen and other rotting vegetable debris underfoot. As he pushed with his right foot to free his left, water was forced from the tangle and pooled on the surface in an iridescent, oily puddle.

The whole swamp smelled of a great, hollow, rotting tree and Joel found himself breathing through his mouth, for his nasal passages felt as if they were packed with sawdust and black pepper.

He sneezed repeatedly until Cotten commanded him to stop, and then sporadically with the occasional glower from his companion. He imagined his lightheadedness resulted from his boots being full of leeches sucking his blood. Then he remembered, with some relief, that it was late in the year and the slimy vampires were probably all dead.

Joel felt a sting on his left hand as they passed the ragged remains of a tree. He looked down and saw his own blood on one of the rapier-like blades of a clump of yellowed sedge growing like wild hair from the stump. To soothe his stinging hand, he rubbed it, but only forced his salty sweat into the scratch, making it burn all the more.

I hate this goddam place. This has to be the most miserable fucking place on the whole fucking planet.

"My little domain is a haunting one, is it not?" Cotten said. "It is my opinion that if we were ever attacked here, the atmosphere alone would be sufficient to drive off half of the intruding force. I'll wager you have never experienced anything so daunting yourself, but, perhaps, for the Bell Spirit herself."

Since Cotten had given him an opening. . . .

"She was indeed terrifying. I asked the spirit about the future, and she said—"

"I'll have none of that! The future is mine! Mine to command and no one else's."

The outlaw, clearly troubled, lapsed into silence as he trudged along the sodden path. He quickened his steps, hurrying ahead. Joel smiled, chuckling silently at Cotten's retreating back.

A wattle-and-daub structure came into view as they crested a slight rise. Pallid blue smoke wafted from its tumbled-down chimney and disappeared into the rust-colored canopy above. The ancient shake roof of the cabin barely supported the litter of stones and mud chinking that had fallen from the chimney. Several turkey buzzards circled in the sky above the cabin and Joel hoped it was merely garbage that had attracted the birds. The cabin was set in the midst of a clearing ringed with tupelos and cypress trees bearing late fall color.

Daylight was failing and Joel heard the strange call of a barred owl in the distance, as well as the rapid-fire tapping of a woodpecker to his left. He turned and saw, perched in a cottonwood tree, the ivory-billed woodpecker, a species extinct in the time in which he was born.

Joel was soaked to the bone, and knew that his sodden and muddy boots would be hard as rocks when they dried out. He was as miserable as he had ever been in his life. Yet Cotten, clearly in his element now, seemed unaffected by the hardship of their travels. Once again, Joel sensed the outlaw's ability to see only what he chose to see, admit into his world only that which pleased him.

Joel was startled by a muskrat that scampered across their path and disappeared into a pocket of water to their left as they approached the cabin. The door was ajar, the last insects of the season buzzing in the thin light that spilled from inside.

"It looks as if anyone could walk right up to 'America's Powder Keg' unchallenged," Joel said, trying to keep the sarcasm from his voice.

"Not so," Cotten said, proudly, "we've been watched for the

last half hour. That barred owl we heard before—that was one of my men, a half-breed fellow named Collins, signaling."

God, that's so dumb. And I used to eat this crap up. But, hell, I was just a kid.

But as stupid as some of this seems, I shouldn't lose sight of the fact that this man is deadly.

"Crenshaw, this is an historic moment for you," Cotten said, "for you are about to enter the sanctum sanctorum of the Mystic Clan."

He stepped up to the doorway and paused, turning to Joel before entering. "Now you will meet the members of the Grand Council. At the moment there are only eleven of them because one, a drunkard of a fellow by the name of Hargus, was recently caught in a botched bit of the 'What If' and is soon to be hanged. We tried to break him from his confinement, but were unsuccessful. Alas, I think he has had it, and so it is my intention to make you the twelfth—if the others are in agreement, of course—for there must be twelve on my jury. You see," he said with a laugh, "the United States of America is on trial, and I am the judge."

When Cotten turned on his heel and swept inside, Joel stifled a laugh. All humor left him, however, when he entered and saw the men assembled there.

Cotten stopped in the center of the cramped room, while five men converged on him, all talking at once. Joel set his portmanteau on the dirt floor beside him and tried to listen to what they were saying. All he could gather was that they were angry with those who hadn't shown up for the Grand Council meeting. Cotten didn't say a word, but Joel saw a look of embarrassment cross his face.

"Excuse me, gentlemen, excuse me." Cotten silenced his men with a broad sweep of his right hand. "Let me introduce someone to you."

Joel felt five pairs of cold, appraising eyes turn on him, like a pack of dogs.

"This is my young protégé, Matthew Crenshaw. I am grooming him for the position recently vacated by our soon-to-be late colleague, Hargus."

Joel blanched under the hostility directed toward him. He removed his hat, gripping it tightly. These men clearly saw him as an upstart, and perhaps as one seeking to someday usurp Cotten's authority. In those cruel eyes, he saw challenges.

"Crenshaw," Cotten said, indicating a wiry, goatish man with a Vandyke beard, "this is John O'Farrell."

All he needs is horns, Joel thought.

Beside O'Farrell stood a short but stout little bear of man. His pitted face was covered in an unkempt carpet of red beard which seemed to extend down his thick neck and disappear into his collar, only to emerge again at the ends of his shirt sleeves and cover the backs of his large blocky hands. Cotten introduced him as Job Hayes, and the man nodded his shaggy head at Joel in greeting.

"This is Attorney General Art Clayton," Cotten said, clapping a hand on the sloping shoulders of a sickly-looking fellow, "my most trusted."

Cotten said he was the former *Attorney General of the State of Georgia,* Joel reassured himself.

The man locked his red-rimmed eyes on Joel's for an instant and extended his hand. Joel grasped it and the man bore down hard, the tiniest of grins touching the corners of his mouth. To look at the frail man, one would never have expected such strength. Joel bore down as hard as he was able, and the man suddenly let go and sprang back, wringing out his hand. Clayton's expression was thoughtful as Cotten went on to the next man.

What the hell was that all about—like that ridiculous handshake

Cotten gave me the first day we met. Must be something stupid they came up with to help them appraise someone's character.

"This is Garrison Sharpe," said Cotten, "our authority on counterfeiting."

Joel offered his hand, but Sharpe didn't return the gesture. *He looks like a snapping turtle,* Joel thought, eyeing the man's sharp beak of a nose, claw-like hands, and thick middle. He looked like he might reach out and bite at any minute.

Joel remembered telling Mark about the snapping turtles in the creek. "They won't let go until it thunders," he'd said.

"And this is Cecil Givens," Cotten said, pointing to a stinking, fat dumpling with a patina of sweat. "He takes care of our negroes."

The man's brilliant, pinprick eyes peered out from beneath dollops of pasty flesh. He wore nothing but a pair of filthy breeches. His massive belly hung pendulously halfway to his knees. Givens was barefoot, his feet gray and bloated from contact with the soggy dirt floor. His ears were almost hidden within the folds of fat on his neck. He smiled unwholesomely, toying with the tuft of hair sprouting from one of his exposed nipples. Joel shuddered, feeling soiled by Givens' gaze, and he had to struggle to keep from turning away from the sight of him. Still harder was extending his hand to clasp the pale and swollen appendage Givens offered for a handshake. He felt as if he were grasping the larval form of some giant insect.

"And lastly, our newest member of the Council, Jamus Cooke." Cotton winked and gestured toward a darkened corner. "We are proud to have him."

Jamus Cooke . . . thought Joel. *Why do I know that name?*

A massive shadow stirred in the darkness, offering a meaty hand. A large raw, red face emerged. Joel's heart leapt in his chest, then skipped a beat.

That's Wesley Pike!

There was no doubt about it. Joel hesitated, briefly gripped by terror. He would never forget the day he saw the big man, along with Thomas Fellowes and Mark Ryder, washed away in the flood that followed the New Madrid earthquake. Wesley had been gravely injured at the time and Joel never expected to see him again, but there was no mistaking his powerful presence within the close, dank room.

Taking a deep breath, he got control of himself, grasped Wesley's hand and shook it. It was a rough, strong hand, just as Joel remembered it.

Then he had the feeling he was shaking his father's hand. Not the drunken father who had abused him all his young life, but one who had, for good or ill, had something to do with shaping his young heart and mind. As much as he feared him, he had the most inappropriate desire to hug Wesley. He tried to make it casual as he looked up into the big man's eyes. They had aged along with the rest of him. Wesley was in his late fifties now. His face, though still an angry red, was heavily lined and his frame was slightly bent, but there was still fire in his gaze. Joel was relieved to realize that Wesley did not recognize him.

"It is a pleasure to make your acquaintance," Joel said, withdrawing his hand.

"Likewise," Wesley said and then returned to the darkened corner.

Cotten leaned toward Joel and whispered, "We are particularly proud, as he is really Wesley Pike. Of course none of these fellows are old enough to remember Wesley by sight, so they think he's Jamus Pike, Wesley's older brother, but no one is allowed to refer to him as anything but Jamus Cooke."

Joel had no idea Wesley had ever had anything to do with the Mystic Clan. There was so much here that was different from the history he knew. Was it safe to make any assumptions at this point?

"Not long ago our man Peyton Boles blew himself up," Cotten continued his whispering. "Wesley was good enough to take over his work, stocking our caches of weapons for the slave uprising, but the name Pike is so steeped in blood that it is best we don't use it."

Cotten grinned wickedly as he surveyed his Council. "Crenshaw, now that you have met the men," he said, "I think it would be apropos if they met you."

He gestured for everyone but Joel to take a seat, and they did so, waiting expectantly.

Joel took a deep breath. He couldn't get Wesley Pike out of his mind. The more time he spent with the man, the more Joel spoke, the more likely it was the outlaw would recognize him.

The words wouldn't come.

Oh shit, what do I do now?

Then it came to him *because* he was thinking about Wesley—he remembered how he had handled himself around the outlaws of the Pirate Cave so long ago. Joel opened his mouth and the words spilled out.

"My lowly beginnings are of no consequence. Let us just say that my life began when I met Jarrett Cotten on the road. And, if I do not seem all that our esteemed leader would have you believe, I pray you forgive me. In matters of speculation, I am sophomoric in the truest sense of the word. But that is why I am here, to be enlightened by this exalted body." He gestured with a flourish toward the gathering of outlaws.

"Here, here," said Cotten, nodding his approval and looking to Art Clayton. The man nodded his head and said something to the others and they smiled. Joel didn't hear what was said, but he could see that some of the men seemed more relaxed, their expressions softening. Once again in shadow, Wesley Pike's features could not be seen.

"I fear I have little to offer but a quick mind and a willing spirit," he said, looking directly at Clayton, "and I look to you for guidance. My thoughts on the ideals of the Mystic Clan may be simply summed up: I believe in and have confidence in all that our illustrious leader has imparted to me concerning your Grand Plot, and am honored that he has entrusted me with such knowledge.

"I feel that Jarrett Cotten is enlightened by a stratum of knowledge to which few men are privy. Indeed, he is something of a Genghis Khan, an Alexander, or even a Napoleon, and those of us who are similarly enlightened owe him unflagging allegiance."

Joel paused to come up for air and could see Cotten swelling under the flattery—and was that an erection he was hiding beneath his clasped hands? No, Joel was remembering Wesley Pike's response to killing. Putting that out of his mind, he plunged ahead with his sycophantic raving.

"The world is ripe with all that we require for a life of comfort and leisure. And should we stand by and not harvest the fruits of the good life, while the dictates of a world, one we neither love nor respect, keep us down? Have we not equal right to the good things of the Earth? Anything—be it air, earth, fire, or water—that we, as a totality, can reach out and grasp, is ours by rights, for the taking.

"God, if there be one, has given his endorsement to the system of 'might makes right.' The fish of the sea and the animals of the field prey upon one another, each in turn taking advantage of the other, as man has preyed upon himself from time immemorial.

"But we have reestablished order, in our own favor, and we owe allegiance to none save *our own.* Let us exult in the fact that we are masters of our own lives and let us revel in all the treasures which we can prise from the grasp of our foes."

Several of the men roared their approval, and Joel had to

gesture for quiet before continuing. Even so, he was shouting as he went on.

"In the fall of Rome there was set a precedent for the success of all our plans. Did not Antony and his two fellow conspirators plot the downfall of that ancient city in just such an isolated place? I say the same applies to us! Jarrett Cotten is our Antony, and where three conspirators succeeded against Rome, so I say the thousands of the Mystic Clan will succeed against America from the swamps of the Ghost River. To suggest otherwise is to insult our heroic master."

Joel paused, his mouth dry and throat sore. He intended to continue, but some of the applauding outlaws rose from their seats and he bowed instead.

Where in hell did all that come from? It was something like what had been attributed to Crenshaw by history, but Joel had no idea if it would ultimately have the same effect.

Cotten approached and clapped him on the back. Others were crowding in as well, all speaking at once. Someone shoved a jug into his grasp and Joel smelled the whiskey fumes rising from the unstoppered mouth. Cotten quickly took it away.

Apparently his speech did not entirely have the desired effect. As the outlaws stepped away to resume their seats, Joel saw Garrison Sharpe, the counterfeiter, still seated and watching him with an expression of mixed skepticism and hatred. And there was Wesley, still seated in the shadowy corner, his features unreadable in the dark. These two were not interested in wishing him well. Had Wesley realized who he was? What had Joel said or not said that Sharpe remained unconvinced?

"Sharpe, Cooke," said Cotten, "aren't you going to welcome Mister Crenshaw into our fold?"

Wesley shrugged.

"There be plenty o' time fer that after his deeds have proven his stripe," Sharpe said. "Let us proceed instead wit' what *Grand*

Council meetin' we can manage wit'out our absent colleagues."

The outlaws drew their chairs together to begin their meeting. Joel dragged his portmanteau to a chair at the outer edge of the circle where he could sit more or less unobserved.

"Well," Clayton said, "how in hell we gonna have a meetin' wit'out Durham here ta report on the law an' Black ta tell us 'bout the disposition o' the niggers?"

"An' I cain't very well give ye a complete treas'ry report," said O'Farrell, "wit'out Puckett ta tell me 'bout the whores."

"Our first order of business," Cotten said, "is whether or not young Crenshaw here is to join our ranks. What say you men?"

"Kin we depend on 'im ta fill Hargus's shoes?" Sharpe asked. "Ye think he'd be any good at searchin' out the wealth we'll be goin' after when the uprisin' begins? Does he know the first thin' 'bout reconnoiterin' towns?"

"Hargus was useful only when he wasn't drunk," Cotten said angrily. "It was the drink that got him into the trouble he's in now." He took a deep breath and let it out before continuing. "Crenshaw will learn quickly enough. When we give him work, he'll find a way to get it done. I've got a good feeling about him. I haven't merely heard him talk—I've seen him act. Why, just yesterday, he killed a negro who was attacking him with a knife—did it coolly and without a second thought."

"That don't convince me. I don't see that shows any gumption at all. Killin' niggers is one thing—like killin' animals—but how's he gonna act when it comes ta facin' a real man?"

Cotten's face was reddening, and he turned a fierce gaze on Sharpe. "I say the young man is of the pure grit!"

Silence filled the cabin and Sharpe fixed his eyes on the floor. None of the others said a word, but all eyes were on the two men, and Joel was relieved that, for the moment, Cotten and Sharpe had diverted attention away from him.

Is that it—am I in?

Watching Sharpe scratch thoughtfully at his two-day growth of beard, something turned over inside Joel. The last time he had felt such a keen sense of foreboding, he was looking at Virgil Pike.

Could be Wesley's the least of my troubles, just like at the Outlaw Cave. Sharpe might have backed down for now, but I haven't heard the last of him.

Looking around the room, he was once again struck by the coarseness of the men with whom Cotten surrounded himself—all but Clayton, who had to be well-educated to have held such a high office. He wondered why the outlaw had taken to him, and why the man would fight for him now the way he did. But perhaps that was just it: Cotten had tired of all the human garbage. He needed another Grand Council member with the level of intelligence and education that he himself exhibited. And perhaps it was that Cotten, just as Wesley Pike, saw himself in Joel. Could it be that this had blinded Cotten to the fact that Joel was not right for the job? He had blocked from his mind those aspects of Joel's character which didn't quite fit. Cotten's grasp of reality was very selective, which made him all the more frightening.

I guess, when it comes right down to it, he's lonely. I know I would be in this crowd.

As the meeting continued, Joel sat back and ignored the proceedings. Wesley had shown no indication he recognized him, and so Joel began to relax. The warmth from the stove conspired with the droning voices of the outlaws to push him from exhaustion to the edges of slumber. He began to nod off and jerk himself awake, each time hoping the others had not noticed. But their somber voices continued without him and, slouching down in his seat, he allowed himself to relax and let go.

The next thing he knew, Cecil Givens had a grip on his thigh, just below the crotch, and was shaking him awake. "Wake up, Crenshaw," he said. "Yer snores are interruptin' the meetin'."

"I'm afraid I have dragged the young man halfway 'round the world to reach our sanctuary," Cotten said, "and he has not yet my constitution. Pray, Crenshaw, go lie down on one of the pallets in the corner—there should be blankets for you there."

"Here," Givens murmured, "let me help ye." The moist suet of his arms embraced Joel, lifting him by the shoulders and turning him toward the darkened corner. The man's smell, a stench of bad cheese, clogged Joel's head.

"Leave 'im be, Givens," shouted Clayton, "you fat, stinking bum puncher." The frail man jumped to his feet and wrested Joel free of Givens' grasp and nudged him in the direction of the pallets. Joel gathered up his portmanteau and, placing it at the end of his pallet to prop up his feet, lay down. He pulled his coat more tightly about him, but made sure the outline of the .45 wasn't evident. He used his hat, clenched tightly in his fist, as a pillow.

Givens sat back down, a sour expression on his doughy face.

Joel awoke late in the night and found the outlaws still at it—all save Givens, who was nowhere in evidence. Cotten seemed to be the only one sober as he sat amidst the others, watching and listening with a sly smile on his face.

To Joel's right, Hayes and O'Farrell, both red-faced, were shucking bloody fists. He winced each time their fists slammed together.

Cotten was staring at him with a distant, daydreamy smile.

In the middle of the room, Sharpe and Clayton were sitting on the soggy floor with a near-empty bottle, giggling in high-pitched voices. They had been there for some time as their clothes, like giant wicks, had soaked up the moisture of the dirt floor and were darkened with dampness.

"Uh—where can I find the outhouse?" Joel asked.

The outlaws—all but Cotten—turned to him as one and began to chuckle and giggle. This mounted in intensity and went on and on as Joel sat on the edge of his pallet turning red.

"Please, where is the goddam privy?" he finally shouted over their guffaws.

O'Farrell fell out of his chair and rolled in the dampness while Hayes pointed at him and laughed until he wept. When their laughter began to subside, Cotten cleared his throat and spoke in a clear, sober voice. "Young Crenshaw, we're in a swamp," he said, his sly smile stretching to a toothy grin. "It is all outhouse."

This started the outlaws back up again and Joel fled their laughter, stuffing his head into his hat and hurrying out the door and into the night. He thought to take his portmanteau with him, but then realized that was ridiculous—what was in there to find—or steal—but a journal with half its pages missing?

Outside, the utter darkness was relieved only by slivers of moonlight that angled out of the trees and cut across Joel's path. He walked forward into a breeze that blew gently, but bitterly cold, carrying with it the swamp's smell of decay.

He tripped on a fallen branch and stumbled forward blindly, caught his balance and moved on, his eyes slowly acclimating to the darkness until he could make out ghostly silhouettes surrounding him. He selected a place at random, unbuttoned his breeches and urinated, all the while looking around, his eyes open wide, the skin on the back of his neck crawling with the eerie sensation that he was being watched.

As he was buttoning up, he spied firelight flickering off in the distance. Curious, he moved toward it, placing his feet carefully. Drawing nearer the source of the light, a meaty slapping came to his ears, followed immediately by two voices, one grunting, one crying out in pain. He almost turned away, but plunged forward in spite of what he feared he would find.

Just ahead he saw a torch, jammed into a tangle of dead vines, and, beyond, a sight which made him stop dead in his tracks. Cecil Givens knelt behind a slave who was on his hands and knees. Naked, his slabs of fat flying, Givens sodomized the man. The slave was rigid, his hands clawing the dirt as he gave voice to the pain of every savage thrust.

A sharp cry of outrage emerged unbidden from Joel's throat. He regretted it immediately as Givens turned and saw him. Givens pulled away from the slave, his bloody penis briefly exposed before the loaves of his belly and thighs swallowed it up.

Givens moved surprisingly fast and was upon Joel before he could put any more distance between them, before he could reach through the tear between his pockets and grab the .45 automatic. Joel's hat flew from his head as the man's shuddering bulk hit him. Givens grabbed his arm and twisted it viciously, bearing Joel to the ground. It flickered through Joel's mind that this was a well-practiced move. Then his face hit the dirt and stars exploded behind his eyes.

"Gonna have me a li'l white man, now," Givens said, centering his mass on Joel's back. The .45 was beneath him, its hard, sharp edges biting into his hipbone.

In spite of the danger to himself, Joel panicked at the thought of losing his hat. He reached out for it, groping wildly, but Givens twisted his arm again and Joel thought it would break. Joel finally found his voice and cried out, but the sound was swallowed up by the swampy night. Givens' weight was overwhelming. Joel was having trouble breathing. With a grunt, Givens tried to rip the breeches from Joel's backside. "No!" Joel screamed, but his brain calmly told him *this is happening, this is going to happen, there's nothing you can do to stop it. . . .*

Then Givens froze, his head pulled up and back, and Joel became aware that someone was standing over them.

"He arrived wit' Cotten," the stranger said. "Don' ye think Cotten will be upset if'n ye foul 'is friend?"

"Why, i's Wesley's dawg," Givens grunted, turning to look at the man. "Ye'd think a man'd be embarrassed ta carry a name like that, 'specially long after his master's dead. Run on now, dawg."

Wesley's dawg! Joel tried to turn and look, but couldn't move his head far enough. *No, it can't be!*

"Let 'im up," said the stranger. "Or Cotten'll use have yer fat fer candle tallow."

"Like yew," Givens said to the man, "he'll be too 'shamed ta say anything. Now take that knife away from my neck, or I'll give ye more ta be 'shamed of."

Givens became rigid and a gurgling came from his throat, and something wet and hot sprayed Joel's back and neck. His grip on Joel tightened for a moment, then began to relax.

"Ye all right?" the man said.

"Yes."

Joel felt him struggling with Givens' dead weight. Joel put his back into it and finally they managed to roll the fat outlaw off him.

Rubbing his bruised hip, Joel stood and looked at the man who had saved him. The torchlight was behind him and in the darkness all Joel could see was a silhouette with a mop of curly hair. Mark had curly hair! But he really had no way of knowing who this was.

"You Mathias Crawshanks?"

"Matthew Crenshaw," Joel replied.

"What I meant ta say is that *I* am Mathias Crawshanks," the silhouette said, offering his hand.

Joel grasped the hand and shook it, turning with the hope the man might turn with him into the light. Yes, he did turn somewhat. Joel could see the shape of his nose. It did not look familiar.

"Thank you for your help." Joel struggled to come up with something else to say. The strangest feeling had come over him. It was so strange, and so unexpected, that it took a moment for Joel to recognize what it was. Fear. He was afraid to ask the man if he were Mark Ryder.

But why? The worst that could happen was that Joel might hear *no, you've got the wrong guy.* Big deal.

The man moved toward the slave, who had remained quiet throughout the struggle. He was belly-down across a fallen log. The cleft between his buttocks glistened with blood.

"You kin git up now," the man said.

"I cain't, suh," the slave said, his voice shaky. "I's still tied down."

The man pulled out a jackknife and cut the slave free.

Joel suddenly remembered his hat, located it on the ground beside a tree trunk, picked it up and put it on his head.

"Th-thank ye, suh, thank ye," the slave said, standing and pulling on his torn breeches.

Joel looked away, shaking his head.

"You go on back to the shed," the man told Givens' victim.

"No—run away," Joel said. "Dammit, just run away!"

"I ain't gwine ta run nowheres in this swamp. Never fin' my way outta here. I'd be dead in a week."

"When they find out what happened, they'll likely kill you."

"He'll be all right," the man told Joel. He turned to the slave. "Go on now. I'll come and tie you back up."

"Much obliged ta ye, suh." The slave turned and walked awkwardly into the darkness.

He won't live long anyway.

The man turned back to Joel. "And I'll tell 'em Givens' attacked me and I defended my life. They won' know anythin' about him."

Why was this man willing to help the slave? This lent more credence to the idea that he was not an outlaw, but indeed Mark. His childhood friend would never tolerate slavery willingly, would he?

What should I say? How can I ask him if he's Mark? Why am I so afraid?

"I'm the one covered in Givens' blood," Joel said. "I'll tell them Givens attacked me and I had to kill him."

"Suit ye'self," the man said. "But ye'd better hurry back ta the cabin now 'fore it gets light. When they find out 'bout this, hell will come here to prey."

Then he took off, running into the trees, and was gone.

Joel wanted to follow, but couldn't see clearly five feet ahead of him, let alone run through such unfamiliar territory.

I should've gotten him to help me dump Givens' body into one of these bogs.

Plucking the torch from the vines, Joel started off in what he believed to be the direction of the cabin.

His torch long since burned out and tossed away, it was dawn before Joel, bedraggled, exhausted, and shivering cold, found his way back. Looking on the bright side, he told himself, getting lost had given him time to practice what he would say. The story wasn't all that good, but it was all he had.

Opening the cabin door, Joel found everyone asleep but Cotten.

When the outlaw saw the blood on him, he became alarmed. "Are you all right, young Crenshaw? Where have you been?"

"I've been lost in the swamp! I went out to relieve myself and Givens attacked me. There I was with my breeches down around my ankles when he slips up behind me and tries to—"

Joel broke off, as if he were ashamed of the memory.

"And what does he do? He attacks me. We fought and I killed him. It was purely self-defense, I assure you. After that, I left him, and wandered through the swamp, lost, until now."

Then Garrison Sharpe was beside Cotten, yawning sleepily, but his eyes as sharp and penetrating as ever.

"Tha's some story, Crenshaw," Sharpe said loudly.

"It's the truth," Joel said. "I swear to it."

"You don't have to come to your own defense, Crenshaw," Cotten said, eyeing Sharpe, "while I stand beside you."

The counterfeiter spat on the floor, but said nothing. By now, the others had awakened and Sharpe filled them in on what was going on.

Joel began to relax. He wanted to ask about the man he had met, the one who was possibly Mark, but how? He didn't want to draw the outlaws' attention to the fact that this man had been with him last night. It would only complicate things.

"Nobody liked Givens," Hayes said, rubbing his bandaged knuckles.

O'Farrell nodded his head in agreement. "He was a disgustin' beast."

"True," Cotten allowed, "but whatever his faults, he *did* control the slaves with a certain . . . aplomb."

"A Plum?" O'Farrell said. "That's not what he called it."

Cotten shook his head in disgust.

"I kin see it now," said Hayes. "Givens was out there doin' what he does best—ye know, plumbing the causative slaves." He chuckled. "An' ye had the misfortune of attractin' his attention."

"Indeed," said Clayton. "There are those among us wit' strange tastes, but Givens would have it only if he could 'take it an' break it' as he had a mind to put it. So Givens tried to take advantage o' the young man an' found it was a mistake. He deserved what he got."

Hayes snickered. "I say good riddance. Givens was more trouble than he was worth."

"And he stunk too," said O'Farrell.

"But now we ain't got nobody ta take care o' the slaves," Sharpe said. "Crenshaw's provin' ta be a heap o' trouble. An' 'nother thin' that bothers me is that he ain't offered us nothin' 'bout his past."

"I don't believe," Cotten said, "that I know any of you by your true names, and that has never cost me a night's sleep. We all have our secrets. And as for finding someone to take care of the negroes, why there are plenty of our confederates worthy of promotion. Clayton, call on Everett Collins to fill the vacancy."

"Now Jarrett!" Sharpe said.

Cotten turned on him, his eyes flashing dangerously. "That will be enough!"

Clayton stepped to the door and called out to Collins.

Joel moved to his portmanteau, looked in it for a fresh shirt, and put it on. He would have to make an effort to wash away the blood crusted on his clothes and body later.

A man of mixed white and Indian blood, dressed in yellowed buckskins, walked into the cabin.

"Collins, Givens is dead," Cotten told him. "You're foreman now."

"Yes sir," Collins said, vigorously nodding a head full of long, greasy black hair. "I'll do my best, sir."

Sharpe, who obviously wanted to say more, walked back to his pallet, muttering angrily to himself.

Cotten clapped Joel on the shoulders, his eyes filled with an approving light.

"Let us get back to sleep," he said, "for we must leave by noon on this day. Collins, you're still—" The outlaw broke off, looking thoughtfully from Collins to Sharpe. "No, I think it would be better if it were you," he said loudly. "Yes. Sharpe, you stand watch."

"Me?" asked the counterfeiter, incredulous and angry.

"You heard me."

The man rose slowly, his venomous gaze flashing from Cotten to Joel and back as he stuck a pistol into his belt, grabbed his coat, and headed outside.

Joel was so exhausted that the threat in Sharpe's eyes did not register. He needed to find and talk to the man who saved him from Givens, but he followed the others back to the pallets and sleep.

17

As he stood outside the cabin with his belongings waiting for Cotten to emerge, Joel couldn't get the man who saved him from Givens out of his mind. He was searching his memory for any clue that might confirm his suspicion that the man was Mark Ryder. Could it be that Wesley had had a whole string of "dawgs" through the years—men who did his bidding and who he looked upon with some affection or just found to be *funny,* as he had once said of Mark?

Cotten and Wesley Pike emerged from the cabin. The big man bellowed into the forested swamp, "Mathias, time ta git outta this shit hole."

"Yes, sir," came the voice from last night from somewhere off in the trees.

"Mister Cooke and his companion will be joining us in our trek out of the swamp," Cotten said.

Now I'll get a good look at him!

Joel watched the trees, wondering where the man might emerge. Had the poor fellow spent the night out in the cold or was there some other structure besides the slave shed?

A lean man with a pack, wearing a heavy, blue cloth coat, calf-length brown breeches and gray stockings, moccasins, and black hat, slipped from the trees and approached. He had dark curly hair, but at first Joel couldn't make out his features in the shadow beneath the broad-brimmed hat.

As he approached and Joel was able to see his face, he

experienced the fear he'd felt the night before when trying to speak to the man. He realized that something inside him didn't want it to be Mark.

But seeing those eyes!—that was all it took, and Joel knew the truth.

This is Mark.

Joel shrunk away, picked up his portmanteau and stood behind Cotten like a frightened child. His heart was pounding wildly in his chest, his mouth dry. He was ashamed of himself. What the hell was going on?

Then it came to him, and he realized it was a large part of why he had drunk so abusively over the years—he was ashamed of having left Mark here in the eighteen-hundreds.

How many times would he have to tell himself there wasn't anything he could have done to help Mark? If he had tried, he might have failed to get Billy back home. They might all have been trapped here. And there was another part to it. If he managed to get Mark alone and talk to him, Mark would have twenty years of adventure to tell him about. And Joel would have twenty years of drunkenness and failure. What would Mark think of him then?

Fuck it. I'm here now. Suck it up, Joel. Act like a man. Leave the little boy and the cowardly drunk behind.

Mark was looking at him curiously.

"Matthew," Cotten said, "this is Cooke's companion, Mathias Crawshanks. Some call him Wesley Pike's dawg." Cotten slipped an arm around Joel's shoulders. "Most of my men believe that Jamus inherited Crawshanks from his brother Wesley. I suppose I understand why Crawshanks keeps the amusing little moniker—the name of the terrible Wesley Pike gives him some small amount of protection and respect from the local thugs and footpads." He gave Mark a condescending smile, which made Joel want to smack him upside the head.

Okay, now, Joel told himself. *It's time to let all the bullshit go.* Joel stood up straight, turned to the man and extended his hand.

Mark shook his hand. "Being his dawg—it's an old joke," Mark said. "I was orphaned and Wesley took care of me because I followed him around like a pup. When he passed on, Jamus was kind enough to take me on as his, er, business partner." Mark had always been a shitty liar.

"Good to meet you," Joel said.

There was no recognition in Mark's eyes. Joel knew he had to communicate his identity to Mark. But how? He'd have to get him away from the outlaws. And what about Mark's status among these thugs? Was he a criminal? How would that affect what Joel would reveal to him?

"Lead the way, won't you, Mister Pike?" Cotten said.

Wesley shouldered a pack and headed up the trail Joel and Cotten had used the previous day. Cotten followed and Joel and Mark brought up the rear.

It would be a while before Joel would be able to talk to Mark, and now that he had made his decision and the fear had left him, he was jumping out of his skin with anticipation. Mark was right there, walking behind him, but Joel couldn't say a thing to him. He tried and failed to come up with small talk to engage the other man in conversation.

Joel looked back, glancing at Mark, trying to make it seem casual. That's when he saw Garrison Sharpe following at a distance.

Wesley turned off the trail onto another barely discernible one, and they all followed. This trail looked different from the the one they had taken when they arrived. Joel hoped they would still wind up at the Paddock. He would hate to lose Hume's good friend Gailey.

Joel noted that Garrison Sharpe turned onto the new trail as well.

Cotten also seemed to notice this, and the fact that Joel was monitoring Sharpe's progress. "Why do you squirm so?" Cotten asked. "Yes, he's still back there, Crenshaw, and what of it? This is one of few routes out of the swamp. To go where he must go, he *has* to follow us."

"Where's he headed?"

"He travels where he will. He has business you don't need to know about. The man is suspicious of you, and by now quite angry with you, but will not do anything against my wishes."

Somehow, Joel wasn't reassured. Wesley Pike hadn't been able to protect him from Virgil.

What Joel needed was to get away from Sharpe . . . and Cotten and Wesley Pike and . . . unfortunately that meant away from Mark as well. Regardless of having found Mark, his goal, his duty now was to try to have Cotten arrested. Hopefully, later on when the dust had settled, he'd be able to hook back up with Mark again.

"I fear we must soon part company for a time," Joel said to Cotten, "while I take care of some business that has gone unattended far too long."

"Nonsense! We travel together. We have friends and confederates throughout the country who will make sure that we want for nothing. I have to break you in. If you're to take Hargus's position, I must teach you how to reconnoiter. Tell me of your business and I'll have it taken care of for you."

Joel hesitated. His plan of slipping away from Cotten and heading for Alexandria and the law, he realized, would be more difficult than he had thought. The man was clinging to him like a hemorrhoid.

"It is a matter that I must take care of myself. It shouldn't take too long, and I will rejoin you, wherever you say."

"I say we head straightaway for Denmark," Cotten said, "for a little taste of the 'What If.' I met a braggart there whom I would like to relieve of his pride and joy. I'm thinking of ways to introduce you to some of the finer points of our business."

He's not paying any attention to me.

Joel turned and looked back at the counterfeiter again. When he faced forward again, Cotten was eyeing him with distaste.

"You're acting just the way he wants you to," the outlaw said impatiently, shaking his head.

"And how's that?"

"Womanish!"

Joel turned red, and Cotten did him the favor of looking away.

"I will cease to play the part for him," Joel said.

"And for the rest of us?"

"Of course."

Joel felt his face flush despite his contempt for Cotten's belief that women were inferior. He just hoped Mark didn't see his embarrassment.

They walked in silence until the swamp of the Ghost River gave out as it funneled into the Wolf River proper. After climbing over several fallen logs crossing the water, they climbed up the bank and into the forest beyond. Soon Joel saw the paddock where they had left their horses.

"There's my big fellow," called Cotton, to his beautiful, caramel-colored stallion. "There's *The King.*"

Just like that, a brilliant, crazy idea popped into Joel's head, one that might kill two birds with one stone. He put his hand to his mouth to cover a manic grin.

"My errand has waited long enough," Joel told the outlaw emphatically. "It is a bit of business given to me by the Bell Spirit herself. I must go to a certain cemetery in Memphis—"

"To what cemetery do you refer?" the outlaw probed.

"It is a small country cemetery called Graceland—I doubt you've heard of it. I am to go there, stand on the grave of a recently departed soul—a man named Presley, who was murdered—and recite a certain passage to communicate with his unquiet soul. The spirit told me that if I do not want myself, and all those associated with me, to be haunted by those we have wronged, I must do this before the moon is full again. The cycle of the moon is almost complete, so I'd better be about it."

"Sounds like nonsense to me." Cotten spoke without his customary cockiness, and his face had gone a little pale. Joel knew he had made a dent in his armor.

"She gives instructions to many who visit her, sending the unfortunate few on these strange errands. If one does not do her bidding, the consequences are terrifying! I've heard tales of walking dead men, and hideous revenge. . . ."

The outlaw swallowed hard. "What are you supposed to say over the grave?"

"Much of it doesn't make any sense and so I just had to memorize the sounds."

Joel turned so he could see Mark's expression while he spoke.

"It goes like this . . . uh, 'Elvis, you should have stuck to TCB with Lisa Marie, fried peanut butter and banana sandwiches, jelly donuts, and your solid gold Cadillac.' "

Mark's brow furrowed and his eyes squinted as he peered at Joel.

"But you let the star trip get you down," Joel went on. "You shot up a bunch of television sets, let Doc Nic pump you full of barbiturates."

Mark's eyes were focused intensely on Joel's. Wesley was watching Garrison Sharpe approach.

"You weren't no fool, but died while straining at stool," Joel concluded. "Rest in peace."

The meter sucked, but at least he'd gotten it to rhyme a bit.

Mark was clearly affected, but would he *remember?*

"Utterly ridiculous!" Cotten said, shaking his head. "I say you accompany me to Denmark and we will travel from there to Memphis together. While I'm reveling in the whorehouses, poking all the cunny there is to be had, you can go to the cemetery alone and recite your strange little poem. We will have plenty of time to do it all before the full moon."

"I'd rather not take any chances. What if I were to fall ill and couldn't travel from Denmark? There are innumerable mishaps that could befall me within that time. I assure you, I am thinking of you when I say these things, for though there are very few of the dead who would have much to say to me, I rather think you might have an army of murdered men visiting you as you sleep."

Cotten paled, and Joel was relieved that the outlaw had not taken offense, or worse, seen through his ploy.

"Well then, I suppose you will have to meet me in Denmark when you have completed your business."

Now all Joel needed was the list of members of the Mystic Clan that history said Cotten provided to Matthew Crenshaw. He was about to ask for that with the excuse that he might need to ask for assistance if he ran into difficulty when Cotten spoke up again.

"Before we part company, I will write you a list of the most trusted and valuable members of the Mystic Clan, in case we were to miss one another and you found yourself in need."

Hot-fucking-damn! This is *history!*

Mark was watching and listening to all of this with great interest. Wesley was busy saddling his horse.

"Mathias," Cotten said, "help Jamus saddle our mounts."

Mark reluctantly moved toward the horses and got to work.

Cotten seated himself on an exposed rock just outside the paddock and rummaged around in his portmanteau. Not finding what he was looking for, he turned to Joel. "Have you any writing accouterments?"

Joel opened his portmanteau, retrieved his writing equipment, and handed it to Cotten, hoping the fact that the journal was nearly empty would not rouse the outlaw's suspicions. Unconsciously, he reached up and forced his hat down tighter on his head. The outlaw did not appear to notice his actions as he bent over the journal, scribbling names.

"Use the phrase I taught you," Cotten said as he wrote, "or the hand signal to identify yourself to any of the men on this list, and they will help you."

At that moment, Joel looked up and, with a knot of tension tightening in his chest, saw Garrison Sharpe approaching.

"Jarrett, what are you doing?" the counterfeiter asked.

"Making Crenshaw here a list of our confederates."

"What?" Sharpe exploded. "Giving our secrets away to an untried cipher?"

Cotten's face became livid and he sprang to his feet, pulling a pistol from beneath his coat. Wesley and Mark turned to see what was going on.

"I'll not be questioned by the likes of you, Sharpe!" Cotten pushed the barrel of the pistol into the man's gut. "Be gone from my sight, *worm,* before I bare your offal to the world!"

Without a word, Sharpe turned his burning eyes away, spun around, and moved to the horses. Mark had finished saddling Sharpe's horse. Sharpe mounted the animal and quickly passed out of the paddock into the trees. Wesley and Mark finished with their work, mounted up, and disappeared into the forest as well.

Damn—I've probably missed my one chance to talk with Mark again after all these years. If he's involved with these outlaws, he's on the opposing team, and, after I turn Cotten in, he'll consider me an enemy and a threat.

Or worse yet, Mark might get arrested with them and hanged.

Cotten, his hand at first trembling with rage, spent a half hour finishing the list—an amazing five hundred some-odd names of men, listed by the cities and states in which they resided. Then he slipped the hackamore over the head of McHenry Lake's red barb mare and mounted his horse. Joel could only hope that the stolen mare would still be in Cotten's possession when he and Mr. Lake brought the law to him in Denmark.

"The road is just over the rise, there. If you follow it west, it will lead you to Memphis within four days. You should have enough provisions with what O'Farrell packed for you. If not, I'm sure you will be resourceful. I shall see you in Denmark within two weeks' time. You will find me at the home of Ephraim Coltrain. Ask anyone, they'll know where to find him."

Having mounted Gailey, Joel clasped hands with the outlaw. "Thank you, sir," he said, "and never fear, I will see you again soon."

He was almost free of Cotten. If he could just survive the next few moments, he would have it made. Joel swung up into Gailey's saddle and started off without looking back. He found he was hardly willing to breathe as he headed through the forest toward the road. He almost passed out from lack of oxygen. When his horse set hoof onto the roadway, he began gulping air.

If his life now went the way of the Crenshaw story, he would never again have to deal directly with the deadly Jarrett Cotten. But Joel knew that if he had the man arrested, he would be looking over his shoulder for the rest of his life, unless he could find his way back to his own time.

And what of his friend, Mark? Would he ever see him again? The questions were endless. Even so, he felt a tension lift from his head, chest, and gut, a tension he'd become so accustomed to, he hardly knew it was there until it was gone. The farther he walked, the more curves in the road he put between himself and Cotten, the better he felt.

He had almost made it to the McHenry Lake Cabin when he heard a rider approaching from behind and his stomach clenched. He hurried off the trail and from the protection of the trees watched as the rider approached. It was Mark, and Joel's heart soared, his blood pulsing audibly in his throat.

Mark stopped where Joel had left the trail and peered into the forest. He had his hand on the butt of a pistol.

"Matthew Crenshaw," he called out, "come out o' there. I mean ye no harm."

Joel hesitated. He stuck his hand into his pocket through the tear, grasped the .45 automatic and pulled the hammer back. "I'm naturally a cautious man, as any man ought to be in this day and age. If you were to put your hands in the air where I could see them, I'll come out."

"I too am a cautious man. Surely you don' 'spect a fellow Clan member ta relinquish his means o' self protection an' place hisse'f at your mercy, knowin' what ye are."

Of course, he thinks I'm an outlaw. Would Mark be this cautious? If he doesn't recognize me, damned straight he would be.

"Then just take your hand away from your pistol."

Mark did this and Joel carefully lowered the hammer of the automatic, removed his hand from his pocket and moved out of the trees.

"Ye say, 'This day an' age,' " Mark said. "Is there perhaps another?"

And now Joel knew for sure. He knew what Mark was asking—had Joel come from another time? *But like me, he's afraid to open up and just ask. He'd have different reasons for his reticence though.*

"I'm from the twentieth century," Joel said, "and so are you."

Mark's face held a troubled expression for just a moment as he regarded Joel, and then his mouth spread in a great smile. "You're Joel Biggs!"

Seeing the smile, Joel's tight chest melted and he slowly nodded his head.

"My lord!" Mark shouted. "It's Joel Biggs!" he spurred his horse and rode in circles around Joel and his mount.

"Don't shout," Joel warned, but couldn't stop himself from laughing.

Mark came to a stop, still smiling and took off his hat. "Never thought ta see ye 'gain. Thought perhaps it was all a dream. Where ye been?"

"Me and Billy made it home. I've been there for the last twenty years."

Now that Joel could get a good look at him, he decided Mark looked like shit. He appeared a good ten years older than Joel knew him to be. His face was creased and weatherworn, and beneath his heavy tan, his skin looked waxy and sallow. His teeth were yellowed and cracked, parasitic sores were evident in the line of his thinning hair, and his red eyes and nose were rheumy. He had the look of a man who didn't practice good hygiene. Joel thought that by twenty-first-century standards, Mark looked ill.

"Get down off o' that horse an' follow me," Mark said. "We gots ta go sit an' talk fer a while."

They dismounted and led their horses into the trees.

"I'm sorry we left you behind," Joel said soberly as they walked.

Mark smiled. "No need to feel that way, Joel. I've had a good life here."

They found a comfortable spot a couple hundred yards off the trail, tethered their mounts to low-lying tree limbs, and sat on rocks amidst fallen leaves.

"I remember Elvis Presley," Mark said, laughing. "I loved 'is music, an' everythin' else 'bout 'im. That was pretty clever o' ye to remember and use that."

"I had to communicate with you, and when Cotten called his horse The King. . . ." Joel chuckled. They were silent together for a moment. Then Joel spoke. "Mark, how did you survive that flood? How did you meet up with Wesley again?"

Mark's eyes grew distant. He smiled, just a little. "So you rec'nized ol' Wes right away, didja? I'm ac-shully surprised when folks b'lieve that Jamus Pike bit." He laughed. "Anyway, ol' Ebbie jumped in after me, y'see. I grabbed onta her, an' we jus' stuck together. We got warshed miles an' miles away from the crick. That dawg saved my life, an' I saved hers. Finally, the floodwaters give out, an' we managed ta crawl outta the flood an' inta the woods. Was we ever lost! We wandered around for a couple a' days, tryin' ta figger out where ta go an' what ta do. Tha's when we found Wes.

"He was near ta death. That gunshot wound he took in the fight with Fellowes was a bad 'un. He's still got a lame leg from it, y'know. Anyhow, he'd just about bled out ever' drop of blood he had. The big man could barely walk. When we come across a little cabin in the middle a' nowhere, it seemed like a miracle.

"My ma—a woman name a' Mary McLean, took us in. Wait—you remember Royce, that man who tol' us all 'bout the Mingit Toad—that was Mary's husband."

"Oh yes, I remember that weirdo—you're kidding! That woman ended up adopting you?" Joel's mouth hung open. *Fate, or coincidence? Oh, that's the question, isn't it . . . ?*

"Yep, she did. Mary was Royce McLean's wife. He had just died o' pneumonia two weeks before we came to her door. She an' the kids—Royce Junior, and Nettie—were stuck out in the wilderness all by themselves, doin' their best ta survive. That woman was somethin'. An' she was good, Joel—good through an' through.

"She nursed Wes back ta health, an' he thought she was his own personal angel, sent from heaven ta save him. She was a deeply religious woman, an' she persuaded Wes ta leave off killin' folks.

"We made a good fam'ly, Joel—Wes and Mary bein' my new parents, Royce Junior and Nettie my brother and sister. Ebbie lived with us for another ten years, finally died in 'er sleep. Mary treated me like her own. Wes was still inta other . . . *trespasses,* as my ma called 'em, but he loved her. He really did. Called himself Jamus Cooke, an' did his best ta make a good life fer us. Until Cotten. . . ."

Mark's brows knit, and he looked Joel in the eye. "What is your business with Cotten?"

Joel only hesitated a moment. He knew he could trust Mark. No, he didn't *know,* but he had to believe. "I mean to turn him in to the sheriff of Madison County as soon as I've assembled enough evidence against him."

Mark's eye got wide. "That's the damndest thing, 'cause that's what I'm about. Ye remember that story ye used to read us in the tree house about the hero Mathias Crawshanks? That's me! Didn't ye rec'nize the name? With Wesley's help, I got all the way ta America's Powder Keg, found out all 'bout Cotten and 'is Clan and I'm writin' that book, the very one ye used ta read from. Ain't that sumpin!"

Joel wanted to stop him, to tell him he was all wrong, but Mark plunged ahead.

"Cotten and his men destroyed Wesley's counterfeitin' operation, y'see. They burned the building, smashed the press, an' killed ever'body. My ma was there that day, takin' the men some lunch. They shot her in the face."

"I'm sorry," Joel said.

"Me too, Joel. Me too." He went silent for a moment. "Cotten thinks he's so goddam smart, but he never knew the name of the man who ran that counterfeitin' shop—never knew it was Wesley Pike or Jamus Cooke neither. Wesley went ta Cotten a few weeks later. . . ."

"Hold on, hold on," Joel said. "I'm getting confused. If most of the Clan thinks Wesley Pike's dead, how come you're still Wesley Pike's dawg?"

"Wesley couldn't seem ta stop calling me that an' folks got curious so he explained that he, Jamus Pike, had inherited his brother Wesley's dawg. Can't say as I mind too much 'cause it affords me a measure of protection."

Poor guy, he's hidden behind bullies his entire life.

"Because Cotten killed his wife and friends, Wesley, he wanted revenge. He's got himself in close wit' Cotten, an' he's plannin' on doin' somethin' stupid, somethin' that'll get rid o' Cotten, most of his men, an' take Wesley right along with 'em. I know the way ta git revenge 'gainst Cotten, 'cause ye done read me all 'bout it when we's younger, but Wesley won't have any o' it. I thought ta hook up with Crawshanks an' he'p 'im out, but turned out there was no Crawshanks. Tha's when it hit me—I mus' be that very man. I pretended I'd help Wesley with his plan and so he got me in the door with the Mystic Clan. Now I'm writing that book, gonna git it published too, an' then Cotten's Clan and their plot for the slave uprisin' will be rurnt, an' my pa—I mean Wesley—won't hafta blow hisself ta kingdom come. An' the damndest part is that yer here wit' me now. Ye'll git ta see it all happen. Like it was meant ta be. I remember Crawshanks was yer hero. Looks like *I'm* yer hero, and I'm damned proud ta be! Mayhaps we should combine our efforts. I could use all the he'p I kin git."

"Why sure," Joel said, not knowing what else to say. Mark's words had come in such a flood, and Joel was still floundering around in them.

Tears welled up in Mark's eyes and he reached out and grabbed Joel and gave him a big hug. Joel hugged him back, though Mark stunk like a bear and was likely transferring all sorts of parasites to him.

This is just crazy, Joel thought, *but what can I do to straighten things out?* Should he at least inform Mark the hero's name was Matthew Crenshaw? No, because then he'd have to argue that *he* was the real Crenshaw. Why else was he going by that name? That was a giant can of worms he didn't dare try to open.

Mark seemed to be considering something for a moment. "I really don't come from this time, do I?" It was as though the idea had finally come home to him and he could relax with it, and for the first time Joel considered that Mark must have struggled with their childhood experiences in a similar way. Mark may even have thought Joel and Billy had died in the flood that day. Joel patted him on the shoulder.

"How has life been treatin' ye," Mark asked. "What brought ye back here? Was it the creek?"

"I have not been very well," Joel admitted. "I have been full of doubt about myself, felt . . . incomplete, all my adult life. I'm a drunk, but lately I've been trying to stay sober. I *did* walk down the creek to get here, thinking that if I could find you, I might begin to feel whole again. You are an important part of me that I abandoned in an effort to save myself."

"Me, a part of yew?" Mark was surprised and he smiled sadly, his eye brimming with tears again. "Abandoned? Ye feel ye let me down? Joel, without you I wouldn't be alive today. The only reason me and Billy survived the Outlaw Cave was 'cause ye were there to take care o' us."

Joel did understand that, but he couldn't feel the truth of it.

"Billy's gone," he said, turning away. "Died in a car accident."

"Cars!" Mark cried.

Startled, Joel turned back to him.

"I love cars. Hadn't thought about cars in years, 'til ye mentioned Elvis' Cadillac!"

Joel was outraged for an instant at what seemed Mark's disinterest in Billy's death. Then he thought about the amount of death Mark had been exposed to in his life.

They were silent for an uncomfortable moment.

Mark put a hand on Joel's shoulder. "I don't remember Billy very well. Tell me about him."

"He was my best . . . hell, just about my only friend these last few years. Got me out of a lot of scrapes. He was always there, no questions asked."

Joel drew a deep breath. "He was driving through an intersection about six months ago when a tractor-trailer rig ran a red light. He was knocked through the windshield and thrown at least fifty feet. It's a good thing he didn't survive—he was torn all to hell."

"Goddam," Mark whispered. "I'd forgotten all 'bout car wrecks too."

"I miss him, Mark. I really miss him."

"What was he like?"

"He was . . . strong. And kind-hearted. He put up with a *lot* from me and forgave me every time. He could always make me smile. I've never had as much fun with anyone else. I think he was a happy guy. I haven't known many people like that. He was a fireman—can you believe that?—saved a lot of lives. I figured he'd get burned up in a fire one day trying to rescue some pet or something, but a goddammed truck hit him."

"I wish I'd gotten a chance to know 'im. Sounds like somebody I'd've liked."

"Yeah, well. . . ."

Another uncomfortable silence.

"Joel, come wit' me," Mark said, rising and untethering his horse. "I've got to catch up wit' Wesley an' stop 'im from killin' himse'f gettin' 'is revenge. Ye know he's in charge o' the munitions fer the slave uprising. He's got it in his head he's gonna git the Grand Council all in one spot fer a meetin'—lately his plan involves gittin' 'em all aboard some steamboat—and blowin' 'em all ta hell wit' kegs o' black powder. He don't figure on survivin' it, as bein' a Council member, he'll have ta be in attendance. He don' seem ta care none either."

Mark would not understand if Joel explained it to him that he had to follow through with his plans to have Cotten arrested. Hell—Mark thought he was involved in the same business!

"I can't go with you. I'm expected elsewhere." Joel attended to his mount and they began walking back toward the trail.

"You don' mean that Elvis Presley shit you were spoutin'."

"No, I'm expected at the home of Hume and Stephen Stogdon in Adairville. When you can break away, will you meet me there?"

"I'll sure try, but fer now I'd best be catchin' up wit' Wesley while the catchin's still good." He stopped, reached out and gave Joel another big hug. "I wasn't aware a piece of me was missin' 'til yew showed up. Let's git back together again as soon as we kin."

"I'll be at the Stogdons in Adairville—don't forget."

"I won't."

Having rejoined the trail, they mounted their horses and reluctantly parted company, Mark riding back the way they had come.

Instead of going to Memphis, Joel turned east to join McHenry Lake and head for Alexandria and the law. He knew that to get to Alexandria, he and Lake would need to travel northeast, the same direction on the same road as Jarrett Cotten. They might catch up with him unless they put some time and road between themselves the outlaw. And Joel knew that time was precious now. Cotten might sell Lake's horse at any time, and then there would be no evidence against him.

18

This was the sloppiest SWAT operation Joel had ever seen—not that he'd ever seen a real one, but he'd seen several played out on the news. Seeing how disorganized the posse was, he had offered some suggestions, but Sheriff Deland Carter had made it clear these were unwelcome.

The early afternoon air seemed a little too crisp, the actions of the men as they settled into positions around the shuttered, two-story cabin too brittle. There were about thirty of them, but most were too young to have any experience in a fight.

Joel and the sheriff were crouched down beside a stone springhouse at the edge of a creek that ran beside the cabin. Word was passed to Joel that a red barb mare bearing McHenry Lake's brand had been seen in the stable out back, and he was relieved. The evidence was here. As for the criminal . . . who knew? If Joel remembered correctly, history said he *would* be here. But the book had not been the best of guides and now he was running on memory of what the book said—a strange hearsay.

Joel did know that five men, not including outlaws, would die during the arrest of Jarrett Cotten. But which five, he wondered. He scanned the faces nearby, thought of those who were out of his line of sight, training their rifles on the windows and door at the back of the cabin. He had tried not to get to know any of them on the twenty-mile journey from Alexandria to Denmark.

When Joel and McHenry Lake had arrived at the Madison

County Courthouse in Alexandria three days ago and introduced themselves and their charges against Jarrett Cotten, they were met with forced skepticism. After listening to them politely, Sheriff Carter had asked, "How do ye know this man is indeed Jarrett Cotten? How do ye know the meetin' ye attended was not the meetin' o' a harmless gentlemen's club where the members tell tall tales an' pretend ta be what they are not?"

"An' how do I know the horse Cotten took from my paddock was my own?" Lake said, mocking the sheriff with an idiot's expression. "I's difficult ta trust the evidence o' yer own eyes, ain't it? If I didn't know I was in the presence o' the sheriff of this county, I might think I was talking to some spineless, night-crawlin' worm?" Lake was red in the face and he leaned in toward the sheriff menacingly.

Carter turned his eyes toward the floor. He nodded his head and cleared his throat, then walked to the door, looked out to see who might be listening to what was said in his office and shut the door quietly.

"Ye understand I mus' be careful," Carter said, his skepticism gone. "I never know who might be a member o' Cotten's Clan. O' course I *know* 'bout them—they are a *plague* hereabouts. However, unless ye're willing ta stand up in court and make yer accusations, I cannot chance an arrest for fear o' retribution."

"You can count on us for that," Lake said. His long neck popped when he nodded his head vigorously once, then looked to Joel for confirmation.

Joel nodded his head and looked at the sheriff expectantly.

There was a long pause. "Well . . . ," Carter said somewhat nervously. "I s'pose I'd better find me some men as kin be trusted."

While the sheriff conducted an appeal for members of a posse, Joel and McHenry Lake were questioned by Judge

Thomas Erwin and their statements were taken. Erwin wrote his witnessing statement. Joel asked for and was given permission to transcribe the Lake and Erwin statements into his journal. The process that would lead to Jarrett Cotten being arrested and brought to justice had begun.

But did Cotten and the outlaws inside the cabin know the law had come to call? Were they even now training their rifles on these young men?

Joel cocked the flintlock pistols he had in each of his hands. Despite the cool air, his palms were sweaty and his grip on them unsteady.

Could it be I am one of those killed during the arrest? Joel suspected that his presence in this time was changing history. *Is that even possible?* Perhaps his part in these events had always been. Even so, this all happened long before he was born. How could he have any effect on it? It was a difficult thing to reason out.

He had played it safe with Lake, insisting the man not accompany them on the arrest—no sense putting him in harm's way when he was to be counted on as a witness. Lake said he would head for his cousin Rolph Gaylord's place in Memphis to spend a few months. He gave Joel the address so that he could be informed about the time and place of Cotten's trial. Joel gave the address to Sheriff Carter.

Once the men were in place, Sheriff Carter cleared his throat. "Jarrett Cotten," he bellowed toward the cabin, "come outta there. We have a warrant for your arrest."

There was no response, but Joel could feel energy being stored up in that silence. He feared the release of that energy and had to force himself to take slow, even breaths.

After a time Carter shouted, "Hiram Glass, go to the door and try to open it."

"No," Joel shouted, unable to stop himself.

Carter turned to him with an expression meant to shut Joel up, just as the cabin door opened as if on its own.

Jarrett Cotten appeared, not quite in the doorway, but further back in the darkness within the cabin. "What can I do for you fine gentlemen?" he asked.

The men surrounding the cabin seemed to relax and several stood up from their hiding places.

"Tell them to get down," Joel shouted, but the sheriff didn't have time to respond.

The shutters on the upper-floor windows flew open and Cotten disappeared from sight. The crack of musket fire filled the air and Joel and the sheriff flattened themselves to the ground. Joel heard cries of shock and fear arise from the men surrounding the cabin, and the unmistakable cries of pain from those struck by lead shot.

"Tell them to get down!" Joel repeated.

"To the cabin, men," Carter bellowed. He rose up as if he were going to charge, but remained stationary.

"No," Joel shouted again, even as he realized that Carter was taking advantage of the outlaws' need to reload.

The men rushed forward from their hiding places just as another volley of rifle fire erupted from the cabin. Joel saw three of them fall, and his experience with the Pikes in the ambush of the Tennessee Militia came back to him in a rush; the overwhelming smells, the intensity of the colors, a horror associated with a time and place, his fear an iron taste in his mouth, outrage at such cruelty a painful grip on his gut, the dizzying shame that came with his feeling of responsibility. It was all he could do to keep from curling into a ball and retreating within himself.

Joel turned away from the charge, looked toward the sheriff.

"Don't look at me!" Carter shouted.

He was full of shame as well, Joel realized.

Reluctantly turning back to the fight, Joel saw that some of the men had entered the cabin. There was a fresh burst of gunfire, no doubt from the posse who had held their fire while advancing. The outlaws would probably be down to pistols and knives at this point. The sounds of hand-to-hand fighting inside the cabin continued for another minute or so, gunshots and the breaking of furniture accompanied by cries of pain. Then all was quiet, and the man Carter had referred to as Hiram Glass appeared in the doorway, motioning for Carter to come in.

Joel and Carter approached and entered the cabin. Two men Joel had never seen before lay dead on the floor beside the stairway to the upper floor. Another outlaw, his long blond hair and beard bloodied, sat on the floor beside the fireplace while some of Carter's men kept an eye on him.

"Hiram's in the loft," one of the posse said to Carter.

Joel and the sheriff took the stairs. The second floor was divided into two bedrooms. They were being trashed by members of the posse. There were no outlaws here.

Joel's heart sank in his chest. How had Cotten gotten away?

Then he remembered! "Follow me, *now!*" he said, grabbing Carter by the arm.

They descended to the ground floor and Joel turned and looked at a corner hutch. He opened it and saw it was empty. It didn't even have any shelves.

"That's strange," Carter said.

"No, it's not," Joel said. "Someone guard this hutch. The rest of you follow me, quickly!"

"What's this all about," Carter asked as Joel rushed out the door, heading for the springhouse.

"No time to explain."

Joel waited in front of the springhouse for the others to catch up to him. He put his finger across his lips to tell them to be quiet. Then he raised his pistols and kicked the springhouse door open.

Jarrett Cotten was struggling to rise from a hole in the floor of the springhouse. He was so surprised to see Joel, his pistol fell from his grasp. Carter pushed past Joel into the cramped stone building, took charge of the prisoner, and dragged the outlaw out.

"This is the man, Jarrett Cotten," Joel told Carter. "He is the one who stole McHenry Lake's mare."

Cotten looked at Joel, his face a confusion of surprise, anger and pain. Then he nodded his head like he understood, and turned away. Joel knew that the outlaw's expression would haunt him until the day he died. The man was a monster, a heartless murderer, but Joel had no taste for deception and betrayal. For a moment, he wished he'd put a bullet in Cotten's head instead.

The sound of curses came from inside the cabin.

"That would be Ephraim," Cotten said, having composed himself and regained some of his smug demeanor. "His penchant for overindulging has left him too fat for his own secret tunnel."

The outlaw was led away.

This was as far as the Crenshaw book went, Joel knew, at least the edition written solely by Matthew Crenshaw; the one he'd read as a child, the same one he'd left on his kitchen table. Since he didn't have it with him, he had been depending on his faulty memory for quite a while, but the history of these events beyond this point in time was sketchy at best. There were accounts of Crenshaw's activities that Joel had read about, incomplete versions of his adventure included in other history texts, with commentary and historical reference, but he knew history well enough to know that it was inexorably changed with the telling; as it was passed first from mouth to ear, and then into text.

19

Joel returned to Alexandria with the posse and saw Cotten jailed. The trial would be in six months.

He stayed at the Laudermilk Hotel, where he got some rest, organized the notes he had once stored in his hat and filled what remained of his journal with all the additional information he had learned about the Mystic Clan. He saw to Gailey's needs at a livery stable, then got on the road, headed back to the Stogdons in Adairville.

Joel wasn't sure if he would be at the trial. What he intended to do in the next few months would, if it worked, remove his need to be there. Even so, he would need to make himself scarce. Perhaps the Stogdon farm was the perfect place to hole up while he wrote the Crenshaw book. Once that was done, he would go to Nashville to have it published.

For now, he was on his own. He knew he couldn't trust any stranger. Even though he was jailed, Cotten would have gotten word out about Crenshaw by now. The Mystic Clan would be everywhere and they would not rest until they had him. They would know he had the list of names Cotton had given him, but they wouldn't know what he planned to do with it. At least the Clan didn't know Joel's real name. Hopefully that would slow them down.

As Joel rode toward Adairville, his worries about Cotten and the Crenshaw book were replaced by thoughts of Rachel. He realized how desperately he had missed her, how badly he wanted to see her again. He lost himself in thoughts of her eyes, her smile, her anger and laughter.

Garrison Sharpe stepped out of the trees into the road, brandishing two double-barreled pistols, one aimed at Joel's head, one at his heart.

Joel reeled from a rush of adrenaline in his system, but did his best to appear outwardly calm. He carefully reached through the tear between his pockets and gripped the .45. Gailey's neck obscured Sharpe's view so that he couldn't have been aware of the movement, but, at the same time, Joel couldn't fire at the outlaw through her neck, and he realized he couldn't pull the pistol out of the pocket swiftly. If he tried any quick moves, the outlaw would immediately fire on him.

"Good evenin', Mister Crenshaw," said the counterfeiter, "I've been waitin' fer ye—hopin' ta give ye the opportunity ta prove yer mettle."

"Stand aside and let me pass," Joel said with as much bravado as he could muster.

"No, I'm gonna kill ye 'ere an' now," Sharpe said, "for I know ye ain't right. Now get you down off'n that horse."

Joel had the presence of mind to know that dismounting would only be the beginning of the end for him. He pulled the reigns gently so that Gailey turned a little to the left. Now Joel had the advantage; he held the automatic fast in his right hand under his greatcoat, and it was aimed right at the outlaw.

"Ye may've duped Cotten, but I kin see right through ye. *He* ain't gonna do nothin' 'bout it, an' I know ye'll bring us all down if *I* don' do somethin'."

He doesn't know I've had Cotten arrested. Where has he been that the news didn't reach him? Joel knew he was thinking in twenty-first-century terms. It still amazed him how slowly news could travel here.

He pulled the trigger just as Sharpe opened his mouth to

speak, but nothing happened!

"If'n ye don' git down off o' that horse," Sharpe said, cocking the pistols and casually bringing them to bear, "I'll have my sweet twins here—"

Joel fumbled for the pistol Hume had given him. He was sure the outlaw would notice, but he didn't.

"—pluck ye down!"

Without removing it from his pocket, Joel managed to cock the gun and aim it, and, hoping the flint struck iron instead of pocket lint, he fired. There was a flash of powder and a blast. The ball tore a hole through Joel's coat and knocked one of Sharpe's guns from his hand. In his surprise, the man fired both barrels of the second pistol harmlessly into the air over Joel's head. Joel put spurs to his mount and charged forward. Gailey's chest slammed into Sharpe and sent him sprawling to the ground. His head struck the road hard.

Joel's pocket was on fire and his thigh was burning. He batted at the smoldering cloth of his coat until it went out.

Unfazed Gailey galloped on, and, as they rounded the bend in the road, Joel looked back to see the outlaw remained where he had fallen. Joel allowed Gailey to continue at that pace for as long as he felt she could stand it.

The remainder of the journey was uneventful, though Joel kept a very wary eye out for anything suspicious in the forest along the road. He scrutinized the one traveler he encountered so obviously that the man, a farmer with a load of apples, apologized for his appearance. By noon, he had arrived at the Stogdon farm and was approaching the house.

"It's Joel," he heard Hume shout. He turned to see the man running toward him from the direction of the barn. Stephen came out of the barn and hurried toward him as well.

The door to the cabin opened and Mark Ryder stepped out.

"I tol' 'em all about our plan to expose Cotten and his Clan and plot."

Joel was surprised to see him here so soon. The thought that Mark had sought him out on behalf of the Mystic Clan flashed through his mind, but he quickly pushed it out.

"We almost turned 'im away 'cause we thought he was moonstruck," Hume said, coming to a stop before Joel and offering his hand. "But we figured we'd better help or you'd do somethin' stupid an' git yerself killed."

Joel took his hand and shook it, then drew him closer and hugged the old man.

"I'm sorry to say that Macklin and Briley were killed." It was a lie of omission he had been practicing on and off the whole trip back to the Stogdons. He hoped they would not be too curious about the circumstances of their deaths. He didn't want to lie to the Stogdons any more than that, but knew that he would if he were pressed.

"I feared as much," Hume said.

Joel was relieved that the old man left it at that.

"I ain't sure I believe all Mister Ryder has said 'bout yer plans," Stephen said, smiling playfully, "but he's a nice enough feller."

Joel gave Stephen and Mark hugs.

"Speaking of doing something stupid," Joel said. "Where's Wesley? I thought you'd be with him by now."

"No tellin'. I couldn't catch up ta him—lost 'is trail, so I come here."

"Where's Rachel?" Joel asked.

Rachel stepped from the cabin. Seeing her, Joel's heart leapt in his chest. After the slow simmering terror of the last few days, he realized he was so glad to be alive and to see her. His emotions overcame him and sudden tears spilled down his face.

20

They all sat around the kitchen table and listened to Joel as he told all about what happened on his journey, including the arrest of Jarret Cotten. Joel played down his role, but it was obviously a bold adventure, and Mark was more than a little sorry to have missed it. After all these years, he realized he still looked up to Joel Biggs.

And then there was that woman. Mark never would have guessed that Joel would have ended up with a fine woman like that. Rachel was beautiful, smart, and obviously crazy about Joel. She sat next to him at the table, clutching his arm, smiling, obviously hanging on his every word. Every now and then, she'd suddenly kiss Joel's cheek, which always seemed to make him blush. Funny that a man would blush over a kiss from his own wife, but Joel had always been a strange one.

Seeing them together gave Mark a wistful, lonely pang. He didn't pine over Rachel, not the way Stephen Stogdon obviously did. But he pined for someone like her. Hell, any woman who'd love him the way she loved Joel.

Mark was no virgin, of course. He'd had women, mostly whores. He still fondly remembered the one who'd made him a man; a big, jovial redhead named Violet whom Wesley Pike had procured for him on his fourteenth birthday. There were others: confidence women, counterfeiters, hangers-on enchanted by Wesley Pike and his outlaw way of life. Most of them meant nothing to Mark; they had just used each other for pleasure and warmth. He'd had feelings for one of them, a small, slender half-Indian girl who forged land deeds and debt vouchers. He'd thought she cared for him too, until she left with a weasely thug from New York.

Mark had long ago come to the conclusion that he wasn't meant to be a husband and father. He was Wesley Pike's dawg. That wasn't such a bad thing to be. Wes had always been good to him, had saved his life countless times over the years. Mark knew he wasn't good for much else. He wasn't smart, wasn't strong, hell, he wasn't even all that brave. But he was loyal. It was all right being Wes's dawg. But sometimes, just sometimes, he longed for something more.

"Hello! Earth to Mark!" Joel was smiling at him. "Anybody in there?"

"Sorry, Joel. I reckon I'm jus' a little tired."

"Me too!" Hume stood up and stretched. "C'mon, Stephen, let's retire an' let Mark an' Joel catch up."

Rachel squeezed Joel's arm. "I guess I'll turn in too. Don't be too late, okay?"

"Okay," Joel said, and kissed her cheek. Joel and Mark watched her go.

"Meanin' no disrespect," Mark said, "but yer wife is an amazin' woman. Congratulations, ye ol' bastard. Where'd ye meet her?"

"Oh hell," Joel said. "She ain't my wife."

Mark felt his mouth fall open, but he had no power to stop it. "Whut?"

"Rachel's not my wife. It's complicated, Mark. She followed me here, from where I come from. She's my cousin Moss's kid. I'm just taking care of her until I can get her home. The wife bit is just so men won't mess with her."

Mark was dumbstruck. When he finally found his voice, he said, "But she's in love wit' ye, Joel."

Joel lowered his head. "She thinks she is. She's just a kid. Seventeen."

"Seventeen's plenty old enough ta get hitched. Girls around here get married up at twelve sometimes. An' that girl knows her mind, Joel. She may be young, but she ain't stupid. If she says she loves ye, she loves ye."

Joel gave an exasperated sigh. "Didn't you hear me, Mark? She's my cousin's daughter?"

"So?"

"Jesus, Mark! You've been living here too long! Cousins aren't supposed to marry, for Christ's sake!"

"Cousins get married all the damn time. An' if I recall, Moss wasn't truly yer cousin."

"You don't understand, Mark."

Mark felt a quick flash of anger, and pushed it down. "Here's what I don't understand, Joel. I don't understand why ye haven't married that girl. You're lucky if ye find anybody in this God-forsaken life what loves ye. If you've got a brain in your whole fool haid, you'll never let Rachel go."

Joel stared at him, eyes unreadable. "Let's talk about something else, okay?"

"Fine, ye jackass. I want to show ye the book I been writin' to expose the Mystic Clan an' their Grand Plot. I was thinkin' 'bout callin' it *A Month Battlin' Eternal Damnation's Foul Emissaries at the Mouth of Hell.*"

Joel looked a bit uncomfortable, but Mark thought that he might just have gas. He led him into the Stogdon's parlor and Joel took a seat in front of the fireplace. Mark sorted through the contents of his pack until he found the cloth-bound journal. As he lifted it out of the pack, he remembered how important this book had been to Joel when they were younger.

This is the Crawshanks Manuscript, written in my own hand.

He was suddenly flushed with excitement, with a sense of being a part of history. He hadn't thought of it in those terms before. Could it be that he was that important? The thought made him uneasy. His hands were shaking and his palms were sweaty as he took a seat next to Joel.

He fumbled as he tried to open the journal, dropped it and it bounced into the fireplace, landing on the hot coals.

"Shit," he cried, grabbing it before it had even begun to smoke. Embarrassed, he cradled it in his arms and looked at Joel. "Sorry."

Joel smiled.

"It ain't much," Mark said, though he didn't think that was the truth. "I ain't no Shakespeare."

"I'm sure it's wonderful," Joel said, but then he had that look of discomfort again.

Dimly aware he was holding his breath, Mark let it out, opened the book and began to read.

> This is the true account of how I took upon myself the duty of bringing down Jarrett Cotten and his Mystic Clan. Throughout my harrowing adventure with that most villainous personage, and his dreaded and most dastardly band of scoundrels, I adopted the name Mathias Crawshanks so as to afford myself a measure of protection.
>
> I am and always have been a man of most modest beginnings, being born of good stock in March of 1800 in Blount County, Tennessee. Despite most abject poverty, my noble sire did endow me with a liberal education in Nashville.

Joel's brow was furrowed and he turned his head this way and that like a puppy might while trying to figure out how best to listen. This made Mark even more nervous and he paused for a moment before continuing.

"I had ta make that first part up," Mark said. "My family—well you know Ma, Wesley, my sister and brother—had been livin' in Nashville for years, but I didn't go to school."

Joel looked at him with a worried smile.

"I couldn't tell the truth, now could I?"

Joel shook his head and seemed to be trying to swallow a mouth full of words before they spilled out.

Mark continued.

> I obtained an appointment to the staff of that prestigious news journal, the *Nashville Sentinel,* where I built a reputation of incisiveness and determinability. By the time I was a quarter of a century old, I was well known as industrious, decisive, and a man of great moral fortitude.
>
> During my employ with the *Sentinel,* I never shrank from casting my penetrating reportorial gaze wherever the truth might lead. In such pursuits, 'tis natural that I would earn the bitter enmity of rogues and incorrigibles, and, to shield myself, I early on donned the nom de plume, Mathias Crawshanks.

"That part," Mark said, "is partially true, but I was really jus' a typesetter, though I did write a story 'bout a giant snake as terrorized Triune that they ran in the *Sentinel* while I was there. I used the Crawshanks name on it jus' fer the fun o' it an', you know . . . rememberin' our hero an' all. The strange thin' is it turned out I *was* Crawshanks all along. So it was natural to use it 'round Cotten an' the Mystic Clan. An' I figured anyone trackin' down my true name would wind up back at the *Sentinel.* I left there on good terms. The editor's a good man, an' he'll do me right. Anyone askin' after me, I know he'll send 'em runnin' in circles."

Joel's eyes were shut and he had a pained expression.

"Do ye need ta visit the outhouse or somethin', Joel?" Mark asked. "I can hold off if'n ye really need ta go."

"No," he said. "I'm fine. You go ahead."

> I had resolved to settle in the savage wilds of west Tennessee, and so to this end, I removed with my properties in the fall of 1833 to Madison County where I met Jarrett Cotten—

Joel let out his breath in a ragged gasp. "Stop for a minute."

Mark put down the book.

"How much of that have you written?"

"There's at least a hunerd pages here."

"Is there anything in your account about following Cotten to try to get some slaves back for a friend of yours?"

"Well, no."

"Mark, this isn't right."

"Whaddaya mean?"

Joel took a deep breath, squeezed his eyes shut, obviously considering his words.

"The beginning is sort of right, but then you've skipped over the part about following Cotten to get the slaves back."

"But that's not what happened."

What was Joel trying to do here? Mark remembered Joel was sometimes mean-spirited. Maybe he was just picking on Mark for the fun of it.

"That's not what happened to *you.*" Joel shifted uncomfortably. "Uh—it's like this, Mark, you're not Mathias Crankshaw . . . or whatever. I wish I had the book here to show you, but it's probably still sitting where I left it—on my *goddammed kitchen table.* The man's name was Matthew Crenshaw."

"What the hell are ye talkin' 'bout? *'Course* I'm Mathias Crawshanks. I went through everythin' he did, didn't I?"

"Well, yeah—I 'spose, but—"

Goddam right, he did. Joel was just jealous!

And I thought he'd be proud of me. Same old Joel—a real mean bastard.

"—Actually . . . no—not really."

"What . . ." Mark said, his eyes blazing, "ye don' believe me?"

"No, no, Mark—relax. It's not that I don't believe you, it's just . . . it's just that this is not the same manuscript." Joel shook his head.

Seeing that Joel was clearly confused and frustrated took the edge off Mark's growing anger.

"Like I said, the first part is kind of right."

"I mus' be a dunderpate, 'cause I don' see yer meanin'."

"I just read most of the book not long ago. It's got the testimonials of Thomas Fellowes, McHenry Lake and Judge Thomas Erwin in it." Joel found the statements of Lake and Erwin and showed them to Mark. He reminded himself to ask Hume if the testimonial letter from Fellowes had arrived. "Let me tell you more about the book, and then maybe you'll remember it better yourself."

As Joel began the telling of the story, Mark was transported back to their time in the tree house. It was a magical memory full of half-remembered, fantastic things—toys, books, magic *electrical* implements and food, even strange smoking material—that seemed somehow beyond belief to him now. He remembered an odd wheeled conveyance that he used to ride. Ebbie was there. God how he missed that dog! The memories were as painful as they were glowing and pleasant.

Despite the flood of images and feelings, he was listening to Joel, and it wasn't long before he recognized the story and he interrupted the reading.

"You're right, dumbass, I'm not Matthew Crenshaw."

Joel focused on him, the sudden surprise on his face turning to delight. Then he laughed out loud. "Me a dumbass! You're the dumbass." He grabbed Mark by the shoulders, pulled him close and gave him a big hug. "I'm really glad you're here, Mark."

Mark was embarrassed, but he felt the same way. He had always hoped Joel would come back. Something in the back of his mind still feared him, but he had great affection for him as well.

Joel sat back down. "Now let me tell you what happened to me."

He launched into his story of the theft of the Stogdon slaves, his pursuit of Cotten, tricking the man into taking him into his confidence and having him arrested. It wasn't exactly the same as the Crenshaw story, but it was close.

"*You* are Matthew Crenshaw," Mark said, a little sad, but somehow relieved that he didn't have to measure up to a hero.

"Yeah, well, maybe we both are."

"I s'pose I should just chuck this," Mark said, referring to the journal.

"No, don't do that. It's a bit flowery in places and it's written in first person—nobody wants to listen to someone brag about himself. But we can use it."

"I thought it was pretty good," Mark said sheepishly, "but maybe I did hurry it a bit."

"Tell you what—I'll go over it, smooth it out a bit, add the stuff that happened to me, and we'll see what we think then."

Mark swallowed his pride. "I s'pose all that matters is we git it in good enough shape to stop the Mystic Clan's Grand Plot."

"We'll need money to get it published."

"I've saved over two thousand dollars in coin for that very purpose."

21

Thomas Fellowes' testimonial letter had not arrived. He hoped the man had at least sent a copy to the Supreme Court of Madison County. With all the work he had to do, Joel tried not to worry about it, but what if he didn't have the letter to include in the Crenshaw book? Seeing his name in it was a pivotal moment in the course of events. Hume agreed to write Fellowes a letter to remind him.

During the two weeks Joel spent going over the book and preparing it for publication, advertisements bearing a crude drawing of him had begun to pop up in Adairville. Hume had been the first to see one, while in town for supplies. He brought it back for Joel to read.

"Notorious steam doctor, Matthew Crenshaw, wanted for slave and horse theft. Reward for information or capture of up to five hundred Spanish dollars in coin offered by Clarence Duhurst." There was an address below that.

Joel found the Duhurst name among the list of Mystic Clan members given him by Jarrett Cotten. He knew that "steam doctors," also known as "Thompsonians," were considered dangerous medical con men in this area at this time. Their approach to medicine centered around what they claimed were the curative properties of heat. Their methods were of little or no value and often wasted precious time while a patient's condition worsened in lieu of legitimate treatments. In some cases patients had died.

The Mystic Clan didn't know where Joel was located. If they did, they'd have come for him by now. These advertisements were no doubt plastered in every community in Tennessee and the surrounding states. If they couldn't find him, the Mystic Clan was at least doing its best to discredit Joel.

Joel had not left the Stogdon farm since returning. Now he was determined to be seen as little as possible outdoors. This being wintertime, there was not much work to do outside, so staying indoors didn't prove very difficult.

Mark spent much of his time in town at the places where the local men gathered. He performed the Mystic Clan's hand signal as covertly and casually as possible for every man he saw, to see what response he got. To those who asked what he was doing, he had a ready explanation. "An ol' injury," he'd say. "It becomes stiff unless I use this combination o' movements ta get the kinks out."

He met up with five men in the immediate area of Adairville who responded to the signal. Though they didn't know his face, they knew what he meant when he introduced himself as Wesley Pike's dawg. One, a fellow named Geof Bilby, passing through the area selling pins and needles, told him the Mystic Clan's hand signals and secret phrases had been changed because their secrecy had been compromised. "I'm not suppose' to tell anyone," he'd said, "but seein' as how yer Wesley's dawg, I don' see no harm in teachin' ye the new ones." Back at the Stogdon farm, Mark taught everyone the new hand signals and secret phrases.

Hume and Stephen were distressed to find out that some of their neighbors were in league with the Mystic Clan. "I never liked that Harlin Russell," Hume said, "but Hank Waggoner and I used to play chess."

Rachel had an idea for casting the Mystic Clan into confusion and paranoia and throwing them off Joel's scent. He was amazed. "Good God, Rachel, you've got a Machiavellian streak a mile wide."

"No big deal," she said, "for a woman from the information age."

She enlisted Stephen's and Hume's help to organize a meeting of families in the area who had been wronged by the Mystic Clan and ask for their assistance.

Rachel had wanted to talk to the families herself, but Joel explained that they wouldn't take her seriously.

"But it's my idea!" she had complained.

"What matters is that *we* all know it is your idea," Joel said, and she had acquiesced.

It was Hume who introduced the plan. Joel thought there would be much concern about its dangers, especially from the older family members, but they showed no fear when several of the young men gladly offered their help. Joel suspected these fellows would take any adventure, however dangerous, over sitting through another winter as Tennessee frontier farmers. And the older ones, he realized, were veterans of making sacrifices for justice during a time when law and order was still a distant dream of the future.

Stephen was given the task of addressing the volunteers. "Ye'll travel ta nearby communities an' use the hand signals ta locate Mystic Clan members. Once ye're sure o' 'em, ye'll tell 'em the signals and phrases have been changed 'gain. Then ye'll tell 'em that under pain o' torture Jarrett Cotten's been betrayin' the Clan, lettin' on 'bout names and plans. Ye won't have to make the stuff up on the spot. We'll teach ye ever'thin 'fore ye head out."

"Shouldn't we jus' tell everyone the falsehoods?" asked an over-enthusiastic short, blond fellow.

"Goebel Price, ye're a talkative one, I know. But I want ye all ta know this has ta be done slyly. Ye're playin' the role o' outlaws. They don' just stan' up in the town square an' announce their bus'ness. Keep ta ye'selves. We'll give ye false names an' criminal aspirations to he'p ye fool the Clan members, but don' tarry long in one place an' don' be overeager. Don't give 'em time ta test yer willingness ta commit a crime. An' remember ta try an' git their names. When ye return we'll want ta record all the names o' those ye contact an' where they live."

"Hopefully the Mystic Clan will become so paranoid," Rachel told Joel and Mark privately, "it'll start to feed on itself."

"It will probably help whittle down their membership a little," Joel said, "but they won't believe that anyone would take Cotten seriously about their Grand Plot. They'll figure it's too outlandish, and they also have too much invested to be willing to give it up so easily. They *will* try to reorganize the plot to happen at a different time, though."

"Why do ye say that?" Mark asked.

"Because it's a part of history."

After the meeting, Mark traveled to Wallace to ask for Thomas Fellowes' help with the plan and tell him all about their effort with the Crenshaw book. When he returned, he gave Joel the letter of testimony Fellowes had prepared. He said that Fellowes assured him he'd be able to organize a large group to spread the false hand signals and secret phrases. He told Joel that Fellowes was angry with him for not revealing himself to be Joel Biggs when they last met, that he'd said they had a lot of catching up to do, and he looked forward to seeing him again when this was all over.

Unfortunately, Joel thought, *for me this will never be over.*

Curious, Joel looked over Fellowes' letter. He found that the old man had indeed put the names J. Biggs and M. Ryder in it, as if knowing this would somehow reach him in the far future of the twenty-first century.

As Joel worked on the Crenshaw book, Mark tried to convince him they should all go together, armed to the teeth, to Nashville to deliver the manuscript. Hume and Stephen agreed. Rachel didn't want Joel to go at all and suggested they could get someone to deliver it for them.

But Joel had already decided to see to it personally. There were specific dangers that history had in store for him now, and he would not jeopardize anyone else's safety by allowing them to accompany him to Nashville. He knew that Matthew Crenshaw would very nearly perish on this journey.

Finally, the book was complete. It was time for Joel to go to Nashville to find Duke & Willis Gargantuan Press, the publisher of the first edition of *The History of Matthew Crenshaw and His Adventure Exposing the Great Land Pirate, Jarrett Cotten and the Mystic Clan.* The book contained everything Joel thought should be in it, although it didn't feel quite right to him. Part of the problem was that, so as not to hurt his friend's feelings, he had allowed large chunks of what Mark had written to remain.

Joel was so frightened about his trip to Nashville that he wasn't sure he could go through with it. Even so, he secretly prepared the provisions he would need for the trip. He tried to locate the .45 pistol that he had asked Rachel to hide upon his return from having Cotten arrested. He would have asked her where it was, but then she would have questioned him about it. Oh well—it was probably for the best if the .45 never saw the light of day again in this era.

One morning he arose very early before any of the others had awakened. He took the stash of money Mark had saved to pay for the Crenshaw book's publication. He gathered up his bedroll and the supplies he'd packed in saddlebags, then put on a thick coat, gloves, and the hat with the repaired quilted lining, and slipped outside in the predawn darkness before his fear of the long journey alone could stop him.

Hoping that Hume would forgive him for taking her, Joel prepared Gailey for travel, and they headed out toward the road that ran beside the Stogdon property. He followed the road into Adairville and through the middle of town, a chill breeze following him. He kept his gaze fixed ahead and tried not to think, trying to allow the horse's movement to rock him into a numb, insensate state. As long as he had stayed at the Stogdons', the Mystic Clan had no good way to find him, but now he was vulnerable to them once again. He tried to put that out of his mind. He would follow through with the task before him, and that's all he would think about—he would do his best to act and not react. Hopefully this would get him through it.

Adairville slipped by, and he moved out into the surrounding farmland. Gradually this gave way, and Joel surprised himself by putting aside his fear for a while and taking simple pleasure in the unspoiled beauty of the wilderness through which he passed. Stopping at a stream, he and Gailey drank and then proceeded on.

Throughout the morning, Joel remained vigilant and wary, was civil to the few fellow travelers he encountered, but kept to himself. By noon he arrived at the junction with the Nashville Road and turned left. He had been told there were inns along this road approximately every twenty miles. The first, Morrow's Inn, he should reach before nightfall.

But as the afternoon progressed and he began to notice the lengthening shadows, he worried that he might not make it and dreaded the thought of sleeping out in the cold wintry night.

Long past sunset, Joel topped a rise and found a rectangular silhouette of darkness against the moonless night sky, a trail of smoke rising from its chimney. He shivered, then looked up and down the road.

He dismounted and, leading the horse forward, stumbled

over a hitching post. He tethered Gailey to it and started for the cabin.

In the utter darkness, he couldn't see the entrance and was forced to feel his way along the splintery wall of logs. His questing fingers also found a sign, a small placard affixed beside the doorframe. Too dark to read, his fingers traced the hand-carved letters spelling out the name, Morrow.

He knocked on the door, stamping his feet against the cold as he waited for a response. After a minute or so, he knocked again and was at last answered by a gruff voice through the door.

"What'cha wan'?"

"Uh . . . Mister Morrow, I'm looking for a room for the night."

"What's yer name an' where ye from?"

"Biggs from Dexter, Tennessee."

"Ye sound strange, like a foreigner."

There was a pause, then the door opened a crack, and a pistol emerged.

"Dexter, Tennessee? Never heard o' it."

"It's a small place up near Reelfoot Lake."

"Reelfoot Lake? Where the hell's that?"

"The northwest corner of the state," he answered, unsure whether Reelfoot was known by that name yet.

"Humph."

There was a long pause, and Joel was ready to walk off when the man abruptly continued.

"That yer horse out there?"

How can he see Gailey, Joel wondered. "Yessir."

"I'll send my boy 'round ta fetch 'er ta the paddock."

"Thank you. I'll just get my gear then."

"Be quick 'bout it. Don' tarry none." Morrow slammed the door.

Joel hurried back to his horse, retrieved his bedroll and

saddlebag, and started for the door. Anticipating him, Morrow opened it and Joel hurried inside. He was greeted by a blast of heat and human stink.

"So you've got a room for me?" Joel asked, doffing his hat.

Morrow was short, in his sixties or seventies, but had a boyish face and a mop of curly white hair. He looked around the cabin as if sizing it up. "Yeah, an' this is it. I kin put ye up. Ye'll git a pallet an' two meals fer two short bits."

Joel wondered if this were an outrageous price to ask, especially since Morrow seemed to be waiting for him to respond, perhaps to haggle. But ignorant of the local economy, he said nothing and paid the man.

He set his possessions against the wall and looked around. In the center of the room stood a large plank table. Two men sat there, reluctantly putting away their card game as a woman and a red-headed boy began setting the table for a meal.

"Rufus," Morrow said to the boy, "run outside an' fetch Mister Biggs's horse ta the paddock."

The pear-shaped lad with the acne-scarred, hangdog face looked to be about fourteen, and wore faded shreds of linsey-woolsey. "Yeah Pa," he answered sullenly.

"Have a seat, Mister Biggs," Morrow said, "yer jus' in time fer supper."

Along two walls were set eight plank boxes filled with hay—the pallets, Joel assumed, eying the structures dubiously. A ladder in one corner led to a loft where he supposed the family slept.

"Food's on," the woman announced in a raspy voice, setting a Dutch oven on the table and removing the lid. She was gray-pink, rail-thin, and wore a strained expression. She was dressed in a faded blue calico dress buttoned tightly at the neck and cuffs. On her head she wore one of those nineteenth-century bonnets Joel thought were so ugly.

Rising with the steam from the pie within the pot was the unmistakable aroma of baked chicken and vegetables.

"Chicken pot pie?" Joel asked, brightening.

She looked at him askance.

He could feel himself blushing as all eyes turned to him. "I-I mean to say that I *love* chicken pot pie."

She grunted and set a wooden plate and spoon before him. A loaf of bread was passed to him, and he tore off a chunk. It was dense and obviously hadn't risen properly, but he was too hungry to care.

Rufus returned from his errand and began setting out the drinks. He put down a bent pewter mug beside each guest. Carefully tasting the contents, Joel was relieved to find his cup contained only water.

Morrow, Rufus, and the woman all sat at the table, and without preamble everyone began to noisily eat. Joel found the chicken and vegetables to be quite good, and only regretted that he couldn't have seconds—the pot had contained just enough to go around.

After the meal Rufus cleared the table, and the other guests went back to their card game. The woman sat by the fire with a sock, stuck a withered potato into its worn-out heel, and proceeded to darn it.

"I'm goin' ta bed," Morrow said after a time. He stood and picked up a candle lamp. "Mister Biggs, yer pallet is third from the end there." He gestured with his lamp. "Rufus, c'mon ta bed. We got early work."

"Yes, Pa," the boy said, joining his father.

Morrow held the lamp in his teeth while he climbed to the loft, Rufus following after him.

Joel stood and went to take a look at his pallet. Toeing the matted straw, he grimaced at the state of the bedding and tried unsuccessfully to not think about the number and types of insects it might contain. He retrieved his bedroll, unrolled it on the straw, lay down, and closed his eyes, hoping sleep would carry him effortlessly from this day into the next.

But sleep did not come quickly.

The card players, having finished their meal, had resumed their game. He could hear their whispering and he looked up to see them staring at him again. They quickly glanced back down at their game.

They're talking about me.

Joel tried to listen in on their whispered conversation, but he caught only suggestive syllables.

". . . eft handed moosing . . . horts?" he thought he heard the bald one say. "Lathered in leather head dressing."

Then he could have sworn the one with the hawkish nose replied, ". . . credible dog running baby farm. . . ."

Are these guys talking in code? No, that sounded like pure paranoia.

Joel's heart was hammering in his chest and his palms were slick with sweat. He looked up to find the one with the nose eying him furtively. The man looked away again.

"When we's . . . an' on the road tomorrow," the fellow said, "we'll have ta . . . an' jump 'im from both sides an'. . . ."

"If 'e's too . . ." said the bald guy, ". . . may 'ave ta put a bullet in 'is head."

They're gonna kill me.

Joel heard his breath rasping in and out. He wanted to mop the perspiration from his brow, but decided it was best to pretend to be sleeping.

They won't kill me here, but tomorrow on the road. . . .

"Cow's eye," said hawk-nose, slapping his cards on the table. "That's it fer me—I'm fer bed."

The two rose and stretched wearily. "I tell ye one thing," the bald one said, "I hate that goddam horse, an' if we have ta kill 'im, so be it. We'll jus' tell Mister Charles we found 'im dead in a ditch."

Joel's sweat suddenly turned cold, and he took a deep breath to relax. He felt *so* stupid.

What was he so scared of? Even if the word was out about him, news traveled only as fast as a man on horseback, and chances were no one around here had ever heard of him.

Shaking his head, he watched the two men retreat to their pallets and sleep. Not long after, the woman left off with her darning, banked the coals in the fireplace, and then ascended the ladder.

The light from the fireplace had become a dull orange, and Joel relaxed and began to drift off.

At some point in the night, Joel was awakened by a banging at the door. Morrow descended the ladder to respond. After a hurried, whispered conversation, he let someone in. Joel was already drifting back to sleep as the man stumbled toward a pallet and Morrow headed back up the ladder.

22

Joel awoke to the clamor of the other guests preparing for the day. Crawling sluggishly from his pallet, he stood yawning and scratching and brushing straw from his hair and clothing. His nose perked up at the smell of coffee and hotcakes.

The two card players were just getting up from the table and gathering their traveling accouterments. As Joel was taking his seat and being served by Rufus, the two were saying their good-byes and walking out the door.

Beside Joel sat a large, hatchet-faced fellow with great chapped paws for hands. Despite his rather rough appearance, the man was nattily dressed in matching double-breasted waistcoat and trousers, crisp linen blouse, and a silk cravat.

"Good mornin'," he said, belching around a mouthful of hot-cake.

Surprised, Joel nodded his head in greeting and took another look at the fellow.

Did he sleep in that uniform?

A piece of straw dangled from the stranger's lapel and his hair stuck out in all directions. His sleeves were far too short, and his waistcoat strained at the buttonholes. The cravat had been tied so roughly and poorly that his chest hairs were caught up in the knot.

Must be the guy Morrow let in last night.

"Good morning," Joel said and turned his attention to his plate, anxious to finish his meal and get on the road. Having inhaled his hoecakes, and scalded his tongue gulping bitter coffee, he got up from the table and gathered up his belongings.

"Rufus, fetch Mister Biggs's horse."

"Yes, Ma."

The boy dashed outside and Joel followed, putting his hat on his head and waiting uncomfortably until his horse was brought to him. He had to relieve himself, but was in no mood to find out what the Morrow outhouse was like. Stopping along the road somewhere in the middle of nowhere—and there was plenty of that around—would suit him just fine.

Within minutes, Rufus reappeared leading the saddled animal. Joel wondered whether or not Gailey had remained saddled throughout the night, but he said nothing about it, thanking the young man instead.

As he mounted up, he caught sight of his breakfast companion just emerging from Morrow's. He started down the road, and just before it carried him out of sight of the cabin, he turned for a look back and saw Rufus bringing the stranger's horse around.

Putting heels to his mount, he hurried on ahead, apprehensive about the fellow. He might be a Mystic Clan member, but, even if he were not, Joel was in no mood to spend any time with some clodhopper on his way to a wedding or something. Joel hadn't gotten far, however, before the man came galloping up and slowed alongside him.

" 'Tis safer to travel together, is it not?" he asked, but Joel merely grunted, keeping his eyes on the road ahead.

The man's trousers were so short, they rode up almost to his knees, exposing his long johns, a hairy length of leg, and the most embarrassing red boots Joel had ever seen. The clothes were probably stolen, Joel thought, but he decided there was no way a Mystic Clan member would draw attention to himself in this way.

"Could I trouble you for your companionship along the road?"

"Suit yourself," Joel said.

For a time they rode in silence, and Joel hoped his attitude would become clear to the stranger, and that the man would go away.

"It'll rain today," the fellow observed, removing a stained and bent high-hat and smoothing back his dark hair. "Where're you heading, stranger?"

As rough as he is, he doesn't sound like such a hick.

"None of your business."

"Well hell, I can see which way you're headed. I bet you're going to Nashville. Now—if it rains before noon, we might make it to Fowler's on Puett's Creek. If not, we'll have to go all the way to Markham's."

Joel tuned him out, hunching down inside his coat as the day turned cold and gray, threatening a wet, miserable ride. Eventually they came to a fork in the road and Joel paused, not knowing which way to go. This was the Nashville Road and he had assumed it ran straight all the way to Nashville. He looked around for a road sign, but found none.

"What're you stopping for?" the stranger asked innocently enough. "Don't you know which way you want to go?"

Joel bit his lip.

"Well now, that one goes north, to Hurley Dale. Now, surely you ain't going there, are you?"

Joel looked at him blankly.

"If you take this one," the stranger said, pointing left, "the road'll lead you north toward Trowbridge's Ferry, and east."

Without saying a word, Joel urged his horse to the left. Although he was unwilling to look around, he heard hoofbeats behind him and knew the man was following. Once again the stranger rode up alongside him, and Joel ignored his efforts at small talk.

"I'm on my way to see my girl. She said she'd marry me if I could put two thousand dollars in the bank. I may be the foreman for the Thorpes at Augustus," he stated proudly, "but it still took me a long while to accumulate the needed funds. Also I've tried to better myself so as to best provide for her future needs. I learned to read and write, and every day I try to increase my vocabulary by using a new word. Today the word is *accumulate.* Did you like the way I worked that into the conversation?"

Conversation? Joel shook his head, disgusted. *If this guy's on his way to Nashville, then I'll be stuck listening to this crap the whole fucking way.*

"You're not much for conversation, are you?"

A distant rumble of thunder punctuated Joel's mood, and he hoped for a lightning bolt to strike the man from his saddle. The fellow seemed to sense this, and for the next few miles they rode in silence. Joel listened to the approaching storm, and reaching a crossroads, heard the first few drops of rain strike the brim of his hat. He plodded on through the intersection, until the man called to him.

"Hey, you there. That goes to Trowbridge's Ferry."

Joel stopped and turned to stare blankly at him.

"You want to turn right, if you want to go to Nashville, that is."

Trying to appear nonchalant, Joel turned his mount and headed to the right. He had ridden only a few yards when the sky opened up and dropped a rain cloud on him.

"Quick, under that tree—I have a tarp," the stranger said, pointing.

They dismounted, and the man led the way beneath a tall elm. They tethered their horses to a branch which hung nearly to the ground. The fellow then removed a tarpaulin from his saddlebag, spread it out amongst the roots, and they crawled under it. Immediately the sharp smell of the pine pitch impregnating the heavy canvas filled Joel's nose.

"Kinda snug under here," the man said apologetically, "but at least we'll keep dry."

The rain drummed fiercely on the tarpaulin, and Joel lifted up the edge to see the droplets gradually churning the road to mud. With both of their bodies huddled beneath the tarp, the air was rapidly becoming warm and muggy. At least the stranger didn't stink. As a matter of fact, Joel was surprised to find he didn't really mind being cooped up with the guy. And come to think of it, he wasn't even certain why he had been feeling so hostile.

"It's all right," Joel agreed, "like you said, we'll keep dry. Thanks."

"Don't mention it. My name's Harvey Phipps."

Huh . . . Worley. Yeah that's it—Worley . . . what? "My name is Worley Knobbs."

"Nice to meet you, Mister Knobbs."

Phipps lifted the edge of the tarp and watched the rain for a while. Then, as if he suddenly felt the need to say it, he burst out with: "My Bonnie, she's just a Indian whore in the Red Bottoms—you know where that is, don't you?"

"Yeah, west Nashville."

"Well, like I said she's just a whore, but she promised she'd give it up if we were to marry. 'Course, I have my doubts, but I 'spose I could live with it if I had to. I know that's easy to say now, as I can't seem to say no."

"Sounds like a lot of heartache," Joel said. He imagined the man's love for his volatile woman as being similar to his own affair with alcohol.

"I love her is what it is. Surely you've had plenty of experience with women, Mister Knobbs?"

"Never anyone I was serious about," he said, then decided that was perhaps a lie.

"It'll change your world I tell you. I've done things in the last two years of knowing her I never thought I'd do."

"I'll just bet you have," Joel said sarcastically.

Phipps gave him a curious look.

"I mean—I can imagine," Joel said, changing his tone.

Phipps turned back to the rain. "Why, just the other day I got a loan for the building of a house. Can you believe that—a rough man such as myself, Harvey Phipps, lord of his own castle?"

Things are sure a lot simpler here.

"That sounds good. Life hasn't exactly been kind to me the last few years, and I . . . it'd be nice to get settled down." He found himself thinking of Rachel, though he knew he shouldn't. "I have to admit I'm envious."

A leak just above his head began drooling water into Joel's hair. It ran down the side of his face, tickled its way into his shirt, and he shivered. He pulled the tarp forward, and the leak piddled between his feet instead.

"So, Mister Knobbs, where're you from? You sound foreign to these here parts."

"I'm from Long Island, New York," Joel said with a smile. "My people are potato farmers, but that's not my kind of life."

"It *does* sound exciting."

"Yeah, I guess so. If you like watching plants grow."

"What brought you down hereabouts?"

Joel looked at the man. "Potatoes," he said chuckling.

"No, seriously, sir," Phipps said, laughing. "What brought you here?"

"A little bit of research."

"Research? What line of work are you in?"

"I'm a writer. I thought to see something of the frontier for my book."

"What's your book about?"

"Outlawry in the Tennessee Basin."

"Ah . . . then you must've heard about the arrest of Jarrett Cotten?"

Joel felt a sudden chill, as if he'd just discovered a snake in his boot. "Something of it."

"And what do you think? Will the man get a fair shake?"

Suddenly it was very crowded under the tarp, and Joel was trying to think of how to most gracefully make his excuses and get away.

"Don't you have any sympathy for a fellow like that?" Phipps asked. "He might've done some wrong here and there, but does he deserve to go to prison? Who's to say?"

Thinking of all that the Mystic Clan had done and planned to do to cause suffering, thinking of the ego of the man behind it all, Joel couldn't hold his tongue.

"Whatever his punishment, he deserves it, and more. That man's no *fellow,* he's a criminal."

"Goddam," Phipps said, turning and grabbing him by the shoulders.

Joel backed out from under the tarp, getting to his feet and dragging Phipps with him.

"No—no," the man shouted, letting go.

Joel wheeled about at a sudden thunder clap. Phipps seized him by the shoulders again and spun him around.

"That's what I was wanting to hear from you. No need for you to get so upset . . . I ain't one of his."

Joel stared suspiciously at him, the rain washing down his face and into his shirt. Phipps lost the tarp to a sudden gust of wind, and it tumbled away as he stood there, gesturing open-handed, wide-eyed, and smiling.

Although Phipps' expression seemed deliberately open and friendly, Joel found he couldn't quite trust the man.

If this guy is one of them, I'm still alive only because he hopes to get something from me. Joel shivered at the unsettling thought.

"I too hate Cotten and his cursed band of cutthroats. He had his hands in everything around here. Hell, his Clan still does. C'mon, let's fetch that tarp and get back under it."

"Forget it—I'm already soaking wet. I'd just as soon get on my horse and move on."

"Suit yourself. If you don't mind though, I'll be joining you."

"Fine," Joel said, wishing he had just said no. He untethered his horse, mounted up, and headed for the road, watching Phipps out of the corner of his eye.

The man turned to look for the tarp, but it was gone. By the time he had given up on it and collected his horse, he had to spur the animal hard to catch up.

With a rumble of distant thunder, the rain began to suddenly taper off, the wind blowing steadily as the flow of water slackened and stopped. Although chilled to the bone, Joel opened his coat to the breeze, knowing that if he could dry his clothes out even a little, they would do a better job keeping him warm.

"You know something, Mister Knobbs? I have to ask myself every blessed day, 'What is this world coming to when such men as Cotten and his ilk are allowed to prey upon decent folk?' "

He paused, waiting for a response that wouldn't come.

"If ever there was an incarnation of the devil himself, it is Jarrett Cotten. Such foul and evil men must be stamped out. This would be a great country to live in if it weren't for those who take advantage of these wilds, hiding in the forest and leaping out to devour the innocent passerby—only to dash back into the wilderness like skulking jackals and so escape their just desserts."

Does Phipps really think, Joel wondered, *that I'm swallowing this line?* The man was certainly going overboard in his effort to show he was an advocate of law and order. But then, this was an era in which men expressed themselves with such passionate rhetoric.

"But there will come a time—" Phipps bellowed fervently, stabbing his left forefinger toward the sky, "mark my words—when the innocent will rise up, band together, and smite all evildoers, rendering a fearsome justice and setting a grim example against all future malefactors."

If only it were so simple. This all seemed hauntingly familiar to Joel, but he didn't have time to reason out why before his thoughts were interrupted by more words from Phipps.

"I think you will agree, good Worley, as would any sane man, that in order for mankind to thrive—" Balling his left hand into a fist, he brought it down onto his horse's neck, pounding in rhythm with his words. "—*nay,* to survive at *all,* we must *selflessly* embrace *law* and *order,* sacrifice unto it *those* who would gainsay it, and do so *fearlessly,* without compunction, and without a *shred* of sentimentality or *mercy.*"

The horse wailed as he continued to pound, and when Phipps did not stop, it turned its head around as far as it could and snapped viciously at him.

"Do you *have* to beat on the poor animal like that?" Joel asked. "It's getting pretty pissed off . . . and I assure you, I *do* get your point. Outlaws pretty much suck all the way around as far as I'm concerned."

Phipps seemed surprised. "Oh, Winifred," he cooed to his horse, stroking her neck, "I do hope you're not injured overmuch. Forgive me, the both of you. I get so passionate about the subject, as you see. I have such *feelings,* I get carried away, and it is fortuitous that I fell in with a man of similar sentiments, or I fear I would be making a fool of myself."

"Yeah, Harvey, whatever you say. I'm with you."

"You're a good man, Worley, and it is a pleasure to travel by your side."

As the road climbed a gentle rise, a creek meandered toward them from the left. A cabin with a waterwheel straddled the stream, and Joel saw smoke roiling from a chimney. Set beside it was another cabin, and Phipps pointed to it.

"Fowler's," he said. "Old man Fowler has run the mill for ten years and longer. 'Bout a year ago, his missus convinced him to open the tavern there. It ain't much, but it's comfortable and the food's good. It'd be my pleasure if you would allow me to buy you dinner."

"I'm not particularly hungry," Joel said, "but I would appreciate something warm to drink."

"Oh, I think Mama Fowler can fix you up," Phipps said with a smile, "but I've never met a man who could resist her ham and hot spoonbread, especially when it is all smothered in honey."

Joel's mouth watered. It had been many years since he'd had soft, buttery spoonbread. "That does sounds good." Joel turned to Phipps and smiled. "You've convinced me."

They tethered their horses to a split-rail fence which paralleled the road along the front of the tavern. Phipps adjusted his ill-fitting clothing and Joel, uncomfortable in his own damp garments, adjusted them as best he could, pulling at the crotch and armpits where they clung too tightly.

Carrying his saddlebag, Joel followed as his companion led the way to the tavern door. Phipps ushered Joel inside with a sweep of his hat. Joel doffed his own hat and looked around at the single room which was warm and inviting. A large fire burned on the stone hearth, and the air was thick with the smells of ham, baking bread, and wood smoke. There were four tables, none of which were occupied. Over the shuttered windows hung gingham curtains, and the tables were covered with the same fabric.

A fleshy middle-aged woman with wiry gray hair was crouched by the fireplace over a bread pan, using a fork to test for doneness. Evidently satisfied, she upended the pan and plopped the loaf out onto a board. Standing up and smiling broadly, she greeted them.

"Please have a seat, gentlemen. I'll be right back." She vanished through a rear door as they chose a table near the fire.

Phipps remained quiet, and Joel heard the low rumble of the millstone next door and the groan of the waterwheel. He felt himself becoming drowsy and knew that he must've dropped off for a moment because suddenly the woman was beside him.

"What kin I git ye, fellers?" she asked.

"We'd like ham and spoonbread, please ma'am," Phipps said. "That is what you want, Worley, is it not?"

"Sorry, boys—no spoonbread today. Not 'nough business ta make it worth my while. I kin bring ye the ham an' some nice crispy corncakes."

"With honey?" asked Phipps.

"Much as ye'd like."

"That sounds fine," Joel said. "Some coffee too."

"I'll bring it right away," she said, shuffling off.

"It'll take three more days to git to Nashville," Phipps said. "I know a tavern there as can provide us with a private parlor. The proprietor is a friend of mine, and I happen to know he stocks some of the finest bourbon in Tennessee. He'll set us up with a bottle or two each, get us some high-class women—hell, I ain't married yet—and we'll have us a grand ol' time. Then you can go with me to the law and make a statement recanting all you've said against Jarrett Cotten—how about that? It's that or I kill you straight away, Crenshaw."

Joel's eyes went wide.

"Now, now, no need to get excited. We're just two gentlemen having a friendly meal and intercourse. See, I know you can repair the damage to the Clan, so I'm not just gonna do you in, not unless I have to. The minute you show yourself to be of no value in that respect, however. . . ."

As ominous as his words were, Phipps, if that was his name, seemed as friendly as ever. Even so, Joel remained focused on the reality of the situation.

When the woman returned with the coffee and bread, Joel had it in his mind to get up and follow her out of the room. Phipps must have read it on his face, because he tapped Joel on the knee with something hard—the barrel of a pistol, no doubt.

"Who are you?" Joel asked, his voice cracking.

"Mort Puckett."

"You're on the Grand Council. You're in charge of extorting from prostitutes."

"Not a piece of pie sold that we don't earn a slice."

Perhaps the greatest, vilest pimp that ever lived.

"It's good that you know me. You'll know I mean business."

Joel caught his breath, tried to relax. Apparently his posturing was not over.

"As a matter of fact, I know a lot about you—quite a lot."

"Such as?" Puckett asked, raising an eyebrow.

"Let's see, you're in charge of not only whores, but gambling operations for the Mystic Clan, and since Cotten's arrest, you have overthrown and killed several of your rivals in the Clan." Joel had nearly forgotten from his history that Puckett took charge after Cotten was arrested. Briefly. It was a strange feeling, knowing the man next to him would soon be dead, shot in the back by Art Clayton.

"Pah! You could have gotten that from what Cotten spilled

about us. And the rest—well, there's always talk."

"I would have thought that Sharpe or Clayton would have taken charge. What happened to them?"

"Clayton's too sickly. Sharpe is recovering from a blow to the head."

I guess the surface of the road took a toll on him.

"I also know you are a bastard of mixed Creole and English blood. Your mother was a house servant for the Crawfords of New Orleans, and your father, Montgomery Puckett, was a British dignitary who visited the Crawfords, a man you've never met."

Puckett's face froze in an expressionless mask. Knowing that he was getting through to him, Joel felt a heart-pounding thrill.

"To continue—you are partial to sex with Indian squaws and contracted the French Disease last year in the Choctaw Purchase. You are addicted to absinthe, and habitually carry a flask of chased silver with the image of a rampant griffin which you stole from the Crawfords when a child. I'll bet it's there in your saddlebag. So you see, Mister Puckett, I *do* know quite a bit about you."

"I could end your life right here, right now." Puckett's voice was shaking.

Joel reigned in his fear. He knew the man was now nearly as afraid as he was. He would be thinking Joel couldn't possibly know these things unless there were supernatural forces involved.

"You do know I come from Adams, Tennessee, don't you?"

"Cotten spoke of it," Puckett said, nervousness evident in his eyes. "What of it?"

"Surely you also know of the dreaded Bell Spirit."

"You?" Puckett's glaring eyes widened the slightest bit, and the wrinkled bags under them quivered uncertainly. "But she—"

"—takes many forms. Would you care to hear something

about your future?"

Puckett's eyes were wide and his mouth hung open. "No!"

"Very well. I will say only that I know you intend to move the date for the uprising to the fourth of July of next year."

Puckett's mouth dropped open.

Joel sat back and smiled smugly. "I want you to know that, dead or alive, I can change your future. I could do it right here, right now. Or later. You'll never know."

Though Puckett's fearful gaze seemed to drill into his head, Joel didn't turn away. He held his expression of arrogant triumph until the man closed his eyes and took a deep breath.

The woman returned, setting a pewter plate loaded with ham and corncakes before each of them.

"I cannot just walk away," Puckett said. "Cotten be damned, but I can't let you stop our Grand Plot."

Joel thought a moment, agonizing over what he was about to do. "I was on my way to a publisher in Nashville with a manuscript. It tells about everything that happened between me and Cotten—the whole story, from meeting him on the road to America's Powder Keg and the plot for the uprising—*everything.* I could give this to you."

If he did this he'd have to rewrite the manuscript from memory, and Mark's contributions would essentially be lost. But he'd made the offer and so he waited for an answer, eaten up with guilt over his impromptu betrayal of his friend. But was it betrayal, or just what was supposed to happen?

"You ain't gonna do that without gaining something in return," Puckett said.

"I want Cotten. You and the Mystic Clan forget about him. He's mine."

"I don't know what you are, but I'll tell you outright—you know things no one should know. You . . . leave me be, and I promise to hold up my end of this. Deal?"

Joel knew that at best he was only buying himself a month or two. When the Mystic Clan discovered the book on the market, they'd continued their efforts to discredit or kill him. "Deal."

Had he just changed history to avoid the threat to his life this trip represented? Perhaps he would never know.

23

Joel had almost given up his search of the fog-laden Nashville waterfront when he stumbled over a mislaid length of hawser on Water Street, slipped on the slick cobblestone incline leading down to the Cumberland River, and slid down to the river's lapping edge. His saddlebag flew out of his hand and skittered into the water. Joel got up and moved to the river's icy edge. He grimaced at the miasma of smells that greeted him. In the wretched liquid right under his nose, there was a dead yellow bass, a cigar butt, tufts of soggy cotton and twine, and a mass of green algae billowing in the slight current like the hair of a mermaid—all mixed with thinned raw sewage. Nauseated, Joel reached for his saddlebag and pulled it from the water.

He heard harsh laughter from the roustabouts loitering on Water Street above and began to shake with unexpressed anger.

Joel reined in his feelings, painfully aware that law and order had at best a tenuous hold on this section of the city—if he were to become involved in a brawl, was murdered and thrown into the Cumberland River, no one would ever be the wiser.

"Goddammit," he muttered, squeezing the water out of his sleeves and kicking a broken bit of axe handle into the foamy litter at the water's edge. Looking back toward Water Street, he saw the roustabouts still chuckling at him. He walked along the river, looking for a way up the cobblestone incline that would take him out of their view.

The shrill cry of a steam whistle snagged his attention and

Joel turned to see, just emerging from the fog, the most overburdened craft he had ever seen. The sternwheeler lumbered into view, its paddle wheel beating the water to froth. It seemed to Joel rather small, and was obviously used for hauling freight, not passengers. He had been hoping to see one of the big sidewheelers, a floating palace, but they would not come into their own for some time yet.

As the cobblestones gave way to rocky bluff, Joel found a well-worn switchback path up the stony face. At the top he found a group of men working with a winch to pull rotten posts out of the ground. Looking at the configuration of the remaining posts and the holes left by those already removed, he realized this was the remains of the first settlement, Fort Nashboro. Just as Daniel Boone had done in Kentucky, James Robertson and John Donelson had led settlers into this area in the early seventeen-eighties. They had built Fort Nashboro for protection against the fiercely hostile Indians who considered the area sacred hunting and burial grounds. For Joel this was a historic treasure, but to the men struggling to remove the rotten posts it was fairly recent history that stood in the way of progress.

Joel crossed Water Street and walked back down the hill toward Broad. He was relieved to see that the roustabouts were gone now. He asked a gentleman standing outside a warehouse smoking a cigar for directions to Duke & Willis Gargantuan Press. "It was suppose' to be somewhere here on Water or Front Streets," he said.

"He moved," the man said curtly. "An' good riddance to 'im! Never met such an ill-tempered man."

"Who?"

"Duke Willis! That's who yer askin' after, ain't it."

"I suppose so."

"Either ye are or ye aren't. What's it gonna be?"

"Yes, sir," Joel said as politely as he could bear.

"Go up Broad 'til ye git to Spruce. Go left until ye see 'is big ugly blue sign."

Joel thanked the man and proceeded up Broad, looking at the uneven wood and brick buildings of the young city. The cobblestones soon gave way to poorly fired cracked brick, then split and rotting planks and finally to a morass of mud and horse droppings. The stench of the town was thick, but it was not nearly as unpleasant as it would have been in the summer, Joel realized, when the flies would have bred in harrying clouds. He stayed near the edge of the road, as close to the buildings as possible, keeping his eyes on his footing and carefully picking his way through the muck.

Joel tried not to make eye contact with anyone until he realized there were no road signs and he'd have to ask someone for the location of Spruce Street. He asked a black fellow carrying what looked to be a thirty-pound catfish.

"Two blocks that-a-way," the fellow said without breaking his stride.

Joel turned onto Spruce. Still trying to be careful of his footing in the manure-laden mud, he didn't see his destination until he was standing right in front of it. Hanging from a frame building that seemed to sag tiredly into the mud, was a brand new, freshly painted sign that proclaimed in bright blue letters, *Duke & Willis Gargantuan Press.*

The door before him burst open, and a man backed out of it bearing a loose stack of paper. He ran into Joel and knocked him down. Paper flew everywhere and Joel looked for the man amidst the cloud. Finally, high above him, he saw a face glaring down while leaves of paper drifted around it and fell to the ground.

"What the *hell* do *you* want?"

Joel grabbed his saddlebag from where it had fallen and

pulled it to him, then looked back up at the man. He'd thought it was a trick of the light . . . but no, this was the largest man he had ever seen, larger even than Wesley Pike.

"*Well?*"

The fellow was in his shirtsleeves, a gray ink-stained waistcoat, and ratty brown trousers. He was plump and big-boned, about seven feet tall, and his head was bald except for ridiculously bushy eyebrows.

"Um . . . I'm looking for Duke Willis," Joel said, squinting upward.

The fellow's eyebrows lowered to form a single, nasty woolly-worm. "You are, are you? I'm Duke Willis." He extended a hand to help Joel up.

The hand was massive, easily twice the size of his own, and Joel felt as if he were five years old again and his father was helping him to his feet—but this time hopefully not just so he could hit him again.

"Let me help you pick up this mess," Joel said, bending and gathering up a few sheets of the paper.

"Leave it be, goddammit. I meant to throw it in the street. It's rurnt. Press is acting up."

"I see," Joel said. He was beginning to back off when the giant suddenly grabbed him by the arm.

"C'mon you mule-sucking nancy boy! You maybe got a book to sell? Let's get you inside and get this over with. I'm a busy man and I can't *stand* interruptions."

He was obviously used to throwing his weight around, and Joel was quite unwilling to stand in his way. He followed the giant's great square backside into the sagging building. The interior was dark, cold, and smelled of fish, and Joel found the odor so offensive he had to remind himself to breathe. A tired-looking printing press sulked in one corner, while a tiny beaten-up stove smoked away in another. The cracked and peeling walls were burdened with tumbledown shelving and ominous stacks of moldering paper. As his eyes adjusted to the light, Joel saw through a doorway toward the rear, stacks of dusty books, some of which were in varying stages of fabrication.

The giant sat at a heavily littered desk. "I know why you're here," he said, "so out with it, *goddammit.*"

Joel, gulping breath, fumbled at the straps of his saddlebag to get the notes for the new book he'd scribbled while on the road. In his haste, he spilled the contents onto the debris-strewn floor.

"I can't abide hardly any man alive, and I sure as hell ain't got time for a lickfinger like you. I assume you've got money."

"I've got two thousand dollars in silver coin," Joel said, stooping to pick up the purse he had taken from Mark.

When he looked up Willis' demeanor had changed subtly. He was almost smiling, but his voice did not reflect the change of mood. "What the hell're you standing there for, you no-account bummer?"

He kicked a chair toward Joel. It slid across the floor and tumbled over sideways. Joel reached down, righted it, and sat.

He knew now the man was all bluster. His leverage in this situation would be money.

"Tell me about this cussed thing you want me to print," Willis demanded.

"I want it distributed as well." Joel stood and handed Willis the journal in which he'd written his notes.

Willis flipped through the ten pages Joel had written, arching his eyebrow here and there as he read, especially when he found the testimonial letters of McHenry Lake, Thomas Fellowes, and Judge Erwin and the list of names penned by Jarrett Cotton. It was a good thing, Joel realized, that he had kept them separate from the manuscript he had given to Mort Puckett.

Then Willis was flipping through the blank pages that filled the rest of the book, looking for more. "What the hell is this?"

"Uh, I haven't got it all written yet . . . I was hoping to finish it up while you worked on the first parts."

"GODDAMMIT!" He turned and hurled the journal at Joel. It caught him on the right shoulder.

Joel picked it up. "This is a true story and I've got two thousand dollars in silver to see it in print," he said, then looked around the room doubtfully, "and what have you got? I could take my business elsewhere."

Willis' bluster collapsed suddenly. "My business may not look like much," he said, somewhat tiredly, gesturing broadly at the filth, "but I won't have no problem seeing your book all over the country in three months." Then his attitude picked up steam again. "Now shut the hell up, you damn fool lick-spittle, and get to work. By the time I get the first signature done, you'd damn well better have it finished."

Willis set Joel up at his desk and made sure he had plenty of paper, quills, and ink.

"What arrangements have you for distribution?" Joel asked.

"Don't get all riled up on that account," Willis answered. "I got contacts. Plenty of places of business as orders books from me."

24

Joel was feeling good as he headed out of Nashville on a bright morning four days later.

He hoped he hadn't rushed the writing of the Crenshaw book too much, but he'd been desperate to get away from Duke Willis. Joel's muse seemed to support this desire to get away—his dipping of quill into ink could hardly keep up with his thoughts flying onto the pages. How much of this was a product of memory, how much of it he would have written without prior knowledge, he could not determine. Although Joel was concerned that he might have left something important out of the tale, when he finally turned it over to Willis, it did *feel* right. Whatever differences there might be between what he'd written and the final form the Crenshaw book took would probably be the result of editing by Willis.

Late on the third day of Joel's trip back to Adairville, four heavily armed men stepped into the road and demanded that he stop. He recognized one of them as Job Hayes. The other three were unknown to him. Hayes went to his left, one remained in front of Joel, and the others boxed him in, one on his right, one behind.

Hayes gestured with his scattergun and ordered Joel to dismount.

"I have a deal with Mort Puckett," Joel said.

"Don't know nothin 'bout no deal, Crenshaw," Hayes said.

Either Puckett had not kept his word or news traveled too

slowly in this century for all the Mystic Clan to have been informed of Joel's deal with the outlaw.

"Couldn't you just shoot me right off my horse?" Joel said, tired and disgusted. Even so, he hoped the man wouldn't take him up on it.

Hayes didn't say anything for a moment, but all four of them drew closer. There was a deliberateness and determination in their expressions, but Joel also saw fear in their eyes. And that made him wonder what *they* had to be afraid of.

Perhaps, he thought, *they think I'm one real tough bastard since Cotten took me under his wing. They may also know I was responsible for Sharpe being injured.*

Joel had two pistols ready, one held in his right hand under his greatcoat. He wished he had Rachel's .45.

The man on Joel's right was within twenty feet and armed with a squirrel gun. The man in front was carrying a pair of horse pistols. Joel was unwilling to take his eyes off the three in front to get a look at the one behind him.

He was burning adrenaline. The reins were moist in his grasp. He was ready to whip Gailey and cause her to bolt, hoping she would pull him away faster than the outlaws could aim and fire their weapons, but he sat frozen, unable to act.

Hayes moved closer, within spitting distance, and again ordered Joel to dismount.

"If I have ta git ye down, boy, yer horse's liable ta git hurt." Then he leveled his piece at Joel. Joel swung his pistol out from under his coat and pulled the trigger in Hayes' face. The outlaw's head snapped back and he was thrown off the road. His scattergun went off between Gailey's legs and struck the fellow on Joel's right in the knees. He sank to the ground, howling. The man in front, advancing on him, fired one of his pistols and missed. Joel heard the man behind pull the trigger of his firearm. There must've been just a flash in the pan, as the firearm did not discharge. Then, the man in front was advancing on Joel, to make certain he didn't miss with his next shot. As he raised his other pistol, Joel threw his firearm. It struck the man full in the face, just above the eye, and he went down hard. Gailey reared in terror and came down on his skull with her hooves. As Joel struggle to stay mounted, he felt something strike the base of his skull. Later he would decide that the man behind him must have struck him with the butt of a rifle. It rattled Joel from head to toe, and he found himself lying across Gailey's neck. She had delivered him from the fight, and when he was fully conscious again, he found he was far from the highwaymen.

His dizziness and nausea might be attributed to an overdose of adrenaline, but he suspected he had a concussion. There wasn't much he could do about it at the moment.

Hoping to dodge pursuit, he guided his horse off the road, his head throbbing like a kettle drum. In the thick forest, he followed random animal trails going in an easterly direction until he felt he'd put enough miles between him and his pursuers. When he finally felt able to relax his guard, he realized he was indeed very ill. His vision swam, and he vomited, causing his head to pound until he thought it would crack open and spill his brains to the forest floor. Exhausted, Joel knew he could not continue farther.

He found a spot where Gailey would not be easily found. He dismounted. Taking his gear, he left her there, and moved off some distance toward a rocky overhang to find a place to sleep.

Even if someone finds her, he thought, in his increasingly delirious state, *they will not immediately find me.*

"Joel, you asshole," Rachel said. "You didn't even brush that horse down."

" 'M sorry, Rachel," he mumbled. "I'll do it later."

She crossed her arms and smiled at him. "Wrap your fool

head up, Joel, so your brain doesn't fall out."

" 'Kay."

He sat on the ground, pawed in his pack for a spare shirt, and wrapped it around his head. He touched the back of his bandage gently, and could feel it was already soaking through with blood.

"I love you," he said to Rachel.

"I love you," said his father, in a shrill, mocking voice. "You make me sick. Go get me a beer, you little fairy."

Joel croaked out a laugh. "No beer out here, Daddy. Go suck some jimson weed."

His father spit on the ground and glared at Joel. "Fuck you, you little bastard."

"Yep," said Joel. "I'm pretty well fucked, all right." He wrapped himself up in a couple of blankets and leaned against a tree.

Virgil Pike nudged Joel's father with a bony elbow. "We oughta kill him right now."

Joel's father nodded. "I guess you're right."

"Go ahead, then," Joel said. The pain in his head had grown until he felt like his skull was in a vice grip and there were ice picks behind his eyes. "You'd be doin' me a favor, Virg."

"You'll die out here," Virgil sneered. "You'll die of thirst. There's water jes' down the way, but you'll be too weak ta get to it. Yer tongue'll swell up 'til it fills your mouth. Yer lips'll crack an' bleed. An' you think your haid hurts now? Wait 'til yer goddam brain starts shrivelin' up in yer skull, Joel Biggs."

Joel grabbed his head with both hands. "Go 'way, Virg. You're dead."

"You will be too. Nobody'll find you, Joel. Not for years. The flesh'll rot off yer bones. Plants an' vines'll grow through yer rib cage, an' a cute little mouse'll make a nest in yer skull."

"Go 'way, Virg." Tears of agony rolled down Joel's cheeks. He dry-heaved, and the pain that shot through his head made him scream.

"Leave the boy alone, Virgil," Wesley Pike's voice rumbled. The big man knelt next to Joel, smiling just a little. "You'll be all right, Little Man. Jes' sleep a while."

"Might not wake up," Joel whispered.

"Thass' a chance we all take ever' night, Joel. But wouldn't it be nice to close yer eyes fer a while?"

"Wesley—"

"You'll live or you'll die, Joel. Settin' here frettin' on it won't change the outcome. Sleep. I'll keep Virgil away from ye."

"Thanks, Wes." Joel reached out for Wesley's hand, but grasped only leaves. He leaned his head against the tree, and his eyes closed.

It wasn't a peaceful sleep. Joel jerked awake many times from the pain in his head, from the taunts of his father, from violent nausea. Half awake, he'd find himself crawling through the underbrush, his father telling him how pathetic he looked, like a dog somebody ought to shoot. At least Virgil wasn't there; Wesley had evidently kept his word to keep him away. Joel wished that Rachel would come back, just so he could see her face for a moment, but she never did.

When the sky became apparent again through the twiggy canopy overhead, Joel knew that morning was approaching. He had survived. Like a malignant spirit, his father faded in the pale predawn light. Joel was alone, both a blessing and a curse.

His neck was frightfully swollen, and when he tried to rise, the pain was unbearable. Only his momentum carried him to his feet. He gripped a nearby tree to keep from going back down. The pain subsided somewhat. He was running a high fever, and he was stiff and miserable, his mind full of the hopelessness of his situation.

He knew if he was to survive, he must eventually find

someone to take him in while he recovered, but who could he trust when anyone he might come across would be a stranger? Even if he did find shelter with honest folks, it was likely that, by the time he healed up, the Mystic Clan would have tracked him down.

The Crenshaw book said that he'd be hounded out of the country and finish his days penniless in Europe. Considering his present situation, that was beginning to sound attractive.

As the sun rose, Joel dug into his provisions and ate a light meal very slowly. Wesley Pike joined him, sitting companionably next to Joel, but refusing any food.

"Don't s'pose there's a Holiday Inn around here," Joel said. Wesley laughed, and turned into a bramble.

Joel rose and started looking for his horse. He had wandered perhaps a hundred yards from the rocky overhang. He climbed up to it, got his bearings and saw Gailey in the distance. She stood impatiently, saddled and ready to go.

"That poor horse, rode hard and put away wet. Just like you, Joel," Rachel said into his ear. He tried to turn his head and look at her, and nearly fainted from the pain.

Joel made his way to Gailey and mounted the saddle with excruciating care, pain throbbing in his head, his limbs quaking. He was so exhausted by the effort, he fell across her neck and his stomach convulsed, trying to expel whatever was causing his nausea, but nothing came out.

Joel had no idea where he was, but once again, struck out in an easterly direction.

By the light of day, he discovered that he was wounded much worse than he had thought. There was a gash in his scalp at the back of his head. It had bled freely in the night and his hair, shirt, and makeshift bandage were soaked through with blood. Much of it was dry and stiff. There were small lacerations on his exposed arms and, he was sure, his face, from crawling through the underbrush in his sleep.

Mark Ryder, sitting high on the limb of a tree, made a face at him. "Eeow, Joel. You look like shit."

"So d'you, but at least I got an excuse, flicto."

Mark laughed and flew away.

Joel drank what water he had and still wanted more. He could also use some water to help clean himself up, he realized. If he were to meet up with anyone in this state, he was liable to attract more attention than he cared to.

His fever had abated and he began to feel a little better.

Before the sun reached its zenith, he chanced upon a road. This he followed for the rest of the day without meeting anyone. Toward nightfall, he came upon a cabin, but fearing that he might run afoul of the Mystic Clan, he passed on by.

He paused several times to allow Gailey to graze and to water at various streams, but he didn't have the courage to face the pain of climbing out of the saddle to wash himself. During the night there were long periods of numbness, when the cold air, the stiffness in his joints, the throbbing pain in his head, did not reach him. His fever had returned. He tried to eat, chewing a bit of jerky and swallowing the juice without swallowing the fiber. Even so, after a short while, he vomited again.

As the night passed, Joel trusted Gailey to carry him where she would. No doubt there were times when she stood stock still and rested, but he was unaware of that.

Whatever the case, by sunrise they were moving again, and came upon a small farm. Joel decided he'd have to take a chance. A middle-aged man was splitting wood beside a cabin. Joel approached.

"Would you be so kind as to provide a meal for me and my horse?" he asked, noting that his words were slurred. "I was set upon by villains on the road, and I am sick and hungry."

The fellow, looking Joel up and down suspiciously, said,

"Hardly enough here for me and mine."

"Blow his brains out and take what ye need, Little Man," said Wesley, standing behind the man's shoulder.

"I can't do that, Wesley. Sir, please direct me to the Adairville Road."

The fellow kept eyeing Joel strangely and asked several questions, but his words made no sense in Joel's ears.

"I'm tellin' ya, Joel, the man needs killin'." Wesley's grin would have scared a mountain lion.

"I'm startin' to think you're right, Wes. Look, mister, I'm in a bad way. I need to get to Adairville and my people. If you can't help me, please point me in the direction of friendlier folks without further ado."

"Return to the road yonder, west," he said. "Take that 'til one meets it from the south. Take that to its end. There be the Adairville Road. Go west again to find Adairville."

"Thanks," said Wesley. "An' may yer manhood wither an' drop off, an' all yer childern be born wit' two haids."

Joel was several miles down the road before something occurred to him; the man might have been acting strangely because of all the blood Joel was wearing. When he came upon another creek, he paused, climbed out of the saddle and washed himself. He dug another shirt out of his saddlebag and found it nearly impossible to put it on. His arms didn't seem to want to work properly, his hands wouldn't grip. The effort left him exhausted and he rested for a half hour before moving on.

Joel reached a crossroads. A strange shadow played across the road, moving slowly in the breeze. Joel looked up, into the bloated, blue face of a hanged man, and realized he had no idea which way to go.

"Straight down," said the dead man, with a ghastly grin. "I'll walk with ye, I'm goin' that way myself."

"Go left, Joel. West, remember?" Rachel's breath was warm

on his ear. He reached up to touch her face, but she was gone.

"My angel," he croaked.

Her laughter was like water. "Come home, Joel."

By noon, he came to an inn on the Adairville Road where he was able to buy refreshment for himself and his horse. The innkeeper and his wife were friendly enough and seemed concerned about his condition, but Joel wore a mask of stoicism to avoid unnecessary conversation, explaining simply that he was feeling under the weather and giving a false name and occupation when asked. They had a room they offered to rent him, but Virgil Pike and a giant toad were sitting at a darkened table in the corner playing cards, and Joel feared to stay too long.

He resumed his journey and soon found himself drifting in and out again. Gailey kept moving, however. He rested his cheek against the smooth hair of her mane and closed his eyes.

"Don't you fall off that horse," Rachel whispered in his ear.

"Okay, sweetheart," Joel breathed. Blackness enveloped him like a thick blanket.

"God Almighty," shouted Hume Stogdon. "It's Joel! Son, help me bring him in."

Someone was pulling him off of Gailey. He tried to struggle, but his arms felt like spaghetti.

"Easy now, Mister Biggs," said Stephen Stogdon. "It's us, we're tryin' ta help ya."

They carried him indoors, pulled off his clothes and wrapped him in a fresh blanket. Hume caught sight of the back of Joel's head and gasped. Rachel let out a little shriek.

Supporting Joel's shoulders, Stephen lowered him into bed. Hume filled a bedwarmer with hot coals and placed it between the quilts. Bundled up like a baby, Joel's mind and body relaxed.

"Well, Little Man, ye didn't die after all," Wesley rumbled. "I always knew ye were a tough bastard."

"It's that thick head of his," piped Billy, sitting on Willawic's shoulders. "Nothin' in there but gristle." The little boy laughed.

Joel smiled at him. "Billy," he said, and reached for his friend's hand.

A small hand gripped his fingers, but it wasn't Billy's. It was Rachel's. Joel opened his mouth and tried to speak to her, to thank her for guiding him home, but he couldn't make his vocal cords work, and his eyes were closing all by themselves. "Angel," he whispered. The last thing he saw was Rachel's tear-streaked face, and then he was asleep again.

25

Mark Ryder tromped in from the fields, shrugging the stiffness out of his shoulders. His breath blew out in great white plumes in the frosty air. He'd been out helping Carver, the Stogdons' sole remaining slave, mend a broken fence. Carver hadn't really needed the help, he was a strong young man. But ever since Macklin and Briley had been gone, the poor fellow had been nervous as a cat. His fears had only grown worse since members of the Mystic Clan had begun to haunt Adairville.

Mark didn't mind helping out. It was smart to watch each others' back, that was for damn sure. And Carver was a likeable fellow, chatty with a good sense of humor.

Mark had heard no word of Wesley Pike, so he'd stayed at the Stogdons', waiting for Joel. They'd been kind enough to put him up and feed him, and he worked hard to make himself useful.

Mark was looking forward to a hot meal and his bed. But there seemed to be a commotion in the main house; folks running to and fro, Stephen out by the pump getting water, Rachel rushing through the kitchen like someone was chasing her. She burst through the door, a cup of water in one hand, a clean rag in the other.

"Somebody hurt?" Mark asked.

"It's Joel! He came back. Mark, he's hurt bad." Her face screwed up like she would cry, but then she didn't. "Come with me, maybe he's awake by now."

He followed Rachel into the small building she shared with Joel. He still couldn't believe his friend was foolish enough that he hadn't married the girl. How could he sleep next to a woman like that and not want her?

Joel lay in the bed, eyes closed. Mark feared for a moment that he was dead, until he saw the rise and fall of Joel's chest. Hume Stogdon sat next to him, face pinched with worry.

"What happened to him?" Mark asked.

"Don' know exactly. He didn' manage ta talk none. Gailey brought 'im home, half dead. Somebody whacked him good." Stogdon gently touched Joel's chin and turned his head to the right. Mark squinted, bent down to look. There was a huge, crescent-shaped gash at the base of Joel's skull, surrounded by swollen tissue and bloody, matted hair. The wound had left a blood spot on the pillow. As Mark watched, it wept a bloody tear which slid down the back of Joel's neck.

"Dear God," he whispered.

Rachel gently but firmly brushed him aside. First, she lifted the cup to Joel's lips, and, although he still slept, he swallowed a little. Then, with the rag and the water Stephen had brought, she began to clean Joel's wound. He didn't so much as twitch.

Mark swallowed hard, his eyes beginning to sting. "Is he gonna be all right?"

Hume cleared his throat. "Nothin' to do now but wait," he said.

Joel did not wake up the next morning, nor by afternoon. He seemed to be in a deep, peaceful sleep. But he didn't stir, not even when Hume stuck his finger with a pin.

"We'd best get the doctor," Hume said.

"No." Rachel's voice was quiet but firm. She held one of Joel's hands in both of hers.

"He's hurt, Rachel," Mark said gently. "We gotta try an' he'p him."

"There's nothing a doctor from this time can do, Mark. And he might make it worse."

Hume and Stephen exchanged odd looks.

"We at least oughta try—"

Rachel cut Mark off. "You remember Abraham Lincoln? You learned about him in school, Mark."

Mark wracked his memory. The name was familiar. . . . "Oh yeah! He was a president, wasn't he, freed the slaves?"

"There's never been no President Lincoln," Hume said.

"It's a story," Rachel said. "And in the story, somebody shot President Lincoln in the head."

"Did he die?" asked Stephen.

"Yes, but not immediately. They brought in doctors. One of them . . . one of them stuck an instrument in his wound, trying to get the bullet out. Stuck it right into the hole in his head. Probably killed him right then."

"A dreadful story," Hume said. "Ye say they taught this ta childern in school?" He frowned.

Rachel stood up. "I had this morbid history teacher, he used to tell us all kinds of godawful things. What's a doctor gonna do for him, anyway? Bleed him? He's done plenty of that on his own. Clean his wound? I've done that. Give him some kind of horrible medicine? I don't think so." She put her hands on her hips, as if challenging anyone to question her.

"She may be right," Mark said. "Besides, it might not be safe. People are sure lookin' fer him."

Hume and Stephen reluctantly agreed.

Suddenly Rachel was all business. "Good. Now, the most important thing is we've got to keep him hydrated."

"Uh, keep 'im what?" Hume frowned.

"We've gotta make sure he drinks water. If you pour a little bit at a time in his mouth, he swallows. If he doesn't drink, he'll die. And he'll need some broth, I'll start making that right away. He's gotta eat. We don't know how long he's gonna be asleep, so we've got to be sure we roll him over in bed from time to time, put him on his side so he doesn't get bedsores or blood clots. And we need to bend his arms and legs every day so his muscles don't shrink up too much."

The men, Mark included, were staring at her in amazement. "How do you know all this, ma'am?"

Her chin tilted up, a little defensively. "Reruns of *St. Elsewhere.*"

Joel didn't wake up the next day. Or the day after that. Mark, Rachel, and the Stogdons took care of him around the clock, but mostly it was Rachel. Her quiet devotion was amazing to Mark. He promised himself that if Joel didn't marry her when he woke up, he'd have to beat the hell out of him.

In the early evening of the third day, he brought Rachel some bread and cheese. It didn't seem like she was eating much of anything lately. He found her cleaning Joel's head wound, her face pinched with worry.

"It's still bleeding," she said, not looking up at Mark. "It shouldn't still be bleeding. It just won't close."

"Haid wounds is like that," Mark said, not knowing what else to say.

"Go ask Hume if he has any whiskey, would you?"

Mark blinked. "Uh, sure, ma'am, sure."

"And please stop calling me ma'am. I'm only seventeen, for God's sake. Call me Rachel, okay?"

"Yes, ma—Rachel."

He brought the whiskey back promptly, with Hume and Stephen in tow. They said they wanted to check on Joel, but Mark was pretty sure they were curious about the liquor. He halfway expected Rachel to guzzle it down; she surely deserved it by now. Instead, he was surprised to see her take out her sewing kit and pour a little over the needle. Without a word, she threaded it up with green cotton thread, and sat on the bed next to Joel. Rachel took a deep, shuddering breath, and started to sew up the back of Joel's head.

Stephen turned quickly away. Mark fought down a wave of nausea, but watched, fascinated, as did Hume. Rachel's face was white, her lips pursed as she worked. Mark wondered if she were trying not to puke herself.

When she was finished, she wiped down the wound with whiskey, and redressed it. Joel hadn't twitched throughout the entire process.

"Well done," Hume said.

"It's the best I can do," Rachel said brusquely. "Now, remember everybody, you wash your hands before you touch Joel's food or his wound. Especially if you've just cleaned up after him. With soap, you understand?"

They all meekly agreed. As Mark watched her bustle about the room, he realized that Rachel was keeping so busy to avoid thinking about what might happen to Joel. Her tough shell was fragile. He silently promised himself that he'd do his best to keep her from shattering.

Days slipped into weeks, and still Joel slept. Rachel seemed pleased with the way his wound was healing. But they were running low on supplies; soap, flour and salt. Mark volunteered to go into town and get it.

Since there had been freezing rain in the night, he took Gailey, who was always sure-footed on the ice. Though he was bundled up in long johns, two shirts and a greatcoat, the icy wind bit his cheeks and chilled him to the bone. He took a back way through the forest and joined the road some distance from the farm. He was nearly to Adairville when he met two men in the road, riding the opposite way.

"Hello, sir," one called out. Mark didn't like the look of them. Big, rough fellows, unshaven and dirty. The one speaking had the flat, glittery eyes of a snake.

"Hello," Mark called back. His hand crept to the pistol hidden in his greatcoat.

"Where are ye comin' from?" asked Snake-eyes. A strange question, Mark thought. It put him even more on edge.

"A farm," he answered. "On my way ta town fer supplies."

"Whose farm?" It was the second man who asked, a watery-eyed redhead with a nose like a potato.

"Why is that yer concern?" Mark was surprised by his own boldness.

The redhead's eyes narrowed, and he looked like he was considering violence. But Snake-eyes smiled, an unpleasant, gap-toothed grin. "Easy, fella. We're jes lookin' fer a man, tha's all. We've got a message fer him."

"An' who might this man be?" Mark asked.

"Who might ye be?" asked Redhead. Mark noticed that the man's hand was under his coat.

"My name is Mark Ryder," he said loudly. "Known as Wesley Pike's dawg."

Redhead's hand slowly emerged from his coat. Snake-eyes had gone a little pale. "Beggin' yer pardon, sir," he said. "Perhaps ye can help us, then. We're lookin' fer a traitorous bastard callin' 'imself Matthew Crenshaw. Ye seen 'im, Mister Ryder?"

"No. But if I do, I'll put a bullet between his eyes."

The two men smiled. One gave him the sign of the Mystic Clan—not the new one that Rachel had come up with and they had passed around, but the one with which the Clan had replaced the original—and, biting back his disgust, Mark gave the returned gesture.

"Ye do that, ye bring his filthy carcass to the Grand Council. There's a bounty out on his haid."

Mark nodded. "G'day, then."

"Good day, Mister Ryder."

Mark's heart pounded against his ribs as he urged Gailey down the road. He wondered how bad this was all going to get.

Two months passed without Joel awakening.

Mark watched as things went rapidly downhill. More and more Mystic Clan members trickled into Adairville, making no secret of the fact that they wanted Matthew Crenshaw, dead or alive. People were scared of them. Many of the Stogdons' neighbors, formerly friendly and helpful, stopped coming around. One family, called the Reynolds, showed up en masse, seemingly for the sole purpose of interrogating the Stogdons about what had become of their tutor, Joel Biggs. Mark wondered how many more of their friends and neighbors were in league with the Mystic Clan.

There were three other families in the area who were under the scrutiny of the Mystic Clan, each having had boarders or workers from outside the area who had recently moved on. As the whereabouts of these individuals was ascertained, the families were left in peace and all scrutiny shifted to the Stogdons. Not only was the mysterious Mr. Joel Biggs still missing, but, according to several unnamed sources, he bore a strong resemblance to the wanted poster featuring Matthew Crenshaw, steam doctor and con man.

Soon the whole community was polarized. Half the townsfolk shunned the Stogdons. The other half, the loyal friends of the Stogdons, began to increase the frequency of their visits to the farm to offer support as they saw the attention the place was getting from the unsavory elements coming in from out of town.

With Hume's permission groups of friends took turns spending the night in order to help protect the family. Soon the barn and outbuildings were being used as sleeping quarters and the farm took on the aspect of a fort, with sentries always on guard. Through it all, they kept Joel's presence a secret. He and Rachel were moved to the loft in the main house. Hume and Stephen took to sleeping in the parlor, while Mark took the dwelling Rachel and Joel had shared.

When Crenshaw was not delivered to them, the Clan members began to take action. It started out small; a broken window at the Stogdon home, a shop belonging to one of the Stogdons' friends defaced with paint, a sheep stolen from a friendly neighbor. It soon got worse. A couple of townsfolk loyal to the Stogdons were beaten and robbed in the night, threatening letters pinned to their chests. A flock of chickens was slaughtered, their carcasses hung in trees near the Stogdon house like Christmas decorations. A barn burned. Some people whispered of rapes, and other acts of barbarism. Rumors and accusations were like weeds cropping up everywhere.

Mark knew that when spring arrived, and that would not be long in coming, the Stogdons' friends, mostly farmers, would be returning to work in their fields. Then he and Rachel and the Stogdons would have to make do for themselves again, and things were bound to get tough. He began to think of ways of sneaking Joel and Rachel away from the farm and perhaps hiding out in Alexandria or Nashville, but, in considering this, he immediately thought of the Stogdons—he couldn't just abandon them to the Mystic Clan.

Rachel came up with another of her wonderfully brilliant and devious ideas, and enlisted a family friend of the Stogdons in Athens, Georgia, to write Hume a letter in Joel's name, filled with news about a sick brother and a new teaching position. Rachel was frustrated with the length of time it took for the plan to play out completely, being used to mail moving over the Internet at light-speed. Finally the letter arrived and news of it was leaked through town. This seemed to take a little of the pressure off the Stodgon family. But not enough.

One day while Mark was in town for supplies, he decided to stop by Brownfort's Inn for a glass of ale. A pint would warm his belly nicely for the trip back, and, besides, the inn was an excellent place to put his ear to the ground for news of the Clan and their doings.

The inn was packed. Not surprising on such a bitter day; many had nothing better to do, and the fires of the inn were welcoming. But there was something going on. Men were clustered in groups, looking at something. Shouts of laughter rose up around the room. Mark sidled over to the nearest group and peered over a chuckling fellow's shoulder.

It was the tabloid, *American Police Gazette,* they were looking at. A notorious scandal sheet, often filled with lies and slander.

The man noticed Mark looking and grinned at him. "Have ye seen this yet?" he asked.

"Don't believe I have," said Mark.

"Why, i's the tale of Jarrett Cotten, an' how he planned ta blow up the whole South on Christmas Day. Gonna start a nigger rebellion, he was." Another of the men guffawed.

"An' . . . an' you don' think it could be true?" Mark asked.

"Hell no! Who's ever heard o' such a thing?"

" 'Sides, i's in the *American Police Gazette.* Any fool knows that most o' what they print is a steamin' pile o' horseshit."

"It does seem ridiculous," Mark said, swallowing hard. "Do they say where they got their information?"

"Oh, some book by that eedjit Matthew Crenshaw folks been askin' after 'round her o' late. D'ye know what Cotten was arrested for? Horse theft. Tha's a far cry from explodin' half the goddam country."

The man and his buddies laughed again.

Mark stepped back, rubbed his face with his hands. He'd never, ever expected something like this to happen. Joel had talked about this event in history countless times. It was the Crenshaw book that brought down the Mystic Clan. He'd been certain of that. But what if Joel had been wrong? What if he hadn't known the whole story, and something else had happened to defuse the horrible plot? Worse yet, what if his or Joel's presence here had changed things forever? What if they'd messed things up so bad that the plot wouldn't be stopped at all?

Mark felt sick to his stomach, and a little dizzy. He decided to take a pass on the ale. He scanned the room once more, and spotted a few men in the corner he knew to belong to the Mystic Clan. They weren't laughing. They weren't laughing at all. Mark made his way quickly to the door.

The Stogdons listened to Mark's story with concern, and they had something to tell him as well. The two thugs who had stopped Mark on the road nearly two months ago had come to the farm, demanding to see Joel Biggs.

"We told them Joel Biggs returned ta his family home in Athens, Georgia," Stephen said with a smile, "and after a time, they moved on."

"I could tell they wanted to search the farm, but I'da shot 'em first," Hume growled.

"I didn't see them because I was hiding with Joel," Rachel said as she came into the parlor.

"Stephen saw 'em comin' an' didn't like the look of 'em," Hume said. "We decided we just as soon they not see a girl as purdy as Missus Biggs here."

Rachel's face was drawn and tired and she chewed her lip as

she listened to Mark's news. She had no comment and there was an awkward silence which Mark broke.

"If Rachel's gonna be up in that loft there watching over Joel," he said, "she oughta have a gun.

"D'ye know how ta handle one?" Hume asked Rachel.

"Not a flintlock," she said, then added quickly, "You can teach me."

Her reaction seemed curious to Mark, but then what about their present circumstances wasn't extraordinary?

"I could teach ye," Stephen offered suddenly.

"Whatever. I want to start today."

It was Mark who gave Rachel her first lesson in early-eighteen-hundreds weaponry.

Hume had given her a small rifle that had been Stephen's when he was a boy. He had also insisted that Stephen help him rebuild a collapsing wall of the henhouse. Mark suspected that Hume had noticed how much Stephen yearned for Rachel, and was trying to save him trouble and embarrassment.

She was a quick study, and a good shot.

"The most important thing," he told her, "is ye can't be afraid ta shoot. If a man is comin' at ye with evil intent, ye've gotta be able ta shoot ta kill. D'ye think ye can?"

Rachel's eyes glinted. "If anyone tries to hurt Joel, I'll blow his goddam head off."

One night Goebel Price and a couple of his friends, some of those who had helped spread the false hand signals and phrases, came to the house. "There's been a gun battle in town among members o' the Mystic Clan," he said. "It seems there was some sort o' disagreement 'bout the hand signals and secret phrases. Five o' the Clan were killed, several others left town. We been seeing this brewin' fer some time."

"Yew an' some o' the boys been stirrin' thin's up?" Mark asked, his eyes narrowed to slits.

"No sir, we was thinkin' 'bout doin' that very thin' though, 'specially now that they're feelin' threatened, but was gonna ask ye fer permission first."

"Gonna git yerse'ves killed!" Hume rumbled.

"Well, what'd we cook that up fer if we weren't gonna stir it an' serve it up?"

Mark put his hand on Goebel's shoulders. "You've done enough, an' yer efforts have begun ta bear fruit. Ye do like we tol' ye an' keep yer haids down while there's so much Clan in the area."

When Mark looked over at Rachel, he saw her smile for the first time in a month.

Late one afternoon, after spending a freezing few hours patrolling the farm with a rifle and a pair of pistols, Mark came into the parlor to sit by the fire and warm up. Hume was taking his turn as watchdog, and Stephen was in the barn cleaning stalls. Mark was surprised to see Rachel there, sitting by the fire, a shawl wrapped around her like a cocoon.

"Afternoon," he said, smiling. She glanced up at him, and her face was streaked with tears.

Mark's heart flip-flopped. "Oh, no. Joel didn't. . . ."

"No. No, he's the same."

Mark closed his eyes and sagged into the nearest chair. "Thank God."

Her eyes were sharp with pain and anger. "Thank God? He might never wake up, Mark. Have you looked at him? He's wasting away. He's lost God knows how much weight. He doesn't respond if you talk to him, touch him, even slap him. He's just not there."

"He's there, Rachel. Joel's in there somewheres. He'll wake

up, ye'll see."

She sighed, rubbed her temples. "Mark, do you remember anything about comas? Do you even remember what the word means?"

"I's where ye fall asleep for a long time," he said, feeling foolish.

"It's not sleep. Your body shuts down. Sometimes, a lot of the time, people don't wake up from a coma. They waste away and die. Or they linger for years, just withering up like a dead leaf."

Her face crumpled, and she let out a miserable sob. Mark got up and sat beside her, taking her hands in his.

"Ye can't think that way, Rachel. He'll wake up. He's a tough son of a bitch. Why, the Joel I know wouldn' dream of doin' somethin' as boring as dyin' of a coma."

That made Rachel smile, a little. "What was he like, Mark? What was he like as a boy?"

Mark frowned, hesitated. Should he tell her the truth?

Yes. He owed her that.

"He was a bully, at first. Meanest little bastard in town." He expected surprise from her, maybe even anger. Instead, she nodded.

"I can see that. He's still got a streak of it."

Mark scowled. "Has he hurt ye, Rachel? 'Cause if he has—"

"No, no. Nothing like that. But he's tried to . . . to control me now and then, I guess. Tried to make me fit into his view of things."

"Yeah, that was Joel all over. He broke my arm when we was kids, just ta prove he was the toughest boy in school. But after that, we became friends.

"He was smart. He still is, but when he was a kid, it really shone outta him. He loved that book about Jarret Cotten an' America's Powder Keg, an' he read it over an' over. Made me read it a bunch o' times too. He was strong. He could take anything, any kinda pain, pro'bly 'cause of the way his ol' man used ta beat 'im."

Rachel's mouth turned down. "Was his dad an alcoholic?"

"Tha's puttin' it mildly." Mark shook his head. "I don' think I ever seen the man sober. But Joel jus' took it, took whatever 'is dad dished out ta him. Joel was brave. Not like me. I was a snively little coward. Not that I'm much better now."

Rachel squeezed his hand. "Don't sell yourself short, Mark. I think you're as brave as they come."

Mark's face got hot, but he grinned. "Thank ye," he mumbled. "But Joel was always the brave one, the one wit' the ideas an' the plans. If he'd stayed here, he'd pro'bly be runnin' this town an' a few others ta boot."

"But he didn't. He went back home, and turned into a drunk." She didn't say the words with any venom or contempt. She said them as a matter of fact.

"Yeah."

"Why, do you suppose, Mark? He had to see what it did to his father. . . ."

Mark rubbed his chin. "Well, at first I s'pose he did it ta prove he was as tough as his daddy. Then after a while, he pro'bly jes couldn't stop. Or—"

Mark cut himself off. *It's not my place to talk of such things,* he thought.

"Or what?"

"Or maybe. . . . A boy's daddy is important in 'is life, Rachel. Mine was like a ghost in my house, a shadow, so I was always hungry for somethin' I didn' have. Tha's pro'bly why I took such a shine ta Wesley. An' why he took a shine ta me.

"Me'be Joel felt like drinkin' was the only way he could be close ta 'is daddy. The only way he had ta be like him. Lord, I sound like an eedjit." He stared into the fire.

Rachel kissed his cheek, soft as summer rain. "You're not an idiot, Mark. You're a man with a kind soul." Silently, she got up and left the room.

Mark stared down at his callused hands in his lap, the memory of her kiss still lingering on his face. For just a little while, everything was all right.

26

Mark watched as their situation got even worse for a little while. Then, suddenly, things got better. Word through the grapevine said that all but the lowest-level Mystic Clan members had been recalled; a huge meeting was being set up to straighten out the confusion over the secret phrases and hand signals once and for all. It seemed to Mark the town of Adairville breathed a collective sigh of relief.

But damage had been done. There were neighbors and friends who would never trust each other again. The place felt different to Mark. Sadder, more cynical. It hurt him to think that, in some way, he and Joel had brought sorrow down on these people.

But he carried on. They all did. The Stogdons and, of course, Rachel, caring for Joel day in and day out.

Early one morning, Mark was bringing a bucket of water up to the loft for Rachel to wash Joel. He watched her finish shaving Joel, her movements spare and neat. She brushed his hair, then began to open his nightshirt for a sponge bath. There was no tenderness in her touch, just efficiency. The sight unnerved Mark—he'd once seen an undertaker wash a dead man in the same way.

She can't fawn over him twenty-four hours a day, he thought. He knew Rachel hadn't given up on Joel. He'd seen her at night, holding Joel's hand, talking softly to him as she stroked his brow.

He poured the water in the washbowl and prepared to leave. It embarrassed him to see Joel naked and helpless.

"Thanks, Mark," Rachel said, as she dunked a washrag in the chilly water.

"My pleasure, Rachel." She rubbed the wet washrag briskly over Joel's chest.

"Sumbish. Thass cole," Joel grumbled.

Joel opened his gummy eyes a slit as he spoke. *What's wrong with my voice?* he thought groggily. *Oh God, I can't be drunk—*

Rachel let out an ear-shattering scream. Then she had his face in her hands, staring at him, her nose inches from his. "Joel? Joel, can you hear me?"

"Yeah," he croaked. She suddenly burst into tears, and threw her arms around his neck, lying across his bare chest. He raised his arms to embrace her. They felt weird; heavy. His hands felt like they were in heavy gloves.

"Whass wrong with me?" he asked into her hair. "Am I sick?" His tongue felt thick in his mouth. Rachel didn't answer, she just held him tighter, her chest hitching. He stroked her hair clumsily, then frowned. Her hair seemed longer. It felt like it was past her shoulders, down almost to her shoulder blades, but that wasn't possible, was it?

Mark's face loomed over Rachel's shoulder. Mark looked tired, haggard and thin. "Joel, you—you've been asleep for a while."

"How long?"

"Three months," Rachel whispered in his ear.

Joel talked quietly with Rachel as Mark ran out to get the Stogdons. His voice was still slurred, and it didn't seem to be getting any better. Rachel helped him sit up. His head whirled for a moment, and he closed his eyes until it passed.

Rachel told him about his head wound. Joel had no memory of that. He had no memory of anything after delivering the book to the publisher. He raised his hand to the back of his head, and felt the thick, raised scar through his hair. It felt strange, like part of someone else's body.

His arms still felt like rubber, and his fingers weren't working quite right. A phrase popped into his head. *Permanent brain damage.* He shoved it quickly from his mind.

Joel wanted to ask Rachel so many questions, about what had been going on in the past three months. But while he had no trouble forming the sentences in his head, they just weren't coming out of his mouth right. Even if he could find the words, Rachel probably wasn't the one to answer him. She kept stopping in midsentence to stare into his eyes, kiss his lips, or give him another bone-crushing hug. "I love you," she whispered in his ear, over and over again.

"Lub you too," he said, his lips against her slender neck. And it was true, God help him.

She threw herself against him, pushing him back down on the bed. Rachel was stretched out on top of Joel, kissing his face and lips, raining hot teardrops on his skin. He quickly realized that at least one part of him was working just fine.

This is wrong, he thought, as his arms slid around her, as he kissed her back hard. *This is wrong,* as his hands slipped down her back to cup her small, perfect ass.

The door flew open, and Hume, Stephen, and Mark burst in. Rachel moved off him, smoothing down her rumpled dress. Joel sat up as quickly as he could, making sure the covers were well over his waist.

Mark had a huge, silly grin on his face. Stephen looked a little sick. "Ah, Joel, glad yer awake, but maybe we should come back later?" asked Hume, trying not to smile.

"No, s'okay," Joel said. Rachel frowned and turned away.

The men bombarded him with questions. Did he feel all right? Did his head hurt? Was he hungry? Thirsty? What was the last thing he remembered? Joel answered, hating his slurred voice.

"That's enough," Rachel snapped, interrupting Stephen. "Joel needs to rest."

Joel took her hand and smiled at her. "Been resting th'ee monz," he said. "Got questions."

Joel's heart began to pound. "Did the book get pullished?"

"It did," said Mark.

Why was he looking at the floor?

"Ever'things 'kay then?"

Silence. Finally, Hume spoke. "Well. Not exactly."

Listening to Hume's voice, hearing about the *American Police Gazette* version of the Crenshaw story, the Clan's assault on the town, the treachery of friends and neighbors, Joel felt himself sinking. He felt like he did that day in the deadfall, limbs breaking beneath him, dropping farther and farther away from the sun.

Hume was finished. Joel said nothing. Rachel still held onto his hand, and he pulled gently but firmly away.

"Don't you worry none, Joel," Mark said. "We've got spies. We'll figger out what them vipers is up to, an' we'll stop 'em. Just 'cause the book didn't work don't mean they won."

Joel let out a deep, shuddering sigh. " 'M tired," he said.

"We'll let ye alone, then," Hume said. He shepherded the men out the door. Rachel sat on the bed beside him, and kissed his cheek.

"I need to be 'lone," Joel said. He couldn't meet her eyes, but he saw the tight, wounded twist of her mouth as she left the room.

Everyone was so goddam happy he was awake. Hume and Rachel cooked special meals for him. Stephen shot him a fat rabbit. Each act of kindness made Joel feel a little more worthless. While he'd slept, men and women had risked their lives for him. Some had even died. And for what? Nothing he'd done had changed a thing. For all he knew, the uprising would still take place, the cities of the South would burn, the fields would turn red with blood. All he had done was worthless. He was worthless.

And then there was his body. Nothing worked right. Days went by, weeks, and still his words were slurred. He could walk, but his gait was wobbly and unsteady, like a sailor on a turbulent sea. His hands were clumsy, his grip weak. He was thin, skinnier than he'd ever been in his life. His ribs stood out like a starving hound's. His hipbones like razor blades. He felt repulsive.

Rachel insisted he wasn't. She said he was handsome, brilliant, brave. Over and over again, she said she loved him. He was sure he could sense pity coming off of her in waves. He spoke to her politely but distantly, never returning her kisses. When they slept, he kept his back to her. When he saw the raw-edged hurt in her eyes, he told himself it was all for the best.

The thing Joel wanted most was to be alone. He wanted to walk the farm and the woods, perhaps to take Gailey and ride the back roads in the cool winter air until his head cleared. But he couldn't. A small but significant number of the Clan was still about, Hume had told him. There was a hefty price on Matthew Crenshaw's head. If he were spotted, his life would be over. If he were found on the farm, Joel knew the Clan would kill them all. Joel Biggs was a prisoner. In his mind he crawled around the depths of that deadfall, sinking ever lower.

One cold, miserable afternoon, Joel crashed through the last few remaining sticks and hit the fetid bottom. He was alone in the parlor, staring into the fire, as Rachel bustled around the kitchen preparing dinner. She'd given up trying to talk with him some weeks ago, and he was grateful for that.

He heard the front door slam, and Mark's voice greeting Rachel. Mark had been to town, and he'd promised to bring Joel a newspaper and some sweet rolls. Joel had thanked him, feeling nothing but bitter envy of Mark's freedom.

Mark was excited as he burst into the parlor, his eyes shining like they had when he was a boy. "I heard some news today!" he said, unsmiling. "I can't say it's good news, Joel."

Joel rubbed his temples. He'd had a throbbing headache all day; he seemed to get them a lot lately. He didn't want to hear what Mark had to say. He wanted a drink.

"The Grand Plot," Mark said. "It's still on. But they've moved it up. Now it's gonna happen on March thirtieth, Easter Sunday. And . . . Wesley's helped the Mystic Clan set itself up in the old Outlaw Cave on the Mississippi."

Mark looked at Joel, waiting for him to say something. Rachel stood in the kitchen door looking pale and shocked.

Joel slowly got to his feet. He walked past Mark, past Rachel, and took his greatcoat from a hook by the kitchen door.

"Joel! Where y'goin'?" Mark asked.

Joel let out a hollow laugh, but didn't turn around.

"Gettin' th' hell outta here, Mark. I b'lieve I'll go to town."

Mark stared after Joel's back in shock. He blinked when the door slammed. Mark turned to look at Rachel. Her face was drawn and desperate.

"Don't worry. I'll get 'im." Mark tried to smile at her, then trotted out into the cold wind after Joel.

"Hey! Hey Joel, wait!" Joel, tromping toward the stables, didn't turn around. Mark put a hand on his shoulder. "Joel!"

Joel kept walking. "Go back inside, Mark."

"I can't let ye go, Joel. Ye'll be recognized in town, ye know that. They'll kill ye soon as look at ye."

"They won't rec'nize me. Looka me, Mark. I've los' thirty pounds. I look like death." He stroked the ratty beard he'd grown since he woke up and Rachel stopped shaving him every day. "They can't even see m'face anyway." Joel turned around and started walking again.

Mark grabbed his arm. "Ye're not goin', Joel. I—I'm warnin' ye, I'll stop ye if I have to." Mark's heart was pounding wildly in his chest, his fists clenched.

Joel wheeled and stared at him, eyes unnaturally wide. He blew white plumes from his nose with a snort, like an angry bull. Mark felt an old, humiliating fear creeping into him. He remembered, suddenly, the greenstick "snap" of his arm breaking as Joel twisted it harder and harder. But he stood his ground. Joel grinned.

"What'cha gon' do, Mark? Gonna knock me out?"

"Yeah, if'n I have to."

Joel's hand flashed out from beneath his greatcoat, and suddenly there was a pistol in Mark's face, the barrel inches from his forehead. "I said go back inside, Mark. I've gotta get outta here or I'll lose my fuggin' min'."

Mark's eyes narrowed. "I can't b'lieve ye're doin' this, Joel."

Joel's hand was shaking, as it always did these days, but the gun stayed in Mark's face. "You'd better believe it."

Mark's stomach knotted up painfully. He could feel a trickle of sweat running down his temple, growing instantly cold in the frigid air. "Ye won't shoot me, Joel. I know that. Now c'mon back in. Rachel's waitin' for ye."

Joel gripped his wrist with his other hand, steadying the gun. He cocked it. "Go 'way, Mark," he said softly, his tone flat and dead. "Go 'way b'fore I blow your brains out."

Mark wondered briefly if Joel's palsy would cause him to pull the trigger whether he meant to or not. Even so, he tried to stare him down. He really tried. But Joel's eyes had grown opaque, like those of a reptile. Finally, Mark turned away. Without looking back, he went into the house.

Meeting Rachel's expectant eyes was one of the hardest things Mark had ever had to do. "He wouldn't come with me," he mumbled.

Rachel's chin tilted up, her small fists clenched. "I'll go get the silly sumbitch."

"No! It ain't safe for ye. Joel—he stuck a gun in my face."

"Jesus." Rachel looked sick with disbelief. Mark knew he couldn't let her down.

"I'll go, Rachel. I'll let him get a little bit down the road, an' I'll follow him. I'll stop him before he can get into any trouble."

"Good idea. I'm comin' with you."

Mark sighed, rubbed his face with his hands. "No, Rachel. Ye can't."

Her eyes flashed. "I can and I will. If you don't take me with you, I'll just saddle up after you leave and follow." She glared a challenge at him.

Mark found himself suddenly weary. "Fine. But ye wear yer coat an' ye keep your face hid, y'hear me? There's rogues an' ruffians ever'where these days. An' if we get inta town, ye let me do the talkin'."

She appeared to be considering an argument, when abruptly, she smiled. "Yes, sir. Just a minute, I've gotta go get something out of the loft." Mark watched her climb up, and wondered if they'd come back to the Stogdon farm in a couple of caskets.

Rachel came back down a few minutes later wearing her jeans, flannel shirt and boots, her hair tucked up under a mangy-looking beaverskin hat.

Good, Mark thought, *she could pass for a boy.*

Without a word, she pulled on her traveling coat, and Mark accompanied her out into the cold.

The Stogdons stopped them on the way to the stables to ask what was going on, and Mark quickly explained. Stephen volunteered to come along. Mark saddled up Ruffian, the Stogdons' aging gelding, and Rachel rode with him. Stephen took the Stogdons' old mare, Beryl. Joel had taken Gailey.

Stephen didn't like the idea of Rachel coming along, and he said so. It wasn't safe, he insisted. She could get hurt.

"Just watch out for yourself, Stephen," she snapped. "I'll be fine." The young man looked wounded, as he always did if Rachel spoke sharply to him. *Poor devil,* Mark thought.

Mark had noticed the bulge at the waistband of Rachel's jeans, and wondered what, exactly, she was packing. He had little doubt that she could hit anything she aimed at, but he wondered, if it came down it, if she could kill a man.

Joel walked toward Brownfort's Inn like he was walking to his own hanging. Some small, rational corner of his brain screamed *what are you doing, stop, stop, stop.* It quickly washed away in a tide of self-pity and anger.

Stepping up onto the puncheon walk surrounding the building, Joel reached for the door. It burst open, the smells of wood smoke, tobacco, cheap liquor, and unwashed bodies assaulting him. A din of noise accompanied the burly man who stepped outside. The fellow paused, looking Joel up and down, then nodded curtly and shuffled out into the night.

Joel took off his hat and stepped into the dim and smoky room, closing the door behind him. He hadn't been off the Stogdon farm in many weeks, and he had thought that the company of other men would make him feel better. But as a fellow passed close by, he shrank away. The other patrons looked like brutes to him, backward rednecks, idiots. He couldn't stand to look at them.

A fire burned on the hearth, heating the room oppressively in the cramped confines. His eyes teared from the heavy, bitter, smoke-charged air, and he took shallow breaths. Through the pall, he could see that the puncheon tables were all taken. He walked up to the bar, his feet crunching on the straw and sawdust strewn across the floor.

It occurred to Joel that he was feeling too much, smelling too much, seeing too much. His eyes hurt. His senses felt besieged. He perched himself on a bar stool—really just an up-ended log—and rubbed his oily face with his hands, ground his fists into his eyes.

What the hell am I trying to accomplish here? What the fuck am I doing? Joel had been desperate to get out, so desperate he'd pulled a gun on his best friend. But now that he was here, he had no idea what he wanted. Back at the Stodgon farm, the possibility of being recognized by the Clan meant nothing to him, but suddenly, it seemed very real. Joel felt like a spotlight was glaring down at him, and he glanced around nervously.

The bartender, a short, bug-eyed little fellow, stood in front of him, staring curiously. Suddenly Joel felt like an idiot. And what was he going to ask for—water? He swallowed hard.

"Uh, um. . . ."

The bartender stared, his eyes like a grounded fish's.

Joel got an idea. "Got any coffee?" He winced at his own slurred voice.

"Certainly," said the bartender. "Vandernoggin," he said to a scrawny teenaged boy, "run git the pot."

The boy slipped out through a back door and returned shortly with a blackened iron pot. The bartender took an earthenware mug from the shelves behind him, and the boy filled it with steaming black liquid from the pot, then set it on the bar before Joel.

"What do I owe you?" Joel asked, holding out a handful of coins.

The bartender smiled and waved it away. "Nothin'. Yer new in town."

Joel smiled grimly. He had seen the man before, several times, before his head injury, but the guy didn't recognize him. *Of course he doesn't. I look like shit. Even Moss wouldn't recognize me.* The thought of Moss gave him a stab of guilt about leaving Rachel alone. *She'll be fine, Mark'll take care of her. I won't be gone that long.*

He picked up his coffee, turned around, and leaned back against his bar stool. A few men were looking at him, including one he recognized as the town blacksmith. Two men put their heads together, still looking at Joel, and began to talk. Joel's heart began to pound. The bar stool log tipped over and slipped out from under him. Joel hopped to his feet, splashing hot coffee on his shirt. The bar stool hit the ground with a loud thump, and then everyone was looking at him.

He felt as if he were standing there naked. Hands shaking more than usual, he uprighted the bar stool. He took a sip of the coffee and made a face; it was bitter, burned, and stale. Joel had about talked himself into leaving, into heading back to the Stogdon farm and apologizing for acting like such an asshole, when someone got up from a corner table and left. Joel wavered a moment, then retreated toward the empty seat. His back to the corner, he scanned the room again.

Dropping his hat onto the table, he sat and sipped the nasty coffee, trying to listen to what was being said around him. There was so much noise, so many voices, but Joel couldn't seem to understand any of them. His ears refused to untangle the voices; they were one massive, intrusive roar.

A group of men at a nearby table noticed him staring and eyed him suspiciously, all but a massive guy with his back to

Joel. Joel dropped his eyes and stared at the oily sheen on his coffee, his stomach fluttering. His hands were slick with sweat. He tried to will himself to relax, but that only seemed to make things worse, and the strong coffee was beginning to rattle his nerves. His eyes jerked from table to table, certain he saw a gleam of recognition, a hostile glare, a gun beneath a greatcoat.

I need a drink, he thought, downing his coffee and getting up. *If I just take half a jigger, enough to settle my nerves, I'll be all right.*

He walked to the bar and ordered another coffee, asking the bartender to add a shot of whiskey to it this time.

I'll only drink half of it, he told himself. *And since it'll go down with coffee, the caffeine will cancel out the alcohol.*

That was utter bullshit, and a part of him knew it, but as he watched the bartender measure the oily, amber liquid into his mug, Joel knew it was just the kind of bullshit he was after right now.

He offered his coins once again, and this time the bartender chose one, a bronze coin bearing a picture of a horse. Returning to his seat, Joel sniffed the coffee. It had the kerosene smell of bad whiskey, but it made his stomach growl hungrily.

It's more medicinal than anything else.

He took the smallest sip he could, trying to swallow before he got a good taste of it. If he didn't taste it, he wasn't truly getting drunk.

I'm not really drinking.

Besides, he told himself, most of the alcohol was evaporating from the hot liquid before he could get it into his mouth.

It wasn't until he'd drunk half the mug that Joel realized he was beginning to relax—just beginning to. And if he drank the rest of it, he told himself, he would be feeling just fine. He would stop right there. It would be all he'd drink. It would be all he'd need.

But he hit the bottom of the mug, and his hands were still

shaking. They wouldn't stop shaking. He stared at the filthy-looking grounds at the bottom of the cup as delicious warmth spread from his stomach to his limbs. *I need one more, for my hands. But Christ, I can't take any more of this fucking coffee.*

So he ordered a shot, and was surprised to hear his mouth asking for a double. He stared at the liquid swirling in the glass, then slammed it back, ordering another before he went back to the table.

He sat down heavily, glaring down into his drink. "Sum-bitch," he said loudly.

"What's the matter, friend?"

The voice came from a slim, rabbit-eyed man standing nearby, seemingly looking for a place to sit. Joel tried to focus on him.

"I blew it," Joel said, chuckling darkly.

The man blinked. "Pardon me?"

Joel let out a loud, raucous laugh. "I messed up. Screwed up. Goofed. I made ter'ble mistakes. *Friend.*" His slur was worse, but at least the world had begun to grow soft, fuzzy edges. It wasn't streaming in at him like water through cheesecloth anymore.

The rabbit-man sat down and smiled solicitously. "Surely cain't be that bad. Let me buy ye another drink, an' we can talk 'bout it."

Joel looked him over. *He's gotta be a con man. Or a preacher. Or a snake-oil salesman. Or maybe he's hitting on me.* Joel snorted out a laugh, and the fellow raised an eyebrow. *But what the fuck, he's gonna buy me a drink.* "Sure, a'right."

Joel greedily drank what the man brought him, then closed his eyes, enjoying the vibration in his head. "I'm ready to listen," Rabbit-man said.

Joel opened his eyes. " 'M a terr'ble person, y'see. I've wasted m'life. 'M a loser. An' a drunk. Obviously." A bitter laugh. "I tried t'do somethin'. Tried to stop somethin' bad from hap'nin'. Wanted to save people, make a diff'rence. But nothin' I did changed anythin', y'see. I even had 'istory on my side an' I blew it. An' now ever'thin's worse than it was b'fore. I BLEW IT!" Joel bellowed the last three words and slammed his glass onto the table.

"My friend—" began Rabbit-man.

The huge man at the table across from him slowly turned around. Joel squinted at the angry, narrowed blue eyes in the big, red face. "You're feelin' awful damn sorry fer yerself, ain't ye, little man," Wesley Pike rumbled.

Joel stared at him. He smiled. *Wesley!*

"What the hell ye grinnin at, ye fool?" Wesley slowly rose to his feet.

Joel suddenly didn't know what to do, he couldn't seem to think straight. The grin slipped from his face.

Wesley took a step toward him. "I'll tell ye somethin', boy. Life is full o' loss an' pain. Life is full o' failure. But if yer a man, ye git up, wipe the dirt an' blood off, an' ye get on with it. Ye don' whine like a child with a bellyache, *Crenshaw.*"

Wesley said the name quietly but clearly. He leveled his raptor gaze on Joel. There was a Bowie knife in his hand. Rabbit-man, who'd been glancing nervously back and forth between Joel and Wesley, got up and scurried away.

Anger flashed through Joel like a lightning strike. "You don' know me!" he shouted. "You don' know anythin' about me! You're jus' a thug, an over-the-hill stickup-man with a bad leg. An' your plans weren't 'zackly a success either, were they? I didn' hear 'bout any spectac'lar revenge agains' Cotten. *You* blew it *too.* An' your brother was a fuckin' cannibal. You did the world a favor when you killed 'im."

That clearly surprised Wesley and he froze, his brow furrowed. But then he closed the space between them in a heartbeat. His huge arms shot out and grabbed Joel by the front of the shirt. He ripped Joel out of his seat and across the table, and suddenly he was inches from Wesley's furious, terrified face.

"Who are you?" Wesley hissed. "Tell me or I'll rip yer goddam head off yer shoulders an' throw it through the goddam window."

Joel felt his bladder let go. "You know who I am," he whispered.

Shaking, Wesley stared into his eyes. Suddenly his mouth dropped open, his eyes went wide. "Joel?" he whispered. "Joel Biggs?"

Joel managed a nod.

The whole barroom was staring at them. Wesley slowly set Joel back down, then stared the other patrons down until they turned back to their drinks. He sat at the table across from Joel.

"Why didn' ye tell me before?" he said, his expression unreadable, his voice still lowered to a whisper.

"I, uh, I didn't wanna reveal my 'dentity . . . the plot. . . ." Joel sounded to himself like he was talking with a mouthful of oatmeal.

Wesley's face twisted with disgust. "Yer sloppy drunk, Joel. An' ye didn't tell me who ye was 'cause ye was scared ta. Ye thought I might kill ye fer makin' me shoot Virgil all them years ago."

Not trusting himself to speak, Joel nodded.

Wesley was quiet for a moment, then he said, "There's Clan in the room, Joel, so keep yer voice low."

Wesley stared at him until he started to squirm. To Joel's immense surprise, tears welled up in the big man's eyes. He quickly blinked them away. "I hated ye fer 'while, Little Man. More fer turnin' yer back on me than fer makin' me kill Virg, I reckon. I got past it, though. I fergave ye fer that long time 'go.

But it looks like ye cain't fergive ye'self."

Hot tears rolled down Joel's face. "I shoulda stayed," he blubbered. "I shoulda stayed behin' with Mark."

"If ye had, ye would've ended up an outlaw like me," Wesley said. "If ye'd've lived that long. I prob'ly woulda killed ye if I'd found ye."

Joel's head swam as he tried to take in what Wesley was saying. He looked restlessly around, wishing desperately for another drink.

Wesley was smiling at him, in a strange, sad way. "But all that's in the past, ain't it. I'm glad ta see ye, Joel, even in this sad state."

"I's good to see you, Wes."

"So Joel Biggs is Crenshaw." Wesley's voice was barely a whisper. "I heard tell my dawg—Mark I mean—was here in Adairville. Knowin' Crenshaw was s'spected o' bein' in these parts, I figured Mark had teamed up wit' him ta make that book 'bout Cotten and the Mystic Clan. Figures it'd turn out ta be yew. Tol' me 'bout his plans ta write the damned thang. Couldn't convince him ta give it up. I tol' 'em I thought it was a damned fool idea, gonna git him killed. But he was smart an' stuck yer name on it—the Crenshaw name anyway. Got yer face fixed ta that name though. None too smart o' yew to let 'im do that."

Joel nodded his head in agreement—he *was* a fool. But dammit, the Crenshaw book had done *some* good and it had been a noble effort. "As ridiculous as folks think that book is, it's got the Mystic Clan so full o' mistrust it's like a snake bitin' at i's own tail. *They* think it's dangerous; dangerous enough they wanna *kill* me."

Wesley stared at Joel, clearly thinking about what he'd said. He seemed deep in thought for a moment, then he sighed heavily. "Rumor among the Clan has it Mark's known the where 'bouts o' Matthew Crenshaw all along 'cause he's been here in Adairville fer so long. I cain't have them thinkin' like that 'bout him. They keep that up, one day soon they come here an' kill 'im. I was sent ta look inta it, seein' as how he's my dawg. I'm s'posed ta capture Crenshaw if'n I kin, but I had it in my mind that I should kill him so's ta confuse the trail that leads ta Mark's part in this here."

Wesley said this so casually that Joel, in his drunken state, had a hard time taking it in. He was already a dead man—he knew that, but just how he would meet this fate had been unclear to him. He realized that death at Wesley's hands would be infinitely preferable to being captured by the Mystic Clan. All he had now were desperate questions with obvious answers, but Wesley didn't give him time to ask them.

"Heard Mark had 'im a woman, an' figured he was tryin' ta settle down an' have a fam'ly."

He's talking about Rachel. I guess Mark was moving in on her while I was asleep for the past three months. That no-good son of a bitch!

"Ye wouldn't know it, but I had a fam'ly once. No I ain't talkin' 'bout Virg . . . but a wife and kids. We raised Mark from jus' a pup. I miss my wife, Mary, somethin' fierce. She saved my life, an' fer all the prayin' she did, maybe my eternal soul too. She was a good woman. Never hurt nobody. Was Cotten's men as killed her."

Joel nodded his head again absently, thinking of Rachel and how she'd be better off with Mark anyway.

"Nothin' I kin do fer her now, but Mark. . . ."

It's true—Mark has a life worth saving. I'm just a worthless drunk, a mean little shit who idolized these brutal bastards. My life has caused nothing but pain. There's something right *about Wesley being the one to end it for me. Probably won't hurt too much being drunk like I am.*

Joel looked Wesley in the eye. "Do it now, Wes. You know what it'd be like if the Clan got a hold o' me."

"Don't interrupt me, boy." There was a troubled look in the big man's eyes. He chewed his lower lip. "Jus' hesh up and let me think."

Was the big man having trouble with the thought of committing murder? Mark had said Wesley's wife had gotten him to give up killing.

The outlaw was quiet for a long moment. Joel looked around nervously. Those who were watching them seemed less intent about it. Wesley still held the power to command by mere presence.

"I's true, what ye say 'bout that book. I's done more against the Clan than I thought it would. He'ped to further my own revenge too. Mark must have tol' ye somethin' 'bout my plans."

Joel nodded his head again.

Wesley leaned back, still turning something over in his mind. "With an extra little shove, that book might cause 'em even more grief. That an' you being Crenshaw makes me consider rethinkin' my own plans. . . ."

Maybe I've got a chance after all. "Wesley, you could help me get out of here."

Wesley ignored him. "If Mark's ever gonna have any peace, then I got ta git the whole Clan, and that book might jus' be the key 'cause it's got all the names and such like. Trouble is if i's gonna do any good, if we're gonna get 'em all, I got to be in two places at once."

"Just get up and walk out of here with me," Joel said.

Suddenly Wesley focused on Joel, his gaze withering. "Shut the hell up. I figure some part a yew wants Mark's plan ta work or ye wouldn't o' he'ped him, ye wouldn't've pretended ta be Crenshaw. Ye want my he'p, you want Mark's plan ta work, then dammit, yer gonna have to make a sacrifice *too.*"

"Mark's plan?"

Wesley ignored him.

"What are you talkin' 'bout?"

"Yer trouble Joel, jus' plain trouble fer Mark. A sloppy drunk like yew around. . . ."

"Don't turn me over to them," Joel said, tears in his eyes. "They'll torture an' kill me."

"There ain't no choice. The inn is full o' Clan, Joel. They came here with me, 'cause I came here ta git Matthew Crenshaw."

Joel lurched to his feet, looking around wildly. Wesley grabbed him and yanked him back down. "Sit down, ye eedjit. Ye cain't possibly get away. They're ever'where. That little fella ye was sittin' wit', the men I was wit', an' that table over there, plus some outside. Ye wouldn't get two steps out the door."

"Why?" Joel whispered.

Wesley's eyes glittered in the firelight. " 'Cause ye turned out ta be the one who was Crenshaw, an' I can see some good that'll come of it, Joel. They ain't gonna kill ye right away. They'll take ye back ta the cave. Couple months ago I cleared out the folks as was livin' there. I tol' the Grand Council that since America's Powder Keg was known ta folks 'cause of Crenshaw's book, that our ol' cave on the Mississippi would be the perfect new headquarters fer 'em. They took me up on it. Ain't that a laugh?"

Joel chewed his lips, trying not to cry.

"Now, listen to me, Joel. I need ye to listen. I think yer still wily enough to pull this off if ye ain't so drunk ye'll fergit what I'm sayin'. When ye get ta the cave, there's somethin' ye mus' do. Git away from 'em any way ye can, an' make yer way ta the dusty chamber where ye had the boys an' the Indian hid."

Joel's eyes widened, and Wesley gave a tiny smile. "Oh, I knew about that, Little Man. I knew it all along. I admired ye for yer resourcefulness. Listen, now. Git ta the chamber, an' bring somethin' ta light a fire wit' ye. Once yer there, ye'll know what ta do. Understand?"

Joel's mind was spinning like a hamster wheel. "Wes, there's gotta be another way—"

"I wish I could talk with ye more, Joel. Hell, I wish we could walk outta here together. But that cain't happen. There's somethin' I've gotta do after I leave here, an' it'll be the last thing I ever do, God willin'."

Joel's heart was hammering. Terror froze him from the inside out. "Wes!"

Wesley reached out and patted his shoulder, almost tenderly. "I wish ye well, Joel. I hope ye get outta this alive, but ye pro'bly won't. Ol' Virg'll have his revenge, most likely. They say his ghost haunts the Outlaw Cave." He paused, then said quickly. "But ye won't die for nothin'. I promise ye that."

Before Joel could say anything, Wesley was on his feet, pointing at him. "This man is Matthew Crenshaw!" he thundered. "Take 'im!"

Mark, Rachel and Stephen burst through the doors of the inn, but no one turned to look at them. Everyone seemed to be watching something going on in a far corner.

"Hang back," Mark told the other two. "I'll go see if I can talk some sense into him." Stephen nodded, looking around warily. Rachel's hand went to the lump tucked into her waistband. Mark grabbed her hand, and she glared at him.

"Be calm," he hissed. "Gettin y'self killed ain't gonna help Joel none." She nodded.

Mark cautiously crossed the barroom floor, glancing around him. He spotted a few men he knew to be Clan, but no Joel.

Then something was happening. A huge man—*Wes, my God, it's Wesley*—stood up in the far corner and roared, "This man is Matthew Crenshaw! Take 'im!" To Mark's horror, the man Wesley was pointing at was Joel.

Mark didn't have time to wonder why Wesley would do such a terrible thing. Everything was happening so fast. A pack of Clan rose up and surrounded Joel. Somebody hit him in the face. Somebody kicked him in the stomach.

"NO!" Rachel screamed. She lunged forward, hand reaching under her shirt. A thin, weasely little man lunged for her and grabbed her from behind, wrapping his arms around her waist and pinning her arms. "That's enough, lad," he laughed. "Crenshaw's a dead man. Ye try to save him, ye'll be one too."

"Let me go!" Rachel yelled, kicking and thrashing. Her hand clawed for the gun beneath her shirt, but she couldn't reach it.

Joel, blinking blood from his eyes, spotted her. "Leave her alone!" he yelled, struggling against the men who held his arms.

"Her?" said the man holding Rachel. Another Mystic Clan member, a short, whiskey barrel of a man, lumbered up to Rachel. Stephen lunged forward to stop him, and was met with a pistol in his face. Grinning, the short man yanked Rachel's hat from her head. Her hair fell to her shoulders in a dark, silky cascade. Laughing, Whiskey Barrel grabbed Rachel's face and tried to kiss her. Stephen shoved him away, and the man hit him in the temple with the butt of his pistol. Stephen crumpled to the floor.

Mark's eyes were wide, his heart pounding as he watched the nightmare scene unfolding. He had no idea what to do. He had a pistol in his belt, but the Clan was everywhere, armed to the teeth. If he drew on them, he'd be cut down in a second. "Wes—Jamus!" he shouted. "Do somethin'!"

Wesley whipped around and spotted Mark. "What the hell's goin' on, boy?" he bellowed. "Who is that girl?"

"I'm his wife!" Rachel yelled, struggling like a demon. A whoop went up from the Clan members, and they began to converge on her.

"Leave her be!" Wesley thundered.

"Don't think so, Jamus," Whiskey Barrel yelled back. "We're gettin' somethin' ta keep us amused on the trip back!" He reached for Rachel's chest. Her boot lashed out and caught him in the nose and he hit the floor, squirting blood.

"I said let her be! We're here for Crenshaw, nobody else!" Wesley towered over the men nearest him, his eyes blazing.

The weasely man didn't release his grip on Rachel. She stomped at his instep, but he was wearing buckskins and heavy boots. "I say we keep 'er," he said, then started chewing on her ear. Rachel screamed.

Whiskey Barrel got up off the floor, wiped at the blood on his face, and snarled at her.

Wesley came out of the corner like an angry bear, closing the distance between them frighteningly fast. He drew two enormous pistols from his belt and pointed one at each man. "Let her go. Now."

Whiskey Barrel let out a nasty laugh. "Jamus, they's one of you, an' fifteen o' us. Ye don' back down, ye'll be so full o' holes the wind'll whistle through yer cadaver when we hang it from the sign o' this here fine establishment."

Wesley jammed the barrel of the gun against the man's greasy forehead. "It's true, Gardner. If I pull this trigger, I'll surely be cut down. But not b'fore I turn yer haid into a purdy red flower."

Gardner stared into Wesley's eyes. "Let 'er go," he said to the weasely man holding Rachel.

With a curse, Weasel Man released her. Rachel spun on him and slugged him in the eye. He fell on his butt, hands over his face.

"Now git on outta here, Mark," Wesley said, his gun still in Gardner's face. "Take yer wife and friend wit' ye. I wish I had time fer a proper introduction and a good-bye, but I don't. Ye've been a good son, boy. I wish yew and yers well."

"Wes!" Mark didn't understand what was going on. What was Wesley trying to tell him, and why did he think Mark was married to Rachel?

"GO!" Wesley bellowed. Mark dragged Stephen to his feet and wrapped his arm around the half-conscious boy's waist.

"Come on, Rachel," Mark said.

"I'm not leaving Joel!" Her eyes were wide, fierce. He saw her hand once again creeping toward her waistband.

"No!" he hissed. "Do that and you'll die! We'll get him, Rachel. We'll go get him, I promise ye. But if we don't get outta here right now, we'll all be dead, ye understand?"

Silent tears welled up in Rachel's eyes and spilled down her cheeks. She took one last look at Joel, who was watching her with a look of sick despair on his bloodied face, and then followed Mark and Stephen out the door.

27

Rachel was silent on the ride home. She'd been near hysterical when the Clan took Joel away. Mark had had to physically stop her from going after them. She had argued long and hard that they could take Joel back if they struck immediately. Mark knew better. Not only were they miserably outnumbered, but Wesley Pike was clearly with the Clan. Going head to head with Wesley was suicide, he'd seen proof of that often enough. Despite the fact that Mary, Mark's adoptive mother, had convinced Wesley to stop killing long ago, the beast was still there, just under the surface. Wesley held it down with an almost supernatural force of will. If it ever broke free—well, God help anybody within range. Mark had grown to love Wesley Pike over the years, but he would never, ever stop fearing him.

Finally, Rachel had calmed down, or rather, given up. Her whole body had sagged, her eyes grown suddenly dull. Mark tried to tell her it would be all right, they could pull together a posse in just a matter of days, and they'd get Joel back from the Clan. But she didn't seem to be listening, and he didn't really believe it anyway. He was certain that Joel Biggs was a dead man. But they had to try.

A fist hit Joel in the back of the neck, and he fell on his face in the icy mud. Again. He'd been beaten, kicked, spit on, even pissed on in the past few hours. He wasn't really feeling it anymore.

As he tried to sit up and get to his feet—which wasn't easy with his hands tied in front of him—he thought back to the beating Mark had taken from Wesley and Virgil Pike in their first few days in the eighteen-hundreds. He thought of how he'd laughed. *Jesus. I was such a little asshole.*

The Clan members around him were roaring with laughter as he staggered to his feet. One of the men tripped him, and he fell heavily onto his side.

"Enough!" roared Wesley. He strode over and shoved the nearest men away from Joel, glaring around until the others backed off. "We promised ta bring him back ta the cave alive. Look at 'im, he's a miser'ble wreck. Ye beat 'im any more, ye'll be haulin' a corpse back. Ye wanna explain that ta Mister Cotten?"

Joel, wiping the mud from his face with his sleeve, couldn't believe what he'd just heard. *Jarrett Cotten? Out of jail? That wasn't anywhere in the history books. Jesus Christ, what have I done?*

Wesley shot him a quick, appraising look. Satisfied that Joel wasn't about to die, he mounted his horse again and turned away.

The potato-nosed Clan member next to Joel shot him a smirk. "Jes' you wait," he said. "They's gonna be breakin' Cotten outta jail any day now. When he gits a hold o' ye, he'll skin ye alive with a drawknife. If yer lucky."

He's not out yet. Thank God. Maybe there's still time to stop it from happening. Relief flooded through Joel, and a tiny smile quirked the corners of his lips. The potato-faced thug saw it, and slapped Joel hard upside the head.

Joel grunted, his ear ringing. He knew that the abuse he'd taken so far was nothing compared to what he would have received if Wesley hadn't been there to call off the dogs. But he knew Wesley would be parting company with the Clan posse soon. He just hoped they feared Cotten enough not to rip him limb from limb.

Joel worried, but in a distant, detached way. Despite the pain of dozens of cuts and bruises and a possibly broken nose, he was oddly serene. He couldn't be angry at Wesley, not after the big man had saved Rachel. His life was over, but Mark and Rachel and the Stogdons were safe. *She doesn't need me. She'll be so much better off with Mark. He'll take care of her.*

He just wished he'd had the chance to say good-bye.

No time was wasted when they reached the Stogdon farm. Hume rode out into the night to recruit as many of their neighbors as possible. Stephen started out for Wallace, to enlist the help of Thomas Fellowes. The man had an almost mystical reputation to the local people—he was the man who had defeated Wesley Pike and his river pirates. Hume and Stephen thought he'd inspire the men, give them the courage they'd need to battle the Mystic Clan. Mark stayed home with Rachel, cleaning the family's guns, gathering together ammunition and supplies. Rachel seemed lost, drifting from room to room, not speaking.

Mark was reassembling his favorite rifle when she came up to him, a big book tucked under her arm, tears in her eyes.

"What is it, Rachel?" He smiled at her, as best he could.

"Will you look at something, Mark? Can I show you something?"

" 'Course. What is it?"

"My—I never showed him. I meant to, but I never showed Joel my drawings. He asked me one time—more than once—but I said no. And now he'll never see them."

"Sure he will! We're gonna—"

She gripped his shoulder, hard. "Don't bullshit me, Mark. If he's not dead now, he will be soon. But you're his best friend.

I—I want you to see them for him. And if you find him, you can tell him, okay? Even if he's—" Her face crumpled.

Mark took her gently in his arms as she sobbed. When she was finished crying, she sat beside him and opened the book across their laps.

Mark gasped at what he saw. Delicate ferns in shades of gray, tiny insects, strange, spiked seed pods like little fanciful creatures. Each page a perfect little world, alive and vibrant in black and white. He looked up at her, astonished that such a secret lived in her small hands.

"They're beautiful," he whispered.

Rachel looked down. "Thanks, Mark. Remember, find Joel for me. Find him and tell him."

But in the morning, her demeanor had changed. She was no longer sad and silent—she was angry.

Men had been trickling onto the Stogdon farm since midnight, and they continued to do so well into the morning. Everyone was excited, talking and laughing as if they were a hunting party rather than a posse. Rachel had come to Mark, fully dressed in her jeans and boots, and told him she was coming with him.

"No," he'd said flatly. "Ye cain't, Rachel. This ain't no trip ta town. We're goin' ta kill men, an' a lot of us—hell, maybe all of us—are gonna end up killed too. Joel wouldn't want ye goin' inta that kind o' danger."

When he wouldn't budge, she'd gone to Hume Stogdon to plead her case. At first he was gentle but firm. Finally, out of character for him, he'd shouted at her. "Ye'd just be in the way, little girl. We'll drop ye off at the MacEwens' farm on the way outta town. They'll take care of ye until we get back. Now let us do what we have ta!"

Rachel had stormed up to the loft, and Mark hadn't seen her

for the rest of the day. He wanted to go to her, but there just wasn't time.

Mark was disappointed with the turnout for the posse. By dusk there were only twenty-five men who had come to the Stogdon farm to join up. He could only hope that Thomas Fellowes would be able to join them and add a few of his trusted friends. There was no way of knowing how many of the Mystic Clan had assembled at the Outlaw Cave.

A day passed, and another. Three more men trickled in. Then the flow of men began to increase. Surprised, Mark mingled with the young men gathering and questioned them. They had all heard that Thomas Fellowes was leading a posse against another band of outlaws. Apparently that was all it took to gather a small army. Soon there were more men than Mark and the Stogdens could keep track of. Since Fellowes had yet to show up, they were becoming restless. The foot traffic alone was making a mire of the grounds around the cabin, barn and other outbuildings. There were a couple of fist fights, and Hume Stogdon had to raise his baritone voice to a blasting roar to get everyone's attention and remind them why they were there. As the crowd began to settle down, Mark began counting heads. He had reached over a hundred and thirty by the time he realized perhaps he had counted a head or two more than once.

The sun was setting once more when Mark heard shouting from the fields that Fellowes had arrived at last. He was riding up to the farm, proud as a conquering king, flanked by a dozen men on horseback. The posse members who'd gathered at the farm muttered excitedly, stealing looks at Fellowes, some outright staring. Mark knew it wasn't the hideous scars they were seeing, but the man who'd led the Tennessee militia against Wesley Pike and his river pirates and brought them down. Apparently no one remembered that Fellowes had lost his command to a mutiny after the battle.

Fellowes greeted Mark and the Stogdons warmly. After he and his men had eaten and warmed themselves, he called an impromptu meeting in the barn. Everyone gathered quickly, excited to hear what Fellowes might have to say.

Mark glanced around, looking for Rachel, but she wasn't anywhere in sight. He wondered what, exactly, Fellowes would talk about. None of the posse members but Mark, the Stogdons and Thomas Fellowes knew about the Mystic Clan's Easter Sunday plot. If any of them had read the Crenshaw book, they almost certainly didn't believe it. None of them, of course, knew that Joel was Crenshaw. The Stogdons had rallied the posse by telling of Joel's kidnapping—the latest outrage in a series of atrocities committed by the Clan. "Who'll be next?" Hume had asked the men. "Yer wife? Yer sister? Yer daughter?" It was time to end the pestilence of the Mystic Clan, and those who could come along did. But that argument alone would not have been enough for most of these young men. It was the possibility that the posse might be led by Thomas Fellowes that was the clincher.

This was all too complicated. Mark rubbed his face with his hands, wishing he were somewhere else.

"Thank ye all for bein' here," Fellowes said, his voice strong and loud. "It's time I told ye exactly what it is yer gettin' into. We're all here ta rescue our friend and comrade Joel Biggs, right?"

"Right," the men shouted back. Mark looked around at their smiling faces, their shining eyes. A bunch of bored Tennessee farmers, out for the adventure of their lives. Mark suspected they would have roared their approval if Fellowes had told them to dive into a volcano. What was this about?

"As some of ye may know, an' some not, we've discovered the Mystic Clan's latest hideout. Like the vermin they are, they're holed up in a cave on the Mississippi River. The very cave where I fought and defeated Wesley Pike's band o' vicious river pirates!"

The noise was deafening. Men talking excitedly to each other, delighted as kids in a candy store. Mark's stomach went cold, a bitter chill crawling up his spine fast as a centipede. He took deep, slow breaths, his head whirling. For a moment, Mark felt like he might faint.

Images flashed through his mind. Horrible, red-soaked images of the battle at the cave. *Holy God. I never wanted to see that place again.*

Fellowes was speaking again, eyes wide, waving his arms like a preacher. "We're goin' ta that cave, men. We're goin' there, an' we're gonna get our friend outta there. But I propose we go farther than that. I say we wash the stain of the Mystic Clan clean out of this world. I say we kill 'em all, ta a man!"

The room thundered with shouts and bloodlust. Mark leaned against the wall of the barn, shocked and stunned. Fellowes was right, of course. The Clan needed to be eliminated. It was unlikely that they could kill all of them, but if they eliminated the leadership, the organization's back would be broken. But the thought of the coming carnage made him feel sad and sick. Mark hoped he had the strength to see it through.

The man riding next to Joel coughed and looked his way. Joel hunched his shoulders, but no blow followed. Wesley had put the fear of God into the Clan members guarding him; or rather, the fear of Jarrett Cotten. Joel listened carefully to the conversations of the men, reassuring himself that Cotten had not, in fact, been broken out of jail yet. The escape wasn't confirmed, but Joel was horrified by the wide reach of the reports coming in. The Clan was everywhere, a venomous octopus with arms in every walk of life.

He shuddered, thinking about what Cotten would do to him

if they really came face to face. *Probably something like Virgil would have done, and I never had the stones to think about that too much. I just hope I don't embarrass myself too bad before I die.*

Wesley was gone, and they'd never had a chance to talk before the big man had ridden away. Joel felt in his heart that he would never see Wesley Pike again. The thought made him deeply sad. *He left thinking I'm nothing but a worthless drunk, good for nothing but cannon fodder.*

Well, aren't I?

He knew it was pathetic to want Wesley's approval so badly. But he seemed to be nothing but pathetic these days.

A small rock hit Joel in the side of the head. He winced, but didn't react. Harsh laughter filled his ears. He sat on a swaybacked horse, his hands tied to the saddlehorn. They hadn't fed him in over a day, but he wasn't hungry. He wasn't anything.

Joel thought about putting his head down on the neck of that horse, and dying. He wondered if, by force of will, he could just make himself die. *Probably not. I can't seem to manage much of anything on my own.*

But he couldn't die, because back at the inn Wesley had told him to do something right before he'd turned Joel over to the Clan.

With growing horror, Joel realized that he didn't remember what it was. Had he been that drunk?

The posse rolled out at dawn. Three wagons and, as far as Mark could tell, about a hundred and fifty men. Mark had been greatly surprised when Fellowes had asked him to be his second in command—he'd expected Hume Stogdon to take that position. "We need somebody young an' strong," Stogdon had said, smiling. "An' besides, ye know the cave an' the surrounding territory."

Mark hoped he did. He hadn't been back there since the

battle, twenty years ago. And what time hadn't faded, his memory might have suppressed. But he kept his fears and uncertainties to himself. He couldn't show any weakness to the men; they were counting on him.

Rachel was strangely calm and resigned as she rode with the posse to the MacEwens' farm. She hugged Mark and the Stogdons when they dropped her off. The MacEwens, a kind, religious older couple, promised to take good care of her. Mark watched her waving to them as the posse rolled on, and wondered if he'd ever see her again. He saw that Stephen was doing the same thing. Mark closed his eyes for a moment, hoping that, when this was all over and done with, Rachel wouldn't be left utterly alone.

Joel squinted into the late-morning sun at the bluff and the old cave mouth, now clogged with rock rubble. Wesley or someone, perhaps those who had settled the cave after the river pirates left it in 1811, had blasted a new entrance. Unlike the broad, high entrance of twenty years ago, the new opening was about ten feet high and eight feet wide, surrounded by moss-covered rock debris.

Looking at it, a shudder shook Joel's skinny body. Suddenly his head was filled with the thundering of cannons and the crack of rifle fire, the screams of men and the stink of blood and gunpowder. He closed his eyes.

One of the Clan cut the strap that bound Joel to the saddle horn and yanked him from the saddle. Landing in the mud protected him from serious injury. Another man pointed a rifle at Joel's head while the rabbit-eyed fellow from the inn conferred with some men who had emerged from the cave.

"Yer lucky," said Rabbit-eyes, after a few minutes. "Cotten ain't here yet. You got a little while longer ta live, Crenshaw." Joel didn't answer. Somebody pulled him to his feet and pushed him toward the cave.

"Take him ta the main hall," somebody suggested.

"No, you eedjit, there's a hundred ways outta there. Take him ta the larder."

"I don't want that vermin in with the vittles! Take 'im ta that room where we got the tackle an' such stored."

They seemed to agree that that was the place for Joel. Two men he'd never seen before marched him off.

After more than a few minutes of twists, turns, and backtracking, Joel realized that these guys had no idea where they were going. *They haven't been here long enough to know the caves,* Joel thought. To his enormous surprise, he realized he *did* remember them. He knew where each passageway they passed would end up, but he kept silent. At last they reached the storage chamber they were seeking—probably entirely by accident. Joel was thrown into the middle of the room, hands still tied. He slumped against a tangle of rope and closed his eyes.

"Sumbitch looks nearly dead," said one man, a dark-haired, rangy fellow.

"Maybe we should git 'im some water," said the other, a sunburned, freckled blond with bad teeth. "We'll be dead men ourselves if he dies 'fore Cotten can get 'is hands on 'im."

Joel kept his eyes closed, listening.

They argued for a moment about who was going to get the water. Then one of them left and the other—the blond, from his voice—poked Joel with the barrel of his rifle. "You alive, you shit worm?"

Joel groaned. The guy gave him a halfhearted kick in the thigh, and backed off. Joel realized that he had a huge advantage if they thought he was near-unconscious and helpless. They probably wouldn't beat him as much, and they might not watch him as closely. So Joel lay still, trying to remember what Wesley had wanted him to do.

Though he did not sleep, he fell into an energy-deprived stupor in which he lost contact with his surroundings and was unaware of the passage of time.

Then somebody kicked him in the gut. Joel coughed and retched, pain lancing through his midsection.

"Git up, you t-t-traitorous bastard," Garrison Sharpe hissed.

Oh Christ. Just what I needed. Joel opened his eyes and struggled to his feet.

Sharpe looked different. One of his eyes had rotated out to the side as far as it could go. The other was staring at Joel with pure, undiluted hatred. "I should k-k-kill you now," Sharpe snarled. His head twitched to the side once, twice.

Christ on a crutch. What happened to him? Realization dawned on Joel, slow and horrible.

Oh my God. I did this. When Gailey reared and he hit his head on the road. . . .

Fuck him. He tried to kill me.

Joel managed a nasty smile. "And what do you think Mister Cotten would say about that?"

Sharpe backhanded him. Joel staggered, but managed to keep his feet. "C-C-C-Cotten ain't here. These morons think he's on his way, b-but he ain't. I'm in ch-charge now, Crenshaw. An' yer a d-d-dead man."

Joel spit out blood. "Kill me then."

Sharpe's hand went to the knife on his belt, then dropped away. He was clearly boiling with frustration. His head twitched so hard that drool flew from the corner of his mouth.

"Uh-huh. You're not in charge, are you. Who is? Jamus Cooke? Art Clayton?" Joel was amazed by his lack of fear. He seemed to have gone numb, inside and out.

"I will k-kill you," Sharpe spat. "In a d-d-d-day or two, when ever'body realizes that Cotten ain't never c-comin' back, I'll drag you out in front of all the men an' I'll sp-split you open like a hawg."

Joel let out a dry, hollow laugh. "You do that. Just be sure you clear it with your boss Clayton first. And don't try to shoot me, you'll probably hit somebody else, what with that fucked-up eyeball and twitching head of yours."

Sharpe roared. He raised his rifle high and brought the butt down on the side of Joel's head. Joel crumpled to the floor. His head and eyes swam as he watched Sharpe's boots stomp from the chamber. He closed his eyes.

Some minutes later, the darker of his guards returned with a smelly skin of water, and some jerky. Joel drank some water, but though he was hungry, he didn't eat. Instead, he feigned sleep.

"Look at 'im," said the blond. "Sleepin' like a goddam baby. If I was in yer shoes, Crenshaw, I'd be prayin' ta God right now."

"Or cryin' like a baby," the other one laughed. The man bent down closer. "Why's his head and goddam nose bleedin'?"

"Aw, who cares. Let 'im rest. He's gonna need his strength for screamin' later on."

Joel hoped they didn't see him shudder.

They'd been on the road for a day and a half, and everyone was exhausted. It was time to stop and rest, but they had difficulty finding enough open ground for a camp. Passing through a small settlement named Perception, northwest of Adairville, Mark and Fellowes found a farmer named Robes willing to allow the men to camp in one of his fields. The place was a mud bath, but they would make do the best they could. The farmer indicated that he and his family were in no mood to socialize with the huge posse and that they had no supplies other than water to offer them.

As supplies for preparing meals were being unloaded, Mark heard a hoarse cry from the back of one of the wagons. He trotted over to see. Floyd Evers, a skinny boy of no more than nineteen, pointed into the wagon, eyes goggling. Mark cautiously lifted the flap of a tarpaulin and revealed a sleepy-eyed Rachel.

"What?" she said grumpily.

The screaming and yelling went on for half an hour, but there was nothing to be done about it. Stephen offered to take her back to Adairville, and she flatly refused.

"We can tie ye hand and foot and throw ye over the back of Stephen's horse, ye know!" Fellowes roared.

"Fine! Then I'll wait 'til he's asleep and whack him upside the head!" she yelled back in his face. Stephen turned sadly away.

"We'll leave her here with the Robe family," Mark said.

"They'd have to tie me up to keep me here. I'll follow after you the first chance I get."

Mark glared at her, unable to fathom such stubbornness in a woman.

"What difference does it make if I come with you?" Rachel argued. "I won't be in the way. You didn't even know I was here, did you? Mark, you know I can shoot as well as any of you. Maybe better."

Mark tried to stare her down. She didn't flinch. It was Mark who finally looked away with an exasperated sigh. "Ye can come with us, Rachel, but when the fightin' starts, ye're stayin' behind. Ye understand me?"

She started to protest, then cut herself short. "Okay," she said. Rachel gave Mark a quick smile, then bustled off to help make supper.

Mark leaned against the wagon, and looked up through the cold night air at the stars. For a brief, painful moment, he wondered what, exactly, Joel had done to deserve this kind of love.

After long, tense and tedious hours of pretending to be semiconscious—Joel couldn't tell if it was eight hours or two days—the ruse finally paid off. The men guarding Joel got careless. The darker man left altogether, leaving the complaining blond to guard Joel. The man settled down against the wall with his rifle propped between his knees. After some minutes, his head dropped down onto his chest, and he began to snore.

Joel opened his gummy eyes, and blinked a few times to clear them. The man seemed to be deeply asleep.

Joel rose up on his haunches, then onto his knees. Slowly, slowly, he crept across the dusty floor toward the man guarding him. So far, so good.

Joel reached his bound hands toward the knife on Blondie's thigh. Ever so slowly, he eased it out of its sheath. The guard didn't twitch, but he drooled a little. Awkwardly, Joel turned the big knife in his grip and began to saw at his bonds.

The blond man coughed, dropped his rifle, and opened his eyes. Joel spun the knife around in his still-bound hands. As the guard lunged for the gun, Joel rammed the knife into his stomach, up under his ribs, and into his heart, as he had seen Wesley do, long ago.

The blond man shuddered and gagged. His pale blue eyes locked onto Joel's. His mouth opened and closed, like a grounded fish's. Joel could smell shit and piss as the guard slumped over sideways and hit the cave floor. Joel turned his head away and vomited.

There was no time to waste. After freeing his hands, Joel used the rope to bind his dead captor's hands in front of him. He dragged the man to the tangle of rope where he himself had been earlier, and propped him up. He grabbed a smallish tow sack and pulled it down over the dead man's face. It wouldn't fool anyone for long, but someone giving a casual glance might believe it was Joel.

He kicked dust over the blood as best he could, and crept out into the tunnels. Strangely, Joel felt as if he had come home.

They were just a few miles from the cave. Mark's fear had peaked during the night, punctuated by horrible, bloody nightmares. Now all he felt was a dull sense of foreboding, a detachment from himself and everyone around him. He supposed it was best that way.

Fellowes seemed oddly excited, his eyes shining in his weatherbeaten face. "You ready for this?" he asked Mark, clapping him on the shoulder.

"Not really," Mark said. "Don't s'pose I ever will be. But I'm gonna do it anyway."

They rode in silence for a while. Mark had only seen Fellowes a few times over the years since the New Madrid earthquake and flood. Even after his "rehabilitation," Wesley Pike had held no love for Thomas Fellowes. Whenever he was traveling with Wesley, Mark had steered clear of Fellowes, for fear of what Wesley might do. When he had encountered Fellowes on his own, the man had always been friendly and open, but Mark was never comfortable around him. He felt that he had in some way betrayed Fellowes by falling in with Wesley Pike. Some small, inner part of him regretted that decision. He wondered, now and then, if he and Fellowes would have gone back to the twenty-first century if they had ended up together after the flood.

"What's on yer mind?" Fellowes asked at last. Mark shot him a sideways glance.

"Why didn't ye ever go back, Thomas? Ye tol' me yesterday ye knew the way. What made ye stay here?"

Fellowes smiled. "I tol' ye that so ye'd know yew an' Rachel could go back if'n ye wanted ta. But ta answer yer question—I've thought about it, from time to time. Did I ever tell ye how I survived the flood, Mark?"

Mark shook his head no.

"I was bleedin' somethin' fierce, ye know." His hand unconsciously rose to his heavily scarred cheek. "I thought I was done fer. It hurt so bad . . . I'd grabbed onto a log an' managed ta stay afloat, but I was growin' weaker an' my grip was slippin'."

"Didn' ye float on a log down the Mississippi ta Natchez just after ye arrived in this time?"

"Yeah—seems I get along with logs fairly well, don't it?"

Mark nodded.

"Anyways—so I was on this log and finally, when I couldn't hold on no more, I got swept inta this great big snarl o' tree roots, kinda hung there like a fly in a spider's web. I lost consciousness, an' when I woke up again, the water had gone down. I hadn't drowned after all. But I was so tired, an' so weak, I jes' hung there. I wasn't plannin' ta die, exactly, but I didn't have the strength or energy ta live. That's when the Indians came along."

"Willawic?" asked Mark, hopefully.

"No, not him. I never saw Willawic again, Lord bless 'im. It was jes' a huntin' party, lookin' fer what they could find after the flood. I could hear 'em debatin' what ta do with me. They seemed int'rested in my scalpin' scar. Finally, they hauled me outta the snag an' took me ta their camp. They treated my wound with herbs, bandaged it with buckskin an' leaves. When I was walkin' an' eatin' on my own again, they wished me well an' went on their way.

"I spent a lotta time wonderin' why they did that, Mark. Why would they help a white man? White men been nothin' but trouble ta the Indians since we showed up. What made 'em do that, d'ya 'spose?"

"They was good men," Mark said simply.

"Yes. Exactly. Good men. Those Indians were proof that there was—that there's goodness in this time. I took it as a sign. A sign that I was meant ta stay here, an' help out the side o' good. I know that sounds a bit high-flown an' conceited. I don't mean it that way. I ain't no goddam Superman."

That made Mark laugh; the name Superman was familiar for some reason.

"I was nobody back home, Mark. As an insurance salesman, I was just a paper pusher. I thought that if I stayed here, maybe I could make things a little better. Even if I helped jes' one man, the way those Indians helped me, it'd be worth it."

"From what I hear," Mark said, "ye've helped a lot more than one."

Fellowes nodded. "I've tried. An' this . . . this is gonna be the end of my career. I know this is bloody business, but it's gotta be done. If we succeed, Mark, we'll be sweepin' a terrible plague outta the world. We'll be doin' good for generations ta come." Fellowes scratched his scarred forehead. "An' dear God, we can't let Easter Sunday happen."

"Yes," Mark agreed solemnly. "The outlaws *are* a plague."

"And yet you ended up with Wesley Pike," Fellowes said with a little smile. "Oh yes, I recognized 'Jamus Cooke' the moment I saw him."

Mark nodded, feeling a little odd.

"Thomas—I know Wes used ta be a monster. But he's changed. He's a decent man now. I know that's prob'ly hard for ye to believe—"

"I'm not judgin' ye, boy. If Wesley had any hand in makin' ye the fine man ye are now, he must have a decent side." That made Mark smile.

"How 'bout you?" Fellowes asked. "You've traveled all over the South with Wesley. I'm sure you coulda found yer way back, Mark. Why are you still here?"

Mark snorted out a humorless laugh. "What the hell did I have ta go back ta?"

Something strange happened to Joel as he prowled the darkened tunnels of the cave. He changed from hunted fugitive to hunter. He had the blond guard's rifle clutched in one bloody hand, his knife in the other, the man's lantern hooked around his wrist. He was no longer afraid of discovery. He wasn't afraid for his life. He wasn't afraid at all. Some dark, predatory part of him hoped another Clan member would appear to challenge him. *I'll kill the fucker. I'll gut him like a fish.*

As he roamed through the dark, Joel roamed through the past. The memories came back so strongly he could nearly see them. Virgil chasing him through the caves. The shivering tower of humanity, always reaching for the hole in the ceiling. Billy's laughter. Ebbie pressing her cold nose into his hand. Willawic's reassuring smile, even as he lay wounded in the dusty chamber.

The dusty chamber!

That was what Wesley had told him to do! Go to the dusty chamber! But why?

That was something Joel still couldn't remember. But the little boy inside him remembered the way to the hidden chamber where he'd spent so many hours. A hard left into a narrow passageway, and Joel was on his way there.

About a mile from the cave, Fellowes stopped the march for a last-minute strategy meeting. He wanted to cross the river in a frontal attack, the way he had twenty years ago. "It worked then," Fellowes grunted. "It'll work now. We'll set out by mid-afternoon."

But Mark remembered the horrible casualties on the front lines of both sides, the cannon fire ripping bodies to shreds, pirates falling from the cliffs like discarded rag dolls.

"I've got an idea," Mark said. His voice was shaking. He cleared his throat and squared his shoulders.

"Let's hear it then," Fellowes said, cocking his scarred head.

"There's a place up ahead where we can ford the river without too much swimmin'. I say we do that, an' circle around the back. We can sneak up on 'em. Go in the back way an' flush 'em out like rats."

Fellowes stared at Mark until he started to squirm. Slowly, a smile crept across Fellowes' ravaged face. "There's a back entrance?"

"Well . . . yes. How'd ye think Wesley an' some o' them got away the last time yew fought here?"

"I guess I figured. . . ." He seemed lost in thought for a moment. "Well, it's been a long time since then, but . . . now that ye mention it . . . it makes sense."

They both nodded solemnly, then Fellowes grinned. "Yeah, that's it—we'll split up inta two groups. A third of us'll go inta the tunnels an' start cleanin' out the vermin. The other two-thirds'll come down from up-river, go up the sloping side o' the ridge and form a firing line there ta git anyone who comes out the hole on top of the bluff, an' be able to fire down on the cave entrance ta seal it off against any tryin' ta escape that way."

"Now, here's somethin' I thought of, and the men aren't gonna like it one bit," Mark said, "but I think it's important that the men goin' inta the cave don' have ta lug their rifles through all them tight passages. They'll listen ta yew if'n ye ask 'em ta trade up their weapons—the men settin' up the firin' line on the ridge'll take all the rifles, the men goin' inta the cave'll take an' stuff as many pistols in their belts as they kin."

"You're better at this than you may think, Mister Ryder."

Mark smiled and turned away, embarrassed.

"We'll be there ta shoot 'em when they come pourin' out," Fellowes said. "We'll get ever' last one of the bastards."

Mark couldn't help it. He grinned like a little boy. Then he caught the bloodthirsty gleam in Thomas Fellowes' eyes. "What's this about for you?" he asked. "Really. Why d'ye want 'em so bad, Fellowes?"

"They're evil," Fellowes said simply. "An' I'm sick of it. I'm sick of lawless savages destroyin' the lives of decent folk. I may never get this chance again, Mark. I'm gettin old. I wanna know that I made a diff'rence here."

Mark nodded. The two men were silent for a moment.

"You remember them tunnels, Mark?"

"I b'lieve I do."

"Good. You'll command the initial attack, then. I'll lead the other men ta the bluff."

Mark stared at him, stunned. Fellowes clapped him on the shoulder. "Ye can do it, Mark. Ye're the only one who can."

Something inside him wanted this, he knew, but then it came to him with a sickening burst of excitement that this was what he'd always wanted.

Then why am I terrified?

Rachel stepped out from behind a tree. "I want to go with Mark."

"No!" Mark and Fellowes cried at the same time.

Mark looked at her, so small and strong, her chin in the air. "Rachel, i's the devil's den in there. I know ye wanna look for Joel. But ye won't do him no good if yer dead. Go wit' Mister Fellowes an' his men. Ye can stay back in the woods durin' the fightin'. Then, if—when we find Joel, ye can take care o' him ye'self."

Her eyes narrowed, but she nodded. Mark hoped to God that

she wouldn't do something stupid.

Joel ducked his head, and entered the dusty chamber. His first thought was, *it's so small, so very tiny.* It had seemed small when he was a child, but now, it appeared to be no bigger than a broom closet. How had they used this as living quarters for so long? Joel shuddered.

He looked around the little chamber, searching for what Wesley may have been trying to tell him. He squinted; there was something written in the dirt on the floor. "THE THIRD BLAST OF THE TRUMPET," in childish block print.

Joel stared. *What the hell does that mean?* He reached out to touch the letters. There was something lying across the "O." A string? Joel picked it up. It was a long string, which came from a crack high in the wall and hung down to the floor.

Suddenly, Joel realized what he was looking at.

Dear God. It's a fuse.

Wesley's rigged this entire place to blow.

He stared at the end of the fuse held between his grubby, bloody thumb and forefinger. Joel felt a wide, maniacal grin spread across his face.

Mark silently led his men to the low, jagged cave opening, the back entrance at the edge of the woods. They paused before entering to light their lanterns.

How was it possible, he wondered, *that the river pirates poured out of that opening on horseback twenty years ago?* At least they would not be riding in through the opening. Their horses were tethered in a clearing a few hundred yards back.

Mark and his men had split from Fellowes' contingent an hour ago. Armed to the teeth, Wesley Pike's dawg and about fifty Tennessee farmers prepared to enter the Mystic Clan's underworld.

Mark wished he knew what they were facing. He doubted if the Clan would be as heavily armed as Wesley Pike's river pirates had been, but there could be more of them. A lot more of them.

He wanted to find Joel, dead or alive. He wanted to know the fate of his friend, one way or another. Mark didn't share Fellowes' lust for the Mystic Clan's blood. He just wanted this to be over with. And then . . . and then what? He had nowhere to go, nothing to do. He couldn't stay with the Stogdons forever. Mark had a strong feeling he'd never see Wesley Pike again. So what, then?

Mark stepped into the maw of the cave.

Maybe I won't have to worry about what happens next. Maybe none of us will.

Lighting the fuse had been so easy. There was no doubt, no fear. Joel had just opened the lantern and held the cord to the fire until it ignited.

It was a slow-burning fuse, slow and deliberate, like a tiny, sparking demon creeping up a rope. Joel watched it eat an inch of fuse, then three, then six. How long before it went through the crack in the wall and hit Wesley's payload? There was no way to tell. Minutes? An hour, or more?

Smiling, Joel walked from the dusty chamber for the last time.

Mark and his men moved quietly through the tunnels. It worried Mark that they hadn't seen anyone yet, not a single man. He was leading his group toward the entrance chamber, or at least he thought he was. With any luck, they'd surprise the Clan in the midst of a meeting. The men they didn't cut down would be driven to the surface like roaches, where Fellowes would blast them off the bluff.

That's the idea, anyway.

Suddenly, the sound of footsteps in a passage off to the right. Voices shouting.

"He's gone!"

"Sumbitch murdered Jeffers!"

"Gotta find 'im!"

Six Clan members were running up the tunnel toward them.

"Git 'em!" Mark shouted. He raised one of his own pistols and fired. The face of the closest Clan member exploded in a spray of red. Three others fell quickly, as the men at Mark's sides blasted away. One man froze, eyes and mouth wide. Hume Stogdon shot him in the throat. The last Clan member turned and ran. Bile rising in his throat, Mark drew another pistol and shot him down.

"They'll know we're here now," Mark told his men as they reloaded their weapons. "We better move fast."

When they were all set, he led the men down the tunnel toward the entrance chamber. The smell of blood and gunpowder followed them like a ghost.

Joel heard the sound of voices from the entrance chamber. His mind flashed back to the days when Wesley's river pirates ruled this underworld. He remembered Wesley's voice booming across the room. He remembered the debauchery, the fights, the death.

He really wasn't sure what he was doing. He wanted to see exactly how many Clan members he was about to blow to hell. And he wanted to see the large chamber one more time. He took the tunnel that cut high into the hill and would end at an opening in the top of the chamber, where he could observe unseen. He remembered sitting in that opening with Mark, watching the river pirates twenty years ago. He could see the opening in the floor just ahead, glowing with the flicker of torchlight from the large chamber below.

Gunshots, distant and muffled. Joel spun around, but, of

course, there was nothing to see. Whatever was happening, it was some distance away. *Stupid bastards are probably killing each other over their hand signals again,* he thought. Joel eased himself over to the opening in the floor of the tunnel, and looked down into the entrance chamber.

Mark led his men through the dark, toward the entrance chamber, he hoped. But the tunnel they were in jogged left, and he didn't remember that. Soon they found themselves at a dead end, a good-sized cavern filled with crates and canvas-covered bundles. Cautiously, Mark and his point men entered. Young Goebel Price reached out and lifted one of the canvas tarps with his rifle. Mark's face split into a wide grin.

"Well. Luck may jes' be on the side of the righteous today."

Joel looked down at the throng of men below him. There were a lot of them—three, maybe four hundred. Nothing organized seemed to be going on. Men were talking amongst themselves anxiously. They seemed to be upset about something.

Joel heard more distant gunshots somewhere within the caverns. The men below seemed to hear them as well. The noise in the entrance chamber grew louder, then abruptly silent as Art Clayton swept in, Garrison Sharpe right behind him. Clayton was dressed in finery worthy of Cotten, puffed up like a peacock, though still unmistakably frail and sickly-looking. He was surrounded by sycophants.

"Gentlemen," he cried, "preparations are almost complete for our Easter Sunday festivities, not a month away. The ranks of our negro armies have swelled in recent days to tens of thousands. What glory and riches they will bring to us through their struggle and death! We must each rehearse in our own minds our part in the coming engagement and make ready for such blood and treasures as no man has ever seen before."

The outlaws were lapping it up, cheering like Clayton was something other than a crooked politician turned thug.

Watching Clayton preen, Joel knew that Cotten was never coming back. If there had been an actual escape plot, Clayton would have sabotaged it. He wouldn't give this up for anything, that much was obvious.

King of the sewer rats, what an honor. . . .

Joel didn't mind the fact that he was going to die with the Mystic Clan. His only regret was that he wouldn't be able to watch them go before he himself was blown to kingdom come. *It could happen anytime now, any moment. . . .*

Someone was at Clayton's elbow, whispering something in his ear. The dapper criminal's face flushed red. "Find him!" he screamed, his voice croaking and high pitched. "Find Crenshaw now, and bring him to me! If he's gotten away, I'll have the men responsible for it skinned alive!" Sharpe, standing next to him, had turned red with fury. Joel thought the man's head might just explode.

Clayton, favoring his left leg in a pronounced limp, stormed through the chamber, his toadies clustered tightly around him. He was almost directly below Joel now. "Find him!" Clayton screamed again. "Now! Now! Now!"

A laugh started low in Joel's throat, and burst out loud and strong. Clayton froze and looked all around him, but not up.

"Here I am, you fucker!" Joel roared. He threw himself out of the tunnel, and then he was falling, falling like a shooting star.

Mark was back on the right track, he was pretty sure. He'd found the large, wide tunnel the pirates had used to bring in large weaponry and crates of supplies. It opened onto the entrance chamber. It was crucial for the posse to not be too cramped—entering the entrance chamber just two or three abreast would be suicide. They could be, and probably were, severely outnumbered. If most of the Clan was in the chamber, as Mark suspected they were, they weren't expecting an attack at all. That would be a huge advantage.

The opening into the entrance chamber was just around the next bend. Mark motioned for his men to stay back, and eased forward to see. The chamber was packed. Clayton was in the middle of the room, blustering away about something.

Dear God. There are so many of them.

Can't think about that now.

Mark slipped back to his men, whispered quick orders. They'd charge into the chamber, split right and left along the walls, and start firing. A few men would hang behind; then, when the Clan was driven back, they'd deliver the little surprises they'd found in the Clan's own storage chamber. It was going to be bloody, brutal, and ugly.

"Now!" Mark shouted. His men charged full-tilt into the entrance chamber.

Mark rushed in, raised a pistol and fired, hitting a young man square in the chest. His other men began firing as well. At that moment, as blood was spilling into the dust and the Clan members were grabbing for their own weapons, something—no someone—fell from the roof of the chamber, directly on top of Art Clayton.

Joel had intended his fall to be his swan song, but his will to survive took over. As he hit Clayton, he grabbed the man by the shoulders and pushed him down, spreading his weight across Clayton's body, and the bodies of the nearest few men.

Clayton hit the rocky floor face first. His head cracked open like a fumbled egg, and his brains spread across three feet of the cavern floor. Joel landed on the man's back. The wind was knocked out of his lungs, and, for a moment, he couldn't take a breath. But he was alive.

He struggled to his feet. His knee sent spikes of agony up and down his leg. It had collided with the head of a Clan member on his way down; that man now lay on the ground with his neck broken. Joel could barely put his weight on it, but he managed.

Two other men lay nearby, dying or grievously injured. One fellow writhed in slow motion, his face in the dust. The other was on his back, twitching as if electrified.

Joel's head stopped ringing, and he realized he was hearing gunfire, and lots of it, right there in the chamber. Someone was attacking the Mystic Clan! He took a step forward for a better view, and that saved his life.

Something heavy struck Joel on the shoulder, sending a jolt of agony through his body. Joel staggered, spun around, and saw Garrison Sharpe, a cudgel in one hand and a knife in the other, lips skinned back from his rotten teeth in rage.

Mark didn't have time to wonder about the man who fell from the ceiling. He was too busy pulling his pistols and firing into the throng of Clan. It was sickening. Some of the Clan had pistols in their belts, many did not. Every posse member had one to three firearms at the ready. It was a slaughter. Mark started to detach from reality as his bullet smashed through a man's forehead. *I'll leave here, after this. I'll go somewhere far away, where no one knows me,* as he shot a man through the heart.

The man who'd fallen on Clayton was on his feet. Mark squinted through the smoke.

Oh sweet Jesus.

"Joel!" he shouted.

Joel's eyes narrowed. The firing had all but ceased, and he could have sworn he heard someone shout his name. And it sounded like Mark. But he couldn't go looking for him now, because Sharpe was intent on gutting or braining him.

Joel sidestepped as best he could, trying to keep the man out of range. He tripped on the corpse of one of the fallen Clan members, and dropped to one knee. The other knee screamed with agony. Joel grabbed the big hunting knife from the dead man's belt and threw himself backwards. Sharpe's thrust was clumsy. Evidently his speech wasn't the only thing affected by that blow to the head on the road.

Joel slashed at him, catching Sharpe's sleeve and nothing else.

"Ye rurnt my life," Sharpe shouted over the sounds of men dying. "Now I aim ta take yours!"

Joel laughed, loud and long, making Sharpe's little shark-eyes narrow with anger and confusion. "My only regret is tha' my horse didn' stomp your ugly head into jelly!"

Sharpe snarled and swung the cudgel at Joel's knife hand. Joel twisted out of range and caught Sharpe on the backswing, slashing his cudgel arm deeply. Sharpe yelled and dropped the club. Dripping blood, he jumped forward and took a stab at Joel's belly.

The blade nicked him, breaking the skin and drawing blood. Joel brought the pommel of his own hunting knife down on Sharpe's hand. Sharpe yelped and the knife flew from his grip. Joel made a vicious upward thrust at the underside of Sharpe's chin.

It would have ended right there, if Sharpe's head hadn't jerked sideways. Instead of skewering Sharpe's head, the knife sliced up the side of his face, grinding against his jawbone. Sharpe howled. The cut was horrendous, and Joel fought back a wave of nausea. Sharpe lunged for him, grabbing Joel around the throat with both hands.

They fell to the ground, fighting on the bodies of the men

Joel had killed in his dive. Sharpe's grip was like iron. Stars began to blossom in Joel's vision as Sharpe squeezed, his blood dripping down on Joel's face like hot rain. Joel blinked, and, through the haze of red, he saw Virgil Pike above him, grinning his devil's grin. Joel closed his eyes, grateful that Virgil was only strangling him. He had gotten off easy.

The sound of breaking crockery and muffled explosions filled the chamber. Suddenly, flames were dancing around them. A man staggered past screaming, his clothes ablaze. Joel's ears were ringing, his eyes felt like they would pop from their sockets. But it wasn't Virgil killing him, it was Garrison Sharpe, and Joel still had his knife in his hand. He brought it up hard, stabbing Sharpe in the side. Sharpe gurgled. His grip on Joel's throat loosened. Joel threw the man off, and left him there on the cavern floor.

Joel stood up, blinking through the smoke, and saw his oldest friend.

"Mark!"

His shout was lost in the gunfire. Joel was delighted to see Mark again for a moment—he thought he'd never see his friend again. Then he remembered.

"Get out!" he screamed. "Get outta here, Mark! This whole place is gonna blow!"

Joel was shouting something at him. Then something flew over Mark's head, several somethings, like heavy birds shot from the sky. It was more of the jugs of whiskey, shredded cotton sacks stuffed in the necks and lit on fire.

They exploded on impact. Flames shot in every direction, scurrying over the floor like vicious animals. Men were engulfed in fire, screaming, flopping on the floor like bright, hot, roasting fish. Hot air and the stink of burning flesh hit Mark in the face. Smoke filled the chamber. It was nearly impossible to breathe.

Had Joel been killed? There was no way to know. Another "cocktail" went off nearby. Nearly blind, Mark was knocked from his feet by panicked men running for their lives.

Joel staggered through the smoke and panicked men to the wall of the entrance chamber. Feeling his way along, he tried to find the way out.

"Retreat!" Mark screamed, his voice ragged. Hopefully his men were already doing that, if they had any sense. The Clan sure as hell were.

We'll all get to the surface at once. I hope to God Fellowes looks before he starts blasting away.

And what happened to Joel? Is he dead or alive?

It was hell getting out. Literally. Mark prayed that his men were behind him. There was no way of knowing; the tunnel had become so narrow and twisting that he couldn't have seen far behind him, even if it weren't filled with smoke, fire, the smell of charred flesh and stink of blood. . . . Mark wondered if this was the smell that greeted the damned when they first plummeted down to Hades.

They're behind me, they're all behind me. . . .

He held a lantern aloft as he made his way through the tunnel and then up, toward the smokehouse where Virgil once cured sides of meat. His goal was to come out on the ridgetop through the old chimney passage.

Mark was certain that some Clan were getting out too, but it couldn't be very many. Quite a few had been killed in the posse's initial attack. More were lost in the twisting tunnels. He could hear their panicked shouts behind and below him. No one was fighting anymore; for the moment, anyway, it was each man for himself.

The tunnel twisted sideways, and Mark found himself in a dead end. He turned around to go back the other way, and faced a solid wall. He couldn't see through the smoke. Someone ran into his back and nearly knocked him down. He felt the walls desperately, and couldn't find a way out. Fighting panic, Mark closed his eyes. When he opened them, he saw a tiny figure in the haze next to him.

"C'mon, flicto." The little voice seemed to come from inside his head. Billy laughed over his shoulder, and started climbing. Mark followed.

Mark climbed until his sides burned with knives of pain. His arm throbbed with agony from holding the lantern high. *I can't go any farther. I can't. I can't.*

At that moment, he burst out into the sunlight and fresh, delicious air.

A shot whizzed past his ear. "Hold your fire!" he screamed.

"Mark?" he heard Fellowes shout. Posse men poured out of the chimney behind him, gasping for air. Along with them, some Clan members. As Mark blinked his burning eyes and tried to get enough air in his tortured lungs, shots rang out. The young Clan member who'd just staggered out and fallen to his knees behind Mark twitched and hit the ground, blood spraying from his side. *Fellowes intends to keep his promise,* Mark thought grimly.

Not every Clan member was a helpless target. More than one man came out shooting. A scream from the far side of the bluff told Mark that one of Fellowes' men had been hit.

Mark shouted to his men to retreat down the slope, into the trees, where they could regroup and reload. As he herded the men toward the trees, he heard Joel's voice.

"Run!" Joel screamed. "Get off the ridge! The whole thing's gonna blow!"

Mark didn't hesitate. "Run!" he roared at his men. "Run an'

keep runnin'! Git ta the horses an' git outta here!"

"I ain't runnin' from no fight!" Goebel Price shouted.

"Then stay here an' die, ye jackass!" Mark yelled as he helped a young posse man to his feet. Price hesitated, then ran downslope.

More gunshots from Fellowes and his men, more Clan fell. "Are you deaf? Run! The caverns are gonna blow!" Joel roared.

Everything had changed. Joel had actually been looking forward to that final, purifying blast. But then Mark showed up. And was that Thomas Fellowes in the distance? Joel shouted out a warning, and Fellowes hesitated.

"GO!" Joel bellowed. "Thomas Fellowes, take your men and RUN before you get blown to hell!" Fellowes squinted at him a moment. Then he barked a retreat order to his men, and they turned and fled. Joel was glad to see that Mark was getting away as well.

"Crenshaw."

The voice behind him was cold, heavy with hatred. Joel turned to see Garrison Sharpe, blood dripping down his face and soaking his side, a pistol leveled at Joel's head. And he wasn't alone. A dozen Clan members stood behind him. Some had knives, some pistols, and they all looked ready to tear Joel apart with their bare hands.

Joel planted his feet and leveled his gaze as Sharpe approached. Sharpe's gun was in his face, but Joel had no fear, and, strangely, that seemed to rattle Sharpe. He hesitated.

Another second, and it'll be over. . . . Joel grinned savagely.

There was a shuddering "boom" from deep inside the mountain. The ground shook. Sharpe fired as Joel lost his footing and fell to his knees.

The bullet grazed Joel's head, leaving a throbbing trail of fire on his scalp. Sharpe pulled a knife from his belt and lunged as another explosion rocked the ground.

Gunshots, loud and rapid, rang through the air. Two red flowers bloomed on Sharpe's chest and he dropped like a sandbag. Another man's eye exploded. A third staggered back clutching his belly. Another man dropped, and then another.

What the hell? No gun made in the eighteen-hundreds can fire that fast. . . .

Joel scrambled to his feet and turned to see. Rachel stood not twenty feet away, feet spread in a shooter's stance, reloading Moss's .45.

The scream came from the very bottom of his soul. "RA-CHEL! RUN!"

"Not without you!" she shouted. Joel started toward her, and someone knifed him in the back.

Joel gasped and dropped to his knees. With a snarl, Rachel started firing again. She hit his attacker just over Joel's left shoulder. Blood spattered the back of his neck. The remaining Clan attackers turned and fled—those who weren't cut down by Rachel's bullets.

She sprinted to Joel and grabbed his wrist, yanking him to his feet. He cried out in pain. Another explosion, much closer to the surface this time, and the ground beneath their feet began to crumble and cave in. The center of the ridge, over the big entrance chamber, collapsed into a great, sucking sinkhole. It looked to Joel like the mouth of hell.

"Run!" Rachel screamed. She hauled on Joel's arm, and his feet began to move. His knee felt like it was full of broken glass, and he had never gotten his full strength back after his coma, but he ran as fast and as hard as he could.

Rachel tripped on a rock and fell. The ground beneath her was sinking. She looked up at Joel as she started to slide backwards toward the ever-enlarging sinkhole. Joel felt blood gush from the wound in his back and run down his spine as he bent and grabbed her wrists. He pulled her up and back, ran backwards with her in his arms for a few steps, then her feet were on the ground and she was running too.

They ran down the side of the bluff and into the trees, and kept running. Joel began to feel faint. Blood ran freely down his spine. The world around him changed from forest green to pale sepia. Joel suddenly realized he was falling.

"Come on!" Rachel was yelling in his ear, pulling on his shirt. On his hands and knees, he crawled after her. She dragged him behind an enormous fallen log.

An earsplitting boom. The ground shook like an earthquake. Rock and dirt sprayed up from the cave in a gigantic inverted cone, blacking out the sun. Rachel and Joel dropped to the ground and covered their heads. Debris rained down on them. Nearby, a rock the size of a cannonball knocked down a small tree. A human arm landed in the underbrush.

Rachel and Joel stayed down until the dust had nearly settled. Joel didn't realize he had lost consciousness until he was awakened by a jab of pain; Rachel was doing something to the wound in his back.

"Ow," Joel said into the leaves.

"You'll live," Rachel said. "It's a nasty cut and you've lost some blood, but, lucky for you, the asshole hit your shoulder blade."

"Doesn't feel like it's bleeding now," Joel said.

"It's not. I taped it shut with Band-Aids."

Joel laughed, which sent a jab of pain through his back. "Ow! You brought Band-Aids to a nineteenth-century battle?"

"Well, I still had some in my backpack. I thought they might come in handy."

Joel rolled over onto his side to look at her. "Have I ever told you how amazing you are? And what are you doing here, anyway? Surely Mark didn't—"

"What I'm doing is saving your mangy butt. I stowed away with the posse. Mark came to save you, you know."

"No. He came to stop Cotten."

"Partly, but he also came for you. We both did."

Her young face was grave and earnest. Joel reached up and touched her cheek.

Rachel lay down beside him. Joel rested his head on her shoulder, and felt himself drift off to sleep.

Sometime later, the sun was low on the horizon, and Joel awoke. Rachel was sleeping beside him. He kissed her gently on the temple, and she opened her eyes. She brushed the hair from his eyes, and kissed him on the mouth.

Joel didn't intend to make love to Rachel. He had never intended to do that. He didn't even feel like it; he was filthy, exhausted, and every part of his body hurt. But it happened anyway. It just happened, as naturally as the rain or the sunrise. First they were kissing, then Rachel was opening his shirt, opening hers, their skin pressing together. Rachel melted into him, wrapped herself around him, and they were one.

28

Joel had expected a festival atmosphere to prevail among the posse after the fight, something like what happened at the cave twenty years ago, but these men were weary and without the anger and mean-spiritedness of that long-ago militia. They had not been promised anything but a fight; there was no squabbling over gold or liquor. Fellowes kept a tight reign on them. He remained in charge, directing a search of what remained of the cave and its contents.

Of the Grand Council members, they found the dead bodies of Everett Collins and John O'Farrell, and of course Garrison Sharpe. Joel knew that Art Clayton's remains were under the rubble filling the collapsed entrance chamber. Unless Job Hayes was somewhere under the rubble too, then he had somehow managed to escape. Joel knew that historically someone was supposed to lead what remained of the Mystic Clan in a failed slave uprising. Perhaps that would be Job Hayes—Joel couldn't remember.

Thinking about the future, about what might happen next, gave Joel a headache. Had they just changed history by breaking the back of the Mystic Clan? Had they changed anything at all? Joel wondered, as he often did, if history was, in fact, flexible. If so, that was terrifying—his slightest misstep could destroy everything these men had worked for. If not, why was he even trying? If everything was fixed, rigged by some cosmic or divine force, why not just sit back and watch?

Because I can't. I can't take that chance. Because if I sat back and let horrors happen without even trying to intervene, what kind of a man would I be?

It turned out that not only was Joel's shoulder blade perforated, but he had two broken ribs and a fractured collarbone and torn ligaments in his knee. He felt miserable, but decided that strangely he would have felt worse if he had not suffered so much after falling off the wagon. Drinking again after so much wonderful time spent sober was something to be feared, he knew, and that he had barely survived it was a powerful object lesson. He hoped he had learned that lesson.

For Joel the journey home was one filled with a strangely appropriate tension; the young men of the posse were pumped up by their accomplishment, but this was tempered by mourning as they remembered their friends lost in the battle. The posse slowly disintegrated on its way back to Adairville. A few of the men, those who had traveled the farthest to join Fellowes in the fight, were the first to part company. The closer they got to town the more of the men went their own way, returning to their families in various small communities. There were promises exchanged to meet in various taverns, especially Brownfort's Inn, to celebrate at a later date.

Mark was different somehow. As Joel watched him, he found Mark's stride more fluid, as if a weight had been lifted from his shoulders, and his eyes were clearer, as if the fear that had always clouded his vision had fled.

Fellowes was obviously happy with the outcome of the attack at the cave, though he worried privately with Joel that the remaining Mystic Clan members might still pull off the slave uprising.

During much of the journey home, Joel kept his distance from Rachel. He felt ashamed of himself for having sex with her. Though he knew it was ridiculous, he felt he had raped a beautiful and innocent young girl. He had to remind himself that she wasn't a virgin, and that she would be eighteen years old in a couple of months. But every time he looked at her, he was lanced with a cold stab of guilt.

Rachel gave him room, filling her time helping others. The two nights they camped, she nursed the wounded, including Joel, and helped with the cooking. Sometimes Joel caught her looking at him with a strange, half-sad, half-amused expression. The look was unnerving—wise beyond her years.

Joel had just drifted off to sleep on the second night when Rachel slid into his bedroll next to him. His eyes flew open, his mouth went dry.

"Are you ready to talk to me?" she whispered.

Joel nodded, having no idea what he would say to her.

"Good. Let's walk."

Quietly, they moved through the sleeping men, to the edge of the encampment. The stars were bright and clear, and the air was sweet with the scent of some night-blooming flower.

"I figure I know what you've been thinking," Rachel said, looking into Joel's eyes. "You think you took advantage of me."

"Yes," he croaked.

"Uh-huh. Well, guess what, Joel Biggs, I took advantage of you. I love you. You know that."

"I know you think you do."

"Oh, fuck that! I'm not an idiot, and I'm not a child. I know how I feel when I'm with you. I feel like—like I'm really myself, for the first time in my life. You make me real, Joel, and it feels so good sometimes I think I'll sprout wings and fly."

He swallowed hard. Tears stung his eyes. She took his hands.

"I knew you were hurt, and traumatized. I told myself I was making love to you to make you feel better, to start healing you. And that was part of it. But there was more. I wanted *you.* I wanted you more than I ever wanted anything before in my life, and I knew you couldn't say no to me right then. So I took advantage of *you,* Joel. I *did.* And I won't say I'm sorry, because I'm not."

She looked up at him, eyes shining in the moonlight, fine jaw tilted up defiantly. He touched her face, her hair. "Rachel, I—"

"You love me, Joel. I know you do." She kissed his palm, eyes locked onto his.

Tears ran down his face.

"You love me, Joel. You love me!"

With a sob, he pulled her into his arms, holding her tight, burying his face in her hair. "I do, Rachel. God, I love you so much."

"Then show me," she whispered in his ear. They slipped down, down. And Joel let go, let go of the guilt and the shame, and gave his heart to Rachel on the mossy Tennessee ground.

They had been back at the Stogdon farm for a couple of days when Mark received word that Wesley Pike was being held by the sheriff of Alexandria on unknown charges. He set out immediately for Alexandria to look into it. He promised to write Joel as soon as he knew the situation.

Joel considered Rachel his wife now, in all but law. They had moved into the outbuilding where they had first stayed, and enjoyed a little bit of a honeymoon. Hume politely gave the couple their space. Stephen became silent and sad-eyed. *He'll get over it,* Joel thought. *He'll meet a girl. He's a good kid.* Joel fought back feelings of guilt and unworthiness. He was worthy, damn it. Rachel thought so, didn't she?

Life had nearly returned to normal at the Stogdon farm. The criminal element was no longer in evidence in the town of Adairville. Joel needed time to heal, but it was easy to settle into the routine on the farm; Joel tutoring Stephen and Hume, Rachel cooking, tending the animals and creating her lovely drawings.

She had shown him those drawings with such shy hope, and, yes, he had been dazzled, but not surprised. It was natural, somehow, that Rachel could create such beauty.

Joel dreaded participating in the trial of Jarrett Cotten. The thought of it darkened his mood every time he thought of it. He knew being there would put him in jeopardy again, and he was seriously considering not showing up. There was no way the law had rounded up and prosecuted all the Mystic Clan. There would always be some who were loyal to Jarrett Cotten. He tried not to let on to Rachel how worried he was about it.

She seemed happy, although he wondered if she would eventually want more than this simple existence could give her.

A knot of fear formed in his gut at the thought of returning to his own time. Joel had been ashamed to find himself thinking on several occasions that here, in this time period, if he failed to stay sober, if he found himself being cruel to those he loved, it would be easier on him; a little more brutality in this time might be more readily excused than in the twenty-first century. He did his best to banish these unwholesome thoughts, and concentrate on being a good mate to Rachel.

The fresh air of spring and the gentle rewards of teaching Hume and Stephen fed his soul, and he looked forward to a time when he'd be healed and could put some of his energy back into the physical labor needed on the farm. He had no desire to drink. He could live here forever. Whenever he felt weak or frightened in the night, Rachel was there to hold him in her slender arms. And when she cried out in her sleep from time to time, tormented by the horrors she'd seen in the battle, Joel was there for her. It was such an incredible thing, to be needed. Sometimes as he held her close, feeling the pounding of her heart subside as he stroked her hair and whispered words of comfort, he silently wept with the power of it.

And then there was the sex. With Joel's injuries they had to settle for slow and soulful, not wild, but it was always joyful and loving. Joel had never experienced anything like it. The sad truth was, he'd never before had sex with anyone he was deeply in love with. He was fairly sure the same was true for Rachel. And she wanted him, she really did. Sometimes she'd give him a look across the supper table that would send a shiver up his spine and suddenly make him have to adjust his trousers. . . .

Life was good.

Then the first letter from Mark arrived.

Dear Joel,

Wesley took it in his fool hed to turn himself in to the law under the name of Jamus Cooke. He aims to bring down whats left of the Mystic Clan by telling about the Grand Plot. I dont think they believe him none. Im going to try and talk to him sos he changes his mind. More later.

Mark

Joel read the letter, then read it again. There was something about that name, about Jamus Cooke, seeing it in writing. . . . Suddenly it all came together in his head from what he had learned of history. *My God, Cooke is the man who "betrayed" the Clan, and dangled for it. But before he was hung, he helped to expose many of the high-ranking Clan members throughout the country. Rumor had it at the time that some of the Clan who were rounded up said he was actually Jamus Pike, but it was never really established that this was true. It was Wesley all along. . . .*

And this was Wesley's plan all along, to try and help our efforts with the Crenshaw book, by being a witness from inside the Grand Council of the Mystic Clan.

But there's some event that's supposed to help corroborate what Cooke tells the authorities. Joel couldn't remember what it was. *Perhaps it's the failed uprising itself.*

Joel considered keeping the news from Rachel, then realized he couldn't do that. She was his wife.

"Does Mark know?" she asked him.

Joel shook his head. "No. I don't think so."

"Shouldn't you tell him?"

Joel closed his eyes, chewed his lip. "No. I don't think so."

She touched his arm. "Don't you owe it to him?"

"Rachel—Wesley is Mark's father. Would you want to know your father was going to hang, no matter what you did, and nothing would change it?"

She blinked. "No, I guess I wouldn't." She turned around, pain in her eyes, and Joel knew she was missing her father, Moss.

With a sigh, Joel put the letter down and went outside to help Stephen repair the wall of the barn.

Almost a week later another letter arrived.

> Dear Joel,
>
> I havent been able to talk to Wes. The stubborn old mule wont see me. But they cant find nothing to charge him with. He told them he was a counterfitter, but he got no shop no more, and no way to prove it. I think theyr about reddy to let him go. I hope so, cause one guard keeps beating on Wes. I heard that from another guard who I bribed, but he is too scart of the other man to stop him. We will come see you when Wes is out.
>
> Mark

The hope in Mark's tone made Joel's heart ache. He tried to put it out of his mind.

Tomorrow was Easter Sunday. Joel wondered if the slave uprising would take place and if so, failed or not, if it would be felt in such a small community as Adairville.

A couple of days went by with no word of a slave uprising, then Mark's next letter arrived.

Dear Joel,

Now Wes has gone and done it. He kilt that guard what beat him all the time. Just snapped his neck like a goddam rabbit.

Theres a rumor going round that Wes is really Jamus Pike. You know, the one thats supposed to be Wesley Pikes brother. That would be funny I guess if they wasnt probly going to hang Wes. His trial is set for May 2 one month from now. Please come Joel I need you here.

Mark

Joel wrote back, telling Mark he'd join him in a week or two. Within a week Mark's next letter came.

Dear Joel,

You remember that I told you Wesley killed that guard? Well, that and something as happened at a plantation, The Thorpes, just south of here fixed it sos the sheriff beleeves Wes's stories now.

Seems there was a slave wet nurse at this plantation name of OChetta as let on about some foolishness. The mistress of the house gave birth to a daughter not too long ago and the baby was put in OChettas care. Having just lost her own baby, OChetta fell in love with the child. When she heared the other house girls talk about a slave uprising, she feared for the safety of the child. Then she heared some of the field hands talking in hushed voice about how the the master, the mistress, and all of the children would be merdered in their sleep, and OChetta couldnt hold her tongue no longer. She told the master of the house and he called on the law.

At first it was just a local thing. Then some slaves at other homes spoke up.

The Sherriff got hold of a copy of our book and he started pairing what Wesley was saying with what the book says and looking at the list of names.

Now theyve rounded up some of the local Clan from that list. A bunch of folks around here have packed up and left town.

The sherriff sent word about this to all the nearby counties and word came back that theres been such foolishness in some of those counties and a bunch of the Clan are being rounded up all over now. I hear in some places theres Clan being tortured for infomation and confessions.

I guess it took all of us—you me and Wes—to drive nails into the Mystic Clans coffin.

I'm pleased our efferts have been fruitfull, but I need you here real bad.

Mark

Joel was so excited about the news, he couldn't wait to tell Rachel. He ran to the stable where she was feeding the horses. By the time he got there he was pale and shaking.

"Honey—you can't be over-doing it like this. You still need time to heal."

Joel brushed her concern aside and told her the news from Mark.

He felt guilty for feeling such excitement as he thought about what Wesley faced. "At least his death will not be meaningless," he said. "We've got to get to Alexandria right away."

"The doctor Hume called to the house this morning said Stephen and Hume both have influenza. We can't leave the farm with everyone laid up in bed. By the look of you, you may have the flu as well. Right now you're going in to rest." She led Joel into the house and put him to bed.

Flu—the word had never meant much to Joel. When you got the flu, you went to bed and took a lot of Tylenol cold capsules. Maybe you got a fever or threw up, maybe your bones hurt and you felt like shit, but it was really no big deal.

But when he thought about the state of medicine in 1834, and remembered that the worldwide flu epidemic in 1918 had killed close to forty million people worldwide, he became afraid. *All those people who died haven't even been born yet.*

He and the Stogdons became very ill, and though the symptoms were painful and even embarrassing at times, they quickly stabilized, and Joel knew their lives were not threatened. Still, there was no one to run the farm except for Rachel and Carver, the Stogdon's remaining slave. Joel wrote Mark again, explaining the situation, saying they'd be there as soon as they could.

Days flew by, then weeks. Joel hadn't realized how much time had elapsed; perhaps he hadn't wanted to think about it. But he was ice-water shocked when a letter from Mark arrived one day:

Dear Joel,

Wesleys trial is all over. It only took one day. They found him gilty of course. Theyr hanging him on May 17.

I hope you and Hume and Stephen are better. I ben praying for you all. I know you arent much for religin but I wish you wood pray for Wes.

Mark

That same day a letter came from Sheriff Deland Carter:

Dear Mister Crenshaw,

I am writing to enform you yoor testimoney at the trail of Jarrett Cotten will not be nessessary cause yoor affidavit taken by Judge Erwin can be read in court and should be more than enough to convay Cottens ententions and enclinations toward horse theft. The part of yoor statemant concerning his Mystic Clan has no baring on a case of simple horse theft.

We have a copey of yoor book about Cotten and the Mystic Clan and this has been usefull against the Clan.

The truth is what promted me to send this letter is a sinse of compasion and duty. All though most of the Mystic Clan what we haven't captuured has fled Alexandria there are stil some here looking for you and I am suure they would murder you on the spot were they to find you and I got all the work I can handel with out ading that.

Not to worry, Mister Crenshaw, Mister McHenry Lake assures me he wil be at the trail to deliver his evidence.

Sincerly,
Deland Carter

After reading this, Joel thought for a moment that the Mystic Clan had probably forced Carter to write the letter. But the more he thought about it, the harder that was to believe. If Carter were corruptible, then the Clan would have been able to get Joel's address from him, confirming their suspicion that Joel was staying with the Stogdons, and they'd have arrived here instead of the letter.

A great weight seemed to be lifted from Joel. He read the letter to Rachel and she too was relieved that he would not have to participate in the trial.

Joel immediately began to feel better, the remnants of flu symptoms passing from his system. The Stogdons were recuperating as well.

Joel made arrangements with the nearest neighbors to check on the Stogdons, and he and Rachel left for Alexandria the next day. He had one stop in mind on the way to Alexandria. He wanted to visit Jarret Cotten in jail. The exact reason for this he couldn't say, but it was a need as primal as thirst or hunger.

Joel and Rachel made their way to the state penitentiary at Occum Field, just west of Alexandria. Cotton was being kept there until his trial because of the fear that the local jails were not secure enough to hold him. His trial had been postponed several times because of various motions the outlaw had made serving in his own defense.

History had told Joel that Cotten would receive five years of hard labor in this same state penitentiary for the theft of McHenry Lake's red barb mare. Based on what Joel knew about nineteenth-century crime and punishment, he could easily understand why the outlaw, according to witnesses, would blanch when the judge handed down his sentence. Regardless of what Joel knew of Cotten's years in prison, however, he was in no way prepared for the reality. In this part of the world, at this time, there were no advocates for prisoners' rights, no proponents for rehabilitation. Punishment was meant to be exactly that, the harsher the better as far as the public was concerned.

Joel hadn't expected getting in to see Cotten would be so easy—a few bits bought him a guard who would lead him through the prison block. Rachel stayed behind as he followed the guard into a limestone cellblock which was sunk into a hillside. It was as dank and dark as a springhouse, thick with the smells of human body odor, mildew, and the high stink of human waste.

As Joel walked, droplets from the ceiling struck his forehead and as his eyes adjusted, he saw rivulets of water running down the walls and into metal grates in the floor.

The only light came from a row of small slit-windows near the two-story-high ceiling. Two guards were posted at either end of the hall-like structure, huddled next to small wood-burning stoves that obviously weren't meant to warm the inmates.

Joel could hardly imagine a more miserable place.

The guard stopped and pointed to the cell at the end of the row. Peering through the heavy timbers of the door, Joel saw Jarrett Cotten staring back at him. He wanted to speak, but his throat seized up and he felt a rash of gooseflesh run along his arms.

The outlaw's former finery had been reduced to moldering tatters, his gaunt face patchy with parasitic discolorations, and he scrutinized Joel with red-rimmed eyes. Cotten's cell was a dismal pit, the stone walls a scant yard apart, moist and unwholesome, furred with moss. There was no pallet for him to sleep on and only a small, reeking hole in the floor, ringed by a green skin of slimy algae, to serve as a toilet.

But what made Joel's eyes widen in horror was the manner in which his childhood hero was held fast like a dangerous beast. An iron ring had been welded around his ankle and was connected to a long chain of stout links, and fastened to the floor by a heavy staple. Even on a monster like Cotten, it seemed inhumane. Grotesque.

Noticing his expression, Cotten spoke quietly and matter of factly. "This is what I got for my foiled escape last week—this and ten lashes. But such are the pitfalls in the life of any great entrepreneur."

Joel still could not speak.

"Have you come to gloat, Crenshaw? Do you dare? You have escaped the Mystic Clan for now, but are you aware of how you will suffer at their hands, given time?"

Joel was amazed the outlaw could be so cocky. Surely he was unaware as yet of the assault against the Clan by the posse led by Thomas Fellowes and Mark Ryder. That, and the outlaw still had his health. His conceit would not last. Joel knew that Cotten would be left chained in this manner for some nine months before money from a family member made it into the hands of one with the power to remove the heavy shackles. In that time, the red and inflamed area he could see on the outlaw's ankle would become an open, infected sore from which Cotten would never fully recover.

Still Joel had not spoken.

"Why is it that you are here, Crenshaw?" Cotten asked. "I presume you have not come merely to gawk."

Joel found his voice. "There is something of you inside of me. I admired you."

Cotten's face soured, the corners of his mouth turning down. "You'll forgive me if I am not over-flattered after what you have done."

"I wanted to see you, bound like this, and tell you that I no longer admire you. It was the child in me, the little bully, who admired you and—"

Cotten's pale face flushed with sudden color and his eyes flashed. *"Silence,"* he tried to shout, but his voice was hoarse from lack of use. He rattled the door to his cell. "You dare to mock me while I am chained to the floor, while this stout door stands between us and I am thus prevented from striking you. Could it be that after all I have shown you, you still do not understand that I command a vast fraternity? One word from me—"

"You are *so* full of *shit,*" Joel barked contemptuously. It had come out of him so suddenly that he didn't question it. "Your precious fraternity, what is left of them, has forgotten all about you. They've left you here to rot." He could scarcely believe the acid in his tone.

Suddenly taut and white, Cotten's face betrayed disbelief.

Frozen in time, the two men eyed each other—*across a century,* Joel thought.

"By Christ, I'll have my fraternity send you to the devil, I will, you impudent wretch. I'll see you flayed alive and boiled in pig fat."

"Oooh, I am *so* scared! I hate to pee on your pancakes, *ass-hole,* but there isn't much left of your little *club.* A posse led by Thomas Fellowes attacked the Clan during one of their meetings at their new clubhouse, the Outlaw Cave. Almost every one of them was killed."

Cotten visibly started, his eyes narrowing. *He didn't know,* thought Joel. *So much for omnipotence.*

"You obviously understand nothing of the complexities of my organization." The outlaw was so furious he was spitting. Realizing this, Cotten swallowed hard, wiped his lips, and continued more slowly and deliberately. "Sharpe and Clayton do my bidding—"

Joel decided it wasn't worth the effort to inform Cotton that Sharpe and Clayton were both dead.

"—They do not make so much as a move without my endorsement. Why, I have guards here who will carry any message to my confederates at a moment's notice."

Glancing at the huge staple that fastened Cotten to the floor, Joel gave a sardonic grin. *I'm sure they do a good job humoring you.*

"Not a young cherry plucked, nor a counterfeit bill passed without my knowing or approving." He was spitting again, heedless now of his lack of decorum. "I've got men in every riverside port controlling the river trade, and road agents patrolling the whole length of the Natchez Trace as well as every other trade route. We get the best prices on horses and slaves as often as we want. There isn't a whore in any of the great cities of the South that doesn't owe us her livelihood. Nobody gambles a penny without my taking a slice of it. Though I am shackled here in this, the basest of prisons, *you* have much of which to be envious, for I have *my* fingers in everyone's pudding."

Joel wasn't sure whether there was anything left to fear from the Mystic Clan. He knew that there were still hundreds, perhaps thousands of members across the country. There were some among them, no doubt, clever enough to reorganize. But Jarrett Cotten was finished. Even the remnants of the Mystic Clan didn't seem to want him anymore.

The outlaw seemed a very small and broken animal trying to lash out at the world from inside his tiny cell. Joel abruptly felt sorry for him. *He's not dangerous anymore. He's just a mean little shit,* Joel told himself, *just like I was as a child; just as I still am deep down inside.*

Throughout his adult life Joel had feared that the mean little shit within him would rise up and destroy his life and the lives of anyone he cared about. How could he render it as powerless as Cotten was now? How could he keep it from destroying what he might have with Rachel?

"And when I get out of here," Cotten continued, his eyes, his voice feverish, "I assure you, I will control not only the United States of America, but eventually the world."

Yes, Joel thought, *but history says that in less than a year you'll be in such a despondent state you'll set fire to your clothes in a desperate attempt to burn down the door of your cell. It'll fail, of course, and you'll receive a hundred lashes on your burned, blistered skin.*

Joel remembered reading about the criminal's last few years of life: *Held fast and hugging the whipping post, Jarrett Cotten was punished with the cat-o'-nine-tails, his flesh flying with every stroke, his blood streaming down his legs and filling his shoes.*

Afterward Cotten would be confined in a new cell, and a steel ring welded around his waist. Chains and an iron bar connected this to wrist and ankle shackles, and the whole contraption would be connected by a stout chain to a bolt in the floor. He would wear this for a year and a half, and by the time of his release, his health would be irrevocably shattered and his spirit crushed.

He may be cocky now, Joel thought, *may still be pumped up on his Mystic Clan, but when he's released, he'll find himself with nothing to command but the army of lice in his hair, and the skill he acquired his last year in prison.*

Jarrett Cotten, who once commanded a criminal empire, would end his days as an impoverished farrier.

"You know, you're really nothing but a *common* criminal," Joel spat.

He was surprised to see Cotten momentarily stunned into silence. Joel took the opportunity to turn on his heels and make his way out of the darkness of the prison.

Cotten will regret not getting in the last word. In years to come, he'll still be here, crouched in the gloom, trying to come up with some clever retort.

Joel and Rachel headed east for Alexandria, where they spent the night in a small, surprisingly clean hotel. In the morning, they headed to the courthouse, where they were married by a justice of the peace, with a beaming cleaning lady as their only witness.

29

Joel wanted to be at the hanging just about as much as he didn't want to be there. With every step toward the gallows in the town square of Alexandria, he felt more like he was headed to his own hanging. He didn't want to see Wesley's neck broken, but he felt an obligation to the man . . . and to Mark.

As they entered the crowded town square the going got a lot rougher. People were pushing and shoving, trying to get closer to the front.

"I can hardly wait until deodorant is invented," Rachel said, giving a sour look.

Joel gave her his most serious expression and she mouthed a simple "Sorry."

As Joel, Rachel and Mark struggled to move through the crowd of spectators to get as close as possible to the gallows, Joel saw Wesley being led by a man dressed all in black—the hangman, no doubt—up to the platform of the gallows. They were accompanied by a preacher. Wesley towered over both of them. He looked larger than life.

Amidst the spectators' catcalls and jeers, Wesley stood on the platform with his arms behind his back—presumably shackled—and craned his neck as he looked out over the crowd. Joel had a feeling the big man was looking for him.

What an ego I've got, Joel thought. *He's probably looking for Mark. He considers him his son, after all.*

"Watch where ye're puttin' yer feet down," cried an old man beside Joel.

Mark turned to the man and glared at him angrily.

"I apologize for stepping on your toes," Joel said, placing a hand on Mark's arm.

The man merely grumbled and turned away.

"Mark, I don't think we can get any closer. Not without riot gear." The crowd was packed as tight as sardines. They were twenty yards from the gallows.

"I guess this'll have ta do, then," Mark said. He stood on tiptoe. "I think Wesley sees us," Mark said.

Wesley's eyes were indeed focused in their direction.

Mark told Joel that when, nearly two months ago, he had told Wesley that Joel survived the destruction at the Outlaw Cave, a great smile had spread over the big man's face.

Joel wanted Wesley to know they were here today. In the last few days, Mark had conveyed messages to Wesley for Joel, through the guard he had befriended with coin. Joel had thanked Wesley for his part in the destruction of the Outlaw Cave and expressed his sorrow that the big man had to come to such a dreadful end. Mark had had no reply to convey from the outlaw.

"Are you sure you want to see this?" Joel asked Rachel. "You could just turn and face the other way. I'll tell you when it's over."

"Joel Biggs," she said, exasperated, "if you can take it, I sure as hell can."

"I'm sorry," he muttered, remembering her courage at the cave. "I didn't mean—I just can't seem to stop trying to protect you."

"Honey," Rachel said more softly, "I know it's hard for you to see Wesley die. The least I can do is be here with you, just like you're here for him." She squeezed his arm. "And thanks for trying to look out for me. I love you for it."

He gave her a brief, hard squeeze.

A plump, nattily dressed man in a top hat—probably the mayor of Alexandria—rose to the platform and addressed the crowd. The noise from the spectators diminished slowly and the man was half way through his speech before Joel began to make out the words. He was reciting the charges and the punishment issued by the court.

He turned to Wesley and spoke, but Joel couldn't hear what he was saying. Wesley opened his mouth to speak and an immediate hush came over the crowd. His voice was clear and strong, the voice of a general addressing his army, not a man about to get his neck stretched.

"I'm here today 'cause it's the right thing ta do. I didn't have ta turn m'self in like I done. Sure, I shouldn't o' killed that guard, but he was not a good man an' so I don' feel too bad 'bout it. Made ye folks sit up an' take notice, I'll say that.

"Truth is I'm feelin' old and wretched-sore. I got ta live fer a good many years, though, with a chunk o' goodness in my heart an' I wouldn't trade that fer anythin' on this Earth. For the longest time, that goodness was somethin' I borrowed from my wife Mary. She cared about others; even me, and that was confusin'. But I tried ta care fer her and there come a time when I knew I loved her an' her childern, Royce Junior and Nettie, who done grown up ta be fine law-abidin' folks, now both married an' raisin' up fam'lies of their own. And, though I didn' deserve it, I was loved by Mary an' the childern and m' son, Mark, who's here t'day."

Wesley was looking at Mark now.

"I'm grateful ye come ta see me off, son. You growed up ta be a good, strong man. Do what ye know is right and ye'll be able ta hold yer head up an' have a good life. I know I sound like a preacher, an' ye prob'ly think it was religion made me change, but I never really believed in any o' that tripe. No, it was you and yer brother an' sister, an' my dear Mary. An' one other as well."

Joel could see Wesley's eyes shift slightly to focus on him.

"When I knew 'im, he was jus' a boy. I called him Little Man fer a laugh, but he proved that was what he was. I'd never had loyalty fer nothin' but m' brother, who wouldn' o' spit on me if I was afire, but that he needed me ta get him through the hard scraps o' life. Little Man taught me 'bout bravery and loyalty; taught me there was somethin' worth fightin' for that was bigger than me an' mine; what it meant ta be hard as stone, tough as they come, but still love an' care for others."

"Yeah . . . right," Joel said under his breath as Wesley paused for a moment.

Mark heard what he said and he turned on Joel with a fierce look. "You feel sorry for ye'se'f all ye want, Joel Biggs, but Wesley's got no cause ta be tellin' anything but the truth. And don't ye fergit, I was there. I know what yer made of."

Joel was stunned silent.

"Little Man *did* like ta fight," Wesley continued. "He had a mean streak wider'n some men twice his size, but when it come ta defendin' his friends, he was willin' ta risk life an' limb ta do it. An' he did it 'cause it was the right thing ta do."

I had that kind of impact on him? Me? Joel looked down, tears stinging his eyes, humbled.

"Thanks, Little Man," Wesley concluded. "I wish I coulda watched ye grow up. I think we both mighta been the better fer it." He bowed his head and fell silent. The catcalls resumed, but not half as strong as before.

As a black hood was fitted over Wesley's head, Joel found himself struggling to revise history, but it was difficult. He was being asked to believe that his example had changed the heart of one of the most callous and murderous criminals of history.

Rachel seemed to notice his confusion. "Is it that hard to

believe that you had goodness in your heart?"

Sure, he could believe it; he could understand in the same rational way that he knew that he was five foot, ten inches tall, had size nine feet and had the beginnings of male pattern baldness that what Wesley was saying was true. But this was a matter of the heart, and only Joel knew what resided there. How could Wesley have known what was in Joel's heart, that Joel had decided to stay at the Outlaw Cave not only because he thought the pirates were so cool, but also because Mark and Billy needed him in order to survive and escape?

With this question came the long-suppressed memory of having made that decision. *Yes. I stayed for them. Yes.*

"I've always chosen to remember Joel, the mean bastard," he said to Rachel somewhat unsteadily, "but I guess there was always more to me than that." He knew this was much bigger than what he'd just admitted, but he couldn't fully wrap his mind around it.

The preacher on the platform beside Wesley opened the Bible he was holding and began to mumble prayers. When he was through, he stepped back and the mayor gave a signal to the hangman.

"Human beings are complex," Rachel said. "You *are* a bastard sometimes, but you're also capable of great sacrifice for those you care about. That's one of the reasons I love you."

The hangman placed the noose around Wesley's neck, and adjusted the knot behind his left ear. He placed his gloved hand on the lever that operated the trapdoor.

"You two hesh up," Mark said, tears in his eyes. "It's time."

Joel was still struggling to believe, to feel the truth of what Wesley had said, when the floor dropped away from the outlaw's feet. The big man hit the bottom of the rope with a grinding snap.

Joel felt a wrench in his gut, a physical pull as Wesley passed from the realm of the living. A part of Joel was carried away with the outlaw—the mean little shit—and for the briefest moment his life passed before his eyes, and he saw all that had led up to this moment. He saw himself with a sharp-edged clarity that had never been there before. He was a victim of his father as a boy; he'd had no choice in that. Later he'd been the victim of his own anger, and a victimizer in turn. But that was over. The bully within him had just been hung. He would no longer be around to beat up on Joel. There would be no more self-destruction.

"Thank you, Wesley Pike," he whispered.

Mark collapsed against him and wept. Joel consoled him for a time, then he and Rachel led him away.

There were things to take care of. The claiming of Wesley's body, the transport to the undertaker's. Wesley would be buried here in Alexandria, where he had made his great sacrifice. Mark had picked out a fine plot for him, beneath a giant oak in a shady little cemetery.

They went back to the boardinghouse where they all were staying, and Joel and Rachel got Mark to bed. Rachel even got a little soup into him, with a lot of coaxing. Soon Mark was asleep, his face exhausted and tear-streaked. Rachel kissed his stubbled cheek, and then she and Joel retired to their room.

Joel kicked off his boots and prepared to fall into bed. His head was full to bursting. He felt like he had just been reborn, but the process of shedding his old, hateful skin had been exhausting. He closed his eyes.

He felt Rachel's small hand on his shoulder.

"Joel. We need to talk."

He rolled over on his back. "What is it, babe?"

Her face was a strange mix of worry and nervous excitement. "We have to decide, Joel. Are we going to stay here, or, you know, go back?"

He groaned. He knew the day would come when they'd have to make the call. But he didn't want it to be now. "Rachel—can't we talk about it tomorrow?"

She smiled a little. "No. I've been waiting, holding it back, because of everything that's been going on, but if I don't tell you now, I'm gonna explode."

Joel swallowed hard. "Uh . . . tell me what?"

Her smile turned into a grin. "I'm carryin' your baby, Joel Biggs."

For a split second, the bottom dropped out of Joel's world. He was terrified. He opened his mouth to speak, but nothing came out. Then he heard the voice of Wesley Pike in his ears, loud as it had been on the gallows this afternoon. *Thanks, Little Man. I wish I coulda watched ye grow up.*

He was going to be a father! *A good father.*

"We have to go home," he said. "This time is wonderful in its way, but it's so brutal and harsh. . . . I want our baby to have everything."

She smiled. "You're gonna spoil her rotten, aren't you?"

"Her?"

"Well, him or her."

"Joel Jr.?"

"Ugh! How 'bout Max?"

"I dunno, I kinda like Mathias Crawshanks. . . ."

Laughing, they collapsed on the bed together.

Joel and Rachel made tearful good-byes with the Stogdons, during which Joel explained that the Biggs's only chance to escape possible retaliation from the Mystic Clan was to depart the United States. They were going to Europe, Joel said, and would write to the Stogdons when they were settled.

Stephen had held Rachel's hand a moment too long. Then he clapped Joel roughly on the shoulder. "You take care of her."

Joel nodded gravely.

The young man walked away, back stiff, head held high.

Now Joel, Mark, and Rachel stood at the end of The New Cut, at the place where Brown's Creek spilled out of the twenty-first century and entered Tennessee of the eighteen-thirties. Mark Ryder had led Joel and Rachel Biggs here, following instructions given by Thomas Fellowes. They had traveled for three days together, chatting like the old friends they were, but now there was silence. It was time to go home.

"Mark," Joel said, holding his friend by the shoulders, "are you sure you won't come with us? You can stay with us as long as you want. I'll help you find a job. . . ."

Mark laughed. "That's only 'bout the fifteenth time ye've asked me, Joel, an' I thank ye fer it. But my place is here. It's where I was raised. An' for the first time in my life, I feel like I'm my own man. It wasn't that Wesley held me down . . . but I was always Wesley Pike's dawg, an' damn proud ta be so." His eyes teared up, and he wiped them roughly with the backs of his hands. "But now . . . now I'm jes' Mark. An' ye know what? I'm startin' my life over again an' I'm feelin' strong. Don't need no more bullies ta back me up. I'm thinkin' I'll buy a little piece o' land with the money I've saved up over the years. Find a sweet, plump little gal an' raise up a bunch o' young-uns."

Joel smiled. "You'll make a great daddy, Mark. You always had such kindness in your heart."

Mark grinned at him, then Rachel. "You'll make a good one too. An' a lot sooner than me, I reckon." Rachel blushed and laughed.

"So I guess this is good-bye." Joel swallowed down the lump in his throat, and it came right back.

"Guess so," Mark replied. The two men hugged fiercely for a moment. Then Rachel squeezed Mark tightly around the waist, and kissed him on both cheeks.

"You take care of yourself," Joel said. "Have a good life, Mark."

"You too. Keep that flicto outta trouble, Rachel." Mark smiled.

"Gonna try."

One more round of hugs, and then Joel and Rachel started walking down the bank. Joel didn't look back. He couldn't. He was afraid he couldn't go through with it if he saw Mark there, waving good-bye. "Have a good life," he said again, under his breath. He looked down, and a teardrop hit his dusty boot.

"He will," Rachel said, squeezing him around the waist. He patted her belly, which had already taken on a gentle curve.

"So will we." Joel kissed her hair.

"Holy Christ. What are we gonna tell my mom and dad? They're not gonna believe we've been in the eighteen-hundreds all this time. They're probably not even gonna believe we're married."

Joel chuckled. "Moss is likely to beat the hell outta me. But when he's done, let's take him down to the archives in Alexandria—I mean Jackson. We'll show him our names on the marriage register and the little note I left him."

"You didn't. . . ." Rachel's eyes were wide and smiling.

"Damn straight, I did. How else are we gonna convince him to take us seriously?"

Rachel threw back her head and laughed. "You're brilliant, Joel Biggs."

"Well, I may not be that, but what I am is a man in love. And I'm gonna do right by you, Rachel, for as long as I live. You have my promise."

She rested her head on his shoulder. "I know you will. We're gonna be so good together, baby."

There was nothing else to say. As the birds and insects sang in the thick of the Tennessee woods, Joel Biggs walked, arm around his bride, into the present.

ABOUT THE AUTHORS

Alan M. Clark grew up in Tennessee near a creek. He is most known for his work in illustration, which appears in books of fiction, nonfiction, textbooks, young-adult fiction and children's books. His awards in the illustration field include the World Fantasy Award and four Chesley Awards. His fiction has appeared in magazines, anthologies and a collection released by Scorpius Digital Publishing. *Siren Promised,* his Bram Stoker Award–nominated novel, written with Jeremy Robert Johnson, was released in 2005. Mr. Clark's publishing company, IFD Publishing, has released six books, the most recent of which is a full-color book of his artwork, *The Paint in My Blood.* He and his wife, Melody, currently live in Oregon. Visit him on the Web at www.alanmclark.com.

Stephen C. Merritt has collaborated with his cousin, Alan M. Clark, on previously published short fiction. He is a native of Nashville, Tennessee, where he lives with his wife, Cynthia. *The Blood of Father Time* is his first novel.

Lorelei Shannon was born in the Arizona desert and learned to walk holding on to the tail of a coyote. She now lives in the woods outside Seattle with her husband and two small land pirates, also known as her sons. Lorelei has two previous books out: a horror novel called *Rags and Old Iron,* and a collection of short stories called *Vermifuge and Other Toxic Cocktails.* Her short fiction has appeared in numerous magazines and anthologies. Visit Lorelei on the Web at www.psychenoir.com.